Making the Best of It

Making the Best of It

Luisa A. Jones

Sign up for the Luisa A Jones newsletter at www.luisaajones.com and receive a free short story as well as news updates from the author.

MAKING THE BEST OF IT

This book is dedicated to the memory of my godmother, Cas, who was always encouraging, kind, and rich in humour, advice and wisdom. She is missed.

"The future belongs to those who believe in the beauty of their dreams."

— ELEANOR ROOSEVELT

Chapter One

Sunday 24th August 2014
The Gower

The old camper van gleamed in the late summer sunshine like a bright orange beacon against the slate-blue sea in the distance. Water dripped from a black wetsuit drooping over its bike rack, and four chairs stood in its shadow: two large, two small. Two bikes had been flung down onto the close-cropped grass, the larger one pink and festooned with stickers; the other purple, its stabiliser wheels pointing heavenwards.

Nearby, Megan Field lay on a striped picnic rug, propped up on her elbows and engrossed in a paperback, only moving now and then to tuck her long, auburn hair back behind her ears or to sweep a stray bug off the page.

Her husband Tom, casual in a loose t-shirt and cargo shorts, stepped down from the van with two mugs of tea.

"Thirsty?" he asked. The question met with silence. She was always like this when she was reading, blind and deaf to everything going on around her. A bomb could go off and she wouldn't notice. "Megan? Hellooooo?"

He tutted and nudged her hip with his toe. Finally he had her attention.

"Tea." He handed the mug over and settled cross-legged on the grass.

"Ooh, lovely." She slipped a bookmark between the pages and sat up, dropping the book into her lap. "I take it Dylan's still asleep in the van?"

"Thankfully, yes. I've never made a cup of tea so quietly. I turned the gas off the instant the kettle came to the boil, so the whistle wouldn't wake him."

He dragged his surfboard closer and examined the fins. He had lost one earlier; it was fortunate that he kept a spare set in the van. With a bit of repair work now, and a fresh application of wax to the board, he'd be ready to head down to the beach again this evening, once the tide had receded.

Loud giggles made him look up at their daughters, Alys and Nia, who were playing in the middle of the field with some other girls they had met that weekend. Squealing and shrieking, they chased each other over the expanse of grass, for all the world like a flock of starlings darting about without any apparent purpose other than to revel in their freedom.

"I wish every day could be like this," he said. "It does us all good to be in the outdoors. Even Dylan sleeps better."

"Mmm. I've enjoyed the family time during the holidays, too. Before we know it we'll be back in the old routine: choir on Wednesdays; swimming on Fridays; ballet on Saturdays; making packed lunches and getting kit washed on time; remembering which days to send homework in to school and reminding Alys to take her violin. Nagging her to practice. Rationing screen time and arguing with Nia because Alys is allowed to stay up later..."

"Don't talk about September," he said, cutting her off. "Just thinking about it makes me want to run away again."

The thought of returning to the daily grind as Head of PE in a busy Cardiff secondary school made his stomach churn. If he could think of a way to escape it, he would. He wasn't as overwhelmed by the pressures of work and family responsibilities as he had been a couple of years ago, when a rocky patch in their marriage had driven him to flee reality and seek solace on a solo surfing trip in Greta, his camper van; but he knew it might not take much to nudge him towards the edge of desperation again.

It was a sobering thought. Their marriage had barely survived his mid-life crisis: he couldn't afford to let himself reach those depths of misery again, not when the aftermath had been so awful. Adjusting to life with a new baby; constantly having to reassure Megan that he wasn't about to make a bolt for it, especially when the baby blues had kicked in and she had looked at him in such despair it was obvious she believed he was only biding his time before leaving her for good.

The mistrust and disappointment in her sister Bethan's eyes, which still hadn't been entirely erased after two years. And of course, braving the contempt of his mother-in-law, who hadn't hesitated to confirm what he'd always felt in his gut: she'd never liked him. There'd always been something shifty about him, she'd said. Too charming, too good to be true with his posh English private school manners, but now his true colours had shown through, inevitably because of course all men were cowardly, feckless shits at heart who didn't deserve to have a good woman at their side and couldn't recognise a good thing when they had it. He'd taken her spite on the chin, because it was at least partly deserved, and he'd been glad when Megan defended him, even if she'd been a bit lukewarm about it sometimes.

They had worked through the rocky patch, thankfully, and Dylan's arrival had focussed their minds on the importance of reconnecting as a couple and as a family. Megan had overcome her initial reluctance to join him on a few camping trips, and hadn't even grumbled much about the lumpy bed, which was more than he had ever dared to hope for, especially as it was a bit cramped with three of them in it. For the first time since their marriage they had neglected the house, repairing the cracks in their relationship instead of their plasterwork. Now their marriage felt almost as solid as it had ever been, and Tom was grateful because he wasn't sure how long he could keep playing the role of perfect husband to atone for his misdeeds when he was only getting five hours sleep at night.

"Look on the bright side," Megan said. "There's only six or seven weeks until half term, and then you'll be a Holiday Husband again."

He grinned in spite of himself. They shared a private joke that each of them was two separate people: a Term-Time Spouse (stressed out, crotchety, constantly on the go and dogged by planning and marking); and a Holiday Spouse (relaxed, more easy-going with the children and far more amenable to sexual advances).

"Ah, yes. And of course you'll still be a Holiday Wife for the next week. I shall make the most of it." He waggled his eyebrows fiendishly, like a lascivious pantomime villain.

"You're insatiable."

"Naturally. You're irresistible."

"I hardly think so. There can't be many men who look at a short, overweight mother of three who's the wrong side of thirty-five and think: ooh, lush."

"You're forgetting a crucial detail. Men and women see different things. *I* see a voluptuous, titian-haired temptress. I see a MILF, and so would any other red-blooded male." He drained the last of his tea and turned his attention back to the surfboard, waggling the fin: it seemed the tiny grub screws were going to hold it.

"A MILF? As in a mummy I'd like to..?" She only mouthed the word, sending a sidelong glance to make sure the swarming children hadn't heard.

"Definitely. Can't think of anything I'd rather do, in fact."

She nearly choked on her tea. "If I'm a MILF, what does that make you?"

"I hope you still see me as a bit of a FILF."

"That's even worse. It sounds like Essex slang for the police."

He stretched out, squinting up at the grey clouds that had begun to congregate among the white. "If you won't accept that you're a MILF, think of yourself as a goddess. Ask Dylan: he'd agree with me."

"No. Not a goddess, thank you very much. This is real life, not *Fifty Shades of Grey*."

By Luisa A. Jones

It was the perfect opportunity to tease her. "Hmmm. I bet you secretly loved *Fifty Shades* – so much more exciting than Jane Austen. Although I can't help feeling a pang of nostalgia for more innocent times, when a man could go to B&Q to buy duct tape and cable ties without the checkout staff sniggering behind their hands."

"Do you honestly imagine that the staff in DIY shops have nothing better to do than speculate about their customers' sexual proclivities?"

"I should think they like nothing better. It probably brightens their day no end."

"What must they have thought of you when you bought that tow rope, then?" she asked with a chuckle.

"Mmm, I'd forgotten about that rope. Laters, Baby."

"Tom, the only fifty shades of grey that applies to you is in your hair. You're not nearly young, rich or kinky enough to make a convincing Christian Grey."

He shrugged. "I could do kinky, I think. Given the right circumstances. If you want kinky, you only have to say."

The skin at the base of her throat flushed crimson, belying her attempts to look prim. It was satisfying to see that he could still make her blush after all these years.

"We haven't the space in our house for a Room of Pain."

"A pity. Of course, if you and I got into S and M, you'd have to be the dominant one. You could be like the Supernanny, and make me sit on your Naughty Step."

She swiped at his knee with her book. "You know, I always suspected your interest in Supernanny was more than just curiosity about parenting techniques. But you're onto a loser with that idea. If I ever feel the need to dominate someone, I've got three kids of my own and hundreds of teenagers at school. I don't feel any need to send you to the Naughty Step or confiscate your toys."

"That's such a shame. You get a minute for each year of your age on the Naughty Step. Imagine it: forty-two whole minutes of solitude and reflection. Sheer bliss."

∞∞∞∞∞

The shrill clamour of Tom's mobile phone rang out from the van, making him leap up and dash to retrieve it. It was too late to prevent Dylan being woken: while Tom carried the handset a few yards away to focus on the caller, Megan caught Dylan up into her arms and patted his back. He had screwed his fists into his eye sockets, purple with outrage at being woken.

"It'll be those silly insurance people again, I bet. Or some rotten sales call. They're a nuisance, aren't they, *cariad*? Waking you up like that, when you were sound asleep. Never mind… Daddy will sort them out."

"Yes, this is Mr Field speaking…. Thomas Field, that's right."

The caller was definitely a stranger, then. She would put money on the odds of it being someone offering him compensation after a car accident. They'd had a few of those calls lately, desperate sales people unwilling to accept their assertions that they had not had any accidents within the past five years, thank you very much. If only Tom had thought to mute his phone, or brought it outside with him, they might have had another half hour or so of peace.

She joggled Dylan in her arms, nuzzling the sleepy smell of his downy cheek. He wouldn't settle again now: he'd opened his eyes properly, and was eyeing the surfboard with interest. Dammit. Another few pages and she might have found out if she'd guessed rightly that the seemingly harmless old woman was actually the villain.

Tom seemed to be listening intently to his mystery caller. Not a sales call, then: he hadn't yet attempted one of his oh-so-polite apologies to get them off the line. And something had made him stand very still.

"I see," he was saying. "Not at all, I quite understand." He had half-turned to cast a glance in her direction. His adam's apple bobbed as he swallowed hard. "Is she absolutely sure about this? Only, she's become… well, forgetful. Confused, even, at times. Have you checked with her carers? They visit morning and evening to help her in and out of bed."

This must be about his aunt Jean, who lived with his dad Hugh in Ludlow and had grown increasingly frail in recent months. Odd, though, that it wasn't Hugh making the call.

"I agree, it is very unusual. Perhaps he's met up with a friend from the Cricket Club?" Tom paused and listened, nodding once or twice. "That's typical, I'm afraid. He never answers his mobile. We've insisted he carries one in case of emergencies, but he only turns it on if he wants to make a call… No, my brother is on holiday abroad, so you won't have been able to contact him. I'm on holiday too, as it happens, but only in the Gower… Yes, I understand… I could get there in about three hours if you really think…" His voice tailed off.

Megan's eyebrows shot up. What could be so urgent that he was offering to cut their trip short? She looked around, working out how long it would take to pack everything up and get going. Three hours to Ludlow sounded a bit ambitious, considering how cranky Greta could be.

Frowning, Tom lowered the handset from his ear.

"What's happened?" she asked, not sure if she wanted to hear the answer. Whatever it was, it seemed it would put an end to their idyllic long weekend by the sea.

"That was West Mercia Police," he said, surprise registering in his voice as if his brain hadn't yet caught up with the ramifications of the telephone call. "It's Dad. He took the dog out for a walk this morning and hasn't been home since. Auntie Jean has reported him missing."

Chapter Two

Sunday 24th August 2014
Ludlow

Hugh's stately Jaguar saloon was parked in its usual spot, polished to a mirror shine in defiance of its advancing age. A rare example of self-indulgence when he retired, in many ways the car resembled its owner: solid, with a kind of restrained, gentlemanly elegance. Dependable. Not the sort to just disappear.

The sight of it was reassuring. No doubt Dad had turned up by now, and Tom's long journey from the Gower, pausing at Cardiff to leave Megan and the children and to swap to their faster family MPV, would turn out to have been a waste of time and petrol. He let himself into the house and strode through to the sitting room, fully expecting to see his dad seated in his usual armchair, remonstrating with everyone for creating such a fuss.

Hugh wasn't there.

Auntie Jean struggled to her feet. "Hugh!" she exclaimed gratefully as Tom entered the room. "You're back!"

Her relief was infectious, making Tom cast a swift glance behind, thinking his father must have followed him in.

"I'm Tom, Auntie," he said.

As confusion and embarrassment swept across Jean's face, Rita Gordon, Hugh's kindly middle-aged next door neighbour, rose from the sofa.

"Hello, Tom," she said. "The police asked me to keep Jean company until Hugh got back, or until you could get here."

He thanked her, then stooped to kiss his aunt's furrowed cheek.

"He's not back, then?"

Jean shook her head, sagging back in her chair, and he perched on her footstool to hold her gnarled hand while she described the day's events.

"When the girl came to get me up this morning there was no sign of Hugh or Dandy. Dandy's lead wasn't on its hook, and Hugh's jacket was gone, so I guessed they must have gone out for their walk. He's always back by a quarter to nine to listen to *A Point of View* on the wireless. The girl – I forget her name – gave me my bath with those lovely bath salts you gave me for my birthday. Or was it Robert..?"

She hesitated, frowning as she tried to untangle her muddled memories.

"I expect it was us," Tom said, although in fact he had no idea what he and Megan had bought for Jean's last birthday. Megan tended to organise cards and presents, especially for female relations.

"Yes, that's what I thought. So – what was I saying?"

"You had your bath while you waited for Dad and Dandy to come home from their walk."

Her expression cleared. "Yes, that's right, I had my bath and got dressed, and then because Hugh wasn't back the girl made my toast before she went. She's always in such a hurry, and you know they always send foreigners and I can hardly understand a word they say."

Tom cringed inwardly but nodded, trying to conceal his impatience. Now wasn't the time to challenge his aunt's prejudices.

"What happened then?"

"Well, nothing. He didn't get back in time for *A Point of View*. He still wasn't back by the time the *Archers Omnibus* finished, and I knew then that something must be wrong. We always have a cup of tea when it starts, and then he takes me to church in time for the morning service. But he wasn't back." Her tone changed from concern to vexation. "I didn't have tea, and I missed the service, but no one's phoned to check that I'm alright. You'd think someone would have phoned, wouldn't you? Hugh should have come back to make my toast and some tea."

He squeezed her hand, a lump of anxiety forming in his throat.

"Have you asked the other neighbours if they've seen him?"

She gestured towards Rita, clearly unable to remember her name. "This nice lady has been and asked them, but they don't know anything. I told her to telephone the man at the Cricket Club, but he hasn't been there. I called the police because I didn't know what to do. I'd missed going to church. He should have been back in time to take me. I hadn't even had a cup of tea since breakfast."

"Don't worry. You did the right thing," he assured her with an enquiring glance toward Rita.

"The police have been looking into it," Rita confirmed, "but up to now, no one has been able to find him." She signalled discreetly towards the door as if there was more she wanted to say out of Jean's earshot.

He took the hint. "You know, I haven't had a cup of tea for a while, either." He squeezed Jean's shoulder as she tried to get up. "No, we'll make it," he told her firmly. "You stay there; I'll be back with it in a jiffy."

"I'll help you carry the cups." Rita followed.

"I won't stop for tea," he whispered, grabbing a couple of digestive biscuits from the tin. He was ravenous, but there was no time to eat. For all he knew, his father could be lying in the woods with a broken ankle or head injury. Time was of the essence. "I must get going. Thank you for keeping her company. She gets – well, as you saw when she mistook me for Dad. I like to flatter myself I don't look seventy-six yet, but perhaps I do after all."

"We thought it best for someone to sit with her after she'd called 999 three times."

Pausing in the act of tying his shoe laces, Tom stared. "Three times?" he repeated.

"She forgot she'd already done it."

He swore under his breath.

"Don't worry; I'm sure they get it all the time. I can stay until about half past five, but after that I shall have to pop back home to sort out some dinner. Bill won't like it if it's late. The police said social services might need to be called..."

"I'm sure there'll be no need for that. Once I've found Dad, we'll take it from there. Do you know where they've already looked for him?"

Rita listed a few places Hugh frequented.

"Alright. I'll head across the river and up the hill towards the fields. He sometimes takes the dog up there and into the woods."

He set off before she could respond, knotting the sleeves of his fleece jacket over his shoulders as he strode with a restless, jittery energy. Marching uphill out of the town, he concentrated his thoughts on maintaining a steady stride, to head off the ideas crowding in on him. It did no good to imagine the worst. Pausing only to cross the road, he dashed off a text to Megan.

No sign of Dad yet. Am out looking, will keep you posted. xx

Within seconds the sudden jangle of his mobile phone made him fumble for his pocket.

"He's still not back, then? How's Jean coping?" Megan asked.

"She's alright. The police have asked one of the neighbours to keep an eye on her and make sure she doesn't ring them again."

"And how about you? You sound like you're walking."

"I am. I'll feel a lot better when I know where the hell he is. Are you okay? Sorry for leaving you to unpack everything, but I couldn't stop -"

She cut him off. "Everything is fine here. Just give Hugh a hug from me when you find him. I'll see you later. There'll be a bottle of wine waiting."

He smiled at her calm air of confidence. The wine would be most welcome, a small compensation for the premature termination of the last long weekend of summer.

Within a few minutes, scanning his surroundings for any glimpse of Hugh or Dandy all the while, he crossed the river and then paused, debating whether to follow the footpath along the riverbank, before deciding to keep to his original plan.

"Dandy! Dandy, where are you?" he called. The dog was more likely to hear him than his dad.

Nothing.

He headed upwards and crossed the fields, calling again. Putting two fingers to his lips he gave a piercing whistle, but although he listened carefully there was no answering movement or sound. Pointless to linger here either, then.

On he went for about half a mile, following the path into the woods and stopping every fifty metres or so to call out in his most ringing teacher's voice. He could bellow like a bull when the need arose, a useful talent when refereeing teenagers on a rugby pitch. Now, it helped in dispelling a measure of the tension that had been growing with every step.

"Dad! Dandy! Can you hear me?"

After a short distance he emerged into a clearing. Something about it struck him, and he paused a moment to catch his breath and grope in his mind for what it might be. A flood of memory struck him in a sudden wave. This had been his playground.

That thick oak had once supported a swing made from nylon rope and a sturdy stick. The ground underneath used to be bare from the scuffing of feet in trainers as he and his friends tested the limits of the rope, yelling like savages as they swooped above the bushes. Tom remembered the excitement of looping in a wide arc at the end of the rope, flying like the boy Icarus, air rushing past his grinning cheeks.

One afternoon the air rushed the wrong way, and the impact as he hit the ground left him disoriented and deflated, unable to suck air back into his lungs. The shock on his friends' faces awoke him to the drama of his sudden crash to earth. As he tried to sit up, his left shoulder slumped forwards and his arm felt odd, too heavy for him to carry its weight. At first he had only felt winded, not hurt; but that quickly wore off, and their long walk home had been tortuous, not only from the pain of cradling his throbbing arm, but from the trepidation of what his parents might say.

His mother had put her medical knowledge to instant use and diagnosed his broken collarbone at a glance. She applied the customary bag of frozen peas, dosed him with junior aspirin and folded his arm into a neat sling.

"Am I in trouble?" he asked as she washed the mud and shameful tears from his face with a flannel.

Amusement smoothed the concern and sympathy from her face like a drop of oil spreading across a puddle. "You were just doing what boys do." He vividly remembered the kisses she pressed onto each of his cheeks, and the toffee she produced from the jar on the shelf for him to suck on; could almost smell her Youth Dew perfume and taste the creamy sweetness of the toffee on his tongue.

His face softened at the self-indulgent pleasure of affectionate memories. His mum had been so lively and pretty then, with her blonde hair fashionably permed, a glowing complexion, and eyes as vividly blue and long-lashed as Tom's own. Her body hadn't yet been ravaged by the illness that would rob her of her hair, dull her skin and make her shrunken and thin. He realised now that he tended to remember her as she was towards the end; but the woman she had been before was still there, in the back of his mind, with the glorious smile that had always warmed him with love and approval.

Almost without hope, he called out again, then tilted his head to hear more easily. Had he just imagined it, or had his ears picked out a distant bark?

Jogging forwards, he shouted again, re-energised, senses alert to any sounds. Now he was certain of it: a distant, high-pitched bark came from the trees ahead. Blood rushed in his head from the giddy anticipation of finding his father.

Picking up his pace, he ran towards the sound, calling at intervals and letting the spaniel's occasional answering barks lead him. All at once there came a crash of twigs and bracken, and the elderly Springer Spaniel erupted out of a gap between the trees, tongue lolling and long ears flapping, aiming straight for Tom. He dropped to his knees and hugged the dog tightly, turning his face to avoid its enthusiastic licks.

Dandy smelled strongly of pee, earth and leaf mould, and the curly fur on his ears was tangled with sticky burrs. His paws left muddy prints as he jumped up at Tom's chest, but Tom didn't care. Now that he had found his father's dog, he felt a new surge of confidence that Hugh couldn't be far away.

"Dandy! Good dog. Good boy! Where's Dad? Where is he, come on!" He urged the dog forwards, but Dandy remained where he was, dancing at his heels and sneezing in the excitement of finding someone familiar.

"Come on, boy. Why can't you be like Lassie and lead me straight to him?" Dandy circled his ankles, brown eyes alight with joy. "Come on, let's find Dad!"

After a fruitless couple of minutes, he gave up and fed the grateful animal his digestive biscuits, nearly losing his fingers to Dandy's uncharacteristic snatching. While Dandy crunched the biscuits one after the other he patted the soft, warm head and gazed towards the trees, hoping in vain that Hugh would emerge in pursuit of the dog. There seemed no other option than to set off in the direction from which Dandy had come.

The woods were quiet, with only the warbling of birds to disturb the silence. Tom's feet and Dandy's paws sounded intrusively loud as they pressed onwards, the lack of any answering cry as he yelled out making Tom's stomach twist into knots. As more minutes passed, the frequent shouting started making his throat hoarse and his mouth dry. If only he had thought to carry a bottle of water. He was parched and could feel his blood sugar levels dropping from the uphill exertion on an empty stomach. It had perhaps been overgenerous to give his biscuits away. He slowed his pace to conserve energy and allowed the dog to run on ahead.

All at once the sound of sharp barking came like a jolt, and by following the sound for a short distance he soon glimpsed a familiar grey-haired figure slumped on the ground against a tree.

"Dad!" He gave a yell and spurred forwards, Dandy tearing ahead.

For a long moment Tom stared blankly, taking in the way his silent, motionless father sat hunched against the mossy green bark of the oak. His chin had sunk onto his chest, as if he was sleeping, with his hands resting limply on the ground at his sides.

He knew, of course. He'd felt it in the core of his chest even as he dashed towards him. Knew, but a part of him refused to recognise the truth.

His knees faltered and he dropped to a crouch. Hugh should have jolted awake with a surprised smile and blinked away sleep to greet his son, giving Dandy's head a familiar pat. He should have pushed back the cuff of his jacket and said "oh, is that the time? I nodded off for a moment there." He should have held out his hand for Tom to hoist him to his feet.

Tom sat back on his heels to look for any sign that his father was injured. There was none. The birdsong and Dandy's panting were drowned out by a rushing noise in his ears, a distant ringing in his brain like tinnitus or a gnat's high-pitched whine.

Hugh's knees were muddy, Tom realised. A regiment of ants marched busily across one of them: he brushed them off the serviceable brown corduroy with a sense that his throat was closing up. Perhaps Hugh had stumbled, fallen down onto the earth all alone, with no one to help him up, and then crawled to the tree to rest. The very idea of it was a knife in the gut.

His father's right hand clutched the mobile phone that he and Megan had bought him two Christmases ago. He held his breath to take courage, then picked it up and unclenched each cool finger, one at a time. Their waxy, purplish colour made him shudder as he released the handset and laid Hugh's hand back at his side – carefully, so as not to drop it. Once, not so long ago, his dad's hand had felt big and warm and safe. It had felt strong: strong enough to carry him, to swing him around, to pick him up when he fell. Now it felt thin. Cold. Lifeless.

The phone's screen remained blank when he pressed one of the buttons.

"Did you get your phone out to call for help, Dad? You should have turned it on when you left the house. Mobiles only work when you turn them on, you bloody fool." He spoke softly, without anger, but then his voice split, curdling like sour milk in his throat, and a sudden desperate paroxysm made him seize the old man in his arms and hold him. He pressed a kiss against the thinning grey hair. His father's neck and shoulders were stiff and unbending as he rocked him gently, whether to soothe himself or the old man he didn't know. Pain hit his chest like a physical blow, making him groan aloud and cling all the more tightly. Breathing hurt, as if the sudden emotion had made his lungs forget how to function.

"Oh God, Dad. God!" He blasphemed helplessly, unable to articulate anything but this half-prayer. The fragments of birdsong and the rustling of the branches above seemed to emphasise the silent stillness of his father's body.

"I was surfing this morning, Dad," he croaked out at last. "We camped in the Gower. It's beautiful there: you'd love the beaches and the coastal path. There wasn't much of a swell today, but it was still exhilarating. I had no fears, no worries. I just kept on ploughing into the waves, enjoying the rush." Gasping out a breath that was almost a laugh, he added: "I thought bashing my ankle against the fin of the board would be the worst thing that would happen to me today."

Dandy had been lying at the old man's feet, muzzle resting on his paws, observing while Tom cradled Hugh in a fiercely tender embrace; but when Tom looked over at him he scrambled up and came to lick his face. For once, Tom let him. He hadn't realised he was weeping, but his cheeks were wet and salty for the second time that day.

"We're alright," he said, to reassure his dad, or the dog, or perhaps himself. "I'm here now, Dad. I'm here, and we're all going to be alright."

Chapter Three

Monday 25ᵗʰ August 2014
Ludlow

Tom's throat was so tight he could hardly breathe. He clutched at the blanket smothering his face, tore it away and sat up. Sweat prickled at the back of his neck like crawling ants. He scratched it frantically. He'd always hate ants after seeing them swarming over his father yesterday.

It was still dark: not even the faintest sliver of light showed between the faded chintz curtains. Rubbing at his face, he swung his legs out of bed and stumbled across the landing. Past Jean's old room, the one she had before the stairs became too much; past his dad's.

Into the bathroom. A splash of cold water onto his face. He forced himself to focus on those physical sensations that were real, rather than those his body had worked up itself. Tiles, cool against his feet; the water trickling off his nose and chin. Gripping the thick porcelain of the wash basin, he counted his breaths in and out. Slowly, now. Slowly. It had only been a dream.

He'd been a little boy again. Three, or four perhaps: certainly no older than that. A little lad in white ankle socks and navy blue shoes with a T-bar and buckle, holding his mother's hand and jigging with impatience. They were in a shop. A big one, with thick carpets. There was a whole wall of television screens, all showing the same man, but only his top half, and although his lips moved within his beard Tom couldn't hear what he was saying. Some of the screens were grey, but Daddy wasn't interested in those. Daddy wanted one of the televisions that showed the man in full colour. He was joking with the smartly-dressed man in the shop about how much better the football and the snooker would be on a colour screen. He'd be able to tell which team was which in future, would know without listening to the commentary which ball had rolled into the pocket.

The shop man didn't talk to Mummy much, but she was still paying more attention to the televisions and to Daddy than to Tom. Robert had brought a toy car with him, tucked away in his shorts pocket; but he only had the one, and he wouldn't share, and it was boring watching him pushing it along the floor below the televisions. Tom didn't like just watching, or standing still. He wanted to play chase or hide and seek, or to have a car of his own to push along. But Rob wouldn't play.

His mother didn't say anything when he slipped his hand out of hers and wandered off. No one stopped him as he meandered across the shop floor, up and down the aisles looking for something more interesting to do, finally reaching the open doors of the lift. The buttons inside were brightly illuminated, luring him in, and he stepped inside and smiled at himself in the mirror before sticking out his tongue and pulling a rude face. He pressed a couple of the buttons. Only then did he notice that the doors had closed. He was trapped.

A grinding, juddering sound heralded a jolting movement. The floor felt unsteady. Tom's reflection in the mirror looked wide-eyed and frightened. He reached out to steady himself, and almost gasped with relief as the doors opened.

But everything looked different now. No televisions. Just racks of clothes, and ladies milling about with their handbags over their arms. One with curly white hair under her hat stepped into the lift and peered at him with beady, dark, witch-like eyes. She said something, but he shook his head and squeezed himself back into the corner, unable to speak. A gnarled hand reached out to catch hold of him. Perhaps she wanted to put him in a cage and eat him.

Mummy. I want my mummy and daddy.

His feet itched to run. His hands flapped the old lady's questing fingers away. Nothing mattered but finding his parents. A dreadful sense of loss overwhelmed him, stifling rational thought.

Now he was awake, and safe in his former home, and an adult, not a little boy; but one thing about the dream had been true: the terror that he would never see either of his parents again. There was no chance of a kindly shop worker hearing his name on the tannoy and coming to crouch beside him in the lift, ready to lead him back to his mother. There would be no breathless, thankful reunion tonight. The knowledge made his stomach lurch, hollow and empty.

He buried his face in the softness of a towel and waited while his breathing slowed. Strange how that childhood memory had surfaced in his sleep. He'd been right back there, on the point of screaming. A little boy again, lost and trapped and afraid.

Crossing the landing, he paused at his father's door and pushed it open. No one had bothered drawing the curtains tonight – what was the point, with the room unoccupied? He flicked on the light and the alarm clock revealed that it was just after three.

He was wide awake, but there were a few hours to go before he could justify getting up. He longed to slip into his running gear and take off into the night, to channel his excess energy into the pounding rhythm of a run. But he didn't have his kit with him, and it wouldn't be fair to risk disturbing Jean by going downstairs, even if he could permit himself to leave her alone in the house during the night.

He padded over to the bedside table, his gaze lingering on the half-empty glass of water that Hugh would never finish, and picked up the book lying next to it. A crime thriller, of all things, with a bookmark about two-thirds of the way through. He'd probably been reading it before going to bed for what would be a final time. Poor Dad. Now he'd never find out how the pathologist would help to identify the murderer. Flipping the book over, he was struck by the picture of police tape across the blurb on the back.

The irony of it almost made him laugh. The police had cordoned off the woods earlier, while they examined the clearing for any clues as to the cause of Hugh's death. A precautionary measure, they'd said. They had no reason to suspect suicide or foul play. As far as anyone could tell he'd just gone out for a walk and sat down under a tree after a while for a rest, as you do – except that he had bloody well gone and *died*. It was so crazy, so earth-shattering, and yet the police hadn't even seemed shocked. He supposed people must die in strange places and in strange ways all the time. It probably wouldn't even make the front page of the newspaper, would get a couple of inches of press on page four or five, along with a missing cat or someone's lawnmower being stolen from a shed. Humdrum. And yet Tom's world had been shattered.

A kindly policewoman had explained that a post mortem would be held in the next couple of days and then, if natural causes had been established, the coroner would be able to release the body. He pushed away grisly thoughts of his father's body in a bag in a fridge, being unzipped to be cut open on a slab. The police had been gentle, as far as such an official process allowed, anyway; but he had never felt so out of his depth as he had in those woods.

He ached for Megan, to put his arms around her and bury his face in her hair. She was good with words: perhaps she'd know the right things to say to Jean, or to the neighbours and friends who would inevitably soon start calling to offer their condolences. But she was eighty miles away, and as much as he needed her, he hoped she would do as he'd asked for once and stay away, shield the kids from everything happening here.

Rob and Linda were thousands of miles away, still a few days away from the end of their holiday. He'd told them not to rush back. What would have been the use? It wouldn't change anything. And he was a big boy now, could surely cope in a crisis without his elder brother to take charge.

He thrust his hands into his hair and sank onto the edge of his dad's bed, his mind a tumult of questions. "Why, Dad?" he whispered into the silence. "What happened to you?"

Had Hugh suffered? He had taken out his phone, so he must have known something was wrong. Had he tried to call for help, realised no one would reach him quickly enough and so stopped trying? Or had he lost his strength so quickly that he hadn't had time to turn the handset on?

Images of the scene in the woods, his dream, his unanswered questions, all swirled around in Tom's head until nothing made any sense and one thought took over, drowning out all others.

Dad is dead. I'm an orphan now. The last person to love him unconditionally was gone. Even his children couldn't love him as unquestioningly as Hugh had done. The sense of emptiness, the confusion of having lost something vital, returned.

He opened his eyes in a daze, noticed a slip of paper lying at his feet. It must have fallen out of the book. Perhaps it would have some significance, contain some clue as to his father's health or state of mind. He reached for it and read the words aloud, slowly deciphering his father's handwriting that fit the stereotype of doctors' illegible writing so perfectly:

B'day card Alys (8)
Toothpaste
T. paper
Bread
Ham

So banal, and yet his throat swelled. Hugh would never write anything again. Those long fingers would never pick up a pen, never write another note or shopping list or birthday card.

He'd never send another message or make a phone call. Tom would never again hear his gruff voice on the phone. Sunday evening was when they generally caught up with the week's news, once the kids were in bed and all the packed lunches sorted. Sunday evenings in the future would be different. They'd have to establish a whole new kind of normality.

So many things would change. Little things. They wouldn't share each other's jubilation when Liverpool beat another team, or when England did well in the Six Nations. He wouldn't be able to ask Dad's advice if one of the kids was unwell, or if he needed to vent about a situation at work. He'd never have the pleasure of hearing his dad chuckling at something the kids had done. Hugh would never again get irate and shout at politicians on the television when they gave slippery responses to questions about the NHS.

Hugh's list mentioned Alys's birthday. Now, though, there would be no more cards from him. Worse, Tom would never again need to buy a greetings card addressed to *Dad*. He wouldn't pass the whisky bottles in the supermarket and notice when Laphroaig was on special offer and get a bottle for Hugh, knowing it was his favourite. There'd be no need to rack his brains in December and fume about how impossible it was to buy Christmas gifts for his dad because really, he had everything he needed and the money to buy anything he wanted. He wouldn't be able to get cross when he asked Hugh for gift ideas and received the inevitable, useless response: "I don't need anything; don't worry about buying for me."

Restless with pent-up energy, he looked around. Dad hadn't changed anything in this room for years. The curtains and bedspread were the ones his mum had chosen more than twenty years ago. The dressing table was hers, although her brushes, cosmetics and perfume were gone. He remembered walking in on her once as she was putting her wig on. He'd been embarrassed and awkward, but she had called him over and shown him where a peach fuzz of hair was just starting to grow back on her scalp. She'd grinned into the mirror and said: "just give me a minute to draw my eyebrows back on and I'll be able to give you my full attention." He remembered marvelling at her, and grinning back in spite of himself, because if she could see the funny side of living with cancer, who was he to argue?

The room was neat and uncluttered. Only one bottle stood on the dressing table now: Aramis aftershave, Hugh's signature brand for years. Tom lifted the cap and sniffed at the woody scent, so evocative of his father. He set it down again next to a small metal tray which he recognised at once: he had made it in metalwork lessons at school and given it to Hugh as a Father's Day present thirty years ago. A pair of cufflinks and a charity lapel pin lay inside. Hugh's had been the last fingers to touch them. He reached out, held them in his hand for a heartbeat, then put them back and trailed his fingers across the smooth surface of the dressing table, staring at the tray for a while longer. Remarkable that his dad had kept it all this time. He swallowed hard and turned away.

How empty the house felt without Hugh's quiet presence, even with Jean and Dandy asleep downstairs.

"I miss you already, Dad," he whispered into the silence.

Chapter Four

Monday 25th August 2014
Cardiff

Bethan raised her eyebrows and skirted around the wooden train Dylan had left like a booby trap in the doorway.

"If you're doing housework, things must be bad. Whoops – sorry. Tactless of me. Of *course* things are bad. Do the kids know what's happened?"

Megan pulled the plug out of the socket: ironing could wait. "I told them this morning. The girls were asking why Tom didn't come home last night and I didn't want them thinking he'd gone off on his own again."

She grimaced, remembering the shock and confusion on their faces. Nia had been puzzled, Dylan oblivious; Alys had taken it badly. She, at least, was old enough to have an inkling about the permanence of death: a year after they'd found her hamster lifeless in its cage, she still hadn't stopped talking about it.

"I'm mortified. The first thing I thought when you texted me to say he'd gone missing was 'like father, like son.' I didn't think for a moment that he'd be *dead*. How is Tom? What a terrible blow, finding his dad like that. It doesn't bear thinking about."

"He's still in shock, I think – and worried about his Auntie Jean. She can't seem to take it in. When I spoke to him this morning he said he'd already had to tell her three times since yesterday. Every time it upsets her as badly as the first."

Again, she was hit by the sense of being too far away. It didn't feel right for him to be dealing with everything on his own, but he had insisted that she should stay at home and keep things as normal as possible for the children's sake, for now at least. She could see the sense in that, but it didn't stop her feeling torn.

"She lives in Hugh's house, doesn't she? And didn't you tell me it's pretty big? Too big for one old lady to live in by herself, I imagine?"

"It's probably about the size of yours and ours put together. High ceilings; beautiful features. The sort of house an interior designer would kill to get their hands on. Freezing in the winter, though, even with the central heating on. Tom and I wore bobble hats to bed when we stayed over one Christmas. Silly for two old people to still be rattling around in a great big icebox like that, really. They should have downsized years ago, but I don't think he could face packing everything up and moving." She sighed, moving a pile of t-shirts from the sofa so that Bethan could sit down. "You're right, she won't be able to carry on living there alone. Hugh had already been looking into residential care for her."

Bethan sank into the sofa and caught up a cushion, hugging it. "Poor old thing. As if losing your marbles and your brother wasn't bad enough, now she'll have to move as well. You're not planning to bring her here, then?"

Megan shook her head, quickly squashing another tug of guilt. With three young children, demanding jobs and a house to run, they couldn't give Jean the attention and care she needed. She'd been telling herself over and over again, whilst lying awake in the small hours, that it would be madness to try to take on such a responsibility, and that Jean would find it traumatic to move eighty miles away from her friends. They didn't even have a spare room. But knowing it was impossible didn't stop her feeling like a traitor.

"The job of packing everything up and selling will be down to Tom and Rob now, then. I presume Hugh left everything to them?"

Megan folded up the ironing board and carried it to the kitchen. She needed a cup of tea and a biscuit. "He could have left it all to the dog, for all I know."

"Hugh gave Tom the money to buy his camper van, didn't he? He'd hardly be likely to do something as generous as that, and then leave his big old house to anyone else. You could be in for quite a nest egg, sis. There I was, thinking you'd married Tom for his good looks and charming personality. Turns out you married into money." She chuckled and accepted the mug of tea, seemingly oblivious to Megan's raised eyebrow.

"Not funny, Beth." This wasn't the right time for one of her sister's jokes. Sighing, she reached into a cupboard for the biscuit tin. It was stupid to think eating would help, yet she'd been in and out of the kitchen gorging on treats like a basking shark hoovering up plankton ever since Tom left for Ludlow. If only she could be one of those people who lost their appetite in times of trouble.

"D'you fancy a chocolate Hobnob? I've eaten nothing but junk since yesterday lunchtime." If Bethan had one too, she wouldn't have to feel cross with herself for giving in to temptation.

"Aww, are you comfort eating? I know you were fond of Hugh."

"Yes, I was. He made me feel welcome whenever I stayed there. He was a bit brusque sometimes, but kind. And he doted on the kids, even if he did seem to be slightly relieved whenever we left. But it's not just Hugh dying. I eat like a pig whenever I do housework. It's such a bloody chore, I have to reward myself every twenty minutes with a treat to keep my motivation up."

"You've been doing the school uniforms, I see. I suppose it's only a week till you're back at work?"

"Yep. I figured I'd better sort it all today, given that I don't know whether I'll have to go to Ludlow this week. I couldn't sleep last night, ended up writing their names in their new uniforms at five a.m."

"*Writing* them in? You mean you haven't spent hours sewing name tapes?"

"As if. When did you ever see me with a needle in my hand? Fortunately, I took the girls to buy all their new stuff at the end of last week. I hate that part of the summer: Dante should've included

Clark's back-to-school shoe shopping in his circles of hell. There we were, queuing for forty-five minutes in a shop full of screaming brats, with Nia refusing to try on anything that didn't have a bow on it, and Dylan getting more and fractious. I did everything I could think of to keep him quiet, but when it was his turn to have his feet measured, he had a total meltdown."

Bethan laughed. "Poor Dylan. And where is he now? He's unusually quiet."

"Shit, he is, isn't he?"

Megan dashed to the bottom of the stairs, a cold sweat breaking out on her brow. "Are you all okay up there?" she shouted. "What's Dylan up to?"

"He's fine," Alys called back. "He's drawing in Nia's bedroom." There was a pause while she went to check. "Oh," she added.

"Oh, what?"

"You might want to come up and see."

What the hell had he been up to? And why had she allowed herself to be distracted for so long? She bounded up the stairs, Bethan following at a more leisurely pace.

The scene confronting her as she pushed past Alys into Nia's room was enough to make an archbishop swear.

"Where in God's name did he find a Sharpie?"

Dylan looked up from his position on the floor, his beaming smile whiter than usual amidst the black ink covering his face. He'd obviously been busy: scribbles decorated not only his legs between his socks and his shorts, but also the varnished floorboards, spreading up the wardrobe door and onto the furniture. Megan sprang forward and snatched the pen from his hand, inducing a roar of protest.

"Mammy! Dat's *mine!*"

"My bed!" Nia exclaimed, finally noticing the commotion and looking up from her sticker book.

"Oh God. That duvet cover is never going to be the same again," Bethan said from the doorway. "Sorry, I know I shouldn't laugh. It isn't funny really."

"No, it bloody isn't. And never mind the duvet cover, what about his face? It's *permanent* marker. I'd have to drown him in bleach to get that lot off!" Megan choked back a furious sob.

"Maybe you could try one of those magic eraser sponges?"

"*Magic?* Merlin himself would struggle to get this off."

"It was just a thought. Wow, look at it. You only sanded those floorboards a couple of weeks ago, didn't you?"

"We did it at the beginning of the summer. It took us hours. And – oh no, Nia, your castle!"

Nia burst into noisy tears at the sight of her wooden fort covered in ink. "You naughty boy, Dylan! I hate you!"

Enough was enough. Megan couldn't allow the kids to shriek hurtful words at each other. Nerves frazzled by the pandemonium, she dredged up her sternest teacher voice.

"Stop that this minute! Beth, take your nephew and give him a bath, please; try to get at least some of that muck off his face. I'll make a start on sorting this room out. Nia, you shouldn't have left him to his own devices for so long – no, I know it's not your fault, but I'm just saying that two year-olds can't be trusted. Stop your wailing. Alys, if I find out this Sharpie belongs to you, and you left it where Dylan could find it, there'll be ructions, believe you me."

She scooped up her son, ignoring his screeching, and dumped him in the bathroom. Let Bethan deal with the reality of having kids, for once.

Alys and Nia backed out of the room, still crying quietly. They could grumble about Dylan – and about their mean mother, no doubt – downstairs.

She stripped the duvet cover from the bed and put it to soak in stain removal powder, along with Dylan's shorts. Not that she expected it to work, but she had to at least try. Then she trudged upstairs with a handful of scourers and bleach sprays, but after a fruitless half hour had to accept that no amount of detergents or scrubbing would remove the marks entirely. The wardrobe door would need to be repainted, the floorboards sanded and varnished again. She dragged a toy box over to a new position atop the scribbles, as temporary camouflage. It wasn't ideal, as they'd have to move it every time the wardrobe door was opened; but at least it hid the worst of the damage.

Alys peeped around the door. "Dad's on the phone," she said sullenly, and passed the handset over.

"How are things?" Tom asked in a colourless voice, bereft of his usual vigour. "Alys didn't sound quite her usual self."

Megan thought it remarkable that he'd noticed, considering.

"Nothing for you to worry about. More to the point, how are you doing?"

"Oh… I'm still numb, really. Social services will look into a place somewhere local for Jean – I've explained the circumstances. And there'll be a post mortem for Dad in the morning… As much as I hate to think of him being cut open like that, at least it should give us some answers."

She winced. "It will be good to be able to understand what happened."

"I suppose… Anyway, the news is obviously spreading. The vicar has been round, and we've had a few cards. I haven't opened them yet. Can't quite bring myself to. God, I miss you. Being without you is hard."

The way his voice snagged over his words made her ache to throw her arms around him.

"I miss you, too," she said. And not just because he would probably have made her a cup of tea and taken over the scrubbing. She told him about the Sharpie incident, choosing her words carefully, anxious not to add to his woes.

"His face will come clean eventually. Take a photo - one day you'll be able to look at it and laugh. As for the rest… well, it's only a bit of varnish and paint."

"And a duvet set. Which matches the curtains, so if we can't get any the same we'll have to replace the whole lot. They're not cheap, you know."

"It doesn't matter. We can live with it for a while, until he's old enough to know not to do it again."

"You're taking it better than I did." She wasn't sure whether to be worried or annoyed by his lack of concern. He was usually the house-proud one.

"They're just things, Meg. God knows, life's too short to get in a state about curtains."

∞∞∞∞

Bethan stayed while Megan prepared a simple lunch of beans on toast for everyone. Megan watched her spooning beans into Dylan's mouth, pretending the spoon was a train or an aeroplane to persuade him to co-operate. After the bean juice and toast crumbs had been wiped off his still-inky face, he was content to sit on her lap with milk and a story while Megan tidied up.

Soon it was nap time. It was hard not to envy his freedom to spend a couple of hours in bed each afternoon.

"I've been thinking," Megan began, glad of the chance to sit down once he was settled in his cot. She hesitated, fidgeting with the wheels on a toy train Dylan had left on the sofa, unsure how to continue without making her sister think less of her.

"Oh yes? Should I be worried?"

"No, don't be daft. It's nothing major. I've just been thinking that it's maybe time for me to go back to work full-time."

"I would have thought three days per week was more than enough when you've three kids to deal with. Especially after days like this one. I couldn't imagine working all day and then coming home to cook tea and scrub Sharpie off the walls and get them all bathed and off to bed before you can even think about sitting down yourself... and then, when you do sit down, you can't relax because you've got marking and prep to do for the next day. Not five days per week. Rather you than me."

"But that's the point, isn't it? Days like today show what a thankless task it can be stuck at home. If Dylan was with the childminder, *she'd* be the one dealing with the chaos and the marker pens. In some ways it's actually easier to be at work, dealing with things that stretch my brain further than just remembering whether Dylan likes his toast cut into triangles or squares. And I could justify paying someone else to do the ironing and a bit of cleaning once a week if I was earning more. Don't get me wrong: my Mondays and Fridays off are lovely, and I'll miss those times when I'm having to cram so much more into my weekends. It isn't that I don't enjoy my time with Dylan and being able to take the girls to school twice a week. It's just that – well, it can get a bit boring. Most of the friends I made when the girls were little have gone back to work full-time now. I get back from the school run and my heart sinks because all I've got to look forward to is another day of running around after a toddler."

She paused and pressed her lips together. Why was it so difficult to explain her need for adult company and mental stimulation without sounding as if she was utterly lacking in maternal instinct? How could she explain to someone who desperately longed for children that being with them all day wasn't all sweetness, sunshine and snuggles? Sometimes it was tears, tantrums and treading on Lego instead. Sometimes she thought she might scream if she heard the Thomas the Tank Engine theme tune even one more time. And it was easier to enjoy the kids' company when she'd been looking forward to it all day.

She sighed, wishing she could explain it even to herself, let alone to anyone else. Why did she have to feel so bloody guilty? Was she mad, wanting it all? Although maybe the mad part wasn't the wanting, but believing that having it all was achievable.

"What does Tom say?"

"I was going to discuss it with him this week, before the beginning of term – but with everything that happened yesterday, I haven't had a chance. I think he'll be fine with it. The extra money will be useful. And he's been with me long enough to know I'm no domestic goddess. He likes a tidy house, and the only time he gets one is when he's cleaned it himself. The main issue will be whether the school will let me increase my hours."

"It sounds like you've already decided." Bethan shrugged, but her expression was tight-lipped and disapproving. "You've got to do what feels right for you, I suppose."

Which should have made Megan feel better, but somehow made her feel worse.

Chapter Five

Friday 29th August 2014
Ludlow

1st January, 2014

*D*ear Robert and Thomas,
If you are reading this, then hopefully I am past caring about you snooping around in my desk. If I haven't yet shuffled off this mortal coil, put this letter back in its envelope at once, and leave it alone until I have…

…Still here? Then I suppose these will be my last words to you. Writing to you as if I am dead feels like an odd thing to do, and I trust it will be some years before you read this letter. I certainly have no plans to depart this life imminently, but it seems only practical to make a few notes, just in case, and New Year's Day is as good a day as any to look towards the future. None of us knows what the future holds (and a jolly good thing too) but one thing I learned from my time as a Boy Scout is that there's no harm in being prepared.

You'll find my will, details of finances/insurances etc. in the safe in my wardrobe. The combination is my year of birth, which you will hopefully remember or be able to work out. I can summarise my will easily here: apart from a few small bequests, everything is to be divided equally between you (that is, all that remains after Her Majesty's Treasury has finished creaming off its portion). Share out your mother's jewellery between our granddaughters, and give Dylan my watch. There are no especially valuable pieces, I'm afraid, as Diana preferred to store up her treasures in heaven, not in her jewellery box. I wish she had lived long enough to know our grandchildren. She would have loved them.

I hope to be around long enough to make arrangements for Jean, as she will almost certainly need residential care within the next twelve to eighteen months. I know I can rely on you to do whatever is in her best interests, if events overtake me.

You have grown into good men - loyal, caring and responsible – and you have made me a very proud father and grandfather. I have no words of wisdom or advice with which to leave you, apart from only one suggestion, learned from my own experience: live while you may. Carpe Diem!

With regard to my funeral, do whatever comforts you. Let Megan choose a poem, if it helps. Make the hymns cheerful, not dreary, and don't waste money on flowers or a fancy coffin. I trust I shall be too busy catching up with your mum to appreciate all the fuss.

God bless you both,
Dad

Megan watched Rob fold the sheaves of paper, his hands shaking. It was the first time he had read Hugh's letter: she and Tom had thought it prudent to wait until Jean had gone to the day-care centre before showing it to him. The way his voice threatened to crack as he reached the end made her heart go out to him.

Witnessing Tom and Rob's grief, and joining in it, was every bit as awful as she had expected it to be. It wasn't that anyone was behaving badly. They weren't a family that went in for overblown displays of emotion, so there'd be no open casket with mourners wailing over the corpse, no blazing rows over money. And yet somehow their quiet and dignified state of shock was no less painful to observe.

Robert had slipped the letter neatly back into its envelope and folded the flap down, creasing it sharply back into place. "Do you think he knew he was dying?" he asked, his voice tight with restrained emotion.

"I don't know." Tom spoke softly from his perch on the sofa, one arm around his knees and his feet up on the upholstery in defiance of his parents' rules.

"I think he must have realised. He wrote this letter months ago. Yet he didn't say a word to us. We went through the whole summer not suspecting anything was wrong. Linda and I would never have booked a holiday in the U.S. if we'd known he could drop dead at any moment. He kept us in the dark and look at the result. I can't believe it." He dropped Hugh's letter onto the coffee table and spun on his heel, glaring out of the window at the Jaguar parked in its customary spot. It was the closest Megan had ever seen him come to losing his temper.

Tom curled up tighter, like a hermit crab retreating into its shell. He would hate any criticism of Hugh, but would inevitably seek to avoid confrontation. Knowing that, she felt obliged to leap in and offer some kind of defence.

"You can't necessarily assume he knew. He wasn't a young man. It sounds to me as if he was just taking precautions, future-proofing things."

Rob's dour look made her drop it. Perhaps it was better to keep out of this, leave it to the brothers to sort things between them. She focused on Dylan, dozing in the crook of her arm like a baby again, blissfully oblivious to the undercurrents of emotion in the room. His head was heavy, his blond curls sweaty against her skin. How glorious to be so peaceful.

"If he knew, he should have told us," Rob insisted to the room at large, his vehemence making Dandy wake up and look around for the cause of the disturbance. Dylan stirred, and Megan hushed him, but Rob didn't take the hint: apparently he hadn't yet finished venting his spleen. "It was wrong of him to withhold information like that from us. And if he knew that he had heart trouble, why didn't he get treatment? That..." He indicated the letter with a dismissive gesture. "...He treats it almost like a joke. As if the only thing he was worried about was us snooping about in his desk, or having gloomy hymns at his funeral. How could he be so flippant about something so important?"

His wife Linda spoke up, taking care to avoid snagging her black tights on her heel as she crossed her legs. Megan focused on Dylan's face again. For some reason, Linda's ladylike airs never failed to annoy her.

"I agree with Robert. If he knew, then saying nothing was inevitably going to cause us all the most dreadful shock. It must have been awful for you, Tom, finding him in the woods like that. And imagine if it had happened at home, with Jean. How would she have coped? I feel quite disappointed in Hugh, I must say."

Tom inhaled sharply. "If he did know there was something wrong with his heart – and that's a very big if, because there's no evidence, and I honestly think he'd have had it treated… *If* he withheld that information then I would say he was protecting us. Not to mention protecting himself. He just wanted to go on living, right up to the end. And that's what he did. He put his affairs quietly in order, wrote his letter, and got on with things. He would have hated having to sit down and agonise over it all with us. He wouldn't have wanted to upset us or to be the cause of any worry. And yes, I suppose he does sound a bit flippant. But it's just like him to make light of things, to avoid any fuss. It's exactly that stalwart, indefatigable, ironic sense of humour that I remember. As much as I wish he wasn't gone, I'm glad he did it his way. Don't we all want to control our own destiny, as far as we may? Life is short, and precious; and we all have a duty to make it the very best it can be. But most of us leave it until it's too late."

Linda's mouth opened and then closed again.

Rob plumped down onto the other end of the sofa as if the air had been pricked out of him. "When you found him… Did he look as if he had suffered much?" he asked, subdued.

Megan's eyes stung. The idea of Tom finding Hugh like that… He'd been struggling to sleep soundly, tossing and turning and adjusting his pillow all night long. She'd heard him muttering about ants last night, flapping his hand as if trying to sweep them away. The thought of it had made her shudder.

"No, he looked quite peaceful," Tom replied. "When I look back on it now, I think he must have stumbled: there was mud on his knees, and on his hands. Maybe he fell when it happened - I don't know. But it looked for all the world as if he just sat down in the woods, nodded off and quietly passed away… He'd taken his mobile phone out, but it wasn't turned on."

"No surprise there," Rob interjected.

"Quite. I'm only surprised he was carrying it, to be honest. By my reckoning, by the time he sat against the tree and took the phone out, he can't have had much time left. When you think about it, Rob, it's not such a bad way to go. We should be pleased for him, really."

Linda looked almost offended at this, but something in the raw pain on his face made her refrain from passing comment, for once. No one seemed to know quite what to say next, and the silence in the room was thick and uncomfortable when Nia came bounding in, her usual high spirits undimmed by the gloomy atmosphere. She bounced next to Megan's chair, holding onto the arm for balance, then could contain herself no longer.

"What is it, *cariad*?" Megan asked, putting her free hand lightly on Nia's cheek and looking her in the eye to assure her of her full attention.

"Please can we bake some cakes, Mammy? Please?"

Megan shook her head, firm despite her daughter's beseeching eyes. "Not today, sorry. We'll bake some another day."

Linda's voice cut across Nia's pleas. "I hadn't realised you'd taken to baking, Megan. You used to profess such an aversion to cooking."

Tom looked relieved at the chance to discuss something other than his father's last moments. "She gets help from Betty Crocker," he said with the smallest of smiles, as if to reassure Megan that there was no criticism implied.

She didn't smile back. Why did he have to make a joke of her lack of domesticity in front of Linda, the perfect country housewife?

"You use cake mixes? Oh, Megan, have you any idea how many additives are in those things?"

"Probably no more than are in that margarine you buy to lower Rob's cholesterol," Megan responded tartly, and shushed her daughter with a discouraging glare.

Nia gave one last whine of protest and turned to her father for support. He enfolded her in his arms for the five seconds or so she could remain still before she scrambled off his lap to head upstairs again.

"How long will you let Dylan sleep across your lap like that?" Linda asked. "I never allowed either of mine to fall asleep on me. They were very good at self-soothing in their cots."

Of course they were. India and Sienna were perfect in every way. To hear Linda tell it, they had sprung from the womb fully trained, not to mention super-intelligent. Future Nobel Prize winners, no doubt.

"He always wakes when I put him down in his travel cot, so it's easier just to hold him. It's fine, I'm only sitting here anyway." In fact, she might have attempted to settle him if Linda hadn't looked so censorious. There was a certain sweetness in defying her sister-in-law's perfect standards. "I don't really go in for all that 'self-soothing' stuff for little ones," she went on. "If I woke in the night feeling upset, and Tom told me I should self-soothe and not disturb him until he decided it was time to get up, frankly I'd kick him. If Dylan needs my attention, he'll get it; and as this is a particularly fraught and stressful time, I'm happy to make an exception today and let him cwtch himself off to sleep to get an hour's peace and quiet."

Rob must have detected the rising hackles, as he intervened to change the subject.

"Have you arranged everything with the cricket club for the catering, darling?" he asked Linda, who confirmed that she had.

"What will you wear to the funeral, Megan?" she asked.

Megan paused before replying. Knowing Linda, there was a barb hidden in the question, but she couldn't work out where it would strike. "I'm not sure yet. I've nothing black to wear," she said.

"Really? Surely black is such a wardrobe staple?"

"It doesn't suit me. It makes me look washed out. And it would look awful when Dylan wipes his nose over it, as he'd be bound to do."

Linda looked her up and down. "What a shame, when black is so slimming. Still, there's a Tesco in Ludlow: I expect they sell black clothes in larger sizes. I could look after Dylan for you tomorrow morning if you want to have a look before you head home."

Megan caught her breath, fuming. She couldn't cause Tom and Rob any further anguish by giving in to the urge to respond in kind, but she guessed her face must have said what her lips couldn't when Tom quickly diverted the conversation.

"Do you remember Mum's funeral, Rob? She didn't want anyone to wear black. She said it should be a celebration: everyone should be pleased that she wasn't ill any more, and she'd be having a party in heaven. You wore a bright red shirt, and Dad wore a flowery tie with a yellow shirt. I think it was the most flamboyant thing I ever saw him wear."

Rob's expression softened. "I loved that red shirt, but I couldn't bring myself to wear it again afterwards. It would have brought back too many memories of that day."

"I was still a student," Tom went on. "I only possessed one smart shirt. A blue one, quite restrained by comparison with yours and Dad's. But I did wear multi-coloured stripy socks, and a jazzy tie. She'd have liked them, I think."

"Yes. She had a good sense of fun."

The two men sat in silence for a moment, sliding into memories. Megan was still reeling from Linda's remark about her size. What was it about her sister-in-law that made her so negative about other people? And what gave her the idea that she could say such unkind things?

"Diana had a rather *inappropriate* sense of humour at times, as I recall," Linda said now, with an arched eyebrow. "I remember being quite shocked when she told me about their honeymoon."

Strangely, instead of seeming annoyed, Tom and Rob were grinning at one another. It seemed everyone was in on the joke.

"What did she say about her honeymoon?" Megan asked, curious to know more about the mother-in-law she had never had the chance to meet.

"Robert and I were planning our wedding, and I was telling her about it. Ours wasn't a shotgun wedding like yours: we spent a couple of years planning it so that we could be sure everything would be perfect. She wanted to know all about my dress, and the flowers, and the venue and so forth. Then she asked about our honeymoon. She said she hoped for my sake that it wasn't a cycling holiday. And then she started giggling like a child. Which I thought very odd. I mean, Diana was very poorly by then. She could hardly breathe for laughing. I was actually quite alarmed."

Megan looked at Tom for an explanation, as Linda didn't seem inclined to provide one herself. She'd overlook the remark about her own wedding for the sake of politeness.

"Mum and Dad loved the great outdoors," he explained. "They used to go off on cycling holidays before they married, staying in little guesthouses - always in separate rooms, of course. I remember she told me once that the fear of being an unmarried mother was a very effective contraceptive back in the sixties. It wasn't all sex, drugs and rock 'n' roll, apparently. Not among the middle classes, anyway." His blue eyes twinkled and she smiled back, glad to see him looking a little happier.

"Dad thought that as they'd enjoyed their other cycling holidays so much, it would be the perfect honeymoon," Rob cut in. "But after their wedding night she didn't feel up to cycling twenty-odd miles the next day."

Megan grinned as she caught his meaning, but Linda's nose screwed up as if she had detected an unsavoury smell.

"It gets worse. She told me she could barely sit comfortably at the table for breakfast, never mind ride, so they spent most of the week in bed, perfecting Hugh's understanding of gynaecology. Actually, I thought it rather poor taste to say something like that to her future daughter-in-law."

"She was a GP, darling," Rob reminded her. "She'd seen just about everything: she was the most unshockable person I've ever met."

Tom shook his head. "I don't know about that. Some of her cases did shock her. I remember coming home one day and finding her in a foul temper. She'd had to deal with a man who asked when his wife's episiotomy stitches could be removed, because they were hurting *him*."

Megan winced. "That's horrific. What did she do?"

"She told him what she would do if she found out he'd touched his wife again before she had completely healed. I believe a scalpel was mentioned… She could be quite fiery if she perceived some kind of injustice: I imagine he was persuaded to leave his wife alone for a while."

"We had sausages for dinner that night. Do you remember, Tom? She'd cut them up into really small pieces, and when Dad asked why she said it was to warn us what she'd do if we ever grew up to mistreat our wives."

"She sounds like quite a character," Megan said, envious of Linda for having been a part of Tom's family long before Megan had even met him. She was sure she would have liked her mother-in-law if she had had the chance to get to know her. There were photographs of her in almost every room, portraying long hair and smiling blue eyes that seemed to radiate warmth, intelligence and humour. Not merely pretty, hers was the sort of face you wouldn't forget in a hurry.

"They were both remarkable characters, in their different ways. I miss them," Rob said simply before lurching out of the room, leaving an awkward silence. To Megan's relief, Linda swept out after him.

Megan eyed Tom, but he wasn't weeping. He had rested his head against the sofa cushions with his eyes closed. With a sigh, she crossed the room to join him. Dylan was heavy in her arms, and she eased herself down gently to avoid waking him. Tom adjusted his position so that she could snuggle into the crook of his arm, and leaned his cheek against the top of her head. He felt warm and solid against her, and smelled comfortingly familiar in the midst of all the strangeness surrounding them.

"Thank you," she murmured.

"For what?"

"For stepping in and changing the subject until my desire to kill her had passed."

"Ah, that. Your gorgon eyes gave you away." He pressed a kiss against her hair. "Anyway, I should be thanking you."

"For what?"

"For not giving her the mouthful she deserved. I don't think I'd have the strength to referee between the two of you if it came to a full-on cat-fight. I'd forgotten how exhausting grief is. And how much it hurts. My head is pounding as if I'd had ten pints of Skull Attack."

"I don't suppose the lack of sleep helps. Whenever I stir at night, you seem to be awake already."

His nod acknowledged the truth of her words.

"Try to be nice to Linda," he said. "At least until the funeral's done and we can go home. I know her parenting approach is very different from yours – ours, I mean - but we're all just doing our best, after all. No one's perfect."

Megan bristled. "It's her conviction that she *is* perfect that infuriates me. With her perfect house in the perfect village, eating her perfect organic food in perfect amounts to keep her perfect bloody figure, and her mini-me daughters in their head-to-toe Cath Kidston who wouldn't dream of putting mucky fingers on her perfect paintwork, never mind creating Sharpie masterpieces in their bedrooms. I've seen her looking down her nose at me because our kids are more likely to wear clothes from Primark than Boden, and because they actually get a bit grubby now and then by daring to go wild and have a bit of fun. She can never resist an opportunity to point out that my standards don't measure up to hers. Did you notice that dig suggesting I should get my funeral clothes from Tesco? Do you know, she said yesterday that I should put a picture of Brad Pitt at the bottom of the ironing basket, as it might encourage me to empty it more often. Cheeky cow."

"Perhaps that's how she gets the au pair to do hers?"

She chuckled in spite of herself. "Honestly, my jaw had dropped so far, I was incapable of saying a word."

"You, speechless? I don't believe it."

"You know she's looked down on me ever since the day I first came here with you. Your dad was lovely: he accepted me straight away and acted as if I'd been part of the family forever. But I've never felt comfortable around her. I can feel her sneering every time I slip up and say 'tea' instead of 'dinner'. Or if I forget myself and do something outrageous like cutting my scone instead of breaking it. Do you remember that time we were joking about our A level results and she said 'Why, Megan, you must actually be quite bright to have those grades with your background. Imagine what you might have achieved if you'd been able to go to a decent school.' Well, excuse me if I don't go along with the view that your school, or the brand of clothing you wear, or what you call your evening meal, defines your worth as a human being."

"I agree."

"Believe me, if you were a snob like that, I wouldn't have stayed with you this long." She pulled away to look up at him, in need of reassurance. "Do I really look as if I need clothes in a large size?"

He dragged a hand across his face. "Megan. You had three children in five years; you have a pathological aversion to exercise; and your sweet tooth would rival the Cookie Monster's. You could hardly expect to look like Twiggy."

"So I *do* look fat, then?"

"That's not what I'm saying…"

She sat up straight, eyes accusing, and he shook his head.

"Meg, please. If that came out badly, then I'm sorry. You know, I'm really not up to this…"

Before she could respond, the door burst open so hard it banged against the wall. The elder of their two nieces ran into the room, her forehead creased in a worried frown.

"What's wrong, India?" Tom asked.

Megan hushed Dylan, who had stirred into wakefulness at the loud noise.

"I'm looking for Mummy and Daddy. I need to tell them about Auntie Jean," India gasped. "She's fallen over, and she can't get up. I think you'd better come.

Chapter Six

Sunday 31st August 2014
Cardiff

Only a week after his father's death and Auntie Jean's collapse from a stroke, Tom had never felt less inclined to celebrate. Unfortunately, there was no way to explain that to a nearly-eight year-old who was desperate to have fun and open her presents. Alys's birthday party had left him exhausted, even though he hadn't done all that much, as Megan had shouldered the burden of the arrangements and he had only had to drive them to the soft play venue and pretend he was enjoying himself. Yet by the time they arrived home he ached with weariness and longed for nothing more than to fall into bed.

Unfortunately, there was far too much to be done: school uniforms to be laid out, lunches packed and hair washed to prepare for the first day of the school term tomorrow. He had to hide his dismay when Bethan called to ask if she might come over to deliver Alys's present and card.

"Oh! Yes, of course you can come over," Megan said into the telephone, forcing brightness into her voice even as her look of horror no doubt matched his own. She started gesticulating wildly towards the pile of toys in the middle of the living room floor. "No, it's no problem at all, as long as you don't mind taking us as you find us. It's the usual madhouse here. When will you be here? Oh, in ten minutes? Yes, that's fine."

Tom sighed and sank to his knees to begin sorting the toys into the appropriate boxes. Megan joined him the instant her sister hung up.

"No time to sort them." Breathlessly, she tossed them all into one box and shoved it behind the sofa before dashing off to the kitchen.

He was gathering up a scattered heap of books when she returned with a can of furniture polish.

"You forgot the duster," he said, puzzled.

"No time," she replied, and squirted a jet of polish into the air.

He screwed up his eyes and coughed, perplexed as she hastened to the hall and threw stray shoes and sandals into the cupboard, willy-nilly.

"What's the point of spraying polish into mid-air?"

She grabbed the heap of coats from the newel post and thrust them into the cupboard along with the shoes. "It'll make it smell as if I've been cleaning. It's what I always do. Like those machines on the wall in public toilets. They puff out little bursts of fragrance and it deceives people into thinking that even the most minging toilets are spotless."

He fetched a duster himself while she headed to the kitchen to load the dishwasher. It was only her sister, for heaven's sake. It wasn't as if the Queen was coming to visit.

"Alys! Nia!" Tom called up the stairs after a quick wipe-round with the duster. "Auntie Bethan is coming over any minute with a present!"

Megan assumed her most beatific, homemaker-like smile to answer the door to her sister and brother-in-law.

"Hiya!" Bethan gave her sister her customary crushing hug and kiss before sweeping in with two enormous gift bags, her husband Matt trailing in her wake.

"Where's the birthday girl, then?" Bethan beamed with anticipation, jiggling the gift bags meaningfully before kicking off her shoes to head into the living room. "Ooh, it smells nice in here. I hope you haven't been cleaning on our account. That would be two housework sprees in one week."

"As if I would. I think Alys is upstairs; I'll give her a shout."

"No, no – I'll go on up and surprise her."

Megan's alarm at the idea of anyone seeing the mess upstairs went unnoticed by all but Tom. Ignoring her protests, Bethan started up the stairs with a grin, obviously looking forward to surprising her niece. Tom watched as Megan dithered for a moment before affecting a brittle laugh and surrendering to the inevitable.

Matt settled on the sofa next to Dylan, who was munching on a pot of mini-breadsticks with his gaze fixed on the TV. "Thomas the Tank Engine, eh?" Matt said and ruffled his hair.

"Dat not Thomas. Dat Percy," Dylan corrected him solemnly.

"Ah, silly Uncle Matt. Of course it is. Can you spare a bread stick for me?"

Tom managed an exhausted smile. Matt and Bethan had longed for a child for many years, but had suffered a succession of disappointments. How sad it was that a couple with so much love to give and the means to provide a secure home had not been able to have their deepest wish fulfilled. Life could be so bloody cruel.

Dylan clambered onto Matt's lap and shoved a breadstick so far into his mouth it almost choked him.

"Steady, now," Matt said with a grin, and they chewed on their breadsticks companionably in front of the television. "How are you doing?" he asked, looking now at Tom.

He drew in his breath. How to answer that? Did Matt really want to know about the aching chasm that had opened up in his belly when he found his dad, the spasms of anguish that periodically overwhelmed him?

"I'm okay, thanks. As well as can be expected."

"So sorry to hear about what happened. Must have been a terrible shock."

"Yeah. Not great. Thanks."

"And your auntie? She broke her hip, didn't she? Is she still in hospital?"

"For the time being, yes, until they can sort out some full-time care for her. I'm hoping it won't take too long, but her fall was caused by a stroke, so she's in a bad way, poor thing."

When Megan appeared with mugs of tea, he took his upstairs with a mumbled excuse. The flood of emotions threatening to envelop him might not stay in check if he had to fend off sympathy and make small talk. No one needed to see or hear him going to pieces. People tried to be nice, but it was obvious they didn't know what to say, any more than he did. He curled himself into a foetal position on the bed, breathing in the fresh scent of lavender laundry powder, and tried vainly to empty his disordered mind and gain some respite in sleep until their visitors had gone and it was time to bathe the children and put them to bed.

∞∞∞∞

Megan flipped through the pages of the television listings, unseeing, until at last, still no clearer about what to do with the rest of the evening, she set the magazine down beside her and looked across the room towards Tom.

He seemed to have shrunk in the past week. It was as if a giant hand had reached down from the sky and crumpled him. Grief had aged him ten years or more, deepening the grooves that bracketed his mouth and smudging the puffy shadows under his eyes as if an artist had rubbed charcoal in the creases.

She had devoted a great deal of energy to persuading him not to go to work for the first week or two of the new academic year. While she knew that taking time off would prick his conscience, dealing with five or six classes of teenagers each day and running a busy department would be too much for him in his current state. When she thought back to the levels of stress and depression he had struggled with a couple of years ago, the consequences of which could so easily have cost them their marriage, she was determined to save him from further demands. He was needed in Ludlow to help Jean, and to share the task of tackling Hugh's affairs with Rob. St Dyfrig's High School could manage without its Head of P.E. for a couple of weeks.

To her surprise, he hadn't wept at all. Or if he had, he hadn't done so in front of her. Initially, he'd seemed to waver between numb disbelief and crushing guilt for not being there when his father died and not finding him sooner. She supposed it was an instinctive fear of further loss that made him follow her from room to room at times like a stray puppy, and cling to her or the children whenever a hug was offered. Yet his tortured moments were interspersed with times when he told her amusing anecdotes about his childhood, smiling warmly at his memories of his parents, family outings and holidays at the seaside or in the mountains.

Passing the remote control to him now, she asked:

"See if there's anything on worth watching. Do you fancy a takeaway? I can't face cooking after such a busy day."

"Whatever. I'm not bothered." He flicked briefly through the channels, then passed the remote control back to her. "You choose. I don't really care what we watch."

It was unlike him to be so listless. Tension curled inside her chest. Compassion, and a sense of obligation to at least make an attempt to cheer him up, warred with irritation and fatigue.

"Right. I'll choose something in a minute. Do you want Indian or Chinese?" She forced a smile to her lips, hauling herself to her aching feet to fetch a menu from the drawer.

"It's up to you."

"Well, which would you prefer?"

"Megan, I'm *really* not bothered."

She bridled. "Alright, there's no need for that tone. It was a simple question; all I wanted was a slightly more helpful answer."

She huffed and plumped back onto the sofa, glaring at the menus. He was ominously quiet. His fingers drummed on the arm of the sofa and when she looked up, he was biting his lip. She looked down at the menus again, remorse needling her for being impatient with him.

"How about a lamb saag balti? You always enjoy that."

To her surprise, he sent her a glare that was almost violent in its intensity: she shrank back instinctively into the corner of the sofa.

"For fuck's sake, Megan – when will you get the message? I don't give a shit! I don't care what we watch; I don't care what we eat. I *can't* care. I've got a lump of ice in my chest and I've had to ignore it all day to put on a pretence of being happy for my daughter's birthday, and to be friendly to your sister who still thinks I've let you down, even after two years, and to watch you telling everyone I'm fine considering, and now…" He tugged at his hair with one hand, looking wildly about the room, slumping as he let out his breath all at once – "Now, I just… I'm sorry, I just don't know."

He covered his face with his hands. As she watched, still paralysed by the suddenness of his display of emotion, a burst of sobbing overwhelmed him and he turned to hide his face in the crook of his arm. The ferocity of his weeping was frightening: this was pain on a level she had not witnessed before. He keened like a wounded animal, clinging blindly to her when she crossed the room and opened her arms to him. It was a while before he could blurt out any words, and when he did they were incoherent.

"I just keep – I just… Oh, God. I just keep seeing him there. It was sunny – there was a ray of sunshine resting on him. And ants; I'll never forget those ants. He was cold, Meg. Even in the sunshine, his hand was cold and his fingers were purple and he felt wrong when I touched him. He was there, but the thing that made him Dad, that wasn't there any more. It was as if he was an empty husk. He's gone. My dad's gone, and I don't know what I'm going to do."

His voice fractured. She held him for a long time, not knowing what to say. She held on tightly and stroked his back, ignoring her protesting neck muscles as she tilted her head upwards to rest her chin somewhere near his shoulder. He rocked back and forth, clinging to her small frame for strength until the outburst of emotion had died down and he finally sat back, trembling and whispering apologies.

"I'm sorry. I keep reliving it in my head, and every time it kills me because I should have been there with him. There I was, enjoying myself at the beach - when he was dying in a wood on his own, with no one to hold his hand or reassure him as he passed. I was surfing and he was dying, Meg – he was *dying.*"

Vainly she tried to reason away the images and feelings that tormented him. She ignored the grumbling of her empty stomach: food would have to wait for now.

"You couldn't have stopped it happening even if you'd been there. You did everything you could. You dropped everything to get there quickly, and it was you who found him, not some passing stranger. He can't have been there all that long… And he didn't really die alone: Dandy was with him. He died doing something he enjoyed, in a beautiful and peaceful place with nature around him. No one could have known this would happen."

Kneeling, she cradled his face in her hands, wanting more than anything to make it better. There was a tissue tucked into her bra, and she fumbled for it to wipe the snot and tears from his face.

He thanked her, calmer now.

With a grimace she folded the wet tissue over on itself.

"I wouldn't put that back in your bra if I were you."

"I won't," she told him, warmed by his small attempt at a joke, and clambered onto his lap to allow him to bury his face where the tissue had been.

Chapter Seven

Thursday 4th September 2014
Ludlow

Tom hesitated on the landing outside his father's bedroom. The door was ajar, the scrape and clatter of coat hangers providing a clue as to what was going on inside. He half-turned to step away, almost bumping into Linda as she arrived at the top of the stairs carrying a roll of black refuse sacks.

"Ah, Tom. Have you come to help?" she asked.

He gestured for her to go in first, then followed. The bed was piled with his father's clothes, the wardrobe already half empty and drawers pulled out haphazardly.

Rob paused in the task of unzipping a suit cover, greying hair sticking up and tension radiating from him like a force field. Grief had exhausted Tom, making him slow and awkward; his brother, it seemed, had become a mass of twisted, anxious energy. Ever since he and Linda had flown back from America he had seemed to take refuge in busying himself with tasks, and Tom had been content to let him take charge. But it was too soon for this. They hadn't even buried their father yet. There was no hurry to start picking over his possessions.

"There are two piles," Linda said, shaking out the bin bag she had just torn from the roll.

He stared blankly at her.

"These are for the charity shop; the others are only fit for the bin. Your father obviously wasn't keen on throwing anything away. Look at this sweater: it's full of holes!"

As she held it up, nose wrinkled in distaste at the stains and holes in the brown wool, Tom snatched it from her hands.

It was childish, of course, but the sight of his father's familiar old jackets and sweaters being bagged up for the charity shop made a flame of fury rise in his chest, threatening to overwhelm him. Soon the smell of his father and any sense of his presence would be gone from the house along with his clothes and shoes. He knew he was being irrational: it wasn't as if he wanted to wear the old man's clothes, after all; and it was better to give everything away than to throw it out. He was entirely in favour of recycling, as a general principle. But the idea of strangers wearing his father's familiar shirts, walking in his brogues, threading his ties around their necks, made bitterness flood his throat like bile.

"What do you think you're doing? You can't throw that one away," he said, knowing he sounded unreasonable. "He used to wear this when he took Dandy out in cold weather. I must have seen him in it hundreds of times."

He pressed the sweater to his face. The lambswool felt soft against his skin. It smelled only of laundry soap; the absence of any residue of his father's scent left him disappointed.

Rob folded his arms, lips grimly thin. "Keep it if it means that much to you." His voice was cool with impatience.

"You can't possibly wear it," Linda pointed out. "Look at the state of it. And anyway, it's the sort of thing my grandpa would wear, not a man in his forties."

Tom opened his mouth, but one look at Rob's face quelled his objections. He held the jumper a little longer, while they awaited his decision.

"It's as if you're throwing Dad away," he said at last, tossing the sweater back to his brother.

Rob snapped back. "What would you do, then? Keep this place as some kind of shrine? Let everything get musty and full of moths, so all we can do is take it to the dump? Grow up, Tom. This jumper isn't Dad. None of this is. It's all just stuff. I'll be back at work on Monday, and there's the funeral tomorrow to get through. I haven't time to wait while you sit around investing sentimental meaning into worn-out knitwear. If you don't want to help, that's fair enough; but just piss off out for a run or something, and let us do what needs to be done here."

Tom clenched and unclenched his fists, then spun on his heel. Let them have it their way. Robert had always been the more forceful and dynamic of the two brothers. If he wanted to take over, let him.

∞∞∞∞

Megan watched from the window as Tom fled to their car. He'd flung open the front door and dashed off so quickly, she'd had no chance to ask where he was going. In the aftermath of Hugh's sudden passing and Jean's illness, no one seemed to be behaving normally.

The bedrock of the world they knew seemed to be crumbling away, making the landscape of their life change in a seismic shift and leaving them all disoriented and confused. Hugh's death was the earthquake, Jean's fall the aftershock that reminded them again how suddenly and shockingly life could change. They had found her whimpering incoherently in her room, half of her face drooping like molten wax, one leg useless and clearly causing her great pain. She had hit her head on her bedside table as she fell. Dazed as she was, she again mistook Tom for his father. The despair in his eyes as he knelt beside the old lady and mopped the blood from her scalp, murmuring reassurances, had made Megan's heart ache even as she ran to the telephone.

Although no one said so, Megan guessed they all felt, as she did, that in a horrible way Jean's injury had made things easier. Instead of having to make arrangements to care for her once the funeral was over, they knew she was being well looked after in hospital, and Social Services couldn't avoid the decisions that would need to be made regarding her future. It was clear that Hugh's letter had been right, and she would be unable to live independently.

When Tom returned, the shadows under his eyes and stoop to his shoulders made his exhaustion obvious.

"Where've you been?" she asked, careful to keep her tone interested rather than accusing.

"I went to see Jean."

"How was she?" Megan filled the kettle to make a cup of tea. He looked like he needed one. He sat at the kitchen table and laid his head on his arms.

"She was upset. She cried, and then when I wouldn't agree to what she wanted, she was furious. I've never seen her behave so aggressively before: with her face still affected by the stroke, it wasn't easy to make out what she was saying, but the anger was loud and clear."

"Why was she angry?"

"She wanted to know why Dad hadn't been to visit her in hospital. I had to remind her twice about what's happened, and as if that wasn't painful enough she couldn't get it into her head that she won't be able to go to the funeral. She's worse than Dylan, Meg: at least I can reason with him. She told me I'd let her down – I presume by refusing to take her to her brother's funeral. I've never seen her like that before. Nothing I said made it any better."

As Megan set the mug of tea down beside him, he sat up a little and rubbed his face with his palms. "The trouble is, she's right. I *have* let her down. I should have been able to say something that would offer some comfort; but it's as if I've been emptied out. I had nothing to give her that would have made the slightest difference."

"Don't be so hard on yourself. It's been a week from hell: you're not your usual self. And she's not her old self, either." She couldn't bring herself to say what she was thinking: that Jean might never be her old self again.

His red-rimmed eyes met hers briefly. "I want to do the right thing by her, but she's changed. I don't want to go back to see her again if she's going to put me through the wringer like she did today."

They both gazed into their mugs of tea as if they might find the answers there.

"Do you know, she actually swore at me," he went on. His eyebrows rose at the memory of it. "I've never heard her say anything worse than 'hell' before, and even then she would have apologised. Yet there she was in the hospital ward, cursing like a navvy, slurring her words so badly anyone passing would have assumed she was drunk. It would be funny if it wasn't so sad."

If only she could say or do something that would make things better; but there was nothing anyone could do. "You will go back," she said, reaching out to stroke his arm. "Maybe you and Rob can work something out, take turns to visit. Even if she had no idea who you were, you'd still go. I know you would, because it's the right thing to do."

She watched the conflicting emotions pass over his face. Just when he finally opened his mouth to speak they heard Rob's swift footsteps approaching along the hall and he stiffened, retreating into himself, a sign that he wanted to avoid some kind of drama.

"We have some decisions to make," Rob said.

As much as Megan liked Robert, she couldn't help finding his manner officious when he took charge of things. She gave him a tight smile. There was something going on between the brothers, that much was obvious.

Tom was eyeing him warily. "What kind of decisions?"

"Have you seen how many photograph albums are in the study? There's a whole shelf full of them. Mum and Dad must have taken snapshots everywhere they went. There are discs full of pictures Dad took more recently with his digital camera, too. We need to decide who gets them. Then there's his laptop: I know his password because

I've fixed it for him umpteen times, but Linda and I don't need another laptop – you can take it if you want it."

"Then there's Diana's jewellery," Linda interjected from behind him. "Hugh said he wanted us to divide it between his granddaughters, but it would be impossible to divide it into four parts of equal value. The most valuable piece is her engagement ring, and I think India should get that, as her eldest granddaughter."

Megan shrugged, conscious of them all watching her. "That sounds reasonable." What else could she say? It irritated her that Linda had staked her daughter's claim so quickly, but she didn't want to provoke a family argument by questioning it. Looking up, she saw Linda nod, clearly relieved that Megan had not demurred.

"Your Dad had jewellery too. Robert and I bought him a few tie pins and pairs of cufflinks over the years, and of course he wanted Dylan to have his watch. I presume he meant his good one, not the one he was wearing when he…" At last Linda had the decency to look uncomfortable. "Are you going to keep it all, or sell what you don't want and divide the money between you?"

Tom looked as if he had swallowed something sour, while Rob pulled at his earlobe in a gesture that made him look eerily like his father.

"We might need to wait for probate…" Rob began.

"Do we really have to discuss this now?" Tom asked, interrupting him. "I know we'll have to tackle these issues at some point, but I'm not sure if the day before the funeral is the most appropriate time."

Rob pulled out the chair opposite and sat down. His tone was brisk, even pompous. "Speaking of the funeral – you weren't here when the funeral director called to confirm the arrangements. I've told them we'll visit the chapel of rest tonight. And I told them to pass on any donations in lieu of flowers to the local hospice, as I know it was a cause close to Dad's heart. They've confirmed the family flowers with the florist, and the cricket club has the catering arrangements in hand. And – I almost forgot - they asked if we want them to provide pall-bearers, but obviously I told them we'd be taking care of that."

"Obviously? What's obvious about it? It would be better to let them do it: at least they know what they're doing."

Rob inhaled sharply. "As his son, I *naturally* assumed that you would want to do it."

"Did you? You seem to have assumed quite a lot today."

"What else was I supposed to do? In case you've forgotten, you weren't there, having conveniently disappeared for the afternoon. So what's the problem, little brother? You couldn't be bothered to help us sort out Dad's things, and now you're objecting to helping at his funeral. You didn't used to be this self-centred; what's turned you into such an arsehole now?"

A dangerous flush suffused Tom's face as he faced his brother across the table.

"Come on, now," Megan said, shocked by the sudden change in the atmosphere. "I've never seen either of you like this before. What would your dad say if he could see you like this?"

"He'd probably say 'I want my sons to carry me on my final journey, not complete strangers, so tell Thomas to stop being a spoiled little twat and grow up." Rob laughed bitterly. "I wish they could see you now. You were always Mum's favourite: you couldn't do anything wrong in her eyes. You barely tried at school, and yet their attitude was always 'oh, as long as he's happy'. I don't think either of them ever cared if *I* was happy; as long as I did well in my exams, that was all that mattered."

"Doing well in exams *was* what made you happy! I certainly was not Mum's favourite. You were the one who made them proud. I was the failure of the family. When I think of you and Dad, chewing endlessly over maths problems and bloody physics - you were both in your element. You were the chip off the old block; I was the disappointment. I was the charming idiot; you were the arrogant high achiever – and let's face it, your arrogance is something that's never changed!"

At the look on Rob's face, Megan put a restraining hand on his arm.

"You're both angry," she said, addressing both brothers as they glowered across the table. "It's understandable. Your dad has been taken away; it's been a dreadful shock... Tell me if I've misinterpreted you, but it sounds as if you feel really strongly about wanting to be a coffin bearer, Rob?" She kept her voice quiet, her tone sympathetic, and looked expectantly at Robert to await his response.

Tom opened his mouth to speak but she nudged him and sent a swift warning glance his way before looking to Rob again. As she held his gaze, he exhaled audibly.

"It's the only thing we can do for him now. We did it for Mum…"

"I can understand why it's important to you," she assured him. "Tom, I get the feeling you weren't happy with the decision being made without checking with you first?"

She looked him in the eye. He'd know exactly what she was doing: he would have employed the same behaviour management strategies many times with teenagers at work. Still, it seemed to be working. He looked anguished now, rather than hostile.

"I hated being a bearer at Mum's funeral," he admitted. "It was awful. I was petrified the whole time that I'd trip up the church steps, or that Uncle Jim would drop his corner of the coffin, or that I'd break down in front of everyone. I know it's an honour to do it, and in a way I was glad afterwards that I had, but I just remember feeling sick the whole time. So no - I can't say I'm in a hurry to do it again."

"You're not supposed to enjoy it," Rob said.

"Would you feel better if Rob asked someone else to take your place?" Meg asked, cutting Rob off before his pompous tone could cause further offence.

Tom paused. "No," he said at last. "If it's so important to you, Rob, then I'll do it. But for God's sake, if there are any more decisions like that to be made, ask me first, will you?"

61

Rob nodded, shame-faced. His words poured forth in a rush. "I'm sorry for getting angry. It's not even really you I'm angry with. It sounds terrible to hear myself saying it, but actually the person I'm really angry with is Dad." He looked down, biting his lip.

"You're angry with *Dad*?"

"It's stupid, I know. It's not as if he could help dying. But if he walked into this room now, I'd yell at him for it, and for not telling us if he suspected he had heart trouble, for not doing anything about it and for writing that ridiculous letter… I need someone to blame. I want to throw things, or hit someone. I want God to change things back again to the way they were. I know it's preposterous and there's nothing I or anyone can do to change it. And it makes me livid. I'm not accustomed to being powerless."

Tom took the few steps needed to close the gap between them and laid a hand on his brother's shoulder.

"I know," he said.

It seemed to Megan that the two words encompassed a whole raft of meaning. She sat back silently, the prickle at the back of her nose making her blink and sniff as she watched Robert squeeze and pat his brother's hand. Blindly, she slipped past Linda and out to the hallway.

"Are you alright, Mam?" Alys had emerged from the sitting room with her favourite teddy in her hand. She watched anxiously as Megan reached for a tissue.

"I'm fine thank you, *cariad*. We're just all very sad about Grandpa, aren't we?"

"I wish he was still here," Alys said, following her to the sofa and snuggling against her with a heavy sigh. "Mam, why did he have to die?"

What could she say to that? "I don't know, Alys. Sometimes life is very hard. When things happen that we can't control, we don't always understand the reasons why."

"I wish I had another Grandpa. India and
told me. Now they've only got one. But I haven't g
fair."

Megan blew her nose and took a deep breath to
"You've still got Mamgu Olwen," she said. "You'll be abl
tomorrow because she's coming to look after you and N
Daddy and I go to the church to say goodbye to Grandpa a
funeral."

"But she's really bossy. Grandpa wasn't bossy. He was fun. He
used to tell me stories, and he let us play with his stethoscope and
bandage up our teddies. He said I'm clever enough to be a doctor one
day, if I work hard at school."

Megan's reply caught in her throat. She patted Alys's back a final
time, kissed her cheek and slipped off the sofa, avoiding eye contact
so her daughter wouldn't see the tears that had jumped into her eyes.
Hastening from the room as if there was somewhere else she needed
to be, she made for the stairs, her cheeks burning.

To her shame, she knew the real reason she was crying was not
sadness at Hugh's passing, or relief that Tom and Rob had patched
up their quarrel before it could escalate. It wasn't even pity for the
depth of their sorrow, or for the children's sense of loss. The real
reason she was fighting back tears as she dashed up the stairs was one
she could hardly even admit to herself.

What kind of person could be envious of those who were in
mourning? Yet it was envy of Tom and Rob's loving relationship with
Hugh that made her throat burn and her eyes feel so full. The
magnitude of their sense of loss had opened her mind to all that she
must have missed out on by never knowing her own father. Perhaps
it wasn't true that you couldn't miss what you'd never known.

One thing was for sure: she couldn't let Tom see how she felt. But
she couldn't leave things as they were, either. Because Alys was right:
it just wasn't fair.

Eight

September
low

e'll take you home with us
over," Tom said. He scratched
brown ears, making the dog
lean into his hand.

"What's that?" Megan set her mug down on the scrubbed pine table. Whilst she was sensitive enough to tread carefully around Tom's heightened emotions these days, that didn't mean she was willing to take on the responsibility of a pet. Dandy's soulful eyes watched her as Tom went on patting his head.

"He'll have to come and live with us. We can't leave him on his own here, can we?"

"Well no, but – can't Rob and Linda take him?"

"You're joking, aren't you? They both work full-time; Rob is away half of every week on business. It wouldn't be fair on Dandy to be left alone so much. He's used to having company. And besides, I can't imagine Linda countenancing dog hair on her soft furnishings, can you?"

She spluttered, alarmed by his firm tone. She quite liked Dandy, but then she quite liked baby elephants: it didn't mean she wanted to live with one. It wasn't reasonable for Tom to make this decision without consulting her.

"I've never had a dog," she said. "I don't think I could cope with the extra responsibility, not with three children to look after. And I'm hoping to go back to full-time work soon, if they'll give me the extra hours."

"Are you? It's the first time you've mentioned it."

"I've been thinking of it for a while, but haven't said because, in fairness, you've been a bit preoccupied."

He pressed on, undeterred. "Well, if that's the case, I'll walk him and feed him, so you won't have to do anything. He's easy to look after, aren't you, Dandy?"

The dog's tongue lolled in a friendly grin.

"There must be other places he can go," she protested. "There's bound to be an RSPCA kennel, or something similar, somewhere around here. They could find someone to give him a home."

His gaze was diamond-hard. "Dad wouldn't want Dandy to go to strangers. I like dogs; I grew up with them. I told you years ago that my dream would be to live near the beach with a couple of dogs. You needn't have anything to do with him, if you can't bring yourself to care for an animal."

"It isn't that I don't like animals…"

"Megan, please. I don't often dig my heels in, but I will in this instance. He's going home with us and that's an end to it."

It seemed she was doomed to lose the battle. Swallowing her resentment at being backed into a corner, she pushed her hair back from her face.

"I'm just not used to pets," she said, trying to keep her feelings out of her voice. It wasn't fair to make her feel like a villain for being reluctant to take on such a burden. "It's bound to create extra work. Dog hair and muddy paw prints all over the place. Vet's bills. Not to mention the fact that he smells. He snores, and he farts really horribly…"

"So do you," he replied in a flash. "But no one's proposing to have you rehomed. Although I suppose, in your favour, your breath is *slightly* better than his."

Cheeky. She slapped his arm, as he had probably known she would, and he grinned as if he sensed she had given in.

"You'll have to make it up to me," she said, and was somewhat mollified by the gratitude in his eyes. His smile warmed his face and made the drawn, wearied look of the past days melt away.

"I'll find a way to make it worth your while," he promised. "Let's just get today over with first."

"You're looking a bit better this morning," she ventured. "How are you feeling?"

"I'm coping. Most of the time. Sometimes I even forget for a few minutes. But then I'll remember something about the day I found him, and it's like turning a corner in the street and being hit in the chest by a burst from a water cannon. I'm drenched in it, unable to catch my breath, reeling from the sheer cold shock; and then it passes and I'm left gasping, terrified of having that feeling again." He shook his head as if to clear it.

Dylan had started laughing, and she realised he was dropping pieces of toast into Dandy's waiting mouth.

"I take it you've finished, young man," Tom said, reaching to lift him out of the highchair. He pressed a kiss against Dylan's silky mop of hair before setting him down to race off with the dog.

Megan watched them, biting her lip until she could hold back no longer.

"You're so lucky. At least you knew your father. I know that makes it harder to lose him, but it does mean that you have happy memories to look back on and share with the children. I have no memory of my father at all. I don't even know if he's alive or dead."

"You've never given any indication that it bothers you before."

"I used to think it didn't matter, but since Hugh died I can't stop thinking about it. You've lost someone wonderful who enriched your life and helped you on the road to adulthood. According to my mam all I lost was a lousy piece of shit; but I still lost him. I hardly know anything about him, except what she's told me, and let's face it, she's hardly an unbiased witness. All week I've been wondering… He might be out there, thinking about the daughters he left behind. Or -

he might have died years ago. He might have another family, for all I know. Alys feels sad that she's only got one grandparent, but maybe she's actually got two? Maybe I've even still got grandparents, or siblings I've never met. The not knowing… I didn't really care before, I just accepted what Mam said - but for the last few days it's been driving me nuts."

"Okay. I think I can understand that. The question is, what do you want to do about it?"

She gazed at the dregs in her mug, her mouth turned down at the corners. She had no answer to that. Her mother was the obvious source of information, but as far as she knew there had been no contact with her father for over thirty-five years. Olwen had never been able to forgive his adultery and rarely spoke about him, unless it was to condemn him and men in general as faithless and unreliable. Her stomach quailed at the prospect of her mother's reaction if she raised the subject.

What did she want to do about it? Could she raise the subject with her mother without invoking her wrath? That was a very good question indeed.

∞∞∞∞

The funeral passed in a haze. The church was packed with people, the last arrivals straining to hear from the porch as the vicar conducted the service. Tom, Rob and their cousins carried the coffin without mishap. Tom stared at it throughout the service, his brain protesting at the idea that his father could be inside it. Surely it was too small to hold the man his father had been? How could someone who had played such a huge part in his life be contained within a box?

He felt a peculiar mixture of pleasure and pain at the vicar's tribute to Hugh, describing his achievements as a student and then as a GP;

how he had met his wife Diana at university; his love of hiking, cycling, rugby and cricket, and how he had brought the family through their grief when Diana died.

"I remember telling him once that I thought he had coped remarkably well during her illness and in the time afterwards," the vicar said. "But he laughed in my face and said: 'Coped? I wasn't coping. I was drunk most of the time. The only things keeping me going were whisky and an unwillingness to let her down.' He was a brave man, and I know he would want his sons and their families to be equally brave now, at this difficult time. Though hopefully without resorting to whisky."

Laughter rippled through the congregation, but Tom gripped Megan's hand tightly, remembering his mother's death. Absorbed in his own grief at the time, he had done his best to concentrate on his studies at university so that he could fulfil her wish for him to qualify as a teacher. His training left little time for visits home, and with no mobile phone or email back then, he had been mostly unaware of how his father got through his lonely days after eight long years of supporting his wife's battle against cancer. He felt a wave of guilt, and tried to fight it back. It was pointless now to waste time on regrets.

He kept his eyes on his hands in his lap while Megan made her way to the lectern and read *Death is Nothing at All* in a voice that trembled but still rang out strongly in her lilting Welsh accent. He tried hard to believe the words, knowing his dad would have approved of their sentiments. But Hugh's death didn't feel like nothing. Even if it was true that his father was just around a corner, or in the next room, he was still gone from their lives. The poem, the eulogy and hymns, bidding his father farewell; Linda's soft sniffing into a tissue and Rob's anxiously fidgeting hands next to him: all of it brought home to Tom the magnitude of their loss. He choked back the feeling as it grew in his chest and throat, and tried to look as if he agreed with his wife when she read the final line: "all is well."

At the crematorium, he barely heard the words as the vicar reiterated the promise of eternal life. He bowed his head and said amen with the rest of the congregation, whether out of politeness, habit or genuine conviction he couldn't tell. Did he believe it? There seemed to be so much he wasn't sure of any more.

"Blessed are those who mourn, for they shall be comforted," the vicar said.

Bring it on, he thought, and the sooner the better, sick at the prospect of the terrible finality of the moment when the curtains would close and it would all be over.

∞∞∞∞

Afterwards, at the cricket club, there were smiles and memories to be shared over the buffet. The absence of both their father and Jean left Tom and Rob the most senior members of their branch of the family.

"I hadn't really focussed on it until today, but it's strange to think we're orphans now," Rob said. "Once Jean has gone, it'll be our generation that's next to go."

Tom was quick to brush off his brother's morbid notions. "Hmph. What a cheerful thought. Still, you're older and fatter than me, so I have the comfort of knowing you'll probably make it across the finish line first."

Rob nodded wryly. "At least we know we've given Dad a good send-off. He'd be sorry to miss all his friends and family saying such nice things about him. He was just getting to the age when he might have enjoyed a good funeral. The elderly do, don't they? I was listening to some of the old ladies over there, talking about who else is dead, or nearly dead, or should be dead if they hadn't made a miraculous recovery. That'll be us in thirty years, you know: going to funerals just so we can celebrate still being one of the few left alive, and get a bit of free grub along with the gossip."

Tom eyed the gaggle of old folks nattering animatedly across the room. "Funny, aren't they? They'll brave any amount of misery and undignified weeping for an egg vol-au-vent and a cup of tea. No wonder Jean is so put out about not being able to come."

Hugh's neighbour, Mr Gordon, approached them with a paper plate piled high with chicken bones and discarded cocktail sticks.

"Such a shame about your poor father," he said in his over-loud voice. "Will you be putting the house up for sale now, or will one of you boys move back in?"

The brothers shook their heads and Rob made an excuse to slip away. With Dad gone, and Jean on the point of moving into residential care, there was nothing to draw Tom back to Ludlow, and he knew Megan would never countenance moving to England. She was keen for their children to have a firm sense of their Welsh identity. And besides, he couldn't start thinking about the future when the present was more than enough to deal with.

"No," he said. "We won't be moving back. I've lived in Cardiff since I was a student. I like it there."

"Each to their own. It's a shame about Jean, though. She'll miss you, now that she's on her own. Rita and I did wonder if you or Robert would have her to live with you. There's something so sad about seeing the elderly put away into care."

"*Put away?*" he repeated, horrified. "Rob and I will make sure Jean is very well looked after. She certainly won't be lonely. We'll make regular visits, and she'll have people around her for company. Now, if you'll excuse me..."

He turned away, the firm finality of his gesture seemingly taking the other man by surprise, and headed for Megan, who was frowning at the pontificating of one of the local dignitaries.

"I find I'm getting more and more right-wing as I get older," the man was saying. As far as Megan was concerned, Tom knew this was not something to boast about.

"I suppose it's one of those unfortunate things that come with age," she said. "Like stress incontinence. Something for which people should be pitied. Certainly not something to be discussed with strangers."

The councillor frowned, uncertain, then let out a guffaw of laughter. Perhaps he thought she was joking. Whatever - it was time to rescue them from one another. Tom caught her elbow to pull her away.

"Ye gods, where did they dredge that dinosaur up from?" she whispered as he led her to a quieter corner of the room.

"Who knows? I thought you would prefer the company of a man with a social conscience, so I came to rescue you. And besides, I want to thank you for reading at the service. It can't have been easy."

"I was a bit worried about whether I'd be able to do it without crying," she admitted with a tremulous smile. "Anyway, you didn't do so badly yourself, considering your fears about being a bearer. Hugh would have been proud."

He scuffed his shoe against a flake of pastry that had been dropped onto the carpet.

"Hmmm... I'm glad it's over. Strange to think we'll be back home tomorrow, and in work on Monday. Back to normal." He sounded unconvinced.

Looking up, he saw Olwen ushering the children into the room, and went over to greet them. He hadn't wanted them to witness the intensity of the church service or crematorium, especially as they would have struggled to keep still and quiet, but seeing them here gave his heart a lift.

Olwen resembled a mole in a black velvet tunic and tight leggings that did nothing to flatter her plump torso and short legs. Unusually, she made an effort to be polite.

"I'm sorry for your loss," she said, though the words sounded more brisk than compassionate. "Your dad was a gentleman, and God knows there are few enough of those in this world."

"Thank you, Olwen," he replied, acknowledging her attempt at sympathy while inwardly noting her inability to say anything nice about a man without qualifying the statement.

He led Alys and Nia to the buffet table and they selected their food carefully while he hovered nearby in case they needed anything more. Nia slid hoop-shaped crisps onto her fingers and held up her hand for him to see.

"Look, Daddy: look at my lovely rings."

He made appropriately admiring noises, remembering how he and Rob had done exactly the same at her age, and guided them towards a table.

Nia munched on a ham sandwich, her expression thoughtful. "Daddy, God is in the sky, isn't he? In heaven. So, if God has taken Grandpa to live with him in heaven, does that mean he's on the moon?"

"No, sweetheart. Heaven isn't on the moon. We say it's in the sky, but we can't see it."

"It's invisible, then? Like God is invisible."

He nodded.

"So is Grandpa invisible now, then?"

"You could say that. We can't see him any more. That's why we miss him so much."

Alys cut in, talking through a mouthful of cake. He hadn't the energy to tell her not to speak with her mouth full, or to eat her sandwiches before starting on dessert.

"If God is invisible, how do we know how big he is? He could be big or small. Is he bigger than an aeroplane?"

"Gosh. I've never really thought about whether God is bigger than an aeroplane. I suppose he must be."

"Is he bigger than a giant?" Her serious green eyes, so like her mother's, gazed up trustingly. He took her napkin and wiped the chocolate cake crumbs from her dress.

"Giants aren't real, of course.... But I imagine he would be quite a lot bigger, darling. Would you like something to drink?"

Eager to change the subject, he made for the jug of blackcurrant squash he had spotted across the room and poured some into two plastic beakers. As he did so, Dorothy Freeman appeared at his elbow with a friendly smile. She was in her seventies, a widow with a kindly nature that guaranteed her popularity. Hugh had appreciated her friendship, Tom knew, but he suspected she might once have harboured hopes of more.

"Your dad would have been very proud of you all today. I will miss him, you know. You must let me know if there's anything I can do to help you and Robert, anything at all."

He debated inwardly whether it was fair to burden her. Her offer had sounded sincere enough, and she looked at him speculatively now, as if she sensed his reticence.

"What is it?" she asked. "*Is* there something? If so, you must say. Your father was a dear friend."

"Well – it's only that the house will be empty most of the time, after we all go home tomorrow. We'll be back from time to time to visit Jean and to deal with Dad's affairs, of course, and Mr and Mrs Gordon next door are quite helpful, but..." He hesitated.

"Would you like me to look in now and again? I could pick up the mail and make sure everything's secure. And if you leave your number, I could contact you in the event of any problem." His obvious relief seemed to please her. "That's settled, then. I'll visit Jean as well, of course. It's quite alarming to see how quickly she has deteriorated over the past few months. My husband was very similar... He was a lot older than me," she hastened to add. She touched his arm for emphasis and spoke softly, eyes earnest with sympathy. "If I might be so bold as to offer a word of advice, Tom, it's this: don't let anyone judge you for arranging residential care. Hugh understood more than anyone that there comes a point at which it really is the kindest option for everyone concerned. And that point would have come very quickly whether he had passed away or not. Trained professionals will be able to help in a way that you can't. Unfortunately, people outside the situation are not always as understanding as they should be. Now, I'll let you go. I can see that young Dylan is attracting quite a crowd of admirers."

∞∞∞∞

"Whatever is the matter with you?" Olwen demanded.

Megan shook her head, wishing her mother could have some empathy, just this once. "Nothing. I'll just be glad when all this is over and I can get back home, back to normal. It's been a dreadful week. There's something about grief that brings out a whole host of emotions."

Olwen raised an eyebrow. "You could hardly expect it to be a pleasant time. But it's Tom who's just lost his father, not you; yet he's out there playing the gracious host while you're skulking in the toilets fixing your mascara and looking like the world has ended."

Megan closed her eyes. She shouldn't snap back, but this was too much. The words seemed to fall from her, beyond her control.

"There's no way of knowing how I would behave at *my* father's funeral, though, is there, Mam? You've told me so little about him. I never had the chance to get to know him. I don't even know what he looks like. I could walk past him in the street and not recognise him. And when he dies, I won't know about it. I won't be able to stand beside his coffin and weep, the way we did for Hugh today, and I won't know where his grave is. He could already be dead, for all I know. How do you think that feels, not knowing if my children still have a grandfather left alive?"

She trembled, dreading her mother's reaction, hoping against hope that she might, for once, understand.

Olwen's cheeks had gone white when Megan began, but now they were an angry shade of scarlet.

"Why should you care about him? Do you suppose he cares about you? Do you imagine it would have been difficult for him to find you if he really wanted to? I still live in the same village – it wouldn't have been that hard to track you down, would it? Do you imagine he spared you or your sister a moment's thought when he screwed that girl in my house, any more than he thought of me? Or when he left me without a penny, and sent not a penny in all the years you were growing up? Not so much as a birthday card; not a Christmas present; not a word to ask whether you and Bethan were well, or how you were getting on at school, or whether you were happy. Face facts, Megan: he didn't give a damn about either of you. He was probably relieved to get away from us all."

The words hurt like a physical attack. How unlovable did a person have to be for their own father to want to get away from them? What did it say about her if her own flesh and blood, the man who had given her life, could care so little? Winded, she held her hands to her cheeks, wishing she could rewind the past couple of minutes and erase them for all eternity.

But Olwen hadn't quite finished. She delivered her final judgment in a voice as hard as flint.

"Keep your tears for your father-in-law, Megan, and for your husband who had a father worth grieving over. Yours doesn't even deserve to be called Father: he took no more responsibility for you and Bethan than a tomcat does for its kittens. If you want to know what I think… Well – I can't lie to you, I hope he *is* dead. I hope he died a really horrible death, in pain and alone, with no one to care about him. I hope he's lying in a pauper's grave, unmourned. You might think I'm harsh, but believe me when I tell you this: it would be no more than a man like him deserves."

By Luisa A. Jones

Chapter Nine

Friday 5ᵗʰ September
South Wales

Olwen fumed as she drove home from Ludlow. Megan had no idea, not even the slightest concept of what she had been through thanks to Idris Parry. Hearing her daughter express the sudden and inexplicable yearning to know her father had hurt more than Olwen cared to admit. For more than thirty-five years she had protected her daughters from the truth, deflected their questions and saved her pride and theirs by giving them as little information as possible about what life with him had been like. And this was the thanks she got.

For all that time, she had lived with the consequences of Idris's selfishness, his lies and his fecklessness. He had poisoned her view of men, soured her feelings for her parents and hampered her chances of success, scuppering her attempts to climb the career ladder by giving her two children in the space of as many years. Children were the only thing he ever had given her, she reflected grimly as she negotiated another roundabout, continuing towards Carmarthen and passing the exit for Swansea.

The signs for the town brought memories surging to the surface. She had met him in Swansea, on New Year's Eve in 1975. It seemed a lifetime ago, yet she could recall the details plainly.

She had been invited to a New Year's Eve party by her friend Susan, who knew students in the town and had blithely assured her that they could sleep on the floor after the party and hitchhike home to her parents' farm in Carmarthenshire the next day. Olwen had never tried hitchhiking before, and was nervous at the prospect of it; but Susan did it all the time, relying on it as her main mode of transport to and from college. She had only ever encountered one creepy driver, she assured Olwen as they walked briskly through the town, and had managed to evade him quite easily by pretending to need the loo. There was no need to worry, no need to be so very *parochial* about it.

Her stomach clenched on hearing that word. She was well aware that she was inexperienced in the ways of the world. Susan, by contrast, had tasted life: experience hung about her like exotic perfume. Not yet twenty-one and all too aware of her own lack of polish, Olwen alternated between fascination and bitter envy of her friend's superiority.

She spent hours making her party dress. Almost all of her clothes were home-made, as her mother demanded the lion's share of her paltry wage from her secretarial job, leaving little money to spare for clothes shopping. She loved the confidence her new dress gave her with its feminine Empire-style bust-line and full sleeves. It was long, with a ruffle at the hem and a bow at the bodice, almost like a real Laura Ashley frock - or so she hoped. Twirling in front of the mirror, she hoped the long gown would lend her an air of sophistication. Admittedly, she hadn't sewn the zip in very neatly at the back… but with her long auburn hair loose hopefully no one would notice.

The air in the student digs was a smog of cigarette smoke that stung at her eyes, making her squint and cough as they entered, although she soon acclimatised and joined in, accepting a cigarette from one of Susan's friends but doing her best not to inhale. The press of bodies around her was overpowering and the music blaring from the record player in one corner made conversation difficult, so she held her cigarette at a lofty angle, her arm tucked against her body, and tried to look more at ease than she felt.

A couple of hours into the evening she realised she had no idea how much she had drunk, but she felt uncomfortably hot and unsteady, as if she was standing up in a rowing boat on a summer afternoon. Olwen's anxiety grew as she shoved her way through the crowd back to her friend. Susan had downed several glasses of brandy and Babycham, growing embarrassingly giggly and attracting the attention of various men who seemed to see it as their right to take advantage. She didn't even push them away when they danced up close, rubbing themselves against her. The look in their eyes made Olwen's mouth go dry.

"Don't you think you've had enough?" Olwen beseeched her, dragging her outside for some fresh air. Susan staggered, almost knocking Olwen over as she teetered in her platform shoes.

"Ooohhhh, I do feel a bit sick actually."

Olwen had just enough time to whip the lid off the dustbin and shield herself with it as Susan vomited into the ash and empty bottles within.

She passed her friend a handkerchief.

A young man with long hair and ginger sideburns almost as wide as his shirt collar tumbled out of the front door. "Had a bit too much, have you love? Come here: I'll look after you."

Olwen scowled at him, but he didn't take the hint, tugging at Susan's arm to take her back inside.

"I dunno…" Susan tried to pull her arm back, but he was stubborn and considerably stronger.

"Come on, I'll get you another drink," he insisted, snaking an arm around her waist.

"Leave her alone!" Olwen protested, as Susan's feeble attempts to push him away were easily foiled by his superior muscle power.

He ignored her, nuzzling against Susan's hair.

"I said, leave her alone!"

He swatted her away, then swept his hand downwards to clasp Susan's buttock. Susan whimpered in protest and Olwen's sense of panic grew.

Another man appeared in the doorway, flinging a coat over one shoulder and reaching for the packet of cigarettes in the breast pocket of his shirt. Would this man help them, or would he be another creep? He seemed to take in the situation at a glance.

"Ah, there you are," he remarked, as though he knew them, even though she'd never seen him before. "I've been looking everywhere for you two… 'Scuse me, mate, they're with me."

He smiled, and Olwen was struck by his eyes – the clearest, calmest, *purest* blue eyes she'd ever seen. Young, with a sandy moustache that she guessed he hoped would make him look older, and short for a man, despite the heeled boots he wore under his flared jeans. Considerably shorter than the leering brute who was still pawing at Susan. Olwen wasn't sure how he did it, whether it was perhaps his apparently guileless, unthreatening features or the strength evident in the sinewy forearm holding his jacket, but at last, thank God, something convinced the other man to let go of Susan's waist.

"Oh, no – I feel sick again," she said; and before the pest could move away she threw up, splattering him with vomit that reeked evilly of alcohol.

"Stupid bitch! You're welcome to her, mate," he said to the fair-haired man in the doorway. Backing away, he inspected his clothes in disgust and spat on the ground before heading down the street.

Shaking, Olwen touched Susan's arm. She had begun to cry quietly, dabbing at her mouth with Olwen's handkerchief. The boy in the doorway scratched behind his ear, as if trying to decide what to do next, then stepped down from the threshold towards them.

"*Duw*, you're in a state. Still, looking on the bright side, you improved the colour of that bloke's jacket no end…" He turned to Olwen, and for once she was glad to be the sensible one, because it meant this rescuer would pay attention to her. "How are you going to get her home, *Cyw*?"

"We weren't planning to go home until morning, but we can't really stay now. Could you take us home? I'll give you money for petrol." She gazed at him, willing him to do something more to help. She was way out of her depth, with nowhere to take her friend at this hour, no shops open and the possibility of encountering more drunken revellers at every turn. Although this boy was a stranger, he had a lazy charm that suggested he wasn't about to try anything improper.

"Well, I was going to head off, but…. Where do you live?"

He whistled through his teeth when Olwen told him, looking suddenly doubtful, but the three pound notes the girls pressed into his hand won him round.

"Come on then, girls," he said, as if giving in to a generous impulse. "Idris Parry's chauffeur-driven limo at your service." He held out both arms, elbows crooked, and they tucked their hands in gratefully.

It wasn't a limousine, of course. It was a builder's van, and none too clean at that, with only two seats in the front. He rummaged among the tools in the back and produced a crumpled paper bag for Susan, "just in case". They debated briefly over who should sit on whose lap while he sprang into the driver's seat, started the rattly engine and lit up a cigarette.

"Hurry up, if you're coming!" he called out.

Taking charge, Olwen climbed in. Susan perched on her lap, clutching the paper bag, and they giggled and gripped each other to steady themselves as Idris crunched the gears and set off towards the outskirts of town. It wasn't long before Susan fell asleep, her head lolling on Olwen's shoulder.

Unable to look directly ahead because of Susan's long hair in her face, Olwen faced towards Idris and watched him as he drove. There was a spark about him, she thought: a cheeky grin lit his face from time to time as he glanced at them. His sky blue eyes were his best feature, she decided, although she found her gaze drawn to his forearms as he drove out of town and headed west. She had felt the subdued strength of his arm muscles when she held on to him earlier. It had given her a curiously excited feeling low down in her gut.

He was a carpenter by trade, he told them, which explained the strength in those arms. He had been working in Swansea recently, but generally went wherever the work took him. He'd been all over the country, it seemed: even to London, which he described as a paradise. It seemed such an exciting way of life to a girl who rarely ventured more than twenty-five miles from the family farm.

He gave away little more than this about his own life, but was disarmingly easy to talk to, taking a flattering interest in her. Olwen found herself telling him about her job, her adoptive parents, and her annoying brother Rhodri who planned to have his own farm one day.

"I wish I could travel, like you do," she admitted.

"With you being adopted, who knows? Perhaps there's a bit of Irish gypsy in you, giving you a wanderlust as well as the red hair… Stick with me, kid. I could show you a few things, let me tell you." He was quiet after that, smiling to himself in a way that she found irresistibly mysterious.

As they drew nearer to the village where Susan lived, Olwen prodded her awake.

"We need to get our story straight. I told Mam and Dad we'd be staying with a friend of yours tonight. If I arrive home at this hour, the dogs will wake everybody up, and Dad will go bananas. He'll want to know why I've come home early, and how I got home, and then I'll have to tell him about you getting drunk and Idris taking us home, and he'll probably never let me out again. He'll stop me going anywhere with you."

Susan's brows drew together as she tried to formulate a plan in her drink-addled brain, but rational thought seemed beyond her.

Idris offered them a simple solution. "Don't go home until the time he was expecting you. That way, you won't need to tell him anything."

Both girls stared at him.

"That would work," Susan began. "But you can't come back to my place. My parents will blame you for letting me get drunk. I'll stay at my sister's tonight: I've got a key, I can just kip down on the sofa. But you can't sleep there, sorry. She won't want me letting anyone else in."

Olwen's eyes widened, and her voice came out as a thin squeak. "What am I going to do, then? I can't just stay out all night."

Susan had the grace to look sheepish. "I'm really sorry, Ol. I brought a friend back once before, and she went loopy. She said I was treating her place like a dosshouse and she'd take her key back if I ever do it again. You'll think of something, though, won't you?"

Idris was cheerful and reassuring. "We'll sort something out, don't you worry, *Cyw*. The last thing we want is for you to get into any bother."

The street was in darkness as they drew up outside Susan's sister's tiny terraced house. They said their goodbyes in stage whispers and Olwen watched her friend silently creep inside.

She turned to Idris, at a loss to know what to do next.

"Where now?" she asked him, croaky with nerves.

His only response was to wink, grin and set off again, driving away from the village and out into the country lanes heading, as far as she could tell, towards the coast.

"You wouldn't…. You know..?" She started to tremble, plucking at her skirt, as it dawned on her how vulnerable her position now was. He seemed nice enough, but he was a stranger after all, and he was a man.

"I wouldn't what?"

She summoned the strength to voice her fears aloud. "You wouldn't hurt me, would you? I mean, Susan would be able to tell the police who you are. You gave us your name, and she's seen the name of the firm on the van. It wouldn't be hard for them to track you down…"

He laughed as if she had made a huge joke. "Don't be daft. I've never forced myself onto a girl. We'll find a nice safe place to stop over, and then you can bed down in the back of the van while I sleep in the front. I can drop you home tomorrow, or take you to Susan's so you can pretend to go home from there. How does that sound?"

"Oh! That sounds very kind. Thank you." She let out her breath in a rush, embarrassed for having doubted his intentions.

He found a farm track after a while, pulled into it and parked just beyond the gate.

"Here we are," he said, pleased with himself. "Safe as houses."

"Are you sure? What if someone comes along?"

"I've kipped here before and never been disturbed. It's cool."

There was a single mattress in the back of the van, roped upright against the side. He untied it, laid it down and lifted a bundle of blankets from a corner, shaking dust from them before tossing them onto the makeshift bed. It smelled musty, but it was more appealing than sitting upright all night in the front seat, as he would be doing.

She hesitated before climbing into the back. "Why have you got a mattress in your van?"

"I told you: I go where the work is. Sometimes I sleep in here, if I've nowhere else to stay, or if I'm a bit low on the readies. Why? What did you think I do with it?"

She was too embarrassed to use the phrase "passion wagon", so remained silent, and he let it go; but again she could sense his amusement.

"I'll leave you to it," he said, and went to answer the call of nature in a hedgerow. She watched the dark shape of him silhouetted against the sky as he strolled back and slipped into the driving seat with a sigh. While she burrowed under the scratchy, fusty blankets, she heard him arranging his coat over himself.

She grew gradually warmer in her woolly cocoon, but intensely aware of his restlessness. He shifted and huffed every few minutes, his obvious discomfort increasing in direct proportion with her sense of guilt for taking his bed.

When she looked back, all these years later, she decided it had all been part of his plan. His seduction technique was cunning. The combination of his admiring looks and the gentlemanly gesture of suffering discomfort on her account had beguiled her. When she heard his teeth begin to chatter, she could bear it no longer.

"Are you cold?" she asked.

"Oh, I'm alright," he replied, teeth clattering together. "Don't worry about me – just so long as you're okay."

She gnawed at the corner of her lip, pondering what to do. He was shifting uncomfortably again.

"I can make room for you in the back, if you like."

There was only a moment's hesitation. "Well… as long as you're sure? It would certainly be warmer, and my neck is getting a bit stiff…"

"It's alright," she said, already wishing she hadn't felt obliged to extend the invitation, but conscious that it would have been selfish to leave him shivering and uncomfortable.

He needed no further prompting, but was out of the driver's door and in at the back of the van before she could change her mind.

"Oh, you're lovely and warm! Thanks, *Cyw*," he exclaimed, squeezing in next to her.

Her voice had stopped co-operating at the moment she felt him lift the blankets, so she nodded and lay looking up at the dark space under the roof of the van, acutely aware of him shivering beside her. After a while, he spoke again in that smiling voice.

"I've got something else that will keep us both warm."

She froze, unsure what he meant. He rummaged under the blankets, then pulled out a hip flask. She could see the silvery gleam of it in the faint glow of light coming in through the front windows as he unscrewed the lid and tipped a slug of the contents into his mouth.

"Ah, that's better. Go on, live a little – it'll warm your cockles."

He nudged her and she reached out to take the flask. As much as she didn't really want any more alcohol, it would be nice to feel a little warmer… And braver, given that she had suddenly ended up in bed with a complete stranger, in the middle of nowhere. Even though they were both fully clothed, the idea of it, and the knowledge of how much her parents would disapprove, made her feel she had stepped far beyond the boundaries of her usual life.

Perhaps he was right: she should learn to relax and live a little. Hadn't she been afraid that she would never know any excitement in her life? Hadn't she been desperate for new experiences? And it would be impolite and ungrateful to refuse his generosity when he had gone out of his way to help her and Susan.

She took a sip from the flask and immediately spluttered from the rawness of the alcohol in her throat. Her coughing made him laugh, though not unkindly, she thought.

"Have a bit more, go on. You can't just sip it like a vicar's wife taking afternoon tea. This is rum: you need to drink it like a pirate. Ooh arrr, Jim lad...." he growled, making her giggle despite herself. She took a bigger sip and handed the flask back to him. The rum warmed its way down to her stomach.

"To tell you the truth, I can't quite believe my own restraint," he said after a while. He had stopped shivering by now, and lay very still beside her.

She couldn't read his expression in the darkness.

"Why?" she asked, finding her voice again.

"To be in bed with a girl like you, all on our own with no one to disturb us, and not do anything. It's taking all the strength I've got not to kiss you, at least."

Her eyes widened. "With a girl like me?"

"Mmmm.... A girl like you."

He'd been so damnably clever, she thought now, as she drew up at another roundabout ready to continue past Carmarthen and northwest towards home. It wasn't actually a compliment, as such. "A girl like you" could mean anything. Yet she had fallen for it. She had felt like a precious gem as she lay there next to him, warmed by rum and soaking up what she imagined was his admiration. And of course, he hadn't even had to make the first move, because she'd fallen so completely under that clever spell that she had oh, so stupidly, moved very slightly as if to kiss him; and that, of course, was the point of no return.

He had flattered her into relinquishing her virginity, fooling her into believing it would be safe by telling her he must be sterile as he'd had mumps as a child. Then came that single ten minute episode of unsatisfying, half-clothed fumbling and brief discomfort that made her wonder why on earth people were so obsessed with sex, if that was all it was, because there was no pleasure in it beyond knowing that a man desired her.

Strange, she thought now, that she had allowed him to see her again, and do it again – but she supposed these things generally only go in one direction. Having been willing to allow it once, she'd felt unable to refuse to do it again. Virgins, at least, had an excuse for saying no.

She'd been such a gullible fool, even fancying herself in love with him – because how else could she justify letting him do what he did?

Desperation - to be loved, to get away from her rural home – must have hung about her like an aura. She'd told herself that he could have taken her home first, instead of Susan: she was so flattered that he had chosen her over her prettier friend that she hadn't paused to ask herself why. He told her the reason much later, when it was too late to extricate herself.

"I never go for the pretty girl. The plainer friend is always so much more grateful, she'll do anything. The pretty ones think they're so fucking entitled; the plain ones are undemanding. Like you, Olwen. You were much easier than I expected you to be." His eyes weren't guileless or smiling any more: they were filled with a boredom and contempt that chilled her.

If only she could travel back in time, warn the girl she used to be against such stupidity and stop her before she ever lay down on that mattress. Then she wouldn't have her daughters, of course; but she wouldn't have chosen the life she ended up with, the life that seized her so suddenly by the scruff of the neck a few weeks after he had lied his way into her naïve affections.

She started being sick in the mornings before she had even known him long enough to introduce him to her parents. The unfairness of it still rankled, nearly forty years later. His story of the mumps hadn't been true, of course. Even the van wasn't his: he had borrowed it from a friend. And he wasn't a proper carpenter at all, but a jobbing labourer who travelled around like a gypsy, picking up work when he felt like it – which was generally when he had run out of beer money. He had spun a web of untruths and half-truths, and she had allowed herself to be dazzled by his smile and the beauty of his eyes into believing whatever he said.

Her mother had been quick to realise what was causing Olwen to look so dreadful in the mornings, and dragged her to the local doctor for her suspicions to be confirmed. Faced with the doctor's disapproving glare and her mother's tears of shame, Olwen had made a private vow never to be taken in by a charming smile and faithless words again.

Her father had to be told, and she was left in no doubt of the depths of her disgrace. Modern ways had passed her parents by: their religious views would not countenance the possibility of an abortion, even though it was no longer illegal; but neither could she be permitted to bring up the baby as an unmarried mother. If she was to remain a member of their family, she must marry the baby's father.

Reality dawned. Idris had never said he loved her. He was charming and fun, but she knew relatively little about him. She confessed the arrangements for their next assignation to her father, who waited at the bus stop with her for the arrival of her unsuspecting lover.

Idris thought he was joking at first when marriage was declared the only possible way forward, but her father's threat to blow away his testicles with a shotgun convinced him otherwise. Olwen's father had tracked down Idris's current employer after interrogating her about everything she knew about him. He assured the young man that he knew exactly where to find him if he failed to turn up at the register office. In case this didn't work, he supplemented the stick with a carrot: if Idris married Olwen within the month, her father would give them a thousand pounds to set up a home. It sounded like a fortune. She watched the panic in Idris's eyes turn to speculation and knew as he agreed to the deal that she would not see a penny of the money.

They were married as soon as it could be arranged, at the register office in Carmarthen, with no wedding breakfast, no new clothes, no flowers or fuss. Their only guests were her parents, her brother, and Idris's older sister Delyth, who had voiced some surprise at her young brother's sudden decision to settle down. Her own family had only attended to prevent any whiff of scandal.

Olwen spent their wedding night alone in a ramshackle cottage on the family farm while Idris drowned his sorrows at a late-night lock-in at the local pub. The cottage was barely habitable, with mould on the walls that would soon give her a hacking cough, and gaps around the windows that sucked out the scant warmth she could create with the coal fire. Despite pleading with her parents to let her stay with them, her father was implacable. She had made her bed, and now she could lie in it. Thankfully they were allocated a tiny council house soon after Bethan was born: the thought of bringing up a baby in such damp conditions had terrified her. The thousand pounds her father gave them was quickly spent.

Idris worked away as much as he could. The first time he left, her assumption that he would send money home turned out to be yet another mistake. He came back periodically when the work dried up and he ran out of money, to plead poverty and to charm her into taking pity on him.

She was so lonely, with the responsibility of a tiny baby to care for and no adult company. It wasn't so bad during the daytime, when she could at least get out for a walk with the pram if the weather wasn't too cold. She eked out each visit to the health clinic or local shop, asking questions she knew the answers to, just for the consolation of human interaction. The walls were thin in her council house: sometimes she could hear her next-door neighbours arguing or having sex, and she was never sure whether the sounds were a comfort, giving her the sense of other people nearby, or if they made her feel even more alone. She would stay up each night, watching her rented black and white television until the national anthem and the test card appeared, just to prolong the sound of grown-up voices in the house. She hated going to bed alone, hated being the only adult in the oppressive quiet darkness of the tiny house.

When Idris came home, he exploited her pathetic longings for human interaction for convenience's sake. To him she was just a convenient warm body, someone to provide an occasional meal and a physical release before sleep. Believing she couldn't fall pregnant while their baby was still only a few months old had been the pinnacle of her stupidity. She would never forget the look on Idris's face when she told him she was expecting their second child. Horror and contempt melted together in his cold blue eyes and finally blurred into rage.

"You stupid bitch! I should push you down the stairs, solve the problem for both of us."

She cringed as he lifted his hand to strike her, making him even angrier, and he punched their bedroom door with a force that made her cower, too frightened even to cry. She was too ashamed to tell anyone, convinced that she deserved his insults and his rage. After all, she was angry at herself for being such a fool.

From then on, on his rare visits home, he made no attempt to sleep with her. He would briefly make a show of affection for their girls, then lose interest entirely and head to the pub to spend what little money they had. The charm she had once perceived in him was reserved for other women: women who had the sense to use contraception; women who would part their legs and demand nothing from him beyond a smile and a brief fuck against a wall after pub closing time.

She put up with it until she found him with one of them. She had been called home early from work to collect Bethan and Megan from the babysitter. Bethan had been sick, and the sitter was uncompromising in her refusal to keep her until the end of the day. Braving the disapproval of her boss, she had collected the two little girls and trudged homewards, her head almost bursting with stress. Four year-old Bethan whined all the way. Upon swinging open her front door, she was startled to hear a squeal and a mumbled curse, giving her just enough time to block Bethan and Megan from seeing their father's bare backside as he hastily rose from his position atop a girl he'd been screwing on the stairs.

The girl was panicking, Olwen saw, trying to hide her face and yank her knickers back up. Infuriatingly, Idris looked more irritated than embarrassed by her sudden appearance. He tugged at his jeans and zipped up his fly while the girl hastened to depart. Her pleated skirt and blazer marked her as a sixth-former from the local school. Olwen seized her arm as she ducked past.

"You've forgotten something," she hissed, and indicated the school tie left on the floor.

Outrage seemed to have empowered her with a strength she had never felt before. She looked straight into Idris's blue eyes and spat in his face.

"I'll give you ten minutes to pack. Don't even think about taking anything that belongs to me: I've worked to make this a home, and I won't have you ruining it. I've wasted too much time on you, Idris Parry. I've been a doormat, and you've wiped the dirt off your shoes on me too many times. You needn't think about ever coming back here. I don't care where you go or who you go with, as long as you never see us again."

"You can't stop me seeing my kids," he began.

"I can, and I will. You've never lifted a finger to put food in their mouths or clothes on their backs. You've taken money that I earned to provide for them. You're like a leech, Idris. We don't want you in our lives. Don't ever try to contact them – they're better off without you. Now hurry up. You've only got eight minutes left to pack."

He left, stepping carefully over the puddle of vomit a sobbing Bethan had left on the doorstep after being made to wait too long. He threw his bags into his van without looking back, and had obviously taken her instructions to heart, as there had been no contact from him in all the intervening years. Not a single letter, card or present had ever arrived for Bethan and Megan while they were growing up.

Since her divorce, Olwen had rarely become involved with men: her faith in them had been shattered. She preferred living alone, being self-reliant. When she felt lonely, she considered this less painful than the humiliations she had suffered while married. No, she was infinitely better off like this, living life on her own terms and never having to compromise to please anyone else.

She drew up outside her house and turned off the engine, fatigued from her long journey and the painful memories that had been sparked off. She felt no sense of regret for the end of her marriage, but some for her words to Megan that afternoon. Still – what was done was done. The sooner Megan forgot about her father, the better.

Chapter Ten

Monday 8ᵗʰ September 2014
St Dyfrig's High School, Cardiff

The bright morning sunshine seemed at odds with Tom's gloomy mood, making him squint as he reversed into a space in the staff car park at just after eight o'clock. He killed the engine and sat still for a moment, summoning the will to get out. Monday morning had arrived all too quickly. He had left Megan packing Alys's school bag, rummaging around for a stray reading book that had to be handed in, pleading with Dandy to calm down as he sensed that they were all going out, and wished he could stay in the relative peace of home; but he had already taken a week off work. Delaying any longer would be pointless. It was time to return to reality.

Across the car park, he noticed one of his colleagues getting out of his vehicle. Ignoring the dull headache that had fixed itself across his forehead like a too-tight sweatband, he grabbed his lunch bag and climbed out of his car, hoisting the corners of his mouth in an effort to smile.

"You're back!" Duncan exclaimed and hurried over to greet him. He twitched as if resisting the urge to throw his arms around Tom in a hug, then settled on a quick, awkward pat on the shoulder. "I was so sorry when I heard. It must have been a dreadful shock."

"Thanks, Duncan. It was."

He didn't elaborate, and to his relief Duncan seemed content to walk with him without asking for more details.

"Have I missed much?" Tom asked guiltily, aware that he had been absent at the beginning of term.

"Only the usual chaos. Everyone looked great at the beginning of term, but they're already starting to look weary. You know what it's like. Oh, and Garin seems to have found love."

Tom's step faltered. "Are you serious? Did I just hear you say the words Garin and Love in the same sentence?"

"Well, maybe love is stretching it a bit. He's found regular lust with one person, at least."

"I'm amazed. Next you'll be telling me he wants to settle down and have babies."

Duncan shook his head vehemently, making the thinning hair slip over his bald patch. "No, we'll all be taking cover to avoid low-flying pigs the day that happens."

Tom stepped aside to let the older man enter the building first. Even this early in the term the air in the corridor was rank with the familiar choking cocktail of stale piss from the boys' toilets mixed with deodorant and adolescent sweat from the changing rooms.

Tom's office was small and multi-functional, serving as a meeting room, storage area and administrative centre for the P.E. department with an old, battered desk, two filing cabinets and a pile of boxes holding a variety of equipment and lost property. There was a kettle on the windowsill, and before tackling anything else he took it to fill it up at the washbasin. He couldn't face the day without coffee.

Duncan had left him to it, heading off to dig out the equipment he needed for the first lesson of the day. Stirring his mug of coffee, Tom peered at the messages and documents that had been left on his desk. A glance at his timetable showed that he would be free during the first hour. Good: that would give him a chance to begin catching up. His computer took several minutes to boot up, and he made use of the time to dump as much paper as he could into the recycling bin. Catalogues, unsolicited marketing material, magazines from the teaching union all went in. There was no point in keeping any: he would never find time to read them. Besides, there was a sense of satisfaction in seeing the heap on his desk shrink, even by a little. He took a final slurp of coffee, then made for the school office to check his pigeonhole.

The administrative staff all expressed their pleasure at seeing him back at work. He shuffled the stack of paper in his pigeonhole, selecting anything that looked important to take back to his desk, and tried to avoid engaging in too much conversation. He wasn't ready yet to talk about finding his dad, or to face the kindly faces of the other staff. He could cope with anything but sympathy – that, he knew, could bring him to breaking point quicker than anything.

Back in his office, his emails had finally opened. He swore under his breath, seeing the number in his inbox. How was it possible for so many messages to have found their way to him? An initial sift still left a daunting number to wade through, including one from his line manager summoning him to a Return to Work meeting.

Let me know when you get back, Tom – we'll need to touch base before the close of play that day. Just to give you a heads-up, there are a few initiatives on the radar that could benefit from some blue-sky thinking, such as how we sustain the momentum following the World Cup.

Sorry to hear about your recent family circumstances BTW – obviously my door is always open if you need support going forward.

Regards – Ken.

Tom swore harshly under his breath. Ken was a small man with an overly large ego and an impressive ability to collect corporate-style clichés. Meetings with him tended to be time-consuming, irritating and usually ended by adding a huge number of unanticipated tasks to Tom's to-do list. He dashed off a reply, offering a chat during the lunch break. It would have to do. He had classes for the rest of the morning, and checking his plan for each group's activities had to take priority.

His first lesson was with a group of thirty-two eleven year-old boys, varying in size, culture and ability to a quite startling degree, and clearly nervous of him. He used the full force of his physical presence to impose his authority, clamping down on the slightest infractions, acknowledging good performance with a few words of praise, and watched them scuttle away after an hour knowing his expectations had been established. Next time should be easier. In a fortnight or so he'd even allow himself to smile at them.

At break time, he headed back to his room to find that someone had already put the kettle on. While he checked his emails again for anything urgent, Garin Pugh came in and flopped his lanky frame unceremoniously into the only spare chair. He looked around the room at the posters, the boxes, the pile of work on the desk; indeed, everywhere but at Tom himself; then hoisted his enormous feet onto the corner of the desk. Annoying as this was, at least it seemed Garin wasn't about to broach the subject of Hugh.

"Not sure about you but I'm gagging for something to eat," Garin said by way of greeting. "I didn't get any breakfast this morning. Although three good things did happen to me before I got to work." He counted them off on his fingers. "One: I had sex before I got up. Two: a BMW driver gave way to me, which has never happened to me before in twenty years of driving. And three: I managed to get my USB into its port at the first attempt, which has never happened to anyone I know, so that has to be a good omen for the day. Of course, if you've got any grub to share, it could get even better."

Not quite the usual opening gambit, especially as they hadn't seen each other in seven weeks; but at least Garin's blunt approach was easier to deal with than effusive offers of sympathy.

"If you get your size thirteens off my desk I'll let you have a finger of my KitKat," he replied.

"Ooh, lucky KitKat. Cheers." Garin held out his hand and Tom dug into his desk drawer for the promised chocolate, taking the first part for himself and pointedly withholding the other until Garin's huge feet were back on the floor.

"You look like you had a rough night," Tom remarked curiously, noting the puffy eye bags and dark shadows that indicated a lack of sleep.

Garin's wicked grin told him all he needed to know. "If I told you, you'd be jealous."

"Seriously? On a Sunday night? With school in the morning? Lucky bastard. Most of us have to wait until Friday or Saturday for any nocturnal action." Presumably the woman Duncan had referred to earlier was the reason for Garin's lascivious grin and tired eyes. Tom busied himself with his emails again, only half paying attention.

"Sunday fun day, mate. Women are like old Volkswagen vans. They need to be turned over regularly, kept well lubed, and thoroughly waxed now and again. The seats may get a bit saggy with age, and the ride gets a bit sloppier, but we still won't say no, will we?" He poked a finger into his molars to release clumps of biscuit that had stuck there.

"You're such an unabashed romantic, Gaz. Who's your lucky lady this week? Anyone I know?"

"Mmm, I doubt it. I met her at the beach back in the spring. She's a few years older than me; a cougar, you might even say. Not exactly the prettiest flower in the bouquet, but boy can she handle a surfboard. She used to be a champion, lived in Oz for a while. Still got a great body, even if it is a bit of a shame about the face. All that sunshine and sea air doesn't help to keep the wrinkles and freckles at bay, does it? But hey, who looks at the mantelpiece when they're poking the fire? Typical Swansea girl, she is. Buy her a bag of chips, she'll give you a shag. And if you get a pot of curry sauce to go with them, she'll let you do anything, if you know what I mean."

"Interesting. Perhaps that's how Michael Douglas wooed Catherine Zeta Jones? Tell me, does this sun-damaged Swansea cougar have a name?"

"Her name's Sharon, but I call her Shaz. Or Kronenbourg, because she looks sixteen from the back, but sixty-four when you see her face."

Tom shook his head in exasperation. "How does she resist your charms?"

"Nah, she knows I don't mean it. And she loves having a toy boy to play with. She rides my stick like a pro, and I think you know I'm not just talking about my surfboard. So you'd better make me a coffee to go with the KitKat, Boss, or I'll be asleep by lunchtime. I can't take the pace like I used to."

Tom measured coffee granules into two mugs and stirred in the hot water. "You know, the worst thing about having daughters is knowing there are men like you out there waiting to pounce when they grow up," he said, handing Garin his drink.

"Get away – you had your fair share of conquests in your time. We can't all be serial monogamists like you: some of us like to live it up. Having daughters only worries you because you know how men think."

"It's a great comfort to me, knowing that you'll be far too old to make a play for either of them when they start dating."

"You might think it'd be a fate worse than death for them to meet a hunk like me, but I doubt they'd agree with you. They won't be little girls for ever, you know."

Tom almost choked on his coffee. "For God's sake, Garin… You're talking about my children."

"Yeah, but in ten years even Nia will be legal, won't she? She could be one of those girls you see in Cardiff on a Saturday night, puking in the gutter, staggering along barefoot through the broken glass and the vomit, trying to keep hold of her kebab and her stilettos at the same time; top down here, skirt up here…" His gestures suggested the skimpiest of clothing.

"Just don't, Gaz. Don't do this to me. You're making me want to take them to an uninhabited island and leave them there surrounded by land mines and razor wire."

"Well, I was just pointing out that there are worse things they could do than go out with a bloke like me."

Tom pinched the bridge of his nose, trying to shake off the images and the cold sweat Garin's words had induced. He pushed away the thoughts of under-age pregnancies, drug and alcohol abuse, violence and trafficking that had entered his mind so easily at the thought of his girls grown up and vulnerable. Such things were simply too horrible to contemplate. No, it was time to lighten the load on his already over-stretched nerves.

"You're right," he began with mock solemnity. "There are worse fates. The *very* worst thing they could ever do would be to support Manchester United. That I could never forgive."

Garin whistled through his teeth. "God, yeah. Imagine how ashamed you'd be."

Unlike Tom, who was a lifelong Liverpool FC supporter, Garin was a Cardiff City fan, but their loathing of United was mutual and deeply felt. He shuddered dramatically, then sighed as the bell rang to herald the beginning of the next lesson. Both men rose and slugged their remaining coffee down in a couple of gulps, then went off separately to greet their classes.

∞∞∞∞

When at last lunchtime came, Tom headed across the campus to Ken Haddon's office. He knocked and glanced at his watch, knowing he could expect to wait a while to be summoned into Haddon's presence. Ken was a short man with a highly developed chip on his shoulder and exercising his authority pleased him. When he was finally bidden to enter, Ken didn't look up, but carried on writing something on a pad. Tom's lips pursed: he didn't have the time or the inclination to play this kind of power game, especially not today.

"Not to worry, Ken. If you're too busy now, I'll come back later."

Ken looked up at last. "Ah, Tom. Do sit down."

He took the nearest chair. It was lower than Ken's, presumably calculated to put other people at a disadvantage. He stretched out his legs and tried to assume an expression that looked relaxed but no-nonsense. A don't-mess-with-me face.

"You said you wanted to see me. Something about sustaining the momentum from the World Cup?"

"Ah, yes indeed." Ken paused with his fingers steepled as if in prayer, for dramatic effect perhaps; Tom tapped against his thigh as he fought to contain his impatience. "You're quite right, Tom. We do indeed need to sustain the momentum after the World Cup this summer. And not only the World Cup, but the Commonwealth Games. Wales won thirty-six medals in Glasgow, you know."

Tom nodded. This probably wouldn't be a good time to mention that England had won nearly five times as many medals. The Welsh tended to be tetchy about their national pride.

"So the Head and I are agreed that we need some new initiatives to ensure that the vigour and spirit of this summer isn't forgotten. That's where you come in. We want you to plan a programme of events and activities which will ensure the continuing progress and achievement of our young people in the sporting arena. We'll call it Keep It Up."

Tom made a conscious effort to lower his eyebrows, realising they had risen to an expression of scepticism that bordered on rudeness. Had Ken considered the double entendre in the programme's title?

Ken hadn't finished, it seemed. "I haven't checked yet how Keep It Up translates into Welsh, but I assume Megan could help with that? She speaks Welsh, doesn't she?"

"Some, yes; but her skills are a bit rusty these days…"

His doubts were brushed aside.

"Well, ask someone in the languages department, then. It's all about networking these days, isn't it? Speaking of which, we need to think about ways to improve our presence on social media. The Head feels very strongly about this. How will the parents know about all the fantastic work we are doing unless we tell them? So we want every department to post at least one photo onto Twitter every day."

"I don't even know how to use Twitter."

"Don't worry about that, we'll cover it on our next training day. There's bound to be someone on your team who uses it. Get them to post the photos. Management is about delegation, Tom."

Wasn't it, just? Haddon was so busy delegating tasks, Tom doubted he had time to do any actual work.

"Now, we also need to discuss the issue of raising attainment in literacy across the curriculum."

Tom's brows flew up again. "Megan is the English teacher, not me. I'm the one qualified to teach P.E."

Ken laughed heartily, as if Tom had been joking.

"This is for all departments. Obviously we're keen to raise standards across the curriculum, but we all need to concentrate on raising achievement in the core subjects, especially spelling…"

"When I've got thirty kids on a rugby pitch practising their spatial awareness, team working and motor skills, exactly when and how am I meant to teach them spelling? In between taking photos of them to post online, I suppose?"

The sharpness of his tone earned him a stern glare.

"I'm not here to tell you how to do your job, Tom. You're the expert in how to teach your pupils. But I suggest an obvious option is a plenary session in the changing room. Provide some key words on a whiteboard, get them to copy them down and then test their spellings next lesson."

Unable to quell his derisive snort, Tom muttered under his breath: "Yes, that would be sure to raise their level of attainment." He tried to breathe calmly; this was starting to feel like a bad dream.

Haddon pressed on, regardless.

"We also need to focus on the white boys. There's been a significant improvement in the performance of both girls and our ethnic minority pupils, but ironically the attainment of white boys is falling behind."

Tom drew in his legs and sat straighter, the muscles in his back twinging with tension. "I didn't join the teaching profession to focus on any particular group, Ken. I've always treated every child without favour or prejudice, whoever they are. My focus is on raising *everyone's* attainment."

"Yes, yes: that goes without saying, Tom – but we are all about value added these days, as I'm sure you appreciate."

Tom interrupted him. "Last term the priority was the monitoring and tracking of the most able and talented pupils. The term before that, it was increasing the amount of homework we set. And in the autumn term we had to make cross-curricular numeracy outcomes a priority, along with – what was it, now? Oh, yes: decreasing the amount of teacher-led activities to make our lessons more pupil-centred. How is it that priorities can change every few weeks, Ken? What possible value is there in that? We're so busy planning our new priorities, we don't stop to consider whether anything we're doing actually works."

Haddon held up one finger to indicate that Tom should stop.

"Negativity doesn't help anyone achieve anything. Now, let's summarise the action tasks. It's agreed: a daily tweet from the PE department to showcase your brilliant work; a new focus on spelling; a plan to support white male pupils in raising levels of attainment; and a new Keep It Up sporting programme for each year group, designed to widen participation and sustain our sporting agenda. Put in some aims and objectives, plan your impact measurement and evaluation, include your costings, and email it to me by the end of lunch on Friday, if you don't mind, so that I can digest it in time for the SMT meeting on Monday morning."

"Friday?" Tom almost choked on the word. He would need to spend every waking hour on this to get it done by Friday lunchtime.

"I have every confidence in your ability, Tom," Ken said, rising to his feet to indicate the end of the meeting.

Anger flashed in his brain like a firework, pure in its intensity.

I don't want to do this any more. The sudden conviction was so startling it left him almost winded. The urge to tell Ken what he could do with his ideas, his initiatives and indeed Tom's job revved behind his teeth, set to burst out of his mouth. Somehow, by a supreme act of will, he kept the words in and turned towards the door, then paused, gripping the handle.

"Is there anything else you'd like on your desk by Friday, Ken? My strategy for walking on water, for instance, or for turning water into wine? Costings for feeding the five thousand? A feasibility study around healing the lame and making the blind see, perhaps?"

Ken resumed his seat hastily, muttering excuses about an important telephone call, and with a final defiant glower Tom took his cue to leave.

Back at his office, Garin was eating a sandwich and browsing a supplier's catalogue. Tom pushed the door open so hard it banged against the wall, making him sit up and remove his feet from the desk without having to be told.

"What's up?" Garin asked, obviously alarmed by his expression.

"Haddon," was his terse reply.

Garin rolled his eyes. "What's Kenny Hard-on done now?"

He summed up Haddon's requests, forcing his words out between lips that were still thin with repressed anger.

"What the fuck? Half the kids are on the protection register. We can't go sharing pictures of them in their PE kit. And I didn't go into this line of work to set spelling tests. Tell him to shove it all up his arse."

"You have no idea how tempted I was to do exactly that."

"I hope you put him straight. You'll never get all that Keep It Up shit done by Friday. You only came back to work today and you're teaching most lessons this week."

"I didn't refuse as such. But I don't think he's in any doubt of my feelings about it."

"If he wanted you to plan something like that, he should have told you in the summer term and at least then you'd have had some time to work on it. Mate, you need to stop bending over backwards to help him out and start bending forwards to invite him to kiss your arse. Listen to me: Ken Hard-on is a twat-faced, shit-brained, lily-livered, wanky arsehole. In fact, to call him that is an insult to arseholes, because at least they perform a useful function. I can honestly say that if I saw him about to step out in front of a bus, I'd give him a good shove to make bloody sure it hit him. Fucking Tory tosspot."

Having listened attentively while Garin exhausted his supply of insults, Tom looked past him towards the doorway and waved.

"Hi Ken," he said.

Garin didn't flinch.

"If that short-arsed, weedy little prick was standing behind me, you wouldn't be able to see him past my biceps," he said with a last attempt at defiance, then turned to look, feigning nonchalance. No one was there.

"Still made you look, though," Tom said with a grin that helped to melt away some of his anger. A glance at his watch had him jumping to his feet.

"Shit, I need to cover the second half of Gym Club..."

"Sit down, before you give yourself a heart attack. You can't go leaping about at your age."

It was an inappropriate joke, given what had happened to his dad, but he let it pass: at least Garin wasn't tiptoeing around him. Five years younger than Tom, he could never resist teasing him about being over forty.

"I don't suppose you've had any dinner yet, have you?" Garin went on.

"I haven't had time." He cast a yearning glance at his sandwich box.

"Then I'll cover for you today. It will give you time to start thinking about Kenny's dumb-assed Keep it Up programme. That's if you can think and eat at the same time, of course: it might be beyond your multitasking capabilities."

∞∞∞∞

Megan was seated at the kitchen table surrounded by exercise books when the excited scrabble of Dandy's paws on the hall floor told her Tom had arrived home. She looked up with a welcoming smile and tried to gauge from his expression how his first day back at work had gone. Not well, by the look of him.

"There's Bolognese in the pot," she said. "The kids have already had theirs."

"Thanks. God, I'm glad to be home." He pressed a kiss onto the top of her head.

She turned her attention back to the essay she had been marking. Moments later, an agonised yelp resonated down the hallway. His gladness hadn't lasted long, it seemed.

"What's wrong?" she called out. It couldn't be play dough on the carpet. That would have evoked a roar of rage rather than pain.

"My bloody foot! If you buy Nia any more of this Little Pet Shop stuff I swear I'll divorce you," he said, limping back to the kitchen with a tiny plastic rabbit in his hand.

"That's not Littlest Pet Shop," she said after the briefest of glances. "That's Sylvanian Families."

"Well, whatever it is, Alys and Nia have left it all over the living room floor. This house is like a death-trap. Whenever I think it's safe to cross a room something small and plastic with sharp corners always finds its way under my feet. It's a miracle that Dylan hasn't choked on anything yet."

"I recommend wearing slippers," she said, deliberately keeping her expression bland in the face of his glare.

"And that's the best solution you can come up with? I suppose teaching the children to tidy up hasn't occurred to you, at all?"

She paused, unimpressed but determined not to bite, however much he might deserve it. "*We* have tried doing that for the past eight years and it doesn't appear to have worked. If it hasn't sunk in by now I doubt it ever will. Just pray to God that none of them ever gets into Lego."

He huffed at her lack of sympathy and turned to walk away.

"I wouldn't recommend praying on your knees, though," she added. "Kneeling on tiny plastic animals is even more painful than standing on them."

"Hmph. Thanks for the support. You know what? I wish our kids could grow up in the country, like I did. Then they wouldn't need so many bloody toys: they'd be outside all the time, running around and climbing trees, being active instead of making a mess indoors."

He headed back down the hallway, muttering, and she put down her pen before following.

"Kids in the country don't play outside these days," she said, watching him from the door jamb while he located a clear patch of rug to kneel on and proceeded to toss a variety of tiny items into the designated plastic box. "They're too busy on their Nintendos or watching the Disney Channel, just like the city kids... Thanks for tidying up, by the way; it's reassuring to see that you're no stricter at making the kids do it than I am. You know as well as I that it's quicker and less aggravating to simply do it yourself."

It was almost midnight when he finally joined her in bed. She snuggled against his back, putting her arms around him carefully so as to avoid his erogenous zones. After Dylan's clinginess all day, she had had enough of being touched; but she guessed Tom might appreciate a friendly hug.

"How's your plan for the Keep It Up programme going?"

"I've made precious little progress, to be honest, even after three solid hours. I don't think I've ever felt so utterly empty of ideas or inspiration. My powers of concentration are shot."

"You'll get there," she murmured. "Duncan and the others will help."

"I came so close to telling Ken Haddon exactly what I thought of him today. I came *this* close to saying 'Fuck you, fuck your spellings and your tweets and your Keep It Up programme and fuck your job, I'm going home.'"

She shuddered. "I'm glad you had the sense to park those thoughts and keep quiet."

"Do you know the worst thing?" he asked suddenly, just as sleep beckoned her into its embrace.

"No," she said drowsily, pushing the wooziness away. He obviously felt a need to talk. "What is the worst thing?"

"There was a time when I would have been all for an initiative like this. I'd have been more than happy to put in the extra work, as long as the kids at school were going to benefit. But now, I'm realising that no one really benefits, and I am past being able to care."

He turned over in her arms to lie on his back, frowning upwards towards the ceiling.

"What kind of teacher doesn't care about the kids in his care, Meg? What does it say about me, that I'm not motivated in the slightest by the idea of getting them fitter and healthier and more enthusiastic about my subject?"

If only he would just let it go and fall asleep. She was aching, and her eyelids were weighed down with fatigue. If he could get some rest he'd feel somewhat better in the morning.

"It says you're tired and grieving," she suggested at last. "It would be more surprising if you were leaping around full of energy and enthusiasm, let's be honest."

"Well, in a way old Hard-on's done me a favour," he said. There was a firmness of purpose in his voice that made her eyelids snap open.

"How's that?" she asked, suddenly wary.

"He's helped me make a decision. This year will be my last at St. Dyfrig's High. I've had enough, Meg. When the summer term comes, I'll hand in my notice. I'm leaving teaching for good."

Chapter Eleven

Saturday 13th September 2014
Cardiff

Megan had been at her sister's house for a whole hour before asking the question that had been gnawing at her for the past month.

"Beth, do you ever think about Dad?"

The sisters' eyes met across the table, each the same shade of dark bluish-green flecked with hazel and amber.

"I've been wondering when you'd bring that up," Bethan said. "Mam told me you'd asked her about him."

"Oh. What did she say?"

"That you had some stupid idea about wanting to find him. She wasn't very pleased about it."

"That's an understatement. She made me feel terrible for wanting to know more about him." Megan leaned forward in her seat. "Don't you ever feel like I do – that it's as if half of your past is missing, not knowing where half of your genetic makeup comes from? And particularly now that Tom's parents are both dead: I want to know if my kids still have a grandfather. It's been more than thirty years since Dad left. He might have changed. But if we don't find him, we'll never know."

Bethan set down her hot cup of coffee and pushed biscuit crumbs across the smooth surface of the table, saying nothing. That stubborn pursing of her lips was an expression Megan knew of old, and it didn't bode well. But she couldn't let it drop, not now she'd plucked up the courage to ask.

"How much do you remember about him? You were only about four, weren't you, when he left? I don't remember him at all, but you were that bit older..."

"I remember the day he left."

She leaned forwards eagerly. "Do you, really? Tell me."

"I was poorly, and Mam was in a temper because she'd had to come home early from work. I suppose she was worried about getting into trouble with her boss or losing pay when she could little afford to, but at that age all I knew was that I didn't want her to be cross with me.

"I felt awful all the way home: I remember being sick on the front doorstep. But she wouldn't let us go in straight away. There was shouting in the house; a girl came out in a hurry and ran off without looking at us. Then Dad came out and walked straight past us with some black bags full of stuff. He threw them in his van and drove away. That was the last time I remember seeing him. And I felt so hurt, because he hadn't stopped to look at me, or to ask if I was alright. He just stepped over the sick on the step and went."

"I didn't know that," Megan whispered. Beth had made their father sound cold and unfeeling. But if he had argued with their mother, he was probably just upset, that was all. They both knew how difficult Olwen could be.

"I don't think he was ever much of a father to us. And he certainly wasn't much of a husband. Nobody talked about him much, did they, but from the little I did overhear he sounded like a deadbeat. Are you sure you want to go looking for him, knowing that? Why would you want to invite someone like that into your life?"

"I don't know if I do want him in my life. I just want to know more about him. Whether we've got any half-brothers or sisters out there whom we've never had the chance to meet. If there are any medical conditions on his side of the family. To find out if, maybe, he changed his ways. I'd like to hear his side of the story. I feel as if everyone else has made the decision about whether we get to have a father, and we had no say in it."

Bethan stirred her coffee slowly, then scooped some of the milky foam from the top and sucked it from the spoon.

"It would be weird to have family we've never met…" she said.

Megan watched curiosity catch in her eyes. This was as good a chance as she was ever likely to get – she had better take advantage of her sister's moment of weakness.

"I looked at my birth certificate to see if I could find any clues. It said he was a labourer, and his place of birth was Aberystwyth. Did you know that?"

"I suppose I must have, it'll be on my birth certificate too. But I'd never really focused on it. What difference does it make?"

"Well, it's just strange that they ended up meeting, given that she was from Carmarthenshire."

"To be honest, I've no idea how they met. I just know it was a shotgun wedding. Literally. She would never have married him otherwise."

"I didn't know anything about that."

Bethan's lip curled. "Tadcu threatened him. Being a farmer, he had a gun, didn't he?"

"Really? Bloody hell. It wasn't exactly a recipe for a happy marriage, was it?" Megan's face fell with the disappointment of finding out how reluctant her father had been to get married. She'd imagined her parents as star-crossed young lovers.

"She was only twenty when I was born, and they were different times. These days girls don't need to be lumbered with men they don't want, just because they've got pregnant. Even then, she could have got rid of me, I suppose, if her parents hadn't been so religious."

"Well, thank goodness she didn't. Neither of us would exist, and neither would Alys or Nia or Dylan." She looked down at him. He seemed content, cross-legged on the kitchen floor with his tower of blocks. He must have rebuilt it a million times already but never seemed to tire of it.

"He doesn't even know he's got grandchildren. He should know that, shouldn't he? And to see what we've made of our lives. If we saw him, we could tell him."

111

Bethan held up a hand. "Whoa, hold it there now. I never said I wanted to see him."

"But if I can arrange a meeting, you can't tell me you wouldn't be curious to see what he's like? He'd be proud of us, given what we've achieved."

"I don't know." She shook her head. "Meg, you need to be very, very careful about following this up. You could be opening a lot of old wounds by finding him. If he'd wanted to see us, he could have tracked us down by now. What if he doesn't want to know you?"

"Then I'll still be better off than I am now, because at least I'll know."

She kept her expression positive, even though she knew it wasn't true. Far from making her better off, it would be infinitely worse, because she'd no longer be able to cling to the hope that somehow it had all been a terrible mistake, and that he hadn't really meant to abandon them all those years ago.

"I don't get it. Knowing you aren't wanted would be awful, surely? And Mam will be really hurt, not to mention furious. I honestly don't think this is a good idea." Bethan stood abruptly and picked up their mugs, taking them over to the sink to wash.

Megan swallowed hard, pushed back her chair and stumped past Dylan to shut herself in the downstairs toilet for a few minutes. She needed time to think, a splash of cold water on her wrists and a few deep breaths to steady herself against Bethan's doubts. Shaking the water from her hands, she stood before the mirror and examined her face. Which parts of it resembled their mother? The green eyes, definitely. The nose, perhaps. And of course the auburn hair. Bethan's was browner than either Megan's or Olwen's: where theirs was a true titian colour, hers was chestnut. But the shape of her face wasn't particularly like her mother's, or like anyone in the family she knew. She was petite, like the other women in her family. None of them were taller than five feet one. Like her mother, she had a tendency to put on weight.

Bethan, though, was slender. She could eat whatever she liked without putting on weight, and had always teased Megan about her buxom figure. Had Bethan inherited her physique from their father?

Try as she might, she couldn't remember what he looked like. Olwen had destroyed any photographs long ago, so there was no possibility of ever finding a picture of him.

He was faceless, little more than a phantom she had constructed in her feverish imaginings. The frustrated longing for knowledge made her want to scream and hammer her fists. But what could she do, without risking upsetting her mother and her sister?

∞∞∞∞

By the time she returned to the kitchen, Bethan was washing up and any possibility of continuing their discussion had passed.

Alys ran over and plucked at her top. "*Please*, can we go to the park? It's sunny outside today, we could feed the ducks."

Bethan shrugged. "I've got some stale cobs in the bread crock. I'm up for it if you are."

A walk would be a welcome distraction, she decided. Quickly she cajoled Dylan into a coat before strapping him into his pushchair. With the girls hopping with excitement, they shoved the bread rolls into the basket under the pushchair, slipped the dog's leash through the handle, and set off. Bethan insisted on pushing, and Megan's hands felt strangely light without the pushchair to hold, as if she had forgotten something; it made her realise how much the physical aspects of mothering became automatic.

She fired off instructions as the girls skipped ahead: wait at each corner, stop before stepping out onto the road. Not all drivers were as careful as they should be, and these residential streets, with their pairs of gable-roofed pre-war suburban villas, flanked by parked cars and ornamental trees, were not as safe as the children might believe. It didn't stop her loving the city, though. Each passing car was a reminder that it bustled with life and activity.

"How's school going, girls?" Bethan asked.

"My new teacher has glasses. I still like her, though," Nia said.

"Oh. Well, I'm glad it hasn't put you off."

The two women exchanged amused glances.

"We've got two Miss Williamses at our school, Auntie Beth. There's Miss Williams who's our teacher, and there's Miss Williams who isn't Miss Williams."

The girls ran off to look for conkers, even though it was almost certainly too early to find any.

"That was clear as mud," Bethan remarked with a grin.

"Tell me about it. We get detailed reports every evening over tea about each Miss Williams. It's very important not to get them mixed up."

"By the way – you got me thinking when you said you're planning to go back to work full-time. A vacancy has come up at work. Just a temporary thing, for nine months or so. I'm thinking of applying for it."

Megan tore her gaze away from her daughters and regarded her sister with interest. "Oh? I thought you loved your job. What's made you want to do something else?"

Bethan grimaced. "I need a new project. I've spent the last five years so focussed on the IVF I couldn't really think about anything else. We've spent every spare penny on it, and look where it's got us. Maybe it's time for me to accept that I'm never going to be a mother, and put my energies into something else."

Pained by the difference in their circumstances, Megan watched her daughters romping ahead. It wasn't her fault that she had conceived so easily – too easily, really, given that two of her pregnancies had been accidental – while her sister had struggled for years to no avail. But knowing that didn't make her feel any less guilty.

"What job are you going for?"

"One of our managers is going off on maternity leave. Lucky cow. So I thought to myself, why not give it a go? It could be good experience, and it will send out a message that I'm interested in moving on."

"True. But you don't sound entirely convinced: I'm sensing there's a big but somewhere?"

"Ooh, that's low. Leave my big butt out of this."

They bumped arms and chuckled. They had nearly reached the side of the lake, and Alys and Nia were running back towards them, faces glowing, to fetch the bag of stale bread. For ten minutes or so they supervised, pulling Nia back gently when she strayed too close to the lake, and holding tight to Dandy's lead to stop him stealing the bread or chasing the ducks.

The teeming urban wildlife was wasted on Dylan, who had been soothed to sleep by the movement of his pushchair. Finally they shook out the last few remaining crumbs and continued their stroll while the girls ran ahead towards the playground to burn off more energy on the brightly-painted slides and climbing frames. They loved it here almost as much as Megan did: she had spent so many happy hours here with the children and with friends, enjoying picnics or coffees from the café in the fresh air and experiencing the changing seasons.

Bethan resumed her musing about the job. "I suppose I'm a bit concerned that lower management could be a bit of a poisoned chalice. My perception has always been that it's a shit sandwich… Shit coming from the senior managers above, shit coming from the team below, and I'd get to be the filling in the middle."

"Tom certainly feels that way about it. He gets pretty fed up at times. But Beth, if you're ready to progress in your career, you can't let a bit of shit get in your way."

Right on cue, Beth manoeuvred the pushchair around a dollop of dark green goose poo.

"You're right. I've got fifteen years of experience, it's about time I started moving up the ladder. I need to feel like I'm achieving something for once. If my body won't do what I ask of it, maybe my brain will? I'm sick of feeling like a complete failure. If I get promotion, the team might hate me… but I might start hating myself a bit less."

Megan put an arm around her. "I think you should definitely go for it. You're bossy enough to make an excellent manager."

"Cheers for the vote of confidence."

Her tone was dry but she laughed, and Megan was glad. She hadn't realised how much the IVF had affected her sister's confidence in herself. It must be depressing, of course, to have so many disappointments, not to mention the physical difficulties of injections and procedures so many times. But to see it as a failure in herself – that was something Megan hadn't considered.

Bethan frowned. "I haven't filled in a job application form or had an interview in years. What if I'm rubbish?"

"I'm sure you'll be great. What did Mam used to tell us when we were kids? 'Put can't in your pocket and try'. Which is a bizarre saying, if you think about it."

"At least it was more encouraging than her other catchphrases: 'You're not going out looking like that' and 'What time do you call this?'"

"Aww, she did her best, I suppose. It can't have been easy bringing up two stroppy girls on her own. Who's to say I'll be any better when my kids are older?"

"I bet you will be. You'll have learned from her mistakes."

"Actually, when you think about it – Nia, leave that alone, please..! When you think about it, all of her feminist indoctrination and nagging must have had a positive effect: I mean, look at us now. Decent jobs, decent homes, foreign holidays, husbands who aren't so bad really…"

"Well, Matt isn't, at least…"

"Behave! Tom's as good as gold. Ninety per cent of the time, anyway. You can't tell me Matt doesn't have his little foibles."

"Oh, he does. They just don't involve blowing twelve grand on a camper van and buggering off in it on his own."

Megan paused and laid her hand on her sister's arm, drawing her to a halt.

"Look, Beth - I know you were cross with him, and you felt protective of me; but that was two years ago. Try to be nice."

Bethan sighed. "I do try. It's just – I remember what it was like for you then. But I suppose he could be a lot worse."

"Things are alright between us now, on the whole. I mean, he's got some stupid idea in his head about giving up his job…"

"He what..? Not giving it up completely, surely?"

Megan shook her head. "I'm not taking it seriously. It's just a reaction to his dad's death. Tom's far too traditional and conscious of his responsibilities to become some kind of dropout. He gets a bit down from time to time, and gets these daft ideas, but it never comes to anything."

The girls had come up for their ice cream money, and she counted it out into Alys' outstretched hand before they charged off towards the ice cream van.

"You know, Beth… I feel a bit like you, job-wise. I've spent eight years having kids and it hasn't done my career any good. In a couple of years I'll be forty. I should be a head of department by now, but here I am working three days a week and I've been at the same school for the past decade. I worry that I've missed the boat because working part-time means I don't give the impression that I'm ambitious, but then when Dylan reaches to me for a hug all I want to do is be a total earth mother and mould him to me, to smell that delicious baby smell of him while it lasts and see the adoration in his eyes. No one else looks at me the way he does, as if I'm just the most wonderful creation in the whole universe, and as long as he's got me his life is complete… When I go back to work full-time I'll have all those hours of prep and marking to do, and it'll have to wait until after the kids are in bed because they'll have missed me all day, and I can't just shut myself away and work when they need me. I know I shouldn't complain, but I know how hard it's going to be to have a life and a career and still be a half-decent, not-too-crazy mother and wife. Being needed like that is the most awesome and the most dreadful thing."

Bethan looked away, across the lake towards the birds which were flocking now to another family with a bag of bread.

"Well," she said, so quietly that Megan struggled to hear her. "Even if it's the most dreadful thing you've ever experienced, I'd still swap with you. I'd swap in an instant."

Chapter Twelve

Tuesday 7th October 2014
Cardiff

After a chorus of *Happy Birthday* with candles stuck into the lemon drizzle cake he had baked on the weekend, Tom bathed the children and got them ready for bed. Megan had seemed genuinely delighted with the spa day voucher, the perfume, the books and the green amber jewellery he had bought her. He wished he could have spent more. He'd give her the world if he could. She deserved it for putting up with his gloominess.

"Relax with a nice soak while I sort something to eat. Use that new bubble bath you had for your birthday," he whispered to her as they tiptoed out of Nia's room.

"Do you mean the bubbles that promise to lift and revive me? Frankly, these days it would take a crane and a defibrillator to do that."

But she smiled, and the look on her face when she walked into the bathroom made his efforts seem more than worthwhile. The girls had helped him set up candles of various shapes and sizes, from miniature tea-lights to the hefty trio of church candles that normally stood on the hearth. The scent of the new bubble bath rose from the steaming water; her book lay on the chair next to the bath, and a champagne flute foggy with chilled Prosecco waited on the window ledge. He had hung her robe on the radiator to warm up, and even tidied the bath toys away so that she wouldn't have to share the water with plastic ducks and mermaids.

"Thank you," she murmured. The candlelight caught the tawny bronze lights in the depths of her green eyes as she reached up to bestow a lingering kiss on his smugly smiling lips.

"You can reward me later," he told her, grinning at the thought of the other things he had in store. She hadn't wanted to go out for her birthday, as it was a school night, but he had determined to make the night a special one, and planning it had provided a welcome distraction from the negative thoughts and feelings that plagued him.

Half an hour or so later, with dinner almost ready, he nudged the bathroom door open and crossed the threshold with the next part of his surprise. She lowered her book and stared.

"What on earth have you got there? It looks like a plank."

"You're almost right. Floorboards, actually. I found them in the shed. But don't worry – I cleaned the spiders and cobwebs off before I brought them into the house."

He lay the boards across the bath so that the ends hung over the edges.

"Are you trying to trap me in the bath?"

"No. I'm laying the table."

Everything was coming together just as he had planned. He fetched the tray he had prepared, setting it down on top of the boards that balanced across the bath, then shut the door and quickly stripped off his clothes, careful not to bump into the overhanging ends of the boards and knock everything over.

By the time he slipped into the water at the other end of the bath, she was giggling. Tendrils of unruly hair that had escaped from her high ponytail were curling in the steam from the water, and he returned her admiring glance before turning his attention back to the food on the tray. He bunched his knees up, his feet slippery with bubbles alongside her hips, and resisted the temptation to caress her with his toes, knowing it might make her jump and upset the tray of food. He'd put in too much effort to risk spoiling this now.

"Baked camembert drizzled with olive oil and studded with rosemary and garlic," he announced, lifting the lid off the ceramic dish with a flourish to release the delicious aromas. "Rustic bread for dipping. And there's a chicken and mushroom risotto waiting when you're ready."

He raised his glass in a toast.

"Happy birthday, Mrs Field."

"You're amazing, Mr Field," she said, dropping her book to the floor and picking up a chunk of bread. He had already begun digging the biggest piece into the cheese, eating with his usual hearty relish. The cheese was as delicious as he had hoped, infused with the pungent garlic and rosemary. It clung stringily to the yeasty brown bread.

"Mmmm... I've never eaten a two course meal in the bath, before. Thank you for thinking of it – what a lovely birthday surprise."

"Three courses, actually. There's a chocolate mousse for dessert... I'm glad you like it."

"I'm glad you persuaded me to get such a big bath. Sod the water bills, it's worth every penny for this."

"An inspired decision, I must admit. Especially the freestanding tap: I don't end up with it digging into my back like I used to. But don't drop any crumbs in the water or it'll end up like soup."

"More like bread sauce," she countered. "Or even stuffing, if we drop too much."

"You know how much I like stuffing," he said at once, waggling his eyebrows at the innuendo. She started laughing, almost choking on her piece of bread.

He chewed rapidly, hastening to swallow. "Are you alright?" he asked, rubbing his chest as the bread and cheese went down in a lump. "I wouldn't want to have to spoil our dinner by administering the Heimlich manoeuvre... Ah, you must be alright: no one could giggle that much if they were choking to death. Come on, eat up."

As she dipped another piece of bread into the softly oozing cheese, the bathroom door swung open. The glare of the landing light was startling after the soft glow of candlelight.

Nia stumbled into the room, rubbing her eyes blearily. Her hair was wild, straggling over her face, and she blinked at the unexpected sight of her parents eating in the bath.

"I need a poo," she mumbled, tugging her pyjama bottoms down and clambering onto the toilet.

Tom hesitated, a piece of bread halfway to his mouth. He set it down again on the tray, dusted his fingers delicately and leaned back in the warm water, mouth pursed wryly, to wait.

How long had it been since they'd had a long, uninterrupted romantic evening together? One in which they could build up slowly, gradually intensifying their intimacy as they delighted their senses with music, food and wine; dressed up to impress, with Megan in stockings and heels perhaps. Both of them easing into the mood for an extended session of lovemaking, then undressing each other slowly and devoting hours to sex with more exotic positions than a yoga retreat. God, he missed it.

He looked at her, wondering if she was thinking the same. She had covered her mouth with her hand to hide the silent laughter that made her shoulders shake as low rumbles echoed around the toilet bowl. In spite of himself, his lips twitched.

"I'm done now," Nia said. "Daddy, will you wipe my bottom?"

He opened his mouth to suggest that perhaps Mummy could do it, then remembered it was her birthday and he was supposed to be spoiling her.

"I get all the best jobs," he grumbled, but rose from the water, hurriedly wrapping a towel around his waist before doing his paternal duty.

With Nia tucked back into bed with the requisite soft toys, kiss and rumple of hair, he padded downstairs to collect the main course.

The risotto was creamy and subtle, just as he had hoped, and thanks to the scented candles the bathroom smelled inviting again.

"This is delicious… but I need to slow down," Megan said, patting her tummy. "I don't want to be too full for dessert."

"If you find you can't eat it, don't worry. I'm sure we can find other uses for the chocolate mousse."

His eyes met hers in a challenge, leaving her in no doubt as to what he had in mind. It amused him to observe that he could still make her blush even after ten years of sleeping together. They hadn't used food as foreplay in years; the thought of it made his groin ache. He leaned back to fully appreciate the sight of her, pink from the warm water, food and wine.

"Another time," she said, but softened the blow with a sultry smile. "We've got work tomorrow, and we'd probably be disturbed by one of the kids anyway."

"I wish you wouldn't use that four letter word. It's horrible, especially just dropped into the conversation like that. It's like turning the cold tap on." He was only half joking.

"What four letter word?" She frowned, going over what she had said. "Oh – work, you mean? Sorry. How was it today?"

His smile died. "Busy, as usual. The morning wasn't too bad, but from lunchtime onwards it was another story. A kid came running into my office to say someone had collapsed in the gym, so I went straight down there to help."

"Oh, no – were they alright?"

"It was one of the year nine girls. The usual thing: they try to lose weight by skipping meals and then wonder why they faint in the middle of their P.E. lessons. Duncan had it under control, but he wanted another adult there to stop the others fussing too much. Anyway, come on – eat up and don't look so worried. We're supposed to celebrating tonight, not talking about work."

"I had hoped you might be feeling a bit better about it now than you were a couple of weeks ago... but it doesn't sound as if you are?"

"Every day I come to hate it a little more." Seeing the way she sighed and set down her wine glass, he hurried to explain. "The job has changed, and so have I. You know what it's like. Just now and then it would be nice to feel less like the lamp post and more like the dog… The priorities shift on an almost weekly basis. If it's not the able and talented, or the white boys, or the gypsies and travellers, it's the kids with special needs or the looked after kids, or the ones who are entitled to free meals. Which, let's face it, is most of them at St Dyfrig's. I'm not saying it's wrong to help those kids along: of course we should. They need all the encouragement and support we can give them. But what about the average kids who end up falling through the net? And then there's this ludicrous issue of having to include numeracy and literacy in all lessons… I trained to teach P.E., for God's sake. So tell me how I can include spelling and sums overtly enough for one of Her Majesty's inspectors to see it, and document it, of course, and yet still make my lessons engaging and challenging, especially for the ones who really need to be stretched – though not too challenging for the ones who struggle - *and* tell the kids their learning outcomes, and include a plenary, *and* cater for the whole gamut of learning styles, without making the whole session a tedious mish-mash that ends up achieving nothing by trying to achieve too much… All that, whilst implementing positive behaviour programmes and without forgetting to keep testing them all regularly and record details of every child's performance – bearing in mind that I teach kids from six year groups, so that's over a hundred and eighty kids I'm dealing with on at least a fortnightly basis. Add to that the fixtures; the clubs; planning and assessing coursework; marking; attending meetings; running revision sessions; and now, of course, taking photos to tweet so that helicopter parents can watch what their little darlings are doing even while they're at school… Is it any wonder I don't feel I can inspire or motivate the kids any more? Every last drop of inspiration, motivation and enthusiasm has been wrung out of me."

He took a gulp of wine, feeling like a heel for allowing himself to vent again – and on her birthday, too. If he didn't get a grip on himself sharpish he risked becoming a bore.

"Sorry," he said. "Take no notice of me."

∞∞∞∞

Megan put down her fork, not unsympathetic to the challenges Tom faced, especially when he was still struggling after Hugh's death, but hard pressed to know what encouragement she could offer. The note of desperation in his voice frightened her more than his anger and resentment because it was this that might push him over the edge. What he needed was a pep talk.

"I know it's hard, but it won't last. So much of all that nonsense is politically driven. It will probably change for the better next year, when it all turns full circle again and some government minister decides it's time to let teachers get on with teaching. Just keep focusing on the students and you'll get through. They are what makes it the best job in the world, in so many ways."

He sighed. "I really am sorry. I wasn't going to talk about this tonight. You might be right, Meg; I hope you are. But I've got a feeling it's just going to go from bad to worse. When I was younger, none of that political shit bothered me. I was motivated, full of dreams of being able to make a difference. I'll admit I was often overwhelmed, but I felt I could keep my head above water. These days, I'm not just overwhelmed, I'm so swamped I feel like I'm drowning. I've never been afraid of hard work, and I didn't enter the teaching profession for an easy life. I'm not a lazy man; and despite appearances I'm not a stupid one. But nor am I Superman. Without the will to keep going, I can't keep doing it. The students deserve better. Frankly, *I* deserve better than another twenty-odd years of this. That's if the stress doesn't kill me before they let me retire, of course."

He picked up her bowl, dropped it into his own empty one and pushed himself up to his feet again. He looked magnificent dripping wet: his hair darkened when damp, emphasising the happy trail leading downwards over a stomach that was still enviably flat, even if the muscles weren't as defined as in his younger days. She lay back, picked up her glass and admired the view until he covered it with a towel.

"Time for dessert," he said, but the gleam in his eye had gone. He quickly rubbed himself dry and went off to fetch the mousse. There was a birthday candle in it; she smiled seeing it, touched by the gesture. This had all been so thoughtful and unexpected. She waited for him to re-join her in the cooling water, then blew out the candle with a gentle puff.

"I thought we'd done all the candles earlier," she murmured, dipping her spoon into the rich, dark chocolate. She closed her eyes briefly at the mixture of sweetness and bitterness on her tongue, and sucked every last smear off the spoon before plunging it back into the pot for more. She was still slowly relishing it long after he had finished and laid down his spoon. Her obvious satisfaction seemed to have pleased him.

"That was wonderful," she said at last, replete. "Thank you so much for thinking of it. I enjoyed it far more than I would have enjoyed sitting in a restaurant worrying in case Dylan was missing us."

"Good." He pulled out the bath plug and gathered up the remaining detritus from their meal while she wrapped herself in a dressing gown. When he returned, he sat on the lid of the toilet to watch while she took off her make-up and slathered on some moisturiser. He had told her once that it pleased him to see her private face emerge as she removed her cosmetics. The face only he got to see, freckled and clean.

"I haven't asked you yet about your day," he said. "Did you get many other presents?"

She smiled, remembering.

"I had some lovely cards in work, and the cakes I took in to the staffroom went down well."

"That's good. And is that the only reason you look like the cat that got the cream?"

She unwound her arms from his neck and got up, fussing with the towels on the heated towel rail so he couldn't see her face.

"I phoned Uncle Rhodri and Auntie Jayne to thank them for my birthday card…"

"And?"

"And while I was on the phone, I asked Rhod about my dad."

He was watching her carefully, very still. It was typical of him to be able to read between the lines and guess that there was more. She faced him, unable to keep the excitement from her voice.

"It turns out they've got some photos. They're going to dig them out and we can go to see them during half term."

"Right…"

"Oh, Tom. I'll get to see what he looked like for the first time ever. And when I talk to them, they might remember things about him. I might get some clues to bring me closer to finding him. How amazing is that?"

Chapter Thirteen

Sunday 26th October 2014
Pembrokeshire

The first thing Megan saw when they arrived at Rhod and Jayne's farmhouse was the photograph album lying on the kitchen table as if it had been waiting for her. She felt a jolt when she saw it, like an electric shock, leaving her momentarily stunned and clumsy. For the first time since she was a toddler, she was going to see what her father looked like. Her fingers fumbled when she stooped to remove the children's coats, her eyes returning to the album again and again as if they were magnetised.

She made a creditable attempt at conversation, the usual small talk between family members who are comfortable together despite rarely meeting face to face. Yes, the journey was fine. A cup of tea would be lovely, thank you. And yes, it was amazing how like his dad Dylan was. Jayne was fine, Rhod was fine, everyone was fine, thanks, including Olwen, as far as Megan was aware: they hadn't actually spoken for a few weeks. And through all the small talk wishing, wishing they would just cut to the chase and show her the pictures.

The earthenware mug of tea felt chunky and heavy in Megan's hands as she sat at the table. She took a nervous sip and winced, as it was still far too hot. Distraction had made her forget to be cautious. Now her tongue felt furry and scorched. She looked at Tom: he was watching the children as they took Welsh cakes from the Tupperware box Jayne held out.

"Use plates," he reminded them, too late to prevent a flutter of crumbs landing on the floor tiles.

Jayne didn't mind, with Dandy and her own dog to lick up the mess almost before it could touch the ground. Out came a plate laden with slices of rich, moist Bara Brith tea bread, the fruit almost entirely concealed by the thick layer of yolk-yellow butter on each slice. Tom and Megan each took a piece, but while Tom clearly enjoyed his, for once Megan's stomach objected to the thought of food. Too tense even to nibble at it, she put it back down on her plate untouched.

Come on. Put me out of my misery. Maybe once I've seen a picture of him my curiosity will be satisfied. It was a faint hope, though, she knew. She'd set herself on a trail, and she wouldn't give up until she arrived at the end goal of either meeting him or standing at his graveside.

"So... I expect you'll be wanting to have a look at these," Rhod said at last, patting the album. It was all Megan could do not to snatch it from him as he opened it and slowly turned the pages, scanning each one until he found the one he sought.

"It's not a very good photo, I'm afraid. And I didn't have as many of him as I thought. Just three, in fact." He slid the album across towards her. "That's Bethan's christening. Your dad is on the right, there."

She was already studying the picture. So this was Idris Parry: looking slightly away from the camera, away from the main group, hands in his pockets as if he wasn't really a part of the proceedings. The photograph was small and square, with wide white edges, and the whole picture had a faintly orange tint from age. The women in the photo had long hair, parted in the centre. Her mother was slimmer than she'd ever seen her: at what point over the years had she got fat? There was Rhod, with a thick head of hair! It made her smile to see it, that and the awful clothes he wore. The collars of his shirt were long and pointed and her father's shirt was similar, with a broad kipper tie in a jaunty red stripe.

Unfortunately it was hard to make out anything of Idris's features from such a tiny picture, taken at a distance. His hair was light brown, or perhaps a dark honey-blond, curling under around his face and onto his shoulders. He looked wiry. Shorter than Rhod, who wasn't above average height himself. Taller than Olwen, though. She swallowed, wishing he had been looking at the camera, and that it had been a close-up. She still had no real sense of his face. This was like seeing him through frosted glass: he was there, but she couldn't get a sense of who he was. She lay her hands in her lap and Rhod took the album back to thumb through the pages again.

Tom gave her hand a sympathetic squeeze under the table.

"This one's a bit better," Rhod said. "That's you, as a baby."

Her heart jumped as she looked at the picture. Her parents stood side by side, not touching. She must be the baby muffled in a shawl in Olwen's arms. It gave her a tingle to see herself with both of her parents for the first time. She never even used the phrase "Mam and Dad" in conversation, couldn't put the two words together comfortably in one sentence unless they related to other people's parents. And yet here was proof that hers had been a couple once.

Bethan was little more than a baby herself, hoisted up in the crook of their father's arm. This time it was Olwen who stood stiff and unsmiling for the camera. She looked tired, her mouth downturned. Idris's face was again turned away from the camera, his attention on Bethan as if he was speaking to her. His profile showed a broad smile, teeth white amid a beard that had presumably been fashionable back then. His eyes had crinkled as if enjoying a joke. His hair curled over his collar onto his shoulders. Slim, but strong looking: his rolled-up shirt sleeves revealed sinewy forearms and big hands that fitted what she knew of his working life. A carpenter, or a labourer, whichever he was, would need to be strong.

"There's only one more," Rhod said when she looked up again. "There you go. It's not a very good picture, just a snapshot."

Megan's breath caught in her throat. Rhod was right: it was a poor picture in terms of its composition. In these days of digital photography, no doubt it would have been deleted and never made it into print. Whoever had taken it hadn't aimed the shot very carefully: while its main focus was little Bethan, opening a Christmas present on Jayne's lap, Idris had been caught in the corner, in the act of rising from his chair. Half-turning to move past the photographer, his gaze was on something behind the camera, eyes wide open.

It was uncanny. Freakish, even. She had believed when she met Tom that she had never previously encountered eyes as blue as his. Yet here was evidence that she had. Her father's eyes were like cornflowers, sandy-lashed like Tom's and just as striking when captured in a photograph. Had she been driven by an instinct to seek out eyes like these, subconsciously missing them since she was small? Could it be a coincidence that the man who had had the most success in snaring her heart bore such a strong facial resemblance to her father? How much of her present situation might have been affected by her past?

"Wow," she said, the word ridiculously inadequate to express her maelstrom of thoughts. "I hadn't realised he looked so much like Tom."

Tom looked startled and dragged the album across the table to stare at it in silence.

Understanding dawned in Jayne's eyes. "Ah, yes. He had lovely blue eyes and fair hair, very much like yours, Tom. Not as tall, though. And nothing like you in character."

There was an uncomfortable pause.

"It makes you think, though, doesn't it?" Megan said at last, sliding the album back to gaze at it again. She needed to drink in the sight of her father's face and commit it to memory. "Was I subconsciously looking for something when we met? I've always had a bit of a thing for fair-haired men with blue eyes. Maybe this explains why?"

The legs of Tom's chair screeched against the flagstones as he rose with an impatient burst of energy. "I'll take the kids and Dandy outside for a bit," he said.

"Do you want me to come?" Megan asked.

"No. You stay here. Get whatever information you need, and then perhaps we can put all this behind us."

She felt deflated, hurt by his attitude. She had expected him to understand, watched him now for a sign that he supported her quest to know more about her father, and felt a niggle of resentment when he whistled for the dog and strode out of the door without a backward glance.

"Look at that wallpaper," Jayne murmured, gazing at the photograph. "And the curtains! It's hard to believe that we all used to think such garish colours were stylish."

Rhodri cleared his throat. "So, what do you want to know?"

She took in a deep breath, finding reassurance in Jayne's sympathetic smile. "I just want to know what he was like."

He paused, then went to fill the teapot with more hot water from the kettle on the range. Megan waited while he rummaged in a drawer for a teaspoon, his face hidden.

"Uncle Rhod?"

He sighed and scratched his beard. "Look, my lovely... I'll do my best to be fair but I can't tell you a lie. I didn't like him. Oh, he was pleasant enough. He could smile and say all the right things. But he was full of crap. He said what he thought people wanted to hear. In the end, if he said good morning to me, I checked my watch. And he was lazy - he never lifted a finger to help anybody, unless there was something in it for him. Your mam was better off without him." He brought the teapot back to the table and sat down heavily. "One thing I never understood was the way women took to him. Like flies around a cow's arse they were, wouldn't leave him alone. Jayne, you met him - what did you think?"

Jayne poured the tea and picked up her mug, eyeing Megan across the rim.

"He was quiet, Idris was. Didn't say a lot at first, but when he did, he had a certain charm," she began, nudging Rhod to silence his derisive snort. "He had a way of looking at a girl as if she had his full attention. He'd compliment you on things like the way your dress suited your figure. And he'd remember little things that you'd mentioned before, or notice if you had changed your hair style. It was flattering, I suppose. And all the more so because he never pushed. A lot of men in those days thought women liked to be groped and wolf-whistled at. Idris never did any of that. He'd sit back in his chair looking like he owned the place, dole out some compliments, and just reel them in. He was attentive, I suppose."

"As long as they weren't married to him," Rhodri remarked.

"Well, yes. I think for Idris the pleasure was in the chase. He liked seeing girls falling over themselves to get his attention. But once he'd had them, he lost interest. There was no shortage of broken hearts in the village by the time he left for good. But Megan, I didn't really know him all that well. Socially, that's all, and that was only because my parents ran the pub. He spent a lot of time in there on the rare occasions he was home. But most of the time, he was away. I always assumed he was working, but if he earned money I don't think your mam got to see much of it."

Megan stared at the photograph again, trying to reconcile the face in the picture with the portrait they had just drawn for her.

"Take those photos home with you if you like," Jayne offered, fetching an envelope from a drawer in the dresser and handing it to her. "We never seem to get the albums out these days, so there's no point in us hanging onto them."

Megan gave a grateful smile.

"Thank you," she murmured. "It means a lot to actually see his face at last." She lined up the three pictures on the table for one last lingering look. "Who's that woman in the christening photo?" she asked.

Jayne peered at it.

"That was his sister, wasn't it?"

Megan's eyes widened. "He had a sister?"

"Yes. We only met her twice, at the wedding and then Bethan's christening. They didn't bother having you christened, Megan. I expect she'd have come again if they had."

Rhod nodded. "Delyth, her name was. She lived down Tenby way. Married an Italian, if I remember rightly. They had a café, didn't they?"

"No, not a café. A fish and chip shop, wasn't it?"

"Aye, that's it. Haven't seen her in forty-odd years, so I've no idea if she still lives there. But if anyone knows where your dad is now, I'd guess it would be Delyth Parry."

∞∞∞∞

Tom leaned on the gate and let the breeze ruffle his hair, conscious of a tight knot of tension in his shoulder muscles. It was stupid to get so wound up by a few photographs. Although it hadn't been so much the photographs themselves, or even the superficial resemblance between himself and Idris Parry, but Megan's suggestion that she'd only been attracted to him because he fitted a certain type.

Perhaps the resemblance explained why his mother-in-law had taken an instant dislike to him. Olwen disliked most men, it had to be said, but Tom had always been aggrieved at her attitude, because it was so unfair. Would she have been less prejudiced if he'd had dark hair and brown eyes? He huffed impatiently: the idea that she might have formed such a strong impression based on a vague physical likeness to her ex-husband was absurd.

The kids seemed happy enough, at least, amusing themselves out in the yard. He had fetched a ball from the car for them to kick about, and from time to time he called out advice.

"Tackle her, Alys! Good manners will never win you the ball!"

He grinned at Dylan's comical attempts to co-ordinate his feet, as he spent more time on his bottom or all fours than making contact with the ball. Dandy had joined in for a while, but soon gave up, his attention caught by a scent he tracked with fascination along the fence. How easily a dog could live in the moment. Tom had half expected him to pine for Hugh, but he had settled easily enough into his new family. He liked to know where they all were in the house, and tended to lie where he could keep a watchful eye on everyone, but he seemed otherwise content. Far more content with life than Tom was himself.

He leaned against the rough surface of the wall, looking out across the fields. A public footpath passed the farm, and his spirits rose as he squinted up at the wooden signpost.

Traeth 1/2m.

He had lived in Wales for long enough to understand a few Welsh words and phrases. When he first arrived at university in Cardiff, Welsh had seemed an incomprehensible jumble of random letters, too many words lacking vowels altogether. He'd been confused when every hotel seemed to be called the Gwesty Hotel, and every beach was Traeth Beach, until the penny dropped and he realised the signs were bilingual. A fellow student once wrote "Ynysddu" on the back of Tom's A4 pad, challenging him to pronounce it. He'd failed, of course. How was an Englishman to know that W and Y are vowels in Welsh, that U was pronounced like an E, or that two Ds made a "th" sound? But he'd soon picked up enough knowledge to be able to decipher road signs, with the help of Angharad, a brunette from Harlech with a stunning figure and a keen interest in wild camping. That had been an adventurous summer, in more ways than one.

"D'you fancy a stroll down to the beach, kids? It's only a few minutes' walk." He always loved the beach, and if they didn't do something else soon Alys would start to whine about Nia's increasingly ruthless fouls.

The girls greeted his suggestion with enthusiasm, so he snapped Dandy's lead onto his collar and then scooped Dylan up into his arms, knowing his son's little legs wouldn't cope with walking so far.

"Come on," he said, breaking into a trot. "Let's see who can spot the sea first."

Alys and Nia eagerly shoved past to beat him to the coast, their competitiveness making him chuckle. He could get them to do most things if he made it a race: going up to bed, washing faces, brushing hair. A simple tactic, and yet they never saw through it.

The path sloped downwards, gently at first and then more steeply as they drew nearer to the beach. Dylan's chubby arms wrapped even more firmly around his neck, and he reached up to adjust them so he could breathe. The air here was so fresh he could almost taste it.

"I can see it!" Alys shouted, earning a disgruntled poke from her sister.

"I saw it at the same time, you just said it faster than I did."

"No, you didn't, you fibber!"

They descended the steep steps carefully, Tom insisting that the girls stay behind him in case they should fall. At last they arrived at the sand and in this deserted cove Tom felt the familiar rush of excitement that he had always experienced at the seaside as a boy. He set Dylan down onto his feet and reached down to unclip Dandy's lead. Both boy and dog tore away, their joy at being released contagious. Seagulls flapped away in alarm, calling out a warning with their harsh cries as Dandy chased after them. Tom's own heart swelled at the pure, raw freedom of the ocean.

"Ha!" he said, kicking off his sneakers with a piratical growl at the girls. "While you two are wasting time arguing, Dylan and I will beat you to the water."

∞∞∞∞

By the time Megan arrived at the beach, disgruntled that they had gone off without her, Dylan's nappy was swollen and perilously close to sliding off his bottom. Alys and Nia had rolled up their leggings to their knees but to little purpose, as they were soaked, and Tom wasn't much better, his cargo shorts drenched at the hem. The girls were charging at each other in the shallows and shrieking at the cold splashes from one another's feet. Tom stooped over Dylan, swinging him from his armpits to hurdle the final surges of the waves where they lapped the shore.

"There you are!" she exclaimed, drawing near, and his head turned.

"It's Mummy!" he said to Dylan, who crowed with pleasure.

She held out her arms to their son, but it was Tom's face that had her attention. He's got his sparkle back, she thought – his wide smile seemed somehow supercharged, transforming his features and making her stomach flip like a schoolgirl with a crush.

"You look happy," she said, picking Dylan up with a grimace at the gritty sand stuck to his cold, wet legs.

"It's this place. Isn't it wonderful?" That euphoric look again, taking years off him. Had he really been so downcast lately that a simple smile could make him look so different? She hadn't been conscious of it, but she hadn't seen him like this in a couple of months. Not since they were in the Gower, when he'd traipsed back to the camper van after a morning's surfing. The morning of the day Hugh died.

"It is pretty, yes."

"Much better than pretty. God, I wish we lived near the sea."

"It's probably a good job we don't, if you're going to let the kids get this wet with no towels to dry them off," she answered, then stopped, cross with herself. How stuffy she sounded.

Tom turned back towards the sea, his smile slipping a little.

Alys and Nia were beckoning her to join them in the water.

"Come on, Mammy! It isn't cold once you're used to it!"

"Of course it's cold – it's nearly November." She dithered, reluctant to get cold feet but also unwilling to disappoint them, and suddenly aware that she was in danger of turning into someone much too boring and sensible.

"Oh, alright." She gave in and slipped her shoes off, just as Dylan toppled flat onto his face in the shallows. "You're okay," she reassured him, setting him back on his feet and holding onto one of his hands to avoid another tumble. "Come on, let's go and splash Daddy."

Drawn to them by Dylan's furious cries, Tom must have heard her gasp when her bare feet encountered the water. His smile was back, appreciative this time, making it impossible for her to look away from his face; and when he leaned down to kiss her, oblivious to Dylan's objections, she felt her pulse quicken.

"You've given me a bit of a James Blunt moment," he murmured in her ear.

"What's a James Blunt moment? Is that a clumsy way to say 'you're beautiful'?"

He pressed his hips against her and said, with that maddening poker face that meant he was teasing her again: "Nope. Although you are, of course. What I meant was, I've got a semi by the sea."

She pressed against him in return, her head tilted backwards to look up as she laughed. He was gazing at her throat, as if he was going to kiss that, too, and her stomach seemed to heat up and make her limbs go weak. The chill of the sea water was forgotten.

"Ugh, Mammy and Daddy are kissing!"

They pulled apart with some reluctance. Dylan had been stamping his feet and soaking their legs, his nappy so swollen now it must have soaked up half of the Irish Sea.

"What's that?" Tom asked suddenly, pointing out to sea. They all looked, just in time to see two grey fins arc out of the water.

"Dolphins!" Alys shrieked, her face alight. "Oh look, aren't they wonderful! I love dolphins."

Megan seized Tom's hand and squeezed it, as delighted by the joy on her family's faces as she was by the local wildlife. "They're bottlenose dolphins. See their long beaks?"

One by one they retreated to the comparative warmth of the sand to watch the dolphins, entranced by their perfectly synchronised dips and lifts as they swam together in the grey-blue waters of the cove.

"I wish I never had to go back to the city. I could stay here for ever," Tom said.

"It's pleasant for a holiday, and we've been lucky with the weather today," she conceded, her toes tingling as they started to warm up. "But give it a month or so and it'll be pretty bleak."

"Even when it's bleak, it must be so beautiful." He had that worryingly wistful look, as if he was going to start making impractical suggestions. Sure enough, he did. "Life is so fucking short, Meg. Look at my dad. He got up one morning, no reason to think it would be different from any other Sunday, and then – bang – all over. Don't you think, with it being so short, that we have a responsibility to live it as fully and as well as we can?"

"Yes, I do. Which is one of the reasons I like living in Cardiff. There's such a variety of things to do, you can fill every minute and never get bored." She picked up her shoes, beckoned towards the children and started threading her way back towards the steps. Perhaps he'd give up if she disengaged.

He hadn't given up, though. "But imagine living here. What more could you need? There's walking, surfing, kayaking, coasteering, swimming, fishing…"

"All very nice for outdoorsy types like you, but not so great if you fancy a trip to the cinema, or a really good museum, or ten pin bowling, or the theatre, or ice skating, or a big swimming pool with slides. We can do all those things in Cardiff, and more. I honestly couldn't imagine a better place to bring the children up than where we live. And on days when they've drawn graffiti all over their bedrooms, at least in Cardiff you don't need to drive twenty miles to buy a pot of paint."

He had scooped Dylan up and was following close behind. "Twenty miles isn't really all that far, Meg. It's not exactly the Outer Hebrides, is it?"

She spun to face him. "No, but it's a moot point, anyway, because we don't live here, and we are very happy with things the way they are."

But his face was mutinous. "You might be," he said grimly. "But some of us are starting to realise that life has a hell of a lot more to offer."

It took every ounce of willpower she had not to stamp her foot, but she was damned if she'd give him a chance to accuse her of being childish. So she glared at him, hands on her hips, daring him to try to convince her that this wasn't lunacy.

"Look - I need to get some life back into my work-life balance. I've got twenty-five years of working left. Maybe it'll be even longer than that, if the pension age keeps going up. Do you really want me to carry on doing something that makes me miserable for the next quarter of a century? How do you think our marriage will fare, if one of us is constantly unhappy? Remember what happened before."

She shook her head. He wasn't going to lay that guilt trip on her. As much as she didn't want a full-blown argument, she wouldn't let him manipulate her into agreeing to a narrow and tedious little life in the middle of nowhere, just so that he could go to the beach more often.

"How do you think our marriage will fare if we can't afford to feed and clothe our children, because the main breadwinner has decided he doesn't like his job any more? When we can't see any of our friends, or go to watch a rugby international, because they're a hundred miles away. When the kids get a bit older and need lifts whenever they want to do anything, because they live in the middle of nowhere and there are no buses. When they grow up and have to move away because there are no jobs for them in the countryside, and it's just you and me left, and the neighbours barely speak to you because you don't speak Welsh, and I'm bored witless and unable to forgive you for uprooting us. Just leave it there, Tom. I'm begging you. Please, forget the whole thing. Leave your job if you must, but don't wreck the rest of our lives to go chasing after rainbows."

Chapter Fourteen

Monday 3rd November 2014
St Dyfrig's High School, Cardiff

A tall shadow loomed in the doorway of Tom's tiny office, making him look up from his emails. It was Garin, looking unusually reticent as he came in and sat on the only spare chair. Tom took in the bags under his eyes and the way he perched restlessly, jingling the keys in his pocket.

"You alright, mate?" he asked.

Garin said nothing, but fished a piece of paper out of his pocket and laid it on the desk, smoothing it out with his long fingers.

"That's for you."

It was a ten pound note.

"What's it for?" He hadn't lent Garin any money recently, and as far as he was aware no one in the department had a birthday coming up. He frowned, trying to remember if an envelope had crossed his desk recently for a whip-round.

"You won our bet," Garin said with a fatalistic air.

A quick scan through his memory revealed nothing. Six months had passed since England beat Wales at rugby, so it couldn't be that. There was only one other thing he could think of, but that had been years ago, just a chance remark on Tom's stag night when he'd bet a tenner that Garin would also take the plunge and marry one day. He hadn't been serious, but it had been a safe bet as he'd be able to wait until Garin was on his deathbed before he'd have to pay up. Surely it couldn't be that...

A glance at Garin's solemn green eyes told him it could.

"Bloody hell – congratulations!" He seized Garin's hand and pumped it vigorously. "I never thought I'd see the day!"

"You and me both," Garin agreed. He dragged his hands down his face as if he could hardly believe it himself. "Got a bit carried away, we did. Went down to Cornwall for half term in her T5. When she suggested it I thought – yeah, great. A week at Fistral – what could be better, you know?"

Tom nodded. He couldn't think of anything he'd like more than to surf Fistral beach for a whole week. Even a weekend would be great.

"The surf was cracking, fair play. And on the Saturday there was this wedding on, see, and they came out of the hotel and had loads of photos taken on the beach, her in her wedding dress and the breeze blowing her veil and all that, and to cut a long story short, Shaz said to me 'if I ever get married, I'd want to do it just like that, right by here, only a bit more casual, like', and I said 'yeah, me too', and the next thing I knew we were saying 'fuck it, let's just book it'. They'd just had a cancellation for next Easter, so we grabbed it. Truth be told I haven't really got my head round it yet, but still, it should be a laugh I s'pose."

A laugh? Tom was unsure whether marriage could realistically be described in such terms, but his pleasure at the thought of Garin finding a kindred spirit was genuine.

"Don't get me wrong - we're not going overboard with all the usual shizzle – none of those crappy little bags of sugared almonds on your plate or table plans or whatever. Just getting together with a few friends and family to get hitched, get pissed and enjoy the day. No ankle-biters allowed, though, sorry. She's got about six million nieces and nephews and if you let one come you have to invite them all. I don't know how that'll leave you fixed, Tommo… But I hope it won't stop you coming, because I'm hoping you'll be one of my best men."

"Best *men*?"

"Yeah, my brother will sort the stag night and that, but I reckon he'll shit himself if I ask him to make a speech on the day, whereas you'd do a respectable job of it and remember to tell the bridesmaid she's looking lush and everything. So I thought you two could job-share, like. And if you bring your van, we can head up a bit of a classic VW convoy through Newquay before the serious drinking starts."

His stomach did a nervous dance at the thought of public speaking, but Garin's faith in him was touching. He hadn't been a best man since Rob's wedding, which had been a large and formal affair, and he'd been so scared he'd been sick before the speeches. This one shouldn't be quite as daunting.

And then, a whole weekend away in the camper van with Megan, no kids in tow, having fun with rugby lads, not to mention the prospect of surfing thrown in... Even with the issue of having to give a speech, it sounded like a trip not to be missed. He'd talk to Megan about getting a babysitter. They hadn't gone away without Dylan before, but by Easter he'd be nearly three, so hopefully she'd be willing. And Bethan was usually up for any opportunity to spoil her nieces and nephew, so they'd be well looked after.

His spirits lifted. This was going to be brilliant.

"Wow," he said. "I'm flattered, obviously. I'm sure I'll be every bit as terrified as your brother at the thought of giving a speech, but yes – I'd be proud to do it. Honoured to be asked. And of course I'll bring the van."

∞∞∞∞

"So ends another day in the Field family madhouse," Megan said with a sigh after the children had finally gone to bed and she could plump down onto the sofa. As usual it had been a busy day, rushing through chores and attending to Dylan. She'd made the most of his nap time to settle down at the computer, but it had been a fruitless hour. She'd found no trace of her father or his sister on social media, and had ended up none the wiser as to their whereabouts, weighed down with the old heavy feeling she'd had as a child when she tried to picture her dad. Now, at least, she had photographs of him as a young man; but what did he look like these days? And where was he?

When she was little, she'd watched men getting off the bus at the stop outside their house, wishing for one of them to turn towards their door and knock. She saw men on the television and imagined her dad was just like them. The tall Blue Peter presenter had a wide, kindly smile, so she'd imagined perhaps Idris's was like that. Or was her father somehow more like Dr Who – landing somewhere to battle evil forces and then taking off when the need was greater elsewhere? It would explain why he hadn't come back. The universe needed him even more than she did.

She had flown into rages at school and pulled other children's hair when they taunted her by saying she didn't have a dad. Of course she had a dad, and he was going to come back, laden with presents and with strong arms to pick her up and tickle her and tuck her into bed at night when Mam was bent over her textbooks downstairs. He'd take their little family away on a holiday to somewhere hot, and Mam would maybe even smile and look happy now and then instead of perennially crotchety and tired.

When singing *He's Got the Whole World in His Hands* at school she would smile as if she'd been lit up, throwing all her efforts into the actions, imagining as she sang that God had her father safe within His hands, and would bring him back to her. It would be like that scene in *The Railway Children* when Jenny Agutter cried out "Daddy, my daddy": she would know him without being told who he was, and she'd run to him, and he'd scoop her up and squeeze her against him in the biggest cwtch she'd ever had. She'd snuggle her cheek against his beard (she didn't know why she pictured him with a beard, except that Uncle Rhodri had one, and so did the headmaster Mr Maybank, so that was how she imagined kind men should look), and he'd call her *cariad*, and tell her how much he'd missed her, but his very important job had kept him away for longer than he expected.

For a while she even wrote him letters telling him what she'd been learning in school, reporting any mean things Bethan had done and asking him all sorts of questions, like whether he had watched *All Creatures Great and Small* this week, and telling him how exciting it was when Mam finally got a VHS video recorder from Radio Rentals, because it meant that she and Bethan could record *Grange Hill* if they had choir or netball after school. Writing to him had been strangely cathartic, even though of course she could never send any of the letters because she didn't know his address. Instead, she folded them up very small and tucked them inside her Sindy doll's wardrobe. She imagined the day he'd come home and she would read them aloud to him, and he'd laugh and ruffle her hair and tell her she was a clever little thing as well as pretty. They helped her feel connected to him. Until the awful day when Bethan found them and showed them to their mother.

She was sent to bed early, boiling over with righteous indignation, alternately sniffling and thumping her pillow until Bethan growled at her from the top bunk to shut up and settle down. At last she crept downstairs to fetch a glass of water, but stopped short in the kitchen doorway at the extraordinary sight of her mam sobbing into a glass of the brandy they kept for Christmas cakes. Megan's letters were spread over the table in front of her.

After that, she didn't write any more letters. She buried all thoughts of her father in a box at the back of her mind, too destabilising to risk bringing out. It got easier in time. She wasn't even troubled when she and Tom were married and Uncle Rhod led her up the aisle to give her away. Rhod had always been there for her.

When she met Tom, he'd seemed as different from her feckless father as any man could be. He was settled, reliable, professional and steady. He'd wanted children, had been ready for fatherhood and stability. She'd congratulated herself on not making the mistake her mother had made. And yet, there had been that time two years ago when he had let her down. He had disappeared with barely a word, and even though he'd fully intended to come back, her long-dormant feelings of loss and abandonment had been reawakened. She had understood her mother's bitterness at last.

Thank goodness they had patched things up and were comfortable again. She looked at him now, the smudges under his eyes that were probably mirrored on her own face. This had been a difficult time for him, what with losing Hugh and his growing dissatisfaction at work. And that was without the emotional demands of his weekend trips to Ludlow, visiting Jean in the care home and tidying Hugh's house with Rob.

"How was work today?" she asked.

He looked up from his magazine. "That depends. Do you want the good news first, or the bad news?"

"Bad, obviously. Then you can cheer me back up with the good."

"It might not turn out to be bad news at all... The Head has called a staff meeting for next Wednesday."

"Isn't that just a nuisance, and a bit boring, rather than bad news?"

"There are a few rumours flying around. Nothing concrete."

"And?"

"The word *redundancies* is being whispered."

She felt a sudden chill, as if cold water had dripped down the back of her neck. She knew that budget cuts had meant some other schools in the region had let staff go. As an English teacher, she'd always felt relatively safe. It wasn't as if she taught some obscure subject that could be considered low on the school's list of priorities. Literacy would always be important. But still. There was no such thing as a job for life any more. And with Tom so disillusioned, this might be the kind of excuse he'd been looking for to give up his job. Where would that leave them?

"Do you believe the rumours?"

"Who knows? We'll find out next week, won't we?"

"Doesn't it worry you?" she asked. That wasn't concern on his face. It should be, though, surely?

He rubbed the stubble along his jaw, making a soft rasping sound. "It sounds as if it bothers you?"

"With a mortgage to pay and three kids to support, and thirty-odd years to go before I can retire, it would come as a bit of a blow, yes. I'd have thought that would be obvious. And even if I get to keep my job, I had been hoping to increase my hours. There's not much chance of that if they need to cut back on staff. Bang goes my hope of furthering my career for another few years." Anxiety knotted in her chest. This was the last thing they needed.

"Unless we move somewhere else…"

Not that again. She opened her mouth to challenge him, but he was still talking.

"…But there's no point in putting the cart before the horse. After all, nothing has been said officially yet. They might get a few people volunteering to go, and then no one will end up being forced out. I'm sure you'll be safe." He picked up the remote control for the television, his nonchalance doing nothing to reassure her.

"Are you *hoping* they'll let you go? Is that why you don't seem even the slightest bit perturbed by the idea? Because you can't wait to get out?"

He shrugged. "Surely you can see that this could work out rather well for us, with my intention to go at the end of the year? I wouldn't need to just resign and move on: with twenty-odd years of service behind me, I'd probably get a pretty reasonable payoff. Enough to buy us a bit of breathing space while I look for something else."

"Like what, Tom? Do you even have a plan for providing for your family?" Her voice had grown shrill and it caught in her throat as fear made her mouth dry up; in her agitation, she jumped up to face him. "I'm really sorry that you're not happy in your job at the moment. God knows I wish things were different, but… you can't mean it when you say you're going to just leave. Not without something else to fall back on. You wouldn't do that to us, would you?"

He rose, reaching out with both arms to tug her into his embrace. Usually she felt safe pressed against the strong wall of his chest, but not this time. She put both palms against him to steady herself, telling herself to take deep breaths.

"Don't you trust me?" he asked, his voice soft and deep next to her ear where he had bent his head. "Do you really think I'd give up my job without a thought, without being responsible?"

There was a pause while he let his question sink in. Gradually, her breathing slowed. He *was* responsible: she had to cling on to that. She looked up, saw the steady sincerity in his eyes. His hands cupped her face, warm and firm, yet gentle.

"For the past few years we've muddled along, making the best of things. You've made a life without your father, but deep down you've longed for more. And I've stuck with a job that no longer satisfies me, for longer than was good for me. It's time for us to do more than make the best of things. It's time to take steps towards making our dreams happen. Our lives can never be complete if we don't."

She shook her head, determined not to surrender to this pipe dream he was so keen to build a life on. How would throwing away their financial security make their lives better? Her shoulders sagged and he gripped them, holding her up.

"I promise I'll be careful. You're my world, you and the kids. But I have to follow my heart, and my heart isn't in St Dyfrig's High School. It wouldn't be in any other school either."

"Tom, follow your heart by all means. But for all our sakes, take your head along for the ride. Promise me you won't do anything until you've got a proper plan. Because you've yet to convince me that you have any clear idea of what else to do. I haven't heard you come up with anything else that would pay you anything close to what you earn now. We have to pay the bills. Don't risk our home. Don't risk *us* for the sake of a fantasy."

"I promise."

He bent his head and touched his lips to hers, the kiss long and gentle, leisurely at first and reassuring, like slipping under a warm duvet on a chilly night. It was a kiss to make them both forget their worries, to shut everything out except their complete absorption in one another. When at last they pulled apart, still close enough for her to see how his eyes had darkened, he smiled.

"We should kiss more often," he said, sweeping her hair back behind her ears. "We used to snog all the time before we got married, do you remember? I can recall whole evenings just kissing and talking. Dreaming of the things we'd do, the places we'd go together."

She snuggled closer, feeling safe again. "You said there was good news as well as bad news. You haven't told me what it is yet."

"Ah! Yes, of course." His lips twitched intriguingly.

"Go on, then. Don't keep me in suspense."

"You'll never believe it."

She tutted impatiently, sending him a warning glare, and he gave in.

"Alright. It's Garin. Apparently he's getting married. And he's asked me to be one of his best men, so we'll need to ask Bethan and Matt to babysit for a couple of nights next Easter."

Of all the people she knew, Garin was the one she would have least expected to settle down. As soon as he had apprised her of the astonishing details, which pushed all thoughts of redundancies out of her mind, she called Bethan.

"Is everything alright?" Bethan sounded distracted, Megan thought.

"Yes, why?"

"It's not like you to ring this late on a school night."

She looked at her watch. Nine forty. Was her life really so boring or busy that she no longer made phone calls at this time?

"It's not that late. I was just ringing to find out if you're doing anything on the next Easter weekend. We've been invited to a wedding in Cornwall, but it's a bit of a pain because we can't take the kids. So I wondered if you'd be able to have them, please? I know it's asking a lot of you to have all three, but Tom's best man so it would cause offence if we don't go. And the other reason I'm ringing is I've got some stuff to tell you about Dad. We went to see Rhod and Jayne last week, but I haven't had a proper chance to talk to you about it until now."

She curled up in the corner of the sofa and Dandy jumped straight up to nestle against her. She tutted at his impertinence, but there was something endearing about the way he liked to steal a cwtch whenever he could, so she scratched the back of his ear and grinned at the way he pressed his head ecstatically against her hand.

"Are you alright, Beth? You've gone all quiet on me; have we been cut off?"

Bethan cleared her throat. "Ummm… Yeah, I'm okay."

"You don't sound it."

"I'm just a bit tense about tomorrow, that's all. And to be honest I'm a bit surprised that you went all the way to Pembrokeshire to ask Rhod and Jayne about Dad."

"Don't get huffy on me. I found out they had some photos, that's all. Do you realise I didn't even know what he looked like? It was really weird, seeing a picture of him for the first time ever. He was quite good looking, wasn't he? He looked a little bit like Tom, actually – which freaked us out a bit."

"I don't remember, and as I told you before I'm not interested. I've got more important things to focus on. Like my job interview tomorrow."

"For the management role? The maternity cover? That's fantastic, good luck. I'm sure you'll get it."

Bethan's tone thawed. "Time will tell. I'm petrified, truth be told. I don't suppose I'll sleep tonight, it's the first job interview I've had in years. So I don't really want to talk about it, if you don't mind. Que sera sera, as Mam used to say… And speaking of Mam, I won't mention your little visit to Rhod and Jayne's. I don't think she'd be very pleased that you went all the way down there and saw them without calling in to visit her, never mind your amateur sleuthing to try to track down the ex-husband she never wants to see again."

Megan pursed her lips at the disapproval in her sister's voice, irked by her lack of understanding. "Aren't you even a little bit curious about him?" she asked, annoyed with herself for sounding so defensive.

"We've been over this." She could imagine from Bethan's tone the way her mouth would be set in a firm line. "I'd rather stay as we are than find out we've maybe got a bunch of losers in the family who'll latch onto us and cause no end of trouble. Not to mention how Mam would feel about it. Just think – what if he's in prison or something? Let sleeping dogs lie, that's what I say. But then, you always were like a terrier with a bone once you got your teeth into something."

Megan bridled. "What's that supposed to mean?"

"This! It's just so typical of you. You won't stop until you've found him, even if you've got to track down his sister to go through her. To hell with the consequences, or what anyone else feels about it. It'll be like when Tom ran off that time: you couldn't just sit at home and wait for him to come back. You had to work out where he was and track him down, even though his note said he'd just be gone for half term and you were pregnant and about to pop. And look what happened there. It nearly ended in disaster. Then there was that time you went ahead and organised the party for his fortieth, even though you knew he didn't want one. Honestly, when you get an obsession about something you can't let it go."

The barb hit home, and Megan couldn't help fighting back. "I would have thought you of all people would know what it's like to obsess about something. Four rounds of IVF tells its own story."

She heard Bethan's sharp intake of breath and cursed herself for rising to the bait.

"I think we'd better leave it there, don't you?"

"Yes, that's probably wise." She felt deflated, her cheeks flaming with shame for the impulsive words she had spoken in anger. "Good luck for tomorrow," she said, hoping to atone for them. "Let me know how it goes."

Chapter Fifteen

Tuesday 4th November 2014
St Dyfrig's High School, Cardiff

om had met the careers adviser once before, when she'd set up a careers fair and he'd provided contact details for a physiotherapist and a rugby coach. Although he worried that it might be considered unprofessional to ask her advice on personal matters, after wrestling with his conscience for a week he had decided it was worth a try. Maybe she'd be able to point him in the direction of some information, at least. Information or inspiration – he wasn't sure which he needed more. He definitely needed something to get his exit plan started. He couldn't stay in the relative safety of his comfort zone for ever – not when sharing it with idiots like Ken Haddon was making it decidedly uncomfortable.

She beckoned him in with one of those pleasantly noncommittal smiles that people give when they want to appear friendly but they've no idea what you're after. She was young, in her late twenties perhaps; deeply fake-tanned, with more eyelashes than could possibly be natural and eyebrows so perfectly shaped he suspected they were stencilled on. Fleetingly it crossed his mind that she'd probably be unrecognisable without all that make-up. The teenaged girls she dealt with on a daily basis would probably envy her style; he didn't like to dwell on what the boys would make of her.

"Eleri," he said, managing to shake her hand without being stabbed by her long, lacquered nails. "Sorry to disturb you during your lunch break. I don't know if you remember me. I'm Tom Field, head of PE. I was just wondering if you have a minute or two?"

"Of course I remember. Nice to see you again, Tom. What can I do for you?"

"It's a bit awkward, actually," he said, casting a quick glance over his shoulder. "I hate to take up any of your time, but I'm in need of a bit of advice. And seeing as you're the expert on career-related matters, I thought I'd ask... But it's not for a pupil. It's for me."

She gave him an appraising look, then glanced at her watch. "Fire away. I've got fifteen minutes or so until my next appointment. Just don't tell any of your colleagues, or they'll be queuing outside my door every lunchtime. It's a bit of a standing joke among advisers that teachers often need career advice more than their pupils do."

"Really? I thought I was the only one."

"You'd be surprised," she said, and picked up a sandwich from the box on her desk. "You don't mind if I carry on with my lunch, do you? It's only cheese and tomato, nothing smelly or anything."

"I can hardly object, given that I'm disturbing your lunch break."

He nudged the door closed before taking a seat. It wouldn't do for anyone else to hear what he had to say. She was watching him curiously, chewing on her sandwich, so he took a deep breath and plunged on, conscious that he needed to make the best use of this small window of opportunity.

"It's hard to know where to start. I've felt for a while now that I need to get out of teaching and do something completely different. Any sense of vocation I ever had has been worn away over the past few years. The question is, what else could I do? I've promised my wife I won't do anything rash, and that I'll make a plan before leaving this job, but I don't know what other options might suit me, so I keep hitting a brick wall."

He frowned, worried that she might think him ridiculous, but she appeared to be genuinely interested.

"Funny things, brick walls. People often feel as if they should smash them down, demolish the whole thing at once, when actually a lot of people can chip away at them bit by bit, see which bricks are salvageable and which should be thrown away."

"That makes sense, but I can't really drop this job gradually. Perhaps it's not so much a brick wall, really, then. It's more like when you've been travelling down the same motorway for too long. It's okay at first, but after a while keeping going in a straight line gets tedious. Maybe something else could be out there if I can get off the road I'm on and try a different route? I'd maybe even try a bit of off-roading for a while, if I could just find the right exit and make sure my passengers are secure first."

He still wasn't convinced by his own metaphor, but Eleri nodded as if it made perfect sense, dabbing at her mouth with a tissue and swallowing the last of her sandwich.

"I understand. So tell me, have you been tempted by any particular exits in the past?"

"I took an outdoor fitness instructor qualification just over a year ago, but I haven't done anything with it. And I've got quite a few coaching qualifications, but there aren't many full-time coaching jobs around. As the main breadwinner with a mortgage and a family, I don't feel free to work part-time or try setting up my own business."

"Do you do anything outside work that could link to a job idea?"

"Most things I do are sport-related. I play a bit of touch rugby. I go to the gym; I enjoy cycling; and I'm involved in parkruns when I can spare the time. I've done quite a few marathons and half-marathons." He didn't mention the money these had raised for charity in case she thought he was looking for praise. "I used to love surfing, but I don't have a lot of time to get away to the beach, except during the holidays; and last time I went – well, let's just say I haven't been for a while. Basically I like getting outside and being active."

"So…" There was a pause while she peeled the foil lid off her pot of yogurt and licked it clean. "I can't help wondering how you ended up getting onto this motorway, and why you've stayed on it for so long even though you say you don't know where it's taking you."

He thought back. "I suppose I've drifted. I let myself be pushed into teaching. It didn't seem all that awful, and it gave me the chance of a job in sport – although it's been a bit more difficult than the fitness instructor job I originally had in mind, especially since I was promoted. These days, I'm drowning in paperwork. The downsides of the job outweigh the upsides."

"What are the upsides? What's kept you getting up in the mornings and coming to work, even though you said you've lost your sense of vocation?"

"Apart from paying the mortgage and putting bread on the table, you mean?"

She nodded encouragement, scraping the last of her yogurt from its pot and sucking the spoon clean before dropping it back into her lunch box.

"Well... I like challenging people; helping them become the best they can be. I get satisfaction from seeing kids achieve things they may not even have realised they were capable of."

"What else?"

"I like my colleagues. We've known each other a long time, and we support each other. If I move on – *when* I move on - I'll miss them."

"And what else?"

He rubbed his face. He'd half expected her to just give him a leaflet and send him on his way, but he'd ended up talking about himself far more than he usually did. It felt odd to have a conversation that was so much centred on his own hopes and dreams.

"Erm... I like the job most when I can work outside, much more than when we're in the gym. I get to keep active. And of course it's convenient, working near to home. The holidays are good. So is the pension. But a pension isn't a reason to stay in a job you no longer enjoy, is it? Teaching demands a bit of passion. If I've lost that, the kids deserve to have someone else who's still got it."

"Alright. Now, I want you to imagine I'm your fairy godmother. If I could wave a magic wand and give you any job in the world, what would it be?"

He gave a rueful smile. The answer was too easy, and completely unrealistic.

"I'd be fifteen or twenty years younger and playing rugby for England. But I was never good enough for that." His cheeks and ears flooded with warmth, making him feel even more embarrassed by his own foolishness. But she didn't seem to find it foolish at all.

"What would it mean to you, to be playing rugby for England?"

Such an odd question. "What would it *mean*?" he repeated.

She nodded.

"I'd be proud, obviously. To be good enough to play for England, I'd have to be the best I could be, at the peak of my fitness. Training with the best people; serving my country. Competing. Pushing myself." He stopped, unsure what more to say.

She sat back in her chair. "So… when you're thinking about what else you might enjoy, you should probably bear in mind that it's important to you to be outside, being fit and active, and pushing yourself with a challenge. Ideally you could look for something that gives you plenty of opportunities to get outdoors, with a minimum of time spent behind a desk. You seem to value things like having autonomy, having a passion for what you're doing, and striving to do your best. And not only developing yourself, but also helping other people achieve their potential and make positive changes in their lives. You have a need to take pride in what you're doing, to feel you're serving some sort of greater purpose."

He blinked, surprised by how easily she had untangled his mess of thoughts and neatly repackaged them. His needs seemed obvious now, but he probably wouldn't have been able to articulate them so clearly by himself.

"Yes. Yes, that is all important to me," he said.

In the corridor, the clamour of the bell told them lunch time had ended. She tapped a pink fingernail on the desk.

"Have a think about what might give you that, then. Your outdoor fitness instructor idea sounds to me as if it could be worth further research. Maybe you could combine it with other things. Although you've had one full-time job for a number of years, a lot of people these days don't earn their living like that. Many people have a couple of jobs, or combine a part-time job with self-employment. If it's scary to think about changing to a job that pays less than you earn now, perhaps it might help to work out the minimum you'd need to earn, and take it from there?" She jotted something on a bright yellow post-it note, and handed it to him. "Normally I'd ask you for your ideas about how you could find out more, but we've run out of time. Here's a couple of web links that should help. And maybe think about talking to people you know who work in sports: find out how they manage to make a living."

A soft knock at the door signified that a pupil was waiting, so he got up to leave. Perhaps it had been unfair of him to interrupt her lunch, but he was glad he had done it. His mind was racing with possibilities. He'd talk to the instructors at the gym, and maybe catch up with some of the other people from the outdoor fitness course to ask what they were up to. And he'd look at the websites she'd recommended, too. Gratefully he held out his hand and shook hers again.

"You're very welcome," she said in response to his thanks. "I hope you manage to find the right exit off your motorway. If you need another chat, you know where I am. And perhaps in return I could come to you for some fitness advice. I keep meaning to try a parkrun one of these days."

Chapter Sixteen

Tuesday 4ᵗʰ November 2014
Cardiff

*"*C*ome to bed," Tom said, resting his hands on Megan's shoulders where the knots in her muscles were so tight they hurt. His thumbs pressed in, gentle but insistent, and she arched her neck to lean against him. Closing her eyes, she gave in to the comforting sensation of his warm hands.

"That feels so nice. Don't stop."

He pressed a kiss onto her forehead. There was a smile in his voice. "We can carry on upstairs if you want. It's late. Time to put the laptop away."

She had been looking for her father again, typing every variant on his name that she could think of into Google and Facebook. Idris Parry; I Parry; Parry Carpenter Wales (that one had led her down a few dead ends); I P Builder; even Idris Parry Aberystwyth, in case he had returned to his place of birth. Nothing. She had spread the photographs out on the tabletop, but however much she looked at them, they told her nothing new.

Her gaze had rested on the other woman in the christening photograph. His sister. What did Rhod say? *If anyone knows where your dad is, I'd guess it would be Delyth.* But there had been no trace of a Delyth Parry on Facebook either. Of course, if Rhod and Jayne were right and Delyth had married an Italian with a fish and chip shop in Tenby, her surname wouldn't be Parry any more. But Tenby could be a good place to start looking for her. Even though she might not still be there, someone might remember her. With so little to go on, it had to be worth a try.

An internet search had quickly revealed that there were no fewer than ten fish and chip shops in the Tenby area, and two of them had

Italian names. There was nothing to say that Delyth's Italian husband had named the business after himself, of course, but they would be a good starting point. Tomorrow, at a more civilised hour. Depending on how the staff meeting went.

She submitted to Tom's kneading fingers and shut the laptop down, then swivelled her chair to face him.

His eyes offered an invitation. She tilted her face up and gave a low sigh of pleasure as he bent to kiss her, those warm hands now stroking her neck and up into her hair, sweeping it back while his thumbs gently caressed her cheeks. As always, his touch was soothing even while desire thrilled her skin and made the roots of her hair tingle.

She stood, sliding her body upwards along his, pressing against the hard bulge below his belt so that he groaned softly.

"Come to bed," he said again, taking her hand in his and leading her towards the stairs.

"Have you locked up?" she asked when he paused to kiss her again.

He grunted confirmation.

At the top of the stairs, he stopped and kissed her again, slipping a hand under her top to cup her breast. Her nipple seemed to come to life under his fingers, hot and hungry for attention. She yanked at his belt, loosened the buckle and seized the button of his jeans, pulling him along with her towards their bedroom.

"I want you," he whispered, nudging the door closed with his toe before she dragged him onto the bed. With one hand he reached under her skirt and she squeezed her eyes shut to relish the moment as he tugged her tights and knickers down past her knees.

"Did you let the dog out?" she murmured, shimmying up the bed so that he could bury his face in her groin, stifling a moan when he made contact. She had clamped her thighs around his head and he lifted it just enough to mumble in the affirmative before continuing, the sensation of his tongue making her buck and clutch at his hair with her fingers.

"And did you check on the kids?"

"*Yes*. Shhh, now. Focus on the moment."

He had kicked off his jeans and leaned over her, his nipples within reach now as he shrugged out of his t-shirt. He smelled faintly of coconut from his shower a little earlier, and she nuzzled her cheek against the soft fuzz of his chest hair, teasing ever closer to his nipple with her tongue and her teeth until at last he swore under his breath and pulled away to slip out of his pants.

By the time she had slid out of her top, dropping it carelessly onto the floor beside the bed, he had turned his attention to the clasp of her bra. Freed from the confines of her underwear, she arched and clung to him, wriggling downwards until he drove himself in, making her gasp and rake her nails down his back.

When they were done she lay spent in his arms, trapping his leg with her ankle so he had to stay close. She snuggled her face against his neck and breathed in the musky smell of their sex, glad he was in the habit of shaving in the evening rather than the morning so he didn't rasp against her skin. She should get up, but wasn't ready to break the intimacy of the moment yet.

"Don't let me go to sleep until I've taken my make-up off and brushed my teeth, will you?" she said.

He'd be wanting to fall asleep now, she knew; but she was far too wide awake to sleep just yet.

∞∞∞∞

Tom teetered on the edge of sleep, drowsily wishing Megan would stop talking so he could tumble right in. What was it that made her more awake and in the mood for chatting after they made love, when all he wanted was to let sleep drag him under?

She was warm against his chest, the duvet making a soft cocoon around their shoulders. "I'm sorry you're unhappy," she said.

He roused himself enough to open his eyes, weighing up possible responses. He could deny it, of course; he could say none of it was her fault, even though some of it clearly was, given that she wanted him to stay in the job that left him so burned out and dissatisfied. He settled upon "thanks", hoping it would be enough to shut the conversation down. He was too tired to grapple with emotions now.

"When you love someone, you just want them to be happy, don't you?" she continued.

"Yes." Which was why he wouldn't press her further to support him in pursuing his dreams. Not until he had a plan that was both practical and tempting enough to guarantee her agreement.

The knot of tension in his diaphragm, temporarily loosened by the hormone rush of good sex, screwed itself tighter again. He shifted onto his side, facing away from her, fighting the bitterness that rose whenever he thought about everything he had lost.

"You used to be happy, didn't you? Or, if not happy, you were at least content with our life. You seemed to be, anyway."

Hearing the warning signs of imminent tears in her voice, he sighed. "People change, don't they? They grow. They tire of the things that used to satisfy them. They lose things that gave them comfort or meaning... Parents. Goals. Dreams. All just memories or vain imaginings. Everything ends, doesn't it?"

"Don't say that." Her arm crept around him and clung.

"I didn't mean you, or us. I'm not your dad, remember. I'm not about to abandon you like he did."

You did once. She didn't say it, but he knew it was what she was thinking. He lay awake for hours, her arm a dead weight strapping him to the bed. He might have lost his dad, and his old belief that he'd be a teacher until the end of his days, but a new dream had just started

163

to percolate into his consciousness. One that could give him everything Eleri had said he needed. And if there was even the slightest chance of achieving it, he would find a way to make it happen.

Chapter Seventeen

Saturday 8ᵗʰ November 2014
Ludlow

This had been Dad's favourite time of year. Hugh had always appreciated the changing colours and crisp, chilly days on the golf course to compensate for the lack of cricket during the autumn and winter.

Mum, on the other hand, had preferred springtime and flowers. Before her illness, she'd planted forsythia, and a magnolia tree that was still only half its full height when she died. It was tall now, and would be a mass of glorious pink and cream goblets in a few months' time, until April winds scattered the petals.

She'd set a pair of apple trees at the farthest boundary of the back garden, for their blossom more than for the fruit; and when she was too ill to do it herself she'd directed Hugh to plant daffodil, snowdrop and crocus bulbs that still came up in ever-greater drifts of cheery colour each year, a living memorial to her joie de vivre.

Would Tom get to see her flowers next spring, or might the house belong to someone else by then? He could only hope they'd appreciate her legacy.

The lawn and borders already looked neglected, without Hugh and Jean around to potter about, raking and pruning and weeding. He'd get the mower out of the shed later, if the rain held off, for what would probably be the last cut of the autumn. It would smarten the place up a bit for the estate agent's photographs. He felt hollow inside thinking of people picking over the house, planning all the things they'd do to change it.

It troubled him that his brother had borne the brunt of dealing with the practicalities required for probate. In the past few weeks Rob had brought in antiques dealers and estate agents, and sifted through

Hugh's system of paperwork. He had even painted a couple of the shabbier bedrooms in neutral shades, despite Tom's insistence that he'd help if it could just wait until the school holidays.

He wandered back towards the kitchen to make a cup of tea while he waited for Rob to arrive. While the kettle warmed he gazed out at the back garden, the emptiness of the house like a weight on his back.

The bird table was deserted, the birds staying away now that no one lived here to replenish the supply of seed and peanuts. Jean had loved to sit and watch the different varieties of birds taking their turns at filling their bellies. Now she only had the sky to look at from her bed in the nursing home. He'd visited her earlier, and had been alarmed to see how rapidly her condition was deteriorating, trapping her confused mind inside a body that could no longer perform the basic functions of standing, walking or communicating. At least Hugh had been spared the sight of her like that, and had not endured the experience of a decline in his own faculties. It was a small comfort, but a comfort nonetheless, and he'd take all the consolation he could get.

A lone robin fluttered down and perched hopefully on the roof of the bird table, glancing about with sharp expectant eyes as if anticipating the arrival of more food. Tom smiled, keeping still so as not to alarm it. If only he could believe, as some people did, that robins were the visiting souls of departed loved ones. Hopefully Dad was having too good a time in the afterlife with Mum to waste even a moment of eternity looking in on their grown-up sons.

The robin fluttered out of sight just as the kettle rumbled to a crescendo and clicked off, ignored. Tea could wait. He fumbled for his phone in the pocket of his jeans.

"How's it going?" Megan asked, sounding out of breath and distracted.

"I needed to hear your voice," he said.

"It's only three hours or so since you heard it nagging you to empty the dishwasher." The warmth in her lilting Welsh voice took away any possibility of a sting in her words.

"I know. I just find it odd being here on my own."

"Isn't Rob there?"

"Not yet; he's due shortly. I'm just rattling about, feeling useless. Dorothy Freeman came earlier, telling me how she and Dad helped each other after they were both widowed."

"It's good that they had each other, then."

He paused at the window, looking out for the robin as the neighbour's cat forced its way through the bottom of the hedge. Green eyes stared glassily at him for a moment before it blinked and stalked away. If Dandy still lived here, it would never have dared to enter the garden.

"I know this is a selfish thing to say, Meg, but I hope I go before you. You'd do better on your own than I would. I want to die in your arms. Preferably with my head in your magnificent bosom."

"That's rubbish. You'd cope far better than I would. I'd fall apart without you around. Who'd get the Christmas decorations down from the attic? Who'd tidy up the kids' mess and empty the bins? Left to my own devices, the house would be like a tip by the time they buried you. I'd be living in misery and squalor within days."

"Misery-yn-Squalor? That's a village just off the A470, isn't it? Not far from Pontypridd." He had kept his voice serious, but permitted himself a grin when he heard her laugh.

"Idiot. Hey, now you've mentioned Dorothy… Do you think she and Hugh had a thing going? Was there more between them than just friendship?"

"She says not, but I sincerely hope there was. He was only in his mid-fifties when Mum died. Not all that much older than me, really. Imagine facing a sexless future at that age. No one ever wanting to touch you or kiss you, except for an occasional peck on the cheek or sisterly hug. It must be awful. I hope I'm still shagging you when I'm a hundred."

There was a cough at the doorway and he turned to see Rob retreating down the hall. He must have arrived while they were discussing Hugh's sex life. Awkward.

"Really, Tom…You say the most romantic things."

∞∞∞∞

Robert was in the study, setting up his laptop on Hugh's desk. He raised an eyebrow as Tom walked in.

"Sorry if I interrupted something," he said, grey eyes twinkling. "I trust it was your wife on the end of the line, not some 0898 number?"

"Definitely Megan. I gave up the sex lines when I took up online gambling…"

Rob chuckled, punching in his password with his index fingers.

"I was wondering, what shall we tackle first? The books in the study, or the stuff in the shed?" Tom asked, keen to do something helpful in the limited time they'd have together. "I vote for the study. Look what I found in here earlier." He hefted an enormous leather-bound volume onto the desk and opened the clasps that held it together.

"The family Bible. I remember Dad showing us that years ago."

"There are photos tucked inside, look." Tom riffled through the initial pages with their carefully handwritten lists of names, and fished out a handful of sepia photographs. "Do you know who these people are?"

Rob shook his head, turning a couple of the photographs over to examine the backs. "Ancestors. Presumably, some of the people mentioned in here. There's nothing to say who they are, though."

Tom gave a huff of frustration. "I wish I'd taken more of an interest and asked questions when Dad was still alive. They're part of our genes, and we don't know anything about them, except that they used to like posing with potted aspidistras, poker-faced in their Sunday best. Look at this one in her fox fur. The way it's staring is enough to give me the willies... I suppose their stories are lost to eternity now." He closed the book and tapped the cover. "I'd like to show this to the kids one day. Knowing where you've come from is a good feeling."

He paused, all at once struck by how disconcerting it would be to know nothing of his roots. No wonder Megan felt the need to know more about her father. The sense of a family past, however hazy, gave a feeling of security.

"You hang on to it, if you like. If I ever want to take a look, I'll know who to come to. This is what I wanted to discuss." Rob pointed at the laptop.

Tom peered at it, but the complicated spreadsheet made his brain feel foggy. "Is this the stuff for probate?"

"Yes. Take a seat." Rob donned his glasses and bent owlishly over the screen.

Obediently, Tom dragged an armchair over from its corner near the window and sank into its sagging seat. Rob clicked something, then swivelled to face his brother, his hands clasped in his lap.

"We should be in a position to start dealing with probate a bit earlier than I had expected to be. Hopefully after Christmas. Dad's efficiency with paperwork has been a huge help."

"I'm sorry I haven't been able to do more. It'll be different during the next school holidays: we haven't booked to go away anywhere, so I can come here to share the burden."

Rob shook his head. "It's fine. I find it helpful to have practical things to focus on. The valuations have come in this week from the antiques dealer and the jeweller. I haven't been able to collect together all of the information about the investments, insurances and savings just yet, but as you know, Dad left everything very well organised, so the task isn't as painful as it might have been. I've instructed the estate agents to value the house as it is, rather than what it could achieve with improvements. I considered replacing the kitchen and bathrooms, but I'm of the opinion it would be better to leave it and let the buyer carry out works of their own choosing. People will probably want to knock through and open the back of the house up to the garden, put in folding doors, that sort of thing. Personally I would prefer not to invest the amount of time or money needed for that."

Tom shifted restlessly in his seat. "I concur," he said. He didn't want to start ripping out things that had memories attached. Their mother had chosen the kitchen units, and in the twenty-odd years that had passed since then Hugh hadn't changed anything, beyond an occasional fresh coat of paint. He hated to think of their childhood home changing so fundamentally. There was still so much of Mum here: photos, furniture she chose; even the bowls of sun-bleached, dusty pot pourri she had placed on the windowsills in the nineties hadn't been moved, despite Hugh moaning about them at the time. *Bloody dust traps. They don't even smell all that nice.* Strange that he'd left them there, really.

He blinked and focused his attention on Rob's words.

"Allowing for the need for some modernisation, I'm expecting the valuations to come in at around £750-800,000."

Tom's eyes goggled. "Are you sure? I'd never have thought it would be as much as that."

"Don't forget, they bought it in the sixties, when rambling old houses that hadn't been modernised were out of fashion. Property prices were more sensible then. They both had good jobs. And if they still had a mortgage when Mum died, her life insurance would have paid it off."

Rob rattled off more figures. He seemed to be taking account of everything, to a bewildering level of detail. Hugh's Jaguar (which was worth surprisingly little, given its age); the paintings he had taken to collecting during his retirement as his only real indulgence apart from golfing holidays; the jewellery, glassware and a few pieces of furniture their mother had inherited from her grandparents; and all this without the value of savings and investments, which still needed to be totted up. Altogether it came to a sum that made Tom's head swim.

"Unfortunately, the money Dad gave us for our fortieth birthdays will have to be included in the calculations for inheritance tax, but as there were no other monetary gifts given to us we can roll over the annual allowance to the next financial year…"

"Inheritance tax?"

"I'm afraid so. It's a bitch, but it can't be helped. And it has to be paid within six months of the death. *Before* the estate is finalised. Don't look so worried, we can make an arrangement with the bank."

"Okay…"

"So, all in all, once the tax is taken off, and the estate costs are taken into account – the solicitor's and estate agent's fees and so on – we could potentially be looking at around three or four hundred thousand. Perhaps even a tad closer to half a million."

"Half a million? Do you mean *each*?"

"Mmm. That'll be more or less right." Rob took off his glasses and folded them.

Excitement flared for a moment, then dimmed. It seemed wrong to feel pleased about gaining from their father's death. Conflicted, he leaned forward, his elbows on his knees.

"Don't go spending it just yet," Rob was saying. "I've already warned Linda not to indulge in too many fantasies about cottages in the Cotswolds… Don't forget that some of the value is in goods, so if we keep the jewellery and antiques, it'll reduce the cash. But if the house sells quickly, it's not impossible that it could all be wrapped up by next summer."

Tom let out his breath in a rush. Within months, everything that tied him to this place would be gone: sent to the charity shop, sold or dispersed. With Jean so frail and sick, it might not be all that long before there would be no reason to visit Ludlow at all. The kids would forget about trips to visit their Grandpa, and life would go on as if he'd never lived in a place so full of history that every brick and stone in the centre of town seemed to have a story to tell. Walks with Dandy past the castle and over the river would be a distant memory only he and Rob would share. The future suddenly seemed dauntingly uncertain.

Chapter Eighteen

Saturday 8th November 2014
Cardiff

Megan weighed the telephone handset in her palm, gnawing at the inside of her lip. All afternoon she'd been putting this off, but if she didn't do it soon the evening would wear on and it would be too late to contact anyone.

Her pen rested on her notebook beside the computer, a list of possible sources of information scrawled down the page. She had already exhausted more than half, crossing them off with each disappointment.

~~Google search~~
~~Mam~~
~~Bethan~~
~~Facebook~~
~~Linked In~~
~~Rhod and Jayne~~
Delyth - Tenby fish and chip shops (Italian?)
Appeal on social media
Salvation Army
Private detective???

On the screen, the web page listing fish and chip shops in Tenby offered tantalising possibilities, especially the two with Italian names. She gazed at it until the screen went dark, then waggled the mouse, impatient with herself for hesitating. She had gone too far to back out now. Whatever the result, she had committed herself to this search, and she'd exhaust every angle she could pursue under her own steam before resorting to expensive options like a private detective.

She cocked an ear towards the door, but the children seemed to have settled. Dylan was already asleep. Nia was also in bed, quiet even if she wasn't sleeping. Alys was reading, winding down until it was time to turn out the light. None of the children needed her attention. There was nothing to prevent her from making the call.

Come on. What's the worst thing that could happen?

"Hi, sorry to bother you but I'm trying to contact someone called Delyth who may be connected with your shop. Her maiden name was Parry, and I believe she was married to an Italian, but it was a long time ago and I'm afraid I don't know her married name." Hopefully her voice sounded brighter than she was feeling. It seemed so unlikely that anyone would still be connected to someone who had worked there nearly forty years ago.

Proving her pessimism to be well-founded, the first two calls drew a blank. Neither of the owners had a clue who Delyth Parry was. That put the shops with Italian names out of the running. Her spirits sank a little lower with each rebuff.

Which to go for next? Alphabetical order seemed the most logical way forward, starting with those in the town itself and then widening the search. *Down Tenby way*, Rhodri had said. The shop might not have been in the town, but in the surrounding area. She tried another number, but to no avail. A knot of desperation was swelling inside her head; she closed her eyes and balled her fists in their sockets for a few seconds to ease it.

A deep breath settled her before she moved on to the next. *A Plaice by the Sea.* Why were fish and chip shop proprietors so keen on bad puns?

She dialled the number, her hopes wilting again as the woman who answered the phone sounded too young to be her aunt. Still, she launched into her request. The answer left her stunned.

"Delyth did work here – but that was years ago. She hasn't lived in Tenby for the past twenty-odd years," the woman said. She spoke slowly, as if puzzling over why anyone would be seeking her after so long.

"Oh! So this is the right shop." But if she hadn't been there for twenty years… The spark was snuffed as quickly as it had been ignited. "Can I ask if you're still in touch with her? Or - do you know anyone who might be? I realise it's been a long time…"

There was a pause while the woman covered the mouthpiece and spoke to someone in the background. Megan strained to hear what she was saying, but couldn't make out the words.

The woman's voice came back on to the line, her tone guarded. "Can I ask who's calling?"

Naturally, she'd be reluctant to give out any details to a complete stranger. Megan rushed to explain her identity.

"My name is Megan Parry. Well, Megan Field these days. Delyth is my father's sister."

The line was silent for several heartbeats, apart from the buzz of chatter in the background. Of course: it was a Saturday evening, probably one of the busiest times for a fish and chip takeaway. Unable to help herself, Megan crossed her fingers; she could hardly breathe with the anticipation.

At last the woman cleared her throat.

"Well, Megan. This is a surprise. To tell the truth, I never thought I'd ever get to speak to you."

"You know about me?" Megan set down her pen, stunned.

"Yes, I've heard your name mentioned. Not sure if you've heard of me, too? I'm your cousin Tina. Delyth is my mother."

∞∞∞∞

Tom's burger was falling apart, bun and filling sliding inexorably away from each other and threatening to land either onto his plate or into his lap. As ketchup and mustard glooped onto his right hand, he reached for a napkin.

"You seem to be struggling," Rob said, amused. His own meal of ribs was no less messy, and he licked his sticky fingers with enthusiasm.

Tom gave a wry grin. It was good to be out, just the two of them in a pub like old times. Ludlow was full of excellent places to eat, but neither had been in the mood for gourmet dining. Without even needing to discuss it, they'd both suggested a need for comfort food. Something hearty and stodgy; somewhere with a lively atmosphere full of chatter and a plentiful choice of real ales.

"Linda wants to move to the Cotswolds, then?" he asked, curious to know how his brother planned to spend their inheritance.

"Mmm." Rob dropped a bone onto the plate in the centre of the table and hacked a rib off the rack on his plate. "She fancies a barn conversion. Property in the Cotswolds will always be a sound investment, so I'm not averse to the idea. Not if we stick to the Gloucestershire side, to make it more convenient for work. I think Linda must be harbouring secret longings for Hunter wellies and a Barbour jacket. And of course India has been pestering us for a pony practically since she could talk." He smiled indulgently. "What about you? Have you any ideas yet about what you'd like to do?"

Tom hesitated, unsure where to start. Rob always seemed perfectly content with his life, scaling the career ladder to ever-loftier heights and never expressing the slightest dissatisfaction. Would he think Tom a fool for wanting to drop out of his conventional, safe career?

"It's difficult," he admitted. "How do you work out where you're going when you're not sure what you want?"

"That all sounds a bit deep, little brother. Have you considered that maybe all you need is a change of perspective? Take me, for example. When I stand on my beautifully manicured lawn right next to the molehill some little bastard mole has dug in the middle of it, I wind myself up like a top. I'd happily nuke the entire species to stop the buggers ruining my garden. But when I go up onto my balcony and look at the whole garden from there, suddenly one little molehill doesn't seem so bad."

Easy for Rob to say, with his big house and his three quarters of an acre. And his balcony.

"Take your work situation. Your manager… Harding, is it?" Rob asked, getting to the nub of the issue.

"Hard-on. No, Haddon! Ken Haddon." Tom shook himself. He'd better not make that kind of slip at work.

"Haddon, then. You can't stop him being a dick, can you? He'll have his own stuff going on, stuff you don't even know about. So maybe the simplest answer, to make your job less stressful, is to change the way you respond to him. Stop fighting the things you can't change; focus on the ones you can. Take a few steps back and look at the situation from your metaphorical balcony."

He grinned. "Can I change it to a real balcony? One with a sea view? I've always dreamed of moving to the coast. Meg isn't sure, but I've become more and more convinced in the last couple of years. And if we're going to do it, I'd rather it was before the girls start high school."

"You want more than just a change of perspective, then? A whole change of situation?" He wiped the barbecue sauce off his chin and whistled between his teeth. "So, let's debate that idea. Would you carry on in your current job? There must be seaside towns not too far from Cardiff. You've taken us to a few beaches when we've visited, haven't you?"

It was typical of Robert to see him as a problem that needed to be solved, but as he did occasionally come up with some useful suggestions Tom figured he might as well make use of the opportunity to pick his brains.

"I want to move further away, right into the country. A lifestyle change. Ideally Devon or Cornwall, but that would be a step too far for Megan. So – although it isn't certain yet – I'm thinking probably

West Wales. She'll want to carry on teaching, but I don't want to. I'll have to come up with something else."

There. He'd said it to his brother, and it was surprising how saying the words out loud made it seem like he'd started coming up with a proper plan. There was a pause while Rob chewed his next mouthful.

"What will you do in the country? This house near the sea. You'll still have to work."

"That's the conundrum. Ideally I'd like to work outdoors a lot of the time, doing something physical." He left out the bit about wanting to help people.

"Alright, let's brainstorm. What do people do outdoors? They have farms, don't they? The other day I was reading about llama farmers, of all things. They left their City jobs and bought some land with a flock. Learned to weave; now they sell llama wool jumpers and whatnot."

Tom quirked an eyebrow. "I don't really see myself dealing with livestock. Or weaving. Or knitting jumpers, for that matter."

"Hmm. Perhaps it isn't quite your style. And llamas spit, don't they, so not ideal. Alright, then. What else..? A park keeper works outdoors. You could wear a peaked cap and yell at kids to get off the grass while you puncture their footballs and tend your petunias." He chuckled, spearing his last few chips.

"I don't know a petunia from a pet unicorn, and I'm hardly the sort of chap to stop kids playing football. If anything I'd like to encourage them to do it."

"So you want an outdoor job that allows you to encourage kids to do sport. I know the perfect job for you: PE teacher! You get paid to run around outside, and you have the perfect skills, experience and qualifications for the job."

Tom pushed his empty plate aside and reached for his beer. "Be serious."

"Well... what do people do when they go to the countryside? They stay somewhere. Hotels. Bed and Breakfast. Holiday lets. You could get a nice, big house, and take in paying guests. A perfect job for the seaside. Not very outdoorsy, unless you do the garden. Of course, if I'm honest, I would struggle to picture Megan making beds and cleaning strangers' hairs off the bath, or asking them sweetly how crispy their bacon should be."

Tom shook his head. He'd already dismissed the idea of running a guesthouse. "We wouldn't be comfortable with strangers staying in our home. Not with the kids so young. But holiday lets... There might be something in that. And that way Meg wouldn't need to be involved in the practicalities."

"What about glamping? That's all the rage now, isn't it? You could buy a couple of yurts, add log burners and woolly blankets, and watch the bookings roll in. People will pay silly money to give up their mod cons and stay in places like that. Better still, get someone in to do yoga or mindfulness and call it a Glamping Retreat."

They called the waitress over and paid the bill, leaving a generous tip. Rob's enthusiasm had picked up and he chatted on while they walked home, their collars turned up against the chilly drizzle.

"Why don't you rent out your camper van? Better still, buy a fleet of camper vans! People pay a fortune for that, don't they? Hiring them for a week or two. You could recommend some campsites, supply all the kit..."

"And have them ringing me from the hard shoulder of the M4, wondering why the engine blew up when they took it up to eighty? I wouldn't put Greta through that. I couldn't trust anyone else to look after her."

"Not even for a thousand pounds per week? That's what they're asking in high season. Strewth, it's daylight robbery." Rob had his mobile phone in his hand and was obviously googling the going rate.

"Not even for a million." He would dig his heels in against that particular suggestion, no matter how many arguments Rob could produce in its favour.

The gate groaned under his hand as he pushed it open. Rob fished in his pocket for his keys and stepped back to use what little light he could catch from the streetlamp to find the right one. They hadn't thought to leave a light on, and the house looked cold.

Tom shivered. Their past was here. Birthdays. Christmases, hanging his stocking on the mantelpiece; coming home to the smell of baking, coloured fairy lights twinkling amongst the tinsel on the tree in the front window. Sticking Athena posters to his bedroom wall; arranging his sporting trophies on his shelves. Bursting in to share his excitement at passing his driving test. Sneaking his girlfriend in and canoodling on the sofa while his parents were in bed. The tedium of exam revision, stuck inside while the sun beamed down, trying to focus on his books instead of the cricket commentary drifting through the window from Dad's radio. Tiptoeing past his parents' room while Mum slept off the latest round of chemo.

Soon, a sale board would be hammered into the lawn, and Ludlow and this house would only exist for them in memories. He and Rob would go in their separate directions to whatever future lay beyond this, with Dad no longer the lynchpin of their different lives, bringing them back to the centre.

"You will keep in touch, won't you?" he said. "When we don't have this any more, I mean."

Rob had found the key. He opened the door, stepped inside, and flicked the switch to flood the hallway with light.

"When you've got your dream house at the seaside? Try keeping me away."

Chapter Nineteen

Saturday 15th November 2014
Cardigan

Delyth seemed younger than her sixty-plus years. Black jeans clung to her slim legs, the sequinned motif at the ankle surprisingly funky combined with her layered vest and shirt. Her thinning dyed brown hair was caught back in a low ponytail with an ornate clip, and beneath her bold make-up her grey eyes were coolly appraising.

"You'd better come in," was the only greeting offered on Megan's arrival. No smile of welcome, no delighted bear hug or squeal of delight at seeing her long-lost niece on her doorstep. The bunch of flowers Megan offered were taken without comment to the kitchen and immediately forgotten. Clearly, Megan's daydreams of joyful family reunions had been naïve. Sinking into the indicated chair and tucking her handbag neatly behind her feet, she made a conscious effort to sit up and smile, and to rest her hands calmly in her lap.

"You're your mother's daughter, alright. The spit of her, you are, with that red hair. Hers was frizzy, though. I suppose you use straighteners, like all the youngsters do these days? Yes, I thought as much. I see you young women all the time on the bus, all with the same poker-straight hairstyle. Like clones, you are: terrified to be different by having a bit of frizz or some curls. Same old same old. To tell the truth, I can't see much of my brother in you. His hair wasn't like yours, nor his eyes. And you've got a bit more meat on your bones. He was built like one of my mother's knitting needles. Not an ounce of fat on him."

Megan's heart sank at the way she referred to Idris in the past tense. Perhaps this visit wouldn't turn out to have the positive result she had hoped for. Fortunately, years of teaching difficult teenagers had given her the ability to sound more composed than she felt.

"People do say I resemble my mam. Bethan is slender, and her hair is chestnut brown, like yours."

"I remember Bethan. A sweet little thing. She must be about forty now, I suppose?"

"She was thirty-nine in September. I'm thirteen months younger, but you probably remember that."

There was an uncomfortable silence, broken by the whirring of a cuckoo clock suddenly stirring into life.

"I got it in Switzerland," Delyth said, following her gaze.

"It's charming. As is your home. Very cosy." The words sounded stilted. She attempted a polite smile, which was not returned.

"Dai chose it. He was my third husband."

"Oh... Uncle Rhodri said you married an Italian. I didn't realise you'd married three times."

"Never found one I could tolerate for long. Salvatore was the first, but he cared more about his chip shop than me. Then there was Johnny. He was a wild one. Fun while it lasted, but not one for settling down with. Tina couldn't stand him: she ended up staying in Tenby with her father. We lived all over the place. Never could settle in one place for long, until I moved here. It's probably the bit of me that's most like your dad: never staying anywhere, or with anyone, for any length of time. After a few years with Johnny I got tired of taking risks. Of all my husbands, Dai was the most reliable, sensible one. He always wanted a bungalow, said when he got old it'd turn out to be the best thing he'd ever bought."

"That does sound sensible," Megan agreed, wondering when they would get around to talking about Idris.

"It should have been a brilliant plan, but he didn't get old. Dropped dead in Tesco, he did. Caused a bit of a stir, as you can probably imagine."

Megan stared. "I'm so sorry to hear that."

"In the middle of the freezer section, he was. He'd been right round the shop. There was only peas left on his list."

"What a terrible shock."

"Well, yes. But it was five years ago now."

"Right." Unusually, she found herself fumbling for words. This sudden deluge of personal history was making her feel as if she had been dragged out to sea by a rip current whilst paddling in the shallows.

"The bungalow came to me, of course. He was the only one who left me better off than I was when he found me... Are you married, yourself?"

At last this felt like safer ground. "Yes. My husband dropped me off outside. I sent him into town so we can talk on our own. I'll text him when I'm ready for him to pick me up."

Delyth's eyes narrowed. She sniffed, seemingly on her guard again. "Well, I'll put my cards on the table straight away. There's no money in the family. The Parrys never had any, and I'll be leaving what little I've got to Tina. Just so's you know, in case that's what you're after."

"Actually, that isn't what I'm after. I've managed without a penny of my father's money for this long, after all. The time for him to provide for me was when I was a child, not now that I'm a grown woman with children of my own."

She had spoken without thinking and wondered if her sharp tone had caused offence, but on the contrary - her prickly reaction seemed to have made Delyth relax. She had settled back in her chair and tilted her head to one side, less hostile now.

"Alright. I appreciate plain speaking. Tell me what you *are* after, then."

Megan fidgeted, twisting the rings on her wedding finger. "I've grown up with only my mam's side of the story, and only the bare bones of that. I don't know why he left. I don't know if he ever tried to keep in touch with us... I don't know if he ever had more children, or even if he's still alive. I have nothing to tell my kids about their grandfather, and it feels like a void behind me. I want to know if he's the villain he's always been portrayed to be, or if there's another side to what happened." She stopped, conscious of the wobble in her voice.

Delyth nodded, apparently satisfied. "I'll make a cup of tea, shall I? And then we can talk properly."

Watching her aunt disappear into the kitchen, Megan let out her breath. Bizarrely, it seemed she had passed some kind of test. When Delyth returned and set down a tray with two mugs and a plate of biscuits, she sensed that the biscuits were a privilege she had earned through straight talking.

"Where do you want to start?" Delyth asked, adjusting the cushion behind her. She hadn't taken a biscuit. Perhaps that explained her slim figure.

Best to get the scariest question out of the way first. "Is he alive?"

"He was a couple of months ago when I last spoke to him. I'd like to think someone would have told me if he wasn't."

Absurdly, Megan's eyes stung with unshed tears. She nodded and bit into a shortbread finger, processing this information as the sweet, buttery flavour melted on her tongue. She'd been steeling herself to hear that he might already be dead, that she'd never get the chance to meet him or ask him any questions. The greatest obstacle was gone… Of course, he still might not want to meet. She mustn't get ahead of herself.

"Does he have any other children?"

"None that I'm aware of. But I wouldn't put it past him. He's always lived life as if it was one long Club 18-30 holiday. Last I heard he was shacked up with some posh piece not far from Cardiff."

Megan's heart thumped. "Cardiff?" Could he really be living so close by?

"Somewhere near there. On the coast, he said. I'm sure he mentioned her place having a view over the Bristol Channel."

"Not far from me and Bethan, then."

"I suppose not."

"Did he ever try to contact us?" In the past, she'd imagined him sending her letters, and Olwen getting to them first and hiding or destroying them. She didn't know which was worse: the idea of her mother being so cruel as to withhold her father's letters or the thought that he never cared enough to send any.

"That I don't know, but I can tell you he isn't really one for sending cards. Usually I'm the one who gets in touch, not the other way round. I ring him in December every year to find out where to send his Christmas card, and then again in June to wish him a happy birthday. Sometimes I ask myself why I bother, but if I didn't I'd probably lose touch with him altogether. So I've taken it upon myself to be the one who makes the effort. It's more of a feminine thing, isn't it, sending cards?"

It seemed Olwen was off the hook. Megan jerked to her feet, suddenly restless. She paced to and fro in front of the window until she could hold the words back no longer.

"I just can't understand it. We've both got children. Could you imagine never seeing Tina, not even speaking to her to ask how she's getting along? He's missed so much. So many of our milestones. Helping us ride a bike for the first time. Fixing bookshelves up in our rooms. Warning our first boyfriends to keep their hands to themselves. Dealing with bullies. He wasn't there to help us through our teenage years, to make sure we felt beautiful and precious and loved. To see us pass our exams and go on to university. How could he bear to lose out on all that?"

"Perhaps it isn't the same for men as it is for us."

"I don't buy that," Megan said with a toss of her head. "My Tom couldn't be parted from our kids. It would break him, I know it would."

Delyth didn't answer. She'd been examining her hands while Megan was speaking, and it was impossible to read her expression.

"Delyth, do you think he'd be willing to meet me?"

At last her aunt looked up. She sighed and reached for a notebook resting on a side table. "Your guess is as good as mine. To be honest, I don't think it would be right for me to just give you his number, not when I don't know how he'd feel about you contacting him out of the blue. But if you give me your details, I'll pass them on to him. I can't really say fairer than that, when all's said and done."

∞∘∞∘∞

Tom slipped his purchase into his coat pocket, feeling smug. Not more than ten minutes after parking the car in Cardigan he had spied the perfect gift for Megan in a shop window, and now it was nestling in the palm of his hand awaiting the perfect moment. He'd been pleasantly surprised by the variety of shops in this bustling old market town. It had more character than he'd expected, and a gratifying selection of independent stores and cafés amongst the usual chains. He contemplated buying a coffee to celebrate his purchase, but then spotted a surfwear shop just along the street. Coffee could wait a while.

Nothing in the surfwear shop caught his eye. He already owned more hoodies and shorts than he needed, and the season for buying flip-flops had passed. Stepping outside into the damp and chilly November air, he noticed an estate agent opposite and crossed the road, curious to compare property prices here with those in Cardiff. He scanned the advertisements in the window. Prices were enticingly low.

A large country house looked remarkably grand for the price, but was too big to be a practical option. A B&B with a sea view caught his attention momentarily, until common sense prevailed. He'd already ruled out running a guest house. But the whitewashed stone

farmhouse with three neat gables in a row, set in six acres of land…
Something about it tugged at him. Before he had time to think about
it, he was inside the shop and requesting the details from the smartly
dressed woman on the reception desk.

"*Y Noddfa* is it, sir? A lovely house, that one. Originally a
seventeenth century longhouse, although it's been altered over the
years. It still has plenty of period features, though, and it's been very
sympathetically and tastefully restored, as you can see from the
photographs. There's a courtyard, with ample parking space, and
three outbuildings, including the barn you can see there, built of
traditional Cardigan brick. The current owners contemplated
converting it to a holiday let, but they never got around to sorting out
the planning permission. The pigsty would make an excellent
workshop: there's already mains electricity and water connected…
Four bedrooms, that's right. Two bathrooms. And very convenient
for the coast. You could walk it in about half an hour, or drive in five
or ten minutes."

Tom leafed through the photographs, each one more appealing
than the last. He told himself to be cautious, not to get sucked in by
olde worlde aesthetics or a price that was only a little higher than the
value of their 1930s semi in Cardiff. But oh, those fireplaces, and the
oak beams; the bread oven in the inglenook and the shutters at the
sash windows; the slate floor in the quirky kitchen: everything had
such quaint character and charm.

He skimmed through the details, forcing himself to look for
important, practical information. *Energy performance… En suite shower
room… Active village community…* Then, in the description of the
exterior: *Ample parking for a boat or camper van.* He read the words
again, his stomach seeming to dance as excitement bubbled and
fizzed inside him.

The pieces of his life, so disjointed and confusing lately, were
slotting into place like the most perfect game of Tetris. Fate was taking
a hand, he was sure of it. It was a sense he'd had all week. During

their staff meeting most of his colleagues, Megan included, had looked concerned or stricken at the announcement of redundancies across the borough. He, though, had felt only relief at the prospect of release from a role that exhausted him. And now, here was this house. A house with the kind of historic character Megan loved, on the coast, within easy walking distance of the sea, where they could start building a new way of life with the kids.

He tore his gaze from the leaflet and addressed the estate agent, who was still hovering helpfully.

"How do you pronounce the name of it, again?" He sounded the words out carefully. "*Uh Noth-va*, is it? What does it mean?"

"*Y Noddfa* means The Sanctuary or Haven," she said. "Or The Refuge."

She couldn't have given him a more perfect answer. A sanctuary. That was exactly what he needed. A place to escape from the pressures of life, to be more at one with the world. A haven for them all to retreat to at the end of each day, to find peace, like weary travellers.

"Would it be possible to view it today? After lunch, if you can arrange it."

The agent looked doubtful. Clearly a charm offensive was required, so he shifted gear and treated her to one of his most winsome smiles.

"I know it's a lot to ask, and under normal circumstances I wouldn't dream of putting you to the bother. It's only because I have to go back to Cardiff this afternoon, and I'm not sure when I'll get another opportunity. Do you think there's any chance at all?"

"It's very short notice, Mr..?"

"Field. But call me Tom. I know, and of course I'll understand if it can't be done. But I'd be so grateful if you could try..?"

She hesitated, softening under his pleading gaze. "Well… take a seat while I note down your details. Then I'll speak to the vendor and see what I can do."

Chapter Twenty

Saturday 15th November 2014
Cardigan

Megan slipped into the passenger seat, grateful for the shelter of the car after waiting in the drizzle for Tom to collect her. "How did it go?"

"Okay, I think," she said. "He wasn't there, of course. I did wonder if he might be, if she'd told him I was coming. Silly of me, really. She hasn't told him about me yet, although she says she'll phone him soon and ask if he'd be willing to meet. Her main concern seemed to be to tell me her chequered marital history. And to make sure I'm not after the family silver."

"Seriously?"

"Apparently there isn't any. She was quite keen to make sure I was clear about that."

His dry laugh was reassuring. At least he understood that money was the last thing she expected from her father. Visiting her new-found aunt had been strangely anticlimactic. Whilst it was a relief to know he was alive, there was still no guarantee that she would get to meet her father. In fact, if Delyth decided not to tell him about her, or if he took fright and refused to meet up, this trip could have been a complete dead end, and all that emotional energy would have been wasted.

"You know, I'm beginning to wonder if I was mad to start all this. What do you think? Have I been stupid?"

His gaze was fixed on the road, making it hard to read his expression. "I think you're doing what you need to do," he said, so carefully that it was obvious he was trying to be diplomatic.

"That means yes, then." She rolled her eyes and fussed with her handbag, hunting for her lip balm. Delyth's bungalow had been oppressively hot, making her feel dehydrated despite the cup of tea.

"I expect you're hungry," he said, as if she wouldn't notice the deliberate change of subject. "I'm ravenous. I noticed a few cafés in town, if you fancy some lunch?"

She frowned. "Shouldn't we be thinking about getting back? We don't want to take advantage of Bethan and Matt too much. She told me last week that she's been going to bed at nine every night since she started her new job. She's shattered, and a morning with Dylan would be enough to wear out the Duracell Bunny."

"Well, I for one could do with something to eat, and it isn't often that we get a chance to get a proper café lunch without the kids in tow. Come on, another hour or two won't make much difference. And we can get a nice bunch of flowers on the way back to thank her."

She was hungry enough to allow herself to be persuaded. Tom seemed to be in a remarkably affable mood considering she had sent him off to wander around Cardigan's small town centre for an hour in the depressing autumn weather. Usually he detested shopping, yet there was an energised, excited air about him as they left the café, not dissimilar from the way he had been when he bought Greta. Could he be up to something? If he was, at least it couldn't be anything as whimsical or expensive as a camper van. Hopefully he'd got such quixotic flights of fancy out of his system after the trouble his last one had caused.

A few minutes into their journey home she realised the sat nav was sending them the wrong way and, inexplicably, he seemed content to drive in the opposite direction, taking them even further away from home, despite her remarking upon it.

"It's fine. There's something I want to see before we head back."

She clicked her tongue, impatient at his lack of concern. Didn't he realise it wouldn't help matters with her sister if they were away for longer than necessary? Bethan was already cross about the trip to see Delyth, had been on the verge of refusing to facilitate it by looking after the children, and probably only acquiesced because she'd realised Megan would go with or without her help.

"How long will it take? We're two hours away from home as it is, and we've already delayed to have lunch."

"It's just a couple of miles - we're nearly there. It'll take half an hour at most. This was the earliest time I could arrange for us to go."

Folding her arms, she pursed her lips in annoyance. He had better have a good explanation for this detour along winding minor roads. They passed fields of sheep with occasional trees punctuating the hedgerows, hunched over like question marks by the prevailing wind. Within a few minutes of leaving the outskirts of town she glimpsed the sea, leaden and forbidding at this time of year even though the rain had finally stopped. Then, just as she was on the point of demanding to know what the hell he was up to, the sat nav's placid voice intoned: "in one hundred yards your destination will be on your left." She craned her neck to look.

They were in a village, and an unexceptional one at that, with a hotchpotch of newly built houses, hacienda-style bungalows, short terraces faced with pebbledash, and older, whitewashed houses. Tom drove slowly past a community centre that looked as if it had once been a village school, and a chapel that had been converted to a house, still with the graveyard at the back. There was a small church, but no sign of a shop or post office or pub. Little to suggest that much would happen here to draw Tom. Yet he stopped the car, grinning as gleefully as if he'd discovered buried treasure, parking alongside a low red-brick barn edging the road.

"You have arrived at your destination," the sat-nav announced.

He reached to turn it off, checking his watch. "Good. We're on time. Come on, out you get."

It was only when they rounded the end of the barn that she spotted the sign. *Ar Werth.* For Sale.

Her steps slowed. Surely he wasn't intending to view a property here? Her heart plummeted as a man in a suit clambered out of a car liveried with the same colours as the sale sign. Tom bounded over to shake his outstretched hand, and then, with Megan trailing behind in disbelief, the men pushed the gate open and entered a concreted yard.

The estate agent turned, jangling a set of keys. "Good to meet you, Mr Field; Mrs Field. I'm Marc Evans. Welcome to *Y Noddfa.*"

∞∞∞∞

Tom's excitement dimmed with one look at Megan's stony expression. *Please co-operate. Don't show me up in front of this stranger,* he begged her with his eyes. She must have got the message, as she gave the agent the barest twitch of a smile and shook his outstretched hand so briefly as to be only just polite.

He tried to win her over while the estate agent fiddled with the lock. "It's a lovely name for a house. Apparently it means sanctuary or haven, did you know that? Perfect for us."

She arched an eyebrow in response. "It can mean that, yes. Alternatively, *noddfa* also means lunatic asylum. Which could be even more perfect, because, let's face it, this is madness."

He gestured for her to precede him. He mustn't let her sarcasm dampen his enthusiasm. Once she saw the inside of the house she'd start to feel differently about it, he knew she would.

The slate floor in the hallway looked as if it had been there for centuries, worn down by who knew how many pairs of feet over the years. Not as spectacular as the tiles she loved at his dad's house, admittedly, but still full of historic character.

They trooped behind the agent into the long, narrow kitchen, listening as he pointed out its many positive features: the oak beams; the restored bread oven in the fireplace which could be used as a pizza oven; the original wooden shutters.

Megan was silent, and although she glanced about each room dutifully it was impossible to tell from her sour expression whether

her thoughts were negative or whether she was just playing it cool for the agent's benefit. She could hardly fail to see that this had infinitely more charm than their dated kitchen at home.

"We could always change the cupboards and the tiles if you don't like them," he said, trying to gauge her opinion. "I can just imagine us cooking while the kids do their homework at the table here. And that utility area would be great for muddy boots when we come in from a walk with the dog."

Her only response was a hard stare before she followed the agent along the hallway to view the dining room and sitting room. Surely the Victorian fireplaces would soften her heart in these rooms, given how much she admired the ones at his dad's? But again she stayed silent, apart from remarking that he'd have to spend most of each day chopping wood to fuel the log burners in the rooms they had seen so far. By the time they had seen the bedrooms and bathrooms upstairs, her continuing resistance was making him jumpy. The house was gorgeous – everything he wanted. He knew in his gut that he needed to buy it. But he'd only be able to if she saw it that way too.

"Time to see the outbuildings and the grounds," Marc announced at the front door, casting doubtful looks from one to the other. He indicated that they should precede him down the few steps into the courtyard.

The outbuildings were a bit ramshackle, but there was electricity and a water supply, and the barn was a good size. Big enough for Tom's purposes. His excitement grew, despite the increasingly pinched expression on Megan's face. Finally, Marc led them around the back of the house, across a terrace bordered by straggly-looking shrubs that he guessed would probably burst into bloom next spring, towards a gently-sloping field edged with hedgerows. An area of woodland was visible in the distance beyond.

Megan fell behind while Tom plied Marc with questions.

"Do you think it would be possible to turn some of this land into a camp site? Just a small one, obviously. Perhaps with a few glamping pods or shepherd's huts, with some pitches for tents and camper vans. We'd need water, maybe some electric hook-up points, and a small toilet block, although maybe we could convert the pigsty for that. These fields don't slope too steeply... What do you think? Is it do-able?"

Marc nodded thoughtfully. "It's a good size for something like that. But you'd need planning permission and a licence, with it being a change from residential use. Obviously it's impossible for me to say whether any of that would be forthcoming. It would depend on a whole range of factors: how much of the year it would be open; the number of pitches; the sort of facilities you planned to have; the environmental impact; access, and so on. My advice would be to consult an expert if you and your wife are thinking along those lines."

"I could imagine this as a perfect haven for people to improve their wellbeing, couldn't you? With a small gym in the barn; organised walks, runs and activities. I could link up with other people in the area, see if there's anyone who could offer yoga sessions, mindfulness and so forth. Maybe even crafts or cooking: anything, really, that helps people switch off from their everyday stress. And obviously I'd want to make sure that all the renovations of the outbuildings were eco-friendly and sustainable. There's something magical about this place. We could create something really special here."

He'd almost forgotten the estate agent and was talking to himself now, picturing the outbuildings patched up and functioning, a gym or yoga studio in the barn and bicycles available to hire from the pigsty.

Y Noddfa could truly live up to its name as a sanctuary, not only for Tom but for people like him who needed an escape from reality, somewhere to get closer to the outdoors and the important things in life. It wouldn't be just a campsite, but could potentially offer a hub for the local community too. He'd like that, to feel he was contributing by offering opportunities to local people, not just paying guests. And as long as he was careful to abide by his licence and get good business advice, he'd be in control. No Ken Haddon giving him pointless orders for stupid initiatives that wouldn't do any long-term good. No staff to manage. He could do the day-to-day maintenance himself, run fitness classes, and ask Matt to set a website up for people to book themselves in.

The house would be their private family space. The kids would benefit from a more outdoor lifestyle, with so much fresh air and little traffic – admittedly, they'd have to travel a bit further to school, but Cardigan was only a few miles away, and they could walk to the beach together on days off. He took in a deep breath, filling his lungs with the fresh, damp air. The only sounds were birdsong and the faint babble of a stream.

This place could give him everything Eleri had identified as important to him in his career, and when his inheritance came through it would be within his reach to afford the necessary investment.

He turned away from the rolling fields and hedgerows towards Megan, who had returned to the patio area. Although the sun had come out, lighting up the garden and the glints in her hair with autumn bronze and gold, she had huddled into her coat looking glumly at her feet instead of appreciating the view.

He had to make her understand the fire in his belly that had been ignited the moment he first glimpsed this place. She wouldn't have to be a part of his plans for the business – in fact, her steady income as a teacher would be useful to keep them afloat until he could start making a profit. She could pursue her own ambitions, maybe even go for a full-time job or promotion if she wanted. He needed her on board if he was ever to turn his dream into a reality. More than that, he wanted her to be happy.

"Would you mind giving us a few minutes?" he asked Marc.

"Be my guest. If you're finished in the house, I'll go and lock up."

He waited a few moments, then he joined Megan on the patio.

"What do you think?" he asked, employing his most devastating smile as his fingers closed around the small box in his pocket.

She sniffed. "It's a nice house. Someone is bound to snap it up."

Not the out-and-out negativity he had feared, but he didn't feel any more confident that she had been persuaded. Couldn't she think of anything more enthusiastic to say than *nice*? He changed tack.

"You know, I've loved you for a long time."

A flicker of consternation crossed her face, as if she was unsure how to handle this new approach. He pressed his advantage, taking her hand and rubbing it to warm her chilled fingers.

"Sometimes I find it hard to believe we've had ten years together. In some ways it feels like a lifetime, as if nothing ever mattered before we were Us; and yet it's passed so quickly. Ten years; three children; good times and bad. Times when I've been a bit of a dick; times when you've been a bit hormonal and illogical." He smiled in case she thought he was criticising, and was rewarded with an answering gleam of those feline eyes - little more than a softening, but he pressed on, encouraged.

"You've been my rock through all those years, and I can't express what it's meant to have your strength behind me. While you were at your aunt's house today I saw two things in Cardigan that stood out. I knew straight away I wanted to give you both of them, as a way of showing you what you mean to me. This house was the first. I saw the details in the estate agent's window and knew we had to come and see it. And this was the other." He reached into his pocket and produced the box, pressing it into her palm. "Go on, open it."

Frowning, she opened the lid. The hinge was stiff, and she pushed it open with both thumbs, then gazed down at the object revealed within the satin lining.

"What's this?"

"Most people would call it a ring." He smiled, wishing she wouldn't make him try so hard. The graceful tendrils of yellow and rose gold, twining as if in a harmonious dance, made him feel proud.

He'd made the perfect choice: it was exactly the sort of thing he knew she'd fall in love with.

She squinted up at him, the sun behind him throwing shadows over her face.

"What's it for?" Her tone stung.

He stuffed his hands into his pockets, hunching his shoulders defensively. "To wear on your finger. Pretty obvious, I would have thought. It's Welsh gold. An eternity ring: the lines go around without ending, signifying endless devotion. I bought it in a jeweller's shop in Cardigan. I thought you'd love it..?"

There were tears in her eyes, brushed away almost before he could see them. Abruptly she snapped the box closed and handed it back to him, her mouth set in the stubborn line he knew so well.

"It's beautiful, of course it is."

"Then why give it back?"

"Why give it to me now?"

He paused, bewildered. "Why won't you take it? Can't a man give his wife something beautiful?"

"Think about it, Tom. Why can't he?"

Her voice had risen and he glanced back towards the house to check the estate agent hadn't heard. With an impatient huff she pushed past him and stomped away, around the corner of the house and back to the car.

Marc was waiting by the gate, looking puzzled.

Tom called to him with as much dignity as he could manage while chasing after his wife mid-argument. "Thanks very much for showing us around. We're definitely interested - I'll give you a call on Monday."

In the car, it was clear that Megan was, inexplicably, furious. Her mobile phone buzzed in her pocket, unheeded, while she scowled out through the windscreen, apparently determined not to discuss what had just happened.

"What's the matter with you, Meg? Talk to me. I don't understand why you're being like this."

"Just start the car and take me home."

"No, I won't. Not until we've discussed this."

They tussled briefly as she tried to grab the keys from his hand, both ignoring the insistent buzz from her mobile.

"What the hell has got into you?" he bellowed.

She wrenched away, eyes pink with unshed angry tears.

"It's emotional blackmail, Tom – that's what this is. You've been trying to make me feel guilty for weeks, just because I don't want to drop everything we've worked for and go chasing after your stupid pipe dreams. Just because you've decided you hate your job, and you suddenly like the west coast after one brief visit to Uncle Rhod's, the kids and I have to come trailing after you to live in some poxy little village in the middle of nowhere, while you blow all our security on some ridiculous vision of a rural idyll! You've dragged me to see this house without even asking me first, wasting valuable time when you know we need to get back for the kids, because you think it'll make me change my mind about leaving the life I love behind; and then, to add insult to injury, you think a bit of bling and a few soppy words will bribe me into melting and cooing over how romantic you are, and agreeing to this – this *insanity*." She scrubbed her hands over her face. "Setting me up like that, trying to manufacture the perfect moment… Well, I won't be manipulated. If you want this house so much, buy it with your dad's money - but you can do it on your own. I'm not putting the kids through the trauma of being dragged to the other side of the country, away from their schools and all their friends and, most of all, Beth and Matt. You go ahead, if it means so much to you. But the kids and I will be staying at home. Our *actual* home. In Cardiff."

Pinpricks of light rushed into his eyes. How could this have gone so wrong?

"You're accusing me of insanity, but what's your reaction if not completely unreasonable? I'm not trying to manipulate you into anything. I'm simply trying to demonstrate that life can be different by showing you a house that could meet all our needs as a family and give me an opportunity to change my career. I'm not expecting *you* to give up teaching just because I need to. There must be plenty of schools around here. You could look for a full-time job, maybe even that head of department job you said you've missed out on. Come on, don't cry. Don't be like this."

Helplessly he touched her arm, willing her to calm down and see things more rationally. She couldn't have meant it when she told him to go it alone, could she? He couldn't contemplate a life without her and the kids, and she of all people would know that. Panic threatened to make his chest burst – he needed her to take her words back, or he'd surely break into pieces.

This could be the end of everything he'd been imagining for himself, the death of the plans that had brought a measure of hope and light into his heart again. Was he wrong to want more from life? If the beauty in this place wouldn't convince her, and if she could so easily misunderstand a simple romantic gesture, what was the point in even trying to have aspirations? She had the power to hold him back, and the mulish set of her mouth now made it clear that she was determined to use it.

His shoulders sagged as he permitted himself one last look at *Y Noddfa*'s whitewashed gables. He couldn't build his dream on his own. It would be meaningless without his family around him. But this intransigence of hers, forcing him to choose between his current unsatisfactory life and the pursuit of his dream – a dream that was within reach, if she'd only come with him - would be hard to forgive. He had put his heart in her hands and she had torn it in two.

"Answer your phone, will you? Someone's obviously desperate to reach you." His voice cracked and he hugged the steering wheel, laying his cheek against his forearms while his emotions threatened to overwhelm him.

"Beth? Are the kids alr...?"

He sensed, rather than heard, the change in her; looked up to see her face turn ashen. Something was wrong. Oh God - don't let it be one of the kids. He'd never forgive himself if one of them had come to harm while they were here.

"It's alright, don't worry. It's not your fault. We were just setting off, we should be with you in two hours, less if we can."

She pointed towards the steering wheel, reddened eyes wide with fright, and mouthed *Go!*

He turned the key and the engine fired into life. With trembling fingers he set up the sat nav to give them the directions home, his mind racing, still reeling from the agony of the past five minutes. There must have been an accident: Dylan probably, with his insatiable curiosity. Only last week he had swallowed a coin Megan left on her bedside table, and had to be taken to the hospital for x-rays.

With his head throbbing he engaged first gear and pulled into the road with only the briefest glance. A horn blasted from behind and made him stop with a jerk, startling him back to his senses. *Shit.* He'd have to take more care, couldn't afford an accident now. He set off again more carefully.

"What's wrong?" he asked, the moment Megan lowered the handset to her lap. "Has something happened to one of the kids?"

"No, it's not them. No one's been hurt."

"What then?" The pressure in his head reduced slightly, but there was still something badly amiss: he could see it in the way she looked at him. If he wasn't mistaken, that was pity in her eyes. He negotiated a junction onto an A road and pressed his foot down hard on the accelerator.

"Dylan and Dandy got muddy at the park so Bethan called back to our place to get some clean clothes and another dog towel. She didn't notice anything wrong, at first. But when she went in the house and looked around, she realised the glass had been broken in the back door."

"We've had a break-in? *Fuck!* Did they take much?" His knuckles whitened on the steering wheel. Just when he'd thought things couldn't get any worse, it seemed life was determined to shit over him yet again. His mind raced through an inventory of their valuables. The laptop was on the dining room table. And there was the television, of course. Megan's jewellery, not that she had much of any real value. But that look on her face had been pity, not anger or distress, which could only mean that he had somehow lost more than she had.

She rested a hand on his knee. "Tom. I think you should probably pull into a lay-by and let me drive home."

"Don't be stupid - we can't stop now. We need to get back."

"I know. But I don't want to tell you while you're driving…"

Fuming, he pulled over sharply and yanked the handbrake up.

"What?"

She swallowed hard. "Oh darling, I'm so sorry. As far as Bethan can tell, only one thing was stolen. Tom - they took Greta."

Chapter Twenty-One

Saturday 22nd November 2014
Cardiff

Aweek had passed since the visit to Cardigan and the break-in, and Megan still found herself jumping at the slightest noise. She and Tom should be preparing for Christmas, their first without Hugh and Jean; but their time and energy had been consumed by house insurance, car insurance and locksmiths. Instead of considering a budget for Christmas gifts, they had ordered a new back door with stronger locks. Every time the telephone rang, they jumped – Tom, hoping for news that his precious camper van had been recovered, and she, still on pins after leaving her contact details with Delyth.

There had been no word from her father, even though he must surely know by now that she was looking for him. But when she wasn't distracted by imagining his voice on the telephone, her thoughts turned as if by default to the burglary. Strangers had invaded the sanctuary of her home. Would it ever feel the way it had felt before?

The police had told them the thieves must have targeted the van, watching the house for an opportunity to steal it. Tom's neatly organised row of key hooks beside the door had made it all too easy for them: they hadn't even needed to go hunting for what they wanted.

She couldn't shake off the feeling of unease. Every time she stepped outside the door, her neck prickled. How long had those people watched their comings and goings, waiting for a chance to sneak inside? While they were in the house, did they see anything that might draw them back for a second time? Had they been upstairs, scouted around amongst her personal things? Would they return to violate the safety and privacy of their home again? And who were they? Were they connected to anyone she knew? Every time she spotted a stranger in the street, her heart skipped. And at night she lay awake, terrified that they'd come back under the cover of darkness.

Tom had been worryingly uncommunicative all week. He hadn't even snapped back at her when she had complained in an unguarded moment that it had been stupid to label the keys. Yet bitterness oozed from his every pore. It was as if a reservoir of icy fury was building up inside him, only just held in check by throwing himself into a punishing exercise regime.

For him, losing Greta wouldn't be like losing any ordinary vehicle. Purchased with Hugh's more than generous fortieth birthday gift of £10,000, at a time when Tom had been sinking into depression, his camper represented happiness. To him, she wasn't just a van: she had meant better times ahead, a way to reconnect with his family and with the outdoors. She had given him an outlet, a sense of freedom and release from responsibilities when work or family got too much. Now some thieving scumbag had taken her, and the police didn't seem to think they had much chance of getting her back. She'd probably be in a shipping container on her way overseas; or in a barn somewhere, having her identifying details excised and replaced with those from a scrapped van.

After their disastrous viewing of *Y Noddfa*, together with his misery at work and the talk of redundancies, and all this so soon after losing his dad, she feared this added strain would be too much. She tried to get him to talk, to tell her about the ideas that had prompted him to view the house, but he refused.

"What's the point? You won't consider it."

"Maybe there's some way we can reach a compromise? Some sort of middle ground?"

She felt so sorry for him, and so guilty for being unable to give him what he felt he needed, that she felt compelled to offer him hope, however small. But he shook his head and huddled back in his chair with his arms folded, keeping his gaze firmly on the television screen to avoid any discussion. And really, what possible compromise was there? He couldn't set up a campsite in their street in Cardiff. He'd never get his rural idyll here.

Alys and Nia had been affected by the situation, too. Every night at bedtime Nia asked where Greta was, and sulked or cried when told that they just didn't know.

"I'll pray to God to bring Greta back," Alys had said last night. "Does He listen to our prayers, Mam? Or is He always busy with things for work, like you and Dad?"

The accusation stung.

"You know you can always talk to me or Dad. However busy we are, we always have time for the things that worry you."

"Why didn't God stop the baddies when they wanted to take Greta away from us?"

She thought carefully about her answer, not wanting Alys to sense her own doubts, but also not wanting her to be fearful of unknown 'baddies'.

"I don't know, *cariad*. Sometimes bad things happen, and often it's because people do bad things. You just have to believe that He knows how you feel and will help you to be strong when times are hard, or when someone has hurt you."

She could almost hear the cogs whirring in Alys's brain as this information was processed.

"We will have to be extra kind to Dad, won't we? Because he loved Greta the most."

"Yes, we will." She swept Alys's hair back and pressed a goodnight kiss onto her forehead.

The question was how to be kind to Tom without giving in to his foolish idealism. She might end up having to accept his increasing determination to follow through on his crazy plan to leave his job, but he should be looking for something else on a similar level, not indulging in pipe dreams. He knew nothing about running a business. They'd both worked in the public sector for so long – they'd never had to worry about tax returns, pensions, insurance, business rules or licences. It was enough to join the union and rely on their employers to sort everything else out. They'd never even had to think about when to take time off, as their holidays were fixed. In fact, the holidays were the main perk of the job. Working for himself, living above the shop, how would he ever have any time off at all?

The idea of him doing something so perilously insecure as to set up his own business, with no salary arriving in the bank each month or pension fund slowly accruing, made her stomach churn. The only person they knew who'd attempted such a move was Claire, whose celebration cake business surely couldn't be bringing in much money. Not compared with her former teaching job. If she could speak to her, and find out how awful working for herself must be, she could use the information to put Tom off the idea of taking such a huge risk.

∞∞∞∞

Claire's Cakes was small, tucked away on a trading estate on the edge of town. Claire emerged from the rear of the shop, looking as happy as Megan had ever seen her with her hair tucked up into a bright scarf and her clothes covered by an apron embroidered with her company logo. Within seconds Megan found herself enveloped in a vanilla-scented, bone-crushing hug.

"Hello stranger. It's so long since I've seen you, I'd actually forgotten how tiny you are. Such a little *dwt*. Next to you I feel like Hagrid's big sister."

Smiling ruefully, Megan followed her to the back room. "Not all that tiny any more. I'm not far off ten stone these days. Never been so big, in fact."

"Ten stone? I'd chop off all my limbs if I thought it would give me a chance of getting down to that."

"But you're a good eight or nine inches taller, aren't you? You can get away with it. At my height, ten stone makes me a porker."

"That's your answer right there. Give up on losing weight and start working on gaining height."

Megan laughed, glad she had come. She had left it too long, must make more of an effort to keep up with friends even when life was hectic.

"Here, I've got some cake offcuts you can try. Save the diet for another day. Coconut mojito flavour for you, and chocolate fudge for Dylan, if he's allowed?"

She rummaged in a couple of plastic boxes while Megan looked about the room. Metal racking bore stacks of wrapped cakes and tall boxes, while on a long stretch of worktop a polystyrene block had been stabbed with the wiry stalks of a multitude of yellow sugar roses, and foam pads were strewn with an assortment of modelling tools.

Automatically, she took Dylan's other hand to stop him reaching for anything. His face lit up when Claire presented him with an alarmingly generous portion of chocolate fudge cake. She tugged his sleeves higher up his pudgy arms while Claire sensibly tied a tea towel around his neck to serve as a bib.

"That should keep him occupied for a bit," Claire said. "Do you mind if I carry on working while we chat? I'm busy making babies today."

"Ooh-er! Fancy being paid to do that."

"More fun than teaching. I'll show you how to do it, if you like."

"No, thank you. I've already made three quite successfully, albeit not always intentionally. Tom would kill me if I made any more."

"Hmmm, fair point. The best bit of making *these* babies is when you get to stick a pin up their noses to create the nostrils. Screwing them up and starting again when they aren't quite good enough is pretty satisfying, too. It's a shame we can't apply the same principle to real children, if you think about it. Especially when they won't sleep. Or when they turn into teenagers."

She revealed the contents of a cardboard box. Inside, nestled on bubble wrap and kitchen paper, were a dozen or more tiny disembodied heads, limbs and torsos. The array of miniature sugar body parts was impressive but strangely gruesome.

"A multiple birth, I see."

"Indeed. They've been drying for a week or so, but now they're ready to put together and have their faces painted on. Baby shower cupcakes, would you believe. More American traditions crossing the Pond. Still, I can't complain if it brings business my way. Have you heard about the latest cake trend?"

Megan shook her head, her taste buds in ecstasy at the flavour of the coconut mojito cake. Dylan seemed equally contented, licking chocolate off his fingers and "mmm-ing" with obvious satisfaction.

"Smash cakes. People pay me a small fortune to bake and decorate a beautiful cake, then they sit their little one down and let them smash it to bits. All for the cutesy photos. Yes, your face says exactly what I think. Such a waste – but hey, if they want to pay me sixty quid to produce something that will end up spread all over the floor, that's up to them."

Megan spotted her opening. "How's business? Is it going well?"

"It's building, thanks. I'm getting repeat custom, which is great. And I'm learning some tricks. I've realised the key is being able to produce something really quickly that looks incredibly difficult and complicated. That's where the best profits are. And I've got a trainee who's a whizz on social media so she runs the online side of the business, processing orders and posting things out."

Megan kept a watchful eye on Dylan, armed with a pack of wet wipes for the moment he finished eating.

"Don't you find it stressful, not having the security that you used to have in teaching?"

"It's a different kind of stress. I have more control over what happens in my job now. I'm used to working long hours if something has to be finished, so that doesn't bother me. Admittedly I get some nightmare Bridezilla customers, and it would be great to be able to send them packing to a head of year when they get arsey, like I used to be able to do with the kids at school. But the pros outweigh the cons. I'm doing something I really enjoy. I get to be creative and make things every day, which is satisfying, and I'm constantly learning. It was scary at first, but there's loads of advice out there. And Pete works, so it isn't as if this is our only income." She eyed Megan thoughtfully. "I've been hearing rumours about St Dyfrig's. Rumours of redundancies. Are they true?"

Megan nodded, wiping Dylan's hands.

"I wish that had been available when I decided to leave. Is anyone tempted to go, do you know? What about you? Here, give him this piece of sugar paste. He can play with it like play dough."

"Not me," she said, crouching to help Dylan roll out the paste like a snake. "On the contrary, I wish they were offering extra hours. Sue and Rachel are thinking about it, though."

Claire nodded as if this wasn't news to her. Of course: she had probably spoken to Rachel about it already.

"Tom's tempted," Megan added, watching Claire's reaction.

"Is he, now? Good on him."

She didn't return Claire's smile. "I'm not so sure it's a sensible idea, personally. Not now that he's a head of department. Turning his back on a job like that to pursue a silly dream seems crazy to me. No, Dylan, don't eat the paste!" She tried to fish it out of his mouth, but he was already mmm-ing with satisfaction and reaching for more. She rolled her eyes. The last thing she needed was him overdosing on sugar and throwing up all over Claire's food preparation area.

"It's perfectly safe," Claire said.

"You only say that because you've never seen him having a sugar rush."

"He can't be any worse than mine used to be. So, back to Tom - your sad, sweet dreamer. What are his plans?"

She explained about *Y Noddfa*, and the campsite idea, and the things he had said to the estate agent when he'd thought she couldn't hear, about turning the barn into a fitness studio. She didn't mention the eternity ring. Claire might not understand that bit. She wasn't sure she understood it herself.

"Fair play to him. It's not such a bad idea, I wouldn't have thought. And ambition isn't always about climbing the ladder, is it? Sometimes it's about taking opportunities to pursue different dreams, even if it means earning less or working harder. New challenges keep us fresh, don't they? It's worked for me so far… touch wood." She reached up and tapped the shelf above her head.

"I know all that, and believe me, I hate seeing him so unhappy. If I could fix things so he enjoyed his job again, and so his parents were still here, and Greta hadn't been stolen, I would do it in a heartbeat. I'd give anything for him to just be content with our life the way it is. I'd even go and give Ken Haddon a bollocking if I thought it'd make any difference…"

"What makes you think he needs you to fix his life? Sounds to me as if he has plenty of ideas for fixing it himself."

Heat flooded Megan's cheeks. Why couldn't Claire just agree with her instead of always seeing both sides of an argument?

"He isn't being realistic. Can you imagine us living out in the back of beyond, like that? This is real life, not an episode of *Escape to the Country*."

Dylan tugged at her top, frowning. "Rah, rah, rah!" he growled, screwing up his little face to look like a scary dinosaur, as he did whenever he thought she was shouting. Obviously she had spoken more heatedly than she'd intended.

"Sorry, Dylan. I didn't mean to sound fierce. Come on, where's that snake we were making? Shall we turn him into a snail instead?"

She coiled up the string of paste into a spiral and he grabbed it delightedly.

"There you go," Claire said, looking smug. "There was nothing wrong with the snake, but he still thinks a snail is sooo much better. You can't blame Tom for wanting more: it isn't human nature to be content with what we have. If it was, no one would ever aspire to anything. There'd be no capitalism. Humans would still live in caves grunting at each other and clubbing each other over the head. Actually, that sounds a bit like me and Pete… He's always been a bit of a Neanderthal."

Megan couldn't help but smile.

"So come on - what's changed you, Meggie? You used to be up for adventures. What happened to the bold little firebrand who left darkest Carmarthenshire to teach in the big, bad city?"

Megan grimaced. "She grew up and had three kids. And before that, she realised she missed her sister too much when she lived away. When she moved to Cardiff, she knew she wanted to stay there for good."

∞∞∞∞

Tom halted so sharply at the end of his driveway that the sudden tightening of his leash made Dandy recoil. Anger rose, as it had done often this past week; but this time Megan wasn't the cause. She had been extra-nice since Greta was stolen, tiptoeing around him being deliberately kind and attentive. Perhaps it made her feel less guilty for trampling on his dreams. Or perhaps she pitied him, for the way fortune seemed so determined to shit on him from on high. He'd had moments when he thought he'd explode with rage against the thieves who had stolen his camper, the police who hadn't found it yet, Megan for her inability to share his vision, and the universe itself. He'd kept it in check, for fear of what Fury he might unleash if he allowed himself to express his thoughts, and had been thankful for the outlet of fierce exercise to siphon off some of the adrenalin coursing through his system.

But now, seeing the hooded figure peering in through the stained glass windows of his front door, the red mist descended and he could be justified in not holding back.

"Stay," he whispered, dropping Dandy's lead to the ground and laying the thin plastic bag of dog shit he had been carrying on top of the garden wall. He needed both hands free.

As he watched, the stranger – a man, judging by the way he was dressed - moved to stare in through the bay window of the living room, shielding his eyes to get a better view. Looking for valuables, no doubt, and none too subtly considering it was broad daylight. Enough was enough.

Tom sprinted up the driveway, grasped a handful of the man's coat and slammed him against the wall.

"What the fuck do you think you're doing?" he snarled, leaning his full weight against him to stop him running off.

Cobalt blue eyes stared up at him, wide with alarm.

"*Duw* – you could have given me a heart attack, jumping on me like that."

"I won't ask you again. Why were you staring in through the windows?"

He shoved the man against the bricks again to emphasise his superior height and strength. Despite the man's almost-white hair and beard, he wasn't inclined to be gentle. Not after the burglary. Not when his wife and daughters had spent such a fearful week, convinced that every creak and groan from the house was an intruder.

"I'm not doing anything wrong, just visiting my daughter," the man blustered. "This is her house. I was checking to see if she's in."

Tom narrowed his eyes and tightened his grip. "What's her name, then?"

"Megan."

He let go. The man brushed himself down, still wide-eyed and wary even when Tom stepped back.

"Do you mean Megan Field?"

"Megan Parry, she used to be, but yes, that's her married name."

So this stranger was Idris Parry. He pronounced her name the way Olwen and Bethan did, giving both syllables equal emphasis: *May-gann.* Tom couldn't stop staring at him. He flexed his hands to loosen them.

"A bit extreme for Neighbourhood Watch, isn't it? Grabbing hold of people in the street, I mean, when they come to visit their family." There was a defiant tilt to Idris's chin, now that he had recovered his composure.

"My apologies if I was heavy-handed. We had a break-in last week and it's got us a bit jumpy."

The other man nodded and dusted his hands down the front of his trendy quilted coat.

Reluctantly, Tom reached out to shake his new father-in-law's hand. Although he didn't feel inclined to be friendly, the last thing he and Megan needed was something else to argue about. He'd better be polite, smooth things over, after getting off on the wrong foot the way he had.

"You're obviously Idris. I'm Tom Field. Megan's husband."

"Ah. Well, then. Aren't you going to invite me in, now that you've decided against beating me to a pulp?"

Dandy was waiting on the doorstep, spinning excitedly while Tom unlocked the door. Tom led the way inside and took Idris's coat to hang it with his own on the hooks in the hallway while Idris moved past him towards the kitchen, glancing into the living room and dining room as he passed.

"Nice house, this. Glad to see Megan's done well for herself."

Tom resisted the urge to point out that it was no thanks to her father.

"Do you know what time she's likely to be back? Only, I'm a bit pushed for time today. I've got about an hour, but then I'll have to be off…"

Was this man in earnest? After abandoning his kids thirty-five years ago, had he really only allowed an hour for his first meeting with one of them?

"She should be back by half past," he said, brushing past to the kettle and hoping his scowl wasn't too obvious. It wouldn't do to alienate Idris before Megan had even had the chance to meet him.

Idris shrugged acceptance, glancing at his watch. It looked expensive. Those designer-labelled clothes and Timberland boots weren't cheap either, considering he'd only been a labourer or whatever when Megan and Bethan were little. Presumably he had gone up in the world since then. A shame his daughters hadn't reaped any of the benefits from the change in his fortunes.

"You'd better take a seat while you wait." Tom motioned towards the kitchen table and swept up the pile of exercise books Megan had left there, depositing them on a corner of the worktop as a temporary measure. He had already decided against texting Megan to alert her to her father's presence. She'd be on her way home by now, and he didn't want to take a chance that she'd glance at her phone whilst driving and be distracted by such momentous news.

Idris blew onto his mug of tea. His request for three sugars and lots of milk had further confirmed Tom's conviction that the man was a moron.

"Do you know why she's been looking for me?"

"Natural curiosity. My father passed away at the end of the summer and it made her reflect on how little she knows about you."

Idris nodded, leaning back in his chair as if this was just any ordinary family visit. "That's pretty much what my sister said when she rang."

"I expect it came as a bit of a surprise after all these years," Tom remarked, fishing for some sign that the older man was even the slightest bit nonplussed.

"Yes and no. I always suspected one or both of them might get in touch one day."

"You do realise she'll ask you why you never maintained contact? She grew up not even knowing if you were alive or dead. Not so much as a card on her birthday. Nothing at Christmas. Not a penny to help her through school or university. Her uncle walked her down the aisle at our wedding. As a father myself, I can't help wondering how any man could do that."

Idris took a swig of his tea, seemingly unfazed by this criticism. "How old were you when you became a father, Tim?"

"Tom. It's Tom, not Tim." He paused, realising he shouldn't have taken the bait so easily. "I was thirty-four."

"I thought so. Old enough to have established yourself. Mature. I expect by then you had a steady job, somewhere to live. I was still a teenager when it happened to me. I liked girls a bit too much, that's all, and got myself caught up in a mess. I never planned for things to get complicated. And then - Olwen. Do you know her? Is she still around?"

"Yes, I know her."

He smirked. "Delightful, isn't she? Imagine yourself shackled in your teens to a woman who possesses all the warmth and charm of the athlete's foot between a yeti's frostbitten toes. Tell me, what would you do if she told you never to darken her doors again? At twenty-one or so, would you have stuck around, or would you have grabbed your freedom while you had the chance?"

Tom emptied the dregs from his mug into the sink. Since the day he first met Olwen, when she had looked him up and down with utter disdain and proceeded to ignore him for an entire afternoon, he had thought of his mother-in-law as the original Welsh dragon. He liked to believe he'd have been brave in Idris's situation, but in all honesty, the idea of defying her made him cringe inside.

"I shouldn't knock her, really," Idris continued. "Not if she stuck by the kids. And I'm not expecting any sympathy from you. I've made many mistakes in this life, and truth be told, hanging around long enough to marry Olwen was one of the biggest."

There was a clatter from the hallway as the front door opened. Moments later the girls burst in, oblivious to the visitor in the kitchen. Idris stroked his beard, watching them. Tom tried to imagine how it would be to glimpse your grandchildren as a stranger. What would Idris be feeling as he saw the girls for the first time? Would he feel any sense of a bond between them? Would he be looking for physical similarities between them and himself? Did he even give a shit, beyond idle curiosity?

Megan's voice reached them from the hall. "Come on Dylan, let's get those shoes off."

There was shuffling and a bit of huffing, then she came in with Dylan on her hip, pink-cheeked from bending.

"Some filthy swine left a bag of dog poo on our garden wall, would you believe? I put it in the bin outside. What is the matter with people?" She stopped as Idris pushed back his chair and rose to his feet. "Oh - hello. Sorry, I didn't realise you had a visitor."

Idris's adam's apple bobbed up and down like a swimmer treading water while Megan continued bustling about, hanging up her car keys and peeling Dylan's coat off. Tom ruffled Nia's hair by way of a greeting; as always, she batted his hand away and retreated. Alys had grabbed an apple from the bowl and headed off to the living room, the door slamming behind her just before the theme tune of her current favourite television programme filtered through. None of them had the slightest clue who Idris was, that much was obvious.

"Actually, he's not my visitor. He's come to see you," he said. Megan finally stilled and looked at him properly.

Idris hadn't stopped staring at her since she came in. He gave a sort of half-smile now, wiping his palms on his jeans as if he was nervous. Perhaps he did feel a few twinges of guilt, after all.

"Hello, *Cyw*. You've grown since I last saw you."

Her mouth opened, then closed again. Wide-eyed, she glanced at Tom as if for confirmation. He gave an answering nod.

"It's you," she murmured.

Awkwardly Idris held out his arms and, after the briefest hesitation, she stumbled forward into them.

This was it: the moment Tom had seen her defy her mother and sister to achieve; the moment she'd brought about with hours spent researching and travelling and tracking down lines of enquiry and questioning strangers. He wrapped his arms around himself, an ominous lump forming in his throat. What a week it had been. However resentful he had felt towards her at times, his heart ached for her now. He blinked back the burning in his eyes, watching the self-conscious way Idris patted Megan's back. Her head rested against his shoulder as if she had never wanted to be anywhere else.

"Alright, *Cyw*?"

A shuddering breath later, she stepped back to look him in the eye, still holding on to his forearms as if she was scared to let him move out of reach.

"I am now. I can't quite believe I'm actually seeing you, right there in front of me. I can't believe I'll have the chance to say the things I've been needing to say to you for years."

He flashed a half-smile. "Well. That's good. Where do we start?"

A tear trickled down her cheek and she dashed it away with the back of her hand, then quickly clutched his arm again as if she didn't dare let it go for more than a second.

"How about we start with me telling you you're a low-down bastard crock of shit?"

Idris's cheeks turned salami-pink and blotchy above the silver of his beard, and he shook off her grasp.

"*Duw*, you're your mother's daughter, alright." He looked towards Tom, clearly rattled. "Is she always like this?"

Tom spoke quietly, ready to move to block the doorway if Idris should try to bolt for it. "I suggest you take it on the chin. You owe her that much, at least."

"I didn't come here to be spoken to like that."

But Megan hadn't finished. "I think we've moved past the days when you could correct my behaviour, don't you? And if I'm like my mam it's hardly surprising, because she's the only parental influence I've ever had. Do you have any idea how much I needed you, growing up? Was I such a horrible, hateful child that you couldn't bring yourself to even write me a letter? Was I really so - so..." her voice cracked on a sob. "So *awful*? So unlovable?"

"No! Don't be silly, now. You were lovely. A smashing little kid. It wasn't you, it was me."

"Ha! How many women have you said that to over the years, I wonder? I bet they all found it pathetic and contemptible, too. Have you *any* idea how much I missed having a dad? How many letters I wrote, telling you the things I needed you to know? I couldn't send them, because I didn't know where you were, or even if you were alive. I didn't know if the few things Mam told me about you were true, or if she'd driven you away. I had no way of knowing if the bitterness and coldness in her was because of you, or if she'd always been like it and that's why you couldn't bear to live with us. Or whether you just didn't like me and Beth, and wanted to get away from us because we weren't good enough for you. I couldn't even remember what you looked like. I wondered constantly whether you thought of me as often as I thought of you. Did you ever think about me at all?"

Like a butterfly on a pin, he had stopped struggling now, accepting his fate as the renewed fierceness of her grip left him no option but to stay and listen.

"Of course I thought about you."

"Prove it. When's my birthday? When is Bethan's?"

"That doesn't mean anything. I never had a head for dates."

"You don't know, do you?"

Tom wasn't sure what seared his heart the most: the despair in her voice or the scorn. *Say something, you bastard. Make her believe that you actually gave a damn.*

"You were born in the autumn. Bethan would have been born in September, and you a bit later in the year, but before Christmas. I remember you smiling at your first Christmas. I gave you a teddy bear."

"What else do you remember?"

"Lots, *Cyw*."

It wasn't enough. She stared him out with that gorgon glare that had always made Tom squirm. It seemed to have the same effect on Idris, as he started to gabble.

"You were a bright little thing. You used to chatter all the time, proper sentences, even when you were small. It used to impress everybody, how forward you were."

That was clever, Tom thought. If anything would win her over, it was praising her intelligence.

"Go on," she said.

"There was nothing you liked more than cwtching up on my lap with a book. We had one about a green parrot, and you used to point to it on every page and say 'Where's the geen carrot?' And we had one about the old woman who swallowed a fly, but you weren't so keen on that one because there was a picture of a spider on one of the pages. You had a shock of curly red hair: like little orphan Annie, you were. Cute as a button. But things were never good between me and your mam. When she said I should never contact you again, I knew she meant it. I knew she'd turn you against me and there was no point in looking back. I just had to hope you'd come looking for me one day."

"Really?" It was no more than a whisper.

The doorbell rang, making them all look around as if they had been in a daze.

"That'll be my lift," said Idris.

Tom went to open the door, Idris hot on his heels and Megan close behind, pleading with him to stay.

"Oh no, don't go yet! You only just got here, and we have so much to catch up on."

The middle-aged woman on the doorstep was smartly dressed, with a cape of beige wool slung over her shoulders; the sort of retired, well-off woman who would spend hours in John Lewis or Debenhams. She eyed Tom cautiously, then relaxed at the sight of Idris, who had squeezed past his elbow to join her.

"This is my friend Celia," Idris said.

"Partner, not friend," she corrected him, batting at his arm. "You must be Megan, of course. It's a pleasure to meet you."

Megan looked stricken as Idris edged towards the sleek silver car parked at the bottom of the driveway.

"When will I see you again? You didn't even get to meet your grandchildren. And I don't have your number."

"Soon," Idris said vaguely, opening the passenger door and slipping inside with a wave. Once in the safety of the car, he seemed to give himself a little shake, dragging his hand over his face before composing his features.

Celia tutted indulgently. She took a notebook and pen out of her handbag, then scrawled a note and pressed the torn-off page into Megan's hand.

"Take no notice of him – he's probably just a bit overwhelmed. This is our number. Let's meet soon. In fact, why don't you come over to us – shall we say a fortnight today? We can have a little pre-Christmas party. Nothing special, just drinks and nibbles. Bring the children and I'll invite my grandchildren too, so they'll have someone to play with. Idris has your number, so I'll get him to send you the address."

"Thank you," Tom called after her, while Megan clutched the paper and fought back tears. He put his arm around her shoulders and drew her closer, resting his lips on top of her head as they watched the car purr away. At such a momentous moment in her life, he felt he should say something. But what? It had been a difficult week: a week in which he had kept his thoughts to himself, for fear of saying something he would regret.

As it happened, she spoke first, saving him the trouble of finding words to fit the moment.

"Oh my God – I've actually met my dad! And he hadn't forgotten me. He remembered all those lovely things from when I was small. Do you think I was a bit harsh to start with? I suppose I was. It took me by surprise, seeing him, and suddenly I felt so bitter about all those wasted years. But now – now, we can make a fresh start, can't we? It's exactly what I've been dreaming of."

She was still high on excitement when they went to bed that night. He lay on his back next to her and listened as she went over and over it, unable to tell her that he couldn't find it within himself to share her joy.

"I still can't quite believe he came to find me, that he's back in my life again. Meeting him was so strange. When I imagined it before, I thought he'd seem familiar, but he didn't. There was no sense of recognition - I could have walked past him in the street or spoken to him before today and had no idea how close our connection was. And yet there was something. When you looked at me, and said he had come to visit me, somehow I just knew. And even in that moment when I felt so angry and let down, there still a bond that I wouldn't have felt with a complete stranger."

He bit his lip, frowning into the darkness. As pleased as he was that she'd had a chance to satisfy her curiosity, Idris's attempts at charm hadn't won him over. Why should this man, who had probably shown more loyalty and commitment to his barber over the years than to his wife and children, still be walking the earth when Hugh, who had always been the rock underpinning his family, wasn't? It didn't seem fair.

But then, nothing this week had been fair. And to top it off, here was Megan, who had stamped on his dreams and called them stupid, having her own dreams fulfilled.

He rolled over and thumped his pillow a few times, but it was no good. He was too tense to sleep. Time to start counting sheep, or deep breathing, or something. Anything to bring him some rest for a change. He hadn't slept properly, or been able to relax, ever since the visit to Cardigan and the burglary.

Megan's arm snaked over his waist and he caught his breath as his cock automatically twitched into wakefulness. *Don't get your hopes up,* he told himself, and waited to gauge her mood by her next move. If she was initiating something, he wouldn't turn it down. He might sleep better afterwards.

She snuggled closer, her cheek warm and soft against his shoulder blade; but her hand remained at waist height.

"I've been thinking," she said, her voice small now as she clung.

He grunted. Better not think about her hand – she obviously wanted talk, not action.

"It's been a tough week for you. Greta meant a lot to me, but even more to you. And I know you're still angry about that house... I'm sorry we can't seem to agree on it."

She paused, as if she was waiting for him to say it was alright, but if that was what she expected he couldn't oblige her. If they hadn't gone chasing off to West Wales on her quest to find Idris, they might not have lost Greta, and he would never have fallen in love with *Y Noddfa*. And if she had more imagination, more vision, for God's sake, she would be able to comprehend how he felt. It was a bit late to start showing him sympathy now.

"Tom, every night when we go to bed, and even in the daytime, I keep going over what happened. What if the burglars come back?

What if they only had time to take Greta, but they're planning to come back and go through the house to see what else they can find?"

Should he tell her about the cricket bat he had hidden under the bed in case of a return visit? If those vile, thieving bastards did come back, they wouldn't be leaving in one piece. But it was probably better for her not to know. She'd only feel worse, imagining all sorts of violent altercations and dangers. She was jumpy at every indistinct sound in the night as it was.

"I'm sure they won't bother coming back. They got what they wanted."

"I expect you're right. But it doesn't stop my mind racing every time I try to sleep. Claire said her Pete knows someone whose car was stolen and used in a robbery before being burned out."

"It's hardly likely that thieves would be planning to use an old camper van as a getaway car. She won't go over fifty-five."

"True. But you heard what the neighbours said: there was another house broken into a couple of streets away last week." She paused, then said: "I don't feel so safe here any more."

"That's the price you pay for living in a city."

If she thought he sounded sour, so be it. He'd given her the option of moving to the countryside, where their vehicles could have been safely locked away in a barn each night, but she'd been very clear that she didn't want that kind of life.

She lay still for a few moments, as if digesting his response. Then her arm slid back and she rolled away from him, onto her own side of the bed, until they were no longer touching at all.

Chapter Twenty-Two

Saturday 6th December 2014
Sully, Vale of Glamorgan

No one could have accused Celia of skimping on her Christmas celebrations. Dylan's face was a picture of childish wonder, his mouth and eyes equally round, when Megan led him by the hand into the spacious, modern bungalow. They passed a trio of illuminated reindeer in the garden, then were greeted in the hallway by a four foot high Santa Claus waving and ho-ho-ho-ing. There was greenery everywhere – real, not fake, smelling evocatively of pine resin, and intertwined with fir cones and twinkling fairy lights. Bunches of dried orange slices and cinnamon, tied with silvery organza bows, added to the festive ambience.

The hall and living room each had their own magnificent colour-themed Christmas tree, festooned with home-made biscuits shaped like stars and tied on with little satin ribbons. A miniature train chuffed around the larger tree, its wagons filled with sweets, and the girls were soon absorbed in pressing buttons to make various toys dance to electronic seasonal songs. It was ridiculously extravagant, and Megan had no idea how anyone would find time to do it all, but the children must have thought they had arrived in a winter wonderland.

The aroma of mulled wine and mince pies drew them into the kind of kitchen Megan could only dream of. The sparkling quartz countertop was arrayed with a lavish spread of party food Mary Berry might be proud to serve, elegantly arranged on Christmas-themed Spode plates. Far from the "drinks and nibbles" Celia had suggested, this was a veritable banquet, crowned by a gargantuan criss-crossed, clove-studded ham. Tom would be bound to drool at the sight of the trifle, and her own stomach juices growled at the sight of a chocolate log so perfectly decorated it would be a shame to cut into it. It was like a scene from one of those aspirational homes magazines: enviable, and utterly unachievable for anyone with a job and young family to manage. Thank goodness they'd brought a decent bottle of wine with them, and flowers purchased from the florist rather than the supermarket.

Idris seemed pleased to see them, and willingly drew her in for a hug that made her spirits soar. This was what it meant to have a dad. Glowing like a child in an old Ready-Brek advert, she felt everyone must be able to see the light of happiness that had been ignited by having him back in her life. How perfect that this should happen at Christmas, the season of peace, love and goodwill to all men. It was as if her world had always been slightly off its true axis, even in the best of times, but now was as it should be. She had her father, and the children had their new Tadcu Parry to help make up for the loss of Grandpa Field. If only Bethan were here - but her sister had obstinately refused to take any part in the family gathering.

Celia, it seemed, had thought of everything. Apparently her son and grandchildren hadn't been able to join them, which she explained with an excuse so convoluted that Megan guessed someone had surely made it up. Idris's smirk suggested Celia's son's absence wasn't an unusual state of affairs, which seemed odd, because who would turn down the chance of such a feast, and to meet Idris's family?

Still, Celia made up for it by showering attention on the children. Each was given a beautifully wrapped present, and she insisted that they should be allowed to open them on the spot, which would no doubt annoy Tom as he had always been a stickler for keeping presents until Christmas morning. Fortunately he was too polite to insist that they wait, and soon they were happily colouring at the dining room table, with *Elf* on the television in the background. The adults were left to their own devices.

"You've gone to so much trouble, it's really very kind of you," Megan said, accepting a glass of prosecco. Tom had offered to drive, so she needn't feel guilty; and besides, the alcohol would help to settle her nerves. She mustn't have too much, though. Despite her delight at no longer being fatherless, this felt a bit like one of those supposedly informal job interviews, when you're supposed to feel relaxed but you know you're being judged every moment, and desperation to make a good impression can cause you to come unstuck.

"Celia loves Christmas," Idris replied with a wry shrug that suggested he thought it all utterly bonkers. He seemed more relaxed tonight, confident in familiar surroundings. Perhaps he had grown accustomed to the idea of revisiting his paternal role.

It was impossible not to stare at him. She wanted to take in every feature of his face, examining it for anything familiar from her own or Bethan's or the children's. The hipster beard - slightly quirky, but fashionable she supposed, like his clothes - blurred the line of cheekbones and chin, but didn't quite conceal a mouth that seemed to smile readily. His sky blue eyes did resemble Tom's: the old photograph hadn't been wrong.

Draping a proprietorial arm around Celia's shoulders, Idris raised his glass of wine in a toast.

"*Nadolig llawen.*"

Beaming, Megan responded in kind while Tom merely mumbled back "Merry Christmas" and sipped his cranberry juice. If only he would cheer up a bit and enter into the spirit of the occasion. He hadn't said so, but she sensed that he hadn't yet welcomed the idea of Idris joining their family. She hoped he wasn't envious of her having her dad around at last. As much as she felt for him on this first Christmas without Hugh, he had had forty-two years to know and enjoy the company of his own father. It would be churlish of him to view this reunion with anything other than enthusiasm.

While Celia busied herself with retrieving yet more canapés from the oven, Idris drifted into the conservatory. Megan followed, reluctant to let him out of her sight. She wanted to make the most of every moment with him.

"It's lovely to have some time to get to know you. We've got so much to catch up on. I don't even know what you do for a living…" She faltered, unsure what to call him. She hadn't called him Dad yet. The word seemed to stick to her tongue, wouldn't roll off comfortably for this stranger. She could hardly address him as Idris, though.

"I'm a property developer," he said, sinking into an armchair.

"Really? That sounds amazing. You were in the building trade when I was little, I think..?"

"Mmm. I do less of the actual building now, more of the buying and selling, project management and so forth. That's how I met Cee, at an auction. She was considering an investment property; I bought another house to do up."

Celia returned and perched on the arm of his chair. "I watched him bid on the most ghastly house. I couldn't understand how anyone would contemplate buying it, the state it was in," she said.

Idris shrugged. "It was mostly cosmetic. I sorted the whole house for less than twelve grand and a couple of weeks of work."

Megan nodded enthusiastically. He'd gone up in the world, it seemed, from his youthful days as a labourer. She'd been quoted more than that amount just to replace their kitchen: it must take real ability to spend the same budget on the renovation of a whole house.

"He's a marvel, your dad. So knowledgeable, with so many contacts. He impressed me by telling me his plans to turn the project around, then asked me out to dinner saying he could help me look for a suitable property for myself… the rest is history." Celia gazed down at him like a love-struck teen, then ruffled his hair lingeringly.

"I've been doing up houses to sell on for a long time. It's all about knowing what you can get away with, and what you can't avoid spending. The sort of knowledge that only comes with experience.

And you've got to understand the market you're aiming at. Take the one I'm working on now: Cee was all for revamping the whole place, putting a new fireplace in, replacing the bathroom and all that. Completely unnecessary. The bathroom only needed a good clean and the pipes boxing in to make it look a bit tidier. New shower curtain and bath mat, a lick of paint and Bob's your uncle. And why waste money on a fire when people think a few logs or candles in the gap looks great? Logs cost nothing. Appearances are everything, *Cyw*. People see what they want to see: you've just got to make them believe in the dream."

A noise drew Megan's attention: Dylan had started fussing about something, making Nia shout back at him. Tom was up and out of his chair as if he had been waiting for just such an excuse to leave the room. His voice drifted back through the doorway, low and authoritative in that quiet way he had.

"Sit with me, I'll help you. No, that one's Nia's. This one is yours."

She felt a pang of thankfulness for his dependability, the strength of his commitment to his family that meant their children would never grow up doubting his love or his keen interest in their ideas, opinions and experiences. Crabby though he sometimes was, especially lately, he could always dredge up a genuine smile for the children. A peek into the next room revealed him sitting at the table with their son on his lap, helping him choose a crayon, murmuring praise as Dylan named each of the colours.

Thanks to Tom, she would have a few extra minutes of peace in which to get to know Idris better. He was examining his glass of wine, holding it up to the light as if the answers to the mysteries of life might be found in its tinkling bubbles. He, who still knew so little about her or Bethan or his grandchildren, hadn't asked her anything about her own life yet. But, she told herself, they had all the time in the world.

∞∞∞∞

To Tom's relief, they were invited to sit at the table to eat, rather than balancing plates on their laps, and Celia produced some colourful plastic plates for the children. His first glimpse of the buffet had brought on nightmarish imaginings of Dylan spilling pastry crumbs and cranberry sauce over the sophisticated pale upholstery, and china plates smashing to smithereens on the creamy floor tiles. With a crisis averted, and the table laden with far more food than they needed, he seated himself between Dylan and Nia. Megan was too absorbed in her quest to find answers to a lifetime of questions to pay much attention to the children.

"After you and Mam separated, did you ever remarry?" she was asking Idris now, cheeks pink as she sent a sidelong glance towards Celia. Tom guessed what this was leading to: she wanted to know if there were any secret siblings to add to this brand new family she was trying so hard to create for herself.

Idris seemed to find her question inexplicably amusing. "Not likely. An animal that's chewed its left leg off to escape a trap would have to be pretty stupid to put its right leg into another, wouldn't it? There's a good reason why the rhyming slang for wife is Trouble and Strife." He chuckled and winked at Tom as if expecting back-up.

Tom stared back at him without cracking a smile. After listening to Idris Parry's self-proclaimed expertise on every topic from cutting corners when renovating houses to the difficulty of getting planning permission for hideous blocks of flats to the necessity to block an incoming "swarm" of immigrant builders, he'd had just about enough. He'd take fashion tips from Jeremy Clarkson before he'd listen to any words of wisdom his father-in-law had to offer about marriage.

"Not in my experience," he said loyally. "For me, marriage is like being signed up to a dream team on a permanent contract. We each bring something different to the game: our own unique perspectives and particular skills. Megan's strengths counterbalance my weaknesses, and vice versa. Together, we're greater than we could ever be as individuals."

There was silence around the table. Megan had paused, fork halfway to her lips, and if he wasn't mistaken she was blushing. Celia was looking at him as if he had suddenly thrown off Clark Kent glasses and turned into Superman. Even Alys sent him a proud smile.

Idris alone looked sceptical. "Very millennial, I'm sure. But I doubt many people would describe it in those terms."

Megan's foot brushed against his ankle under the table, making him glance up again. She spoke quietly and with obvious sincerity. "I can only speak for myself, and I'm no good at sporting metaphors so I'll leave those to Tom. For me, being married is like being one of conjoined twins. There's bound to be times when the other person gets on your nerves and you end up wishing you could get away from them to be on your own for a while. But then you remember that the other person has your heart. Without them, you couldn't keep going. Maybe you could live your life alone. You might survive the process of being separated; but deep down you know the trauma would be so great, you'd never feel complete again."

It was Tom's turn to redden. He nodded towards her, warmed by the look in her eyes. He'd wondered sometimes, especially during the past few weeks, whether she still felt that way. The conviction behind her words made him feel ten feet tall.

"Why don't you tell Idris a bit about yourself?" he suggested. His father-in-law's apparent disinterest had irked him more and more as the evening wore on.

"Oh – there isn't all that much to tell, really."

"Yes, there is. Go on."

He reached out to stop Dylan's little hand from grabbing another cake, managing to catch Alys's beaker of squash before it got knocked over. The fierceness of his son's pout made him grin. He was promising to grow up to be every bit as fiery and wilful as his mother.

While Megan gave a potted history of both her own and Bethan's educational achievements and careers so far, Tom had to concede that Idris gave an almost plausible show of listening. He kept up eye contact, nodded and used enough mmm's and ahs to suggest that he was paying attention; but Tom wasn't buying it. At first it was hard to pinpoint what was missing from this show of paternal interest. Perhaps it was the way he kept interrupting to ask Celia to fetch things from the kitchen: another drink here, a plate of food there, as if he was more interested in his stomach than his daughter. Perhaps it was that he didn't offer Megan any praise for all that she had achieved, despite the fact that she'd done it with very little financial support: Olwen certainly hadn't been in a position to help out much. Or perhaps it was the lack of any questions to probe out more information. He seemed to feel no need to know any more than he was being told.

Whatever it was, Tom found he couldn't take to the man. He had tried to imagine being separated from his own children for years, not knowing what they were doing, and found it too upsetting to contemplate. One thing he was sure of, though: he'd want to know everything about them the minute he got the chance. The things they loved to do. The things that frightened them. What he could do to help them. He'd be hammering their doors down, if necessary, to get the chance of more time with them and more insights into their lives. He knew he was far from perfect, but for all his faults he could still search his own heart and know he was an infinitely better father than Idris would ever be.

When everyone had finished, he helped Megan clear the table and load the dishwasher while Celia sorted the remaining food into plastic boxes and stacked them in the fridge and cupboards.

"Tom, would you carry the highchair back to the room next to the guest bathroom, please? It's nice and clean again now. Just pop it in the wardrobe on the left."

Celia indicated a room at the end of the long hallway, and he headed that way obligingly, holding the highchair away from his shirt as it still smelled strongly of bleach. The wardrobe filled one wall, mirrored doors bouncing light back into the room. He slid the one on the far left open and saw the space where the highchair would slot in.

With the door open, a low, deep voice drifted through the thin plasterboard wall adjoining the next room. It must be Idris. Long pauses suggested he was speaking on the telephone, but it was odd because Tom could have sworn Celia had said their bedroom and en-suite were at the other end of the bungalow. What was he doing, sneaking off to the guest bathroom to talk to someone? In spite of himself, he found himself listening.

"You know I would if I could, but it's Christmas. I'd have to be some kind of monster to do it at this time of year. I'll tell her after the New Year, I promise… I know, it's torture for me, too. Soon, *Cyw*, I swear. As soon as the timing's right."

Nia bounced through the bedroom door, her high voice carrying. "There you are, Dad. Mam says it's time to go home. Dylan's getting grumpy."

"Got to go, *Cyw*," Idris muttered in the next room, then emerged, unruffled, into the hallway.

"Tadcu! We have to go, but we'll see you soon, won't we?" Nia cried, throwing her arms around his waist with the affectionate abandon of a Labrador puppy.

Alys was more reserved, offering only a brief hug as they said their goodbyes.

Tom merely shook his father-in-law's hand, unable to reconcile the clear, guileless blue gaze with the skulking and plotting he had heard. For all his smilingly nonchalant air, there was no doubt in Tom's mind: Idris was up to no good.

Chapter Twenty-Three

Saturday 6th December 2014
Cardiff

Megan perched on the edge of the bed, rubbing hand cream vigorously into the dry skin on her fingers. She was still euphoric, an excess of prosecco combining with the thrill of getting to know her father a little better this evening. And Celia had been so welcoming, not to mention generous, with her cooking and gifts for the children. Megan's stomach was still uncomfortably full, her waistband straining by the time they'd headed home to flop into pyjamas. Self-control had never been her strong point, especially when faced with so many treats.

It had failed her in other ways tonight, too. She had deliberately avoided catching Tom's eye after blurting out a last-minute invitation for her father and Celia to come for Christmas dinner. She wanted so much to look after them and spoil them as Celia had done for her tonight. To have a family Christmas with her father, husband and children at its centre, the way it always should have been.

Picturing it, she beamed. They'd spend the afternoon opening presents, and her dad would start to relax with the increased familiarity. Things were still a little stilted now, but it would get easier as he adapted. Maybe she could persuade Bethan and Matt to come over at teatime for turkey sandwiches and drinks? It was the season of goodwill, after all. Even Beth might mellow towards Idris with enough wine and sherry flowing to make everyone relax.

Tom had been predictably cautious about her plan during the drive home. They couldn't talk much, not in front of Alys, who had a habit of eavesdropping. Their elder daughter's seemingly endless fascination with adult conversation had led to awkward questions more than once before.

"What about your mother?" he said, and she'd squashed the immediate feeling of guilt that threatened to choke off her happiness.

"She'll be fine. She's had me and Bethan to herself for the past thirty-eight Christmases. Now's as good a time as any for her to learn to share." And she'd gazed out of the window to avoid seeing him shaking his head.

He obviously hadn't finished, though, entering their bedroom now with a towel wrapped around his waist, droplets of water still clinging between to the curve of his lower back where he couldn't easily reach.

"Had any second thoughts about Christmas yet?" he asked.

"Why would I? What could be more normal than inviting one's father for dinner?" His negativity was so wearing, even when he didn't say much.

He shrugged now, rubbing himself down briskly with the towel.

"We both know there's nothing normal about your family," he said, and stalked off back to the bathroom.

She glowered and dropped her dressing gown on the floor, catching her breath from the chill of the sheets as she slid her feet in. After turning off the lamp she huddled under the duvet with her back to him, letting her body language do the talking as the bed dipped under his weight.

"Good night, then," he said, obviously taking the hint as he didn't make any attempt to snuggle against her back the way he usually would.

She scowled into the darkness before rolling to face him and letting her resentment spill out.

"I'm sorry you think my family is so *abnormal*. We can't all come from blissfully happy homes like you did, you know. And given that you've had the misfortune of losing your own father, I'd have thought you of all people would understand my desire to make up for lost time with mine."

He sounded tired. Resigned. "I do understand it. I just think, for your own wellbeing, and for the sake of the kids, you should go slowly. It's easy to think someone's great when they're never there. You don't get to see their flaws. They don't fail you. They don't get to lie to you or break the promises they made."

"What a cheerful view of the world. Is that how you think of your dad? Do you only remember the times he let you down?"

"Of course not. If he ever failed me, he more than made up for it by always being there."

"Because he could. My dad couldn't be there, and now that he can be, we have to give him a chance." She groped for his hand. "I love him, Tom. I know you think that's silly because I don't really know him. But I do. There's a bond between us that can't be denied. He's my dad."

There was a pause, then he squeezed her fingers.

"Alright. I get it."

That was better. She shuffled nearer so that they lay hip to hip.

"Something has been puzzling me, though," he said after a moment. "Why does he keep calling you Q, as if you were a character from a James Bond film?"

"Sometimes I can't believe you've lived in Wales for more than twenty years. It's not the letter Q, you idiot. *Cyw* is the Welsh word for chick. It's a term of endearment." The thought of it made her smile. She loved that her dad had a pet name for her already.

"Interesting."

She rested her cheek against his arm and he moved to put it around her, drawing her in. The knot in her neck muscles eased just a little.

"I liked what you said to my dad about marriage. It made me feel quite emotional."

"I liked what you said, too. Apart from the bit about me getting on your nerves, making you want to amputate me so you could get away. That was a trifle harsh."

She poked him in the ribs, making him laugh.

"As far as I remember, I didn't actually say it like that."

"Near enough. Still, I'm sure you can make it up to me."

It wasn't a bad idea, now that she was feeling better disposed towards him. He did smell good, fresh out of the shower. And he was warm, his body reassuringly solid next to hers. She tucked her nose in closer, breathing in the scent of his chest, savouring it.

"I daresay I probably could," she said.

Her hand glided lower, barely touching at first, no more than a whisper over the soft hair trailing down his abdomen. His stomach muscles tautened in anticipation and she slowed, trailing one fingernail in tiny circles around to his thigh, prolonging his torment.

"That's a good start. And – oh, God. That's even better."

Leaning in, she nipped the skin around the rigid peak of his nipple with her teeth, feeling the tension build in him until her tongue finally laved over its tender areola. She suckled there for several heartbeats, then pulled back. He whimpered softly.

"You should probably learn some relaxation techniques," she said, mock-serious, rising onto her elbow to flick her tongue in a trail across his chest to the other nipple. "Your breathing has gone quite rapid and shallow all of a sudden."

"Funny, that. I can't imagine why…"

He groaned as she hovered her mouth over his erection, breathing heat onto it. One dart of her tongue against the tip, then back up to his chest, grinning through the darkness as he grabbed her hand in desperation.

"You're a tease."

"And you love it."

The duvet slipped away as he flipped her onto her back, holding onto her wrists.

"What's this? I thought I was supposed to be making it up to you, not the other way round?"

"Believe me, you are," he said fervently.

Her breath caught as his lips lingered over her breast, making her belly turn to liquid.

"Hmmm, you should probably keep a better hold on the duvet on a cold night like this," he said, mimicking her earlier words. "Your nipple has gone quite erect all of a sudden."

"Ouch - you're hurting my wrists," she lied, squirming under him.

He released her instantly, as she'd known he would, and she seized the moment to shove him onto his back, straddle him and pin him down.

"This is a better way to make up for it, I think."

"I'm inclined to agree." His voice was no more than a gasp, strangling in his throat as she leaned forward, slithering her hips to press her heat onto him.

She wanted the joining as much as he did, but there was more pleasure in delaying, feeling how he strained against the urge to thrust upwards and claim her. He'd have what he wanted in her own good time.

The pulse at his throat, so tender and vulnerable, was salty under her lips, his skin as delicious as it was familiar. At last, when she couldn't bear the anticipation any longer, she adjusted the angle of her hips and with a final push they were one. Firmer she pressed, nudging downwards and deeper, until his filling of her made her ache for completion.

Moving slowly at first, dancing kisses along his jaw, then building, she moved on him, making the pace her own and revelling in his helplessness beneath her. He was concentrating, she knew: every fibre and sinew focused on self-control. His hands lifted to cup her breasts, but she swept them aside and leaned forward, her nipples brushing the hairs on his chest. Stretching out, gripping his thighs between hers, she ground herself on him and rocked until her own orgasm made her gasp and pause, her hair veiling his face in silken twists until she could catch her breath enough to shake it back over her shoulders.

"I trust this is making up for what I said?" she asked when she could speak again.

His voice was thick with the effort of holding back. "For this, I'd forgive you anything."

She built a rhythm again, her neck arching and the swell of sensation growing until it flooded over them both, making them buck, panting and shuddering with the release. At last she sank down onto his chest, within the circle of his arms, and nestled there awhile until he rolled them both over onto their sides.

With her ear against him, she listened to his heartbeat gradually slowing, mirroring her own. He was easing into sleep, she realised, so she shifted a little, catching the duvet back up and tucking it around their shoulders.

"You know, I've been thinking," she murmured.

"Mmm?"

"That ring you bought me." She paused, hoping he had forgiven her for their argument at *Y Noddfa*. She had the sense that he was holding his breath. "It was a beautiful ring. I'm sorry I got so angry with you that day. It was just a lot to cope with all at once."

His chin bumped against the top of her head as he nodded. "It's in my sock drawer. Put it on in the morning, if you want."

"Thank you," she whispered, pressing a kiss onto his skin.

Part of her wanted to say more. It hadn't just been a beautiful ring. The house had been beautiful too, its character and aged charm undeniable. She'd been frightened by how much she liked it, how peaceful and safe its village setting had seemed. She'd heard him describing his vision for it to the estate agent and felt a cold wave of panic because the word-picture he drew was so seductive, and she could hear in his voice how much he wanted it: it wasn't just wishful thinking or an idle dream, but an actual plan. So she'd pushed him away, turning her anxiety into anger, and tonight was the closest she'd felt to him since. With his arms heavy around her she felt secure. She could almost forget about the burglary. Confusingly, as she drifted to join him in sleep, it was the cosiness of *Y Noddfa* that filled her mind and made her dreams that night happy ones.

Chapter Twenty-Four

Friday 19th December 2014
Cardiff

Megan had to laugh at her boss's expression, and the way Sue harrumphed at the sight of the waiting staff delivering a multitude of wooden boards and slates to their tables. Now that Sue's children were grown up, she was probably more accustomed to fine dining than gimmicky chain restaurants.

"*Pizza?* At a Christmas party?"

"You must admit it looks very tempting, Sue."

"Perhaps. But this is a sure sign that it's time for me to retire. When I was your age, a work Christmas party involved either a sit-down meal, which was always roast turkey with all the trimmings, or a stand-up buffet with sandwiches and cheese and pineapple on sticks. Most things were served on sticks back then: it was considered the height of sophistication. Nowadays it would appear that a sprinkling of pizza-laden chopping boards constitutes a party. And when did slate roof tiles start being used as plates?" She sighed and shook her head, then helped herself to several slices of pizza. Apparently she wasn't going to let her disapproval of the presentation get in the way of a good meal.

"There's a pancetta and mushroom one over there: it's delicious," Rachel reported with her mouth still half full. "And a roast pepper and olive one over there, where Duncan is sitting. Although Garin's wolfed most of that one down already. Help yourself, Meg. They'll bring more out in a minute."

Garin loomed behind Rachel, leaning over her shoulder to see what delights lay on their table. "Meat," he bellowed. "I need me some meat. Did someone say pancetta?" One long arm snaked past to seize a slice of pizza. "Lush, apart from all this green shit. Who needs greenery on fucking pizza?" With that, he grasped the rocket leaves and dumped them unceremoniously back onto the board.

Sue raised an eyebrow. "On this one matter, it seems we concur."

"Really? Woah, we should celebrate. Everybody! For the first time ever, Sue agreed with me!"

Good-natured laughter rolled across the bar at this booming announcement. Even Sue had to smile.

"It's so strange to think it'll be your last Christmas party with us, Sue," Megan said, feeling a pang of nostalgia. "You'll still come out with us next year, though, I hope?"

"Just send word and I'll be there. Provided I'm not halfway around the world, of course."

Rachel plopped down on the bench next to her. "You've definitely decided, then? No doubts?"

"None. I've done my time, and I'm ready to hand over the reins to someone with more energy. I sent off my redundancy paperwork today; no point waiting until the thirty-first."

"What will you do with all that time on your hands? I can't imagine you taking to retirement. You're always so busy: won't it drive you crazy, having nothing to do?"

Another pizza was delivered to their table, and they all reached to snatch up another slice before Garin could get to it.

"Oh, I think I might travel a bit, find myself a hunky toy boy in the Greek islands, then settle down to write filthy novels and drink ouzo on a veranda overlooking the Aegean."

"No plans to spend your retirement pottering about in your greenhouse, then?" Rachel asked.

"Only once I've made my millions and exhausted the toy boy. I'm not ready for a greenhouse just yet."

Megan smiled, but the pizza suddenly felt dry in her mouth, her throat almost too constricted to swallow. It went down in a lump and she sipped her prosecco to drown the wave of sadness that suddenly engulfed her.

Why couldn't people just be satisfied with what they had? Sue seemed so excited about leaving the job that had engaged her passionate dedication for so many years. If only she would stay, and all the others who were deliberating the option of taking redundancy and going off in their separate directions. St Dyfrig's High would be irrevocably changed: the loss of so many colleagues would feel like a thousand cuts. The survivors would be left with not only more work but also the pain of staff meetings without those familiar faces. Teams would be depleted, needing to regroup. It made her want to stand up and howl like a child: why can't things just stay the same?

The others were laughing now at Sue's outrageous ideas, so she forced herself to lift the corners of her mouth into something approaching a smile.

"I wish I was brave enough to go," Rachel was saying. "Another couple of years and I probably could do it, but I'm not quite ready yet. And then there's the pension: where would I get another package like that? Mind, it upsets me that I've reached the age when that even enters into my considerations… I know you've said from the start that you won't be going either, Meggie, but what about Tom? Has he made up his mind yet?"

She shook her head. "Sore point, Rach. I'm still hoping he'll see sense. Perhaps I should send you over to talk to him."

Tom was chatting to Duncan, who looked almost unrecognisable in smart clothes instead of his usual tracksuit and trainers. Come to think of it, everyone looked great, and there was a buzz in the air among the gathered teachers that only ever came at the beginning of a school holiday: a sort of exhausted hysteria, combined with an adrenaline rush from knowing they had two whole weeks of lie-ins and laziness to look forward to.

Perhaps one week would be more accurate, once the Christmas festivities were out of the way. She'd have more than the usual preparatory work to do this year. Although Tom had expressed doubts about her plan for Christmas Day, there was no reason to think it wouldn't work out… provided everyone stuck to the schedule she had laid down.

Lying to Bethan and Mam hadn't been one of her proudest moments, admittedly, but it had been in a good cause. By discreetly telling them she wanted to keep Christmas dinner quiet for Tom's sake, and save their family time for the evening, it meant Idris and Celia could come for dinner. Olwen had been taken aback at first, suggesting Tom was being overly selfish by wanting Megan and the children to himself until tea time; but Bethan and Matt had agreed to host her for dinner, so in the end she had little option but to go along with Megan's request.

For the first time ever, Megan had planned a menu for Christmas dinner, ordering a fresh, free range turkey at a price that made her feel hot and cold all over, and digging out the copy of Delia Smith's cookery book which had languished unthumbed in the bookcase since the five or six Christmases ago when Linda and Rob gave it to her. She had even chosen separate wines for the starter and the main course, and a dessert wine to go with the Christmas pudding, which she had gone to the trouble of making herself, seeing as the recipe only seemed to call for nothing more complicated than stirring up a surprisingly long list of ingredients. Although it had to be steamed for what seemed an inordinately long time, she had managed to mark a couple of batches of exercise books while it cooked, leaning over the hob to check the water level every time she got up to stretch her limbs and make another cup of tea. It had worked out satisfyingly well.

She drained her glass and was accosted on her way to the bar by Garin, who had been circulating and now seemed to be more than a little tipsy, his feline eyes shining like a child's in a toy shop.

"Fifty types of cider to choose from, and eighty-odd craft beers. It's like trying to work out which DVD to order from Lovefilm: I could spend a whole evening just making my mind up."

"Really? You look as if you might have sampled quite a few of the drinks already."

He spread his hands artlessly. "Faced with such delights it would be rude not to, wouldn't it? Now then, what can I get you? And, more to the point, what are we going to do about your Tom?"

"What do you mean?"

"He's in agonies over there, you know, thinking about this deadline for the redundancy paperwork. Not long until the thirty-first, is it? Now, now - don't stare at him so obviously. He'll guess that we're talking about him, if his ears aren't already burning."

"I wasn't staring," she insisted, although she had been. Tom was still deeply engrossed in his conversation with Duncan.

"For my own part, I hope he stays on. I'll miss the Saxon bastard if he goes, and I've told him so."

"Surprisingly, now I agree with you, too."

"Yeah - he told me you're not keen on him jacking it in. The thing is, though, *I* know I'm being selfish. Do I want him to go? No. I don't want to have to get used to things being different. But do I think it would do him good to keep going? Also no."

Their short-lived alliance died.

"Easy for you to say. It may have escaped your notice that I only earn sixty per cent of a full-time salary. If you had to pay a mortgage and feed and clothe five people on that, I doubt you'd be so quick to say he should give up everything he's worked for."

"Come off it. It's not like he'd sit on his arse and expect you to be the sole breadwinner, now, is it? He'd get a job. Maybe not with the earnings you're used to, but he'd work his bollocks off to keep you afloat. One thing Tom isn't afraid of is hard graft."

She gritted her teeth. Everyone seemed to have an opinion about her life. And it was her life, not just Tom's, that would be affected.

"We'll just have to see what he decides to do, then, won't we? I can assure you, I'm as concerned for his wellbeing as you are."

He slid a glass of wine towards her and took a swig from his cider. It looked cloudy and dark, like a urine sample from someone with a nasty disease.

"Good scrumpy, this," he said, wiping his lip on the back of his hand.

"I'll take your word for it. Look, Garin, I know you mean well, but I'm getting fed up with other people telling me what Tom needs. He's a grown man, perfectly capable of making his own decisions. He doesn't need my permission to leave or stay in his job."

"Except he does, and we both know it. He'll do what he thinks you want him to do, and to hell with what he needs for his own peace of mind. That's the way he is."

"You obviously don't have much respect for him if you think that."

"I have complete respect for Tom. Which is the only reason I've never tried to shag you. Not once in all these years, even though you're pretty hot. Especially in that dress. I keep telling myself, bros not hoes. *Down, boy.*" He slapped at his groin as if it was a dog, then sent her a look through narrowed eyes. "Mind you, if I thought you'd be up for it..."

His lupine grin made her arch a disapproving eyebrow. How much had he had to drink?

"You're supposed to be getting married, aren't you?"

"Aye. I'll be off the market all too soon. You need to grab it while it's still available, babes."

She tutted. The only part of him she'd ever be tempted to grab was his throat, in a firm and unyielding grip. "You should give up the alcohol, Garin. It really does nothing for your social skills."

"Rubbish. Surely nothing could be more sociable than the offer of a nice, friendly shag?"

"Well, thanks for the offer, but I'll have to decline."

He eyed her mournfully over his cider, then sent her a wink.

"I can see you're tempted. Shall I take that as a yes, then?"

∞∞∞∞

244

"Flirting with my wife again, Garin?" Tom appeared at Megan's elbow, sneaking a proprietorial arm around her waist. She flashed a smile up at him, but her eyes were troubled, for some reason which he suspected had nothing to do with Garin's attempts at charm.

She looked ravishing tonight with her auburn curls tumbling over her shoulders and her new frock clinging in a way that made him feel ten years younger. He'd zipped it up for her earlier, unable to resist nuzzling her nape when she lifted her hair out of the way, and had been perplexed by her inability to see how gorgeous she was.

"Does my bum look big in this dress?" she'd asked, turning this way and that to examine her reflection, and he'd had to be extra careful to mind his words rather than tell the truth, which was a very definite yes. Oh yes. It did look curvier than usual, in a way that sent the blood racing to his groin. In fact, he'd like nothing better than to pull the zip all the way back down again. But experience told him she wouldn't understand the workings of the male mind sufficiently to forgive a truthful answer. Discretion being the better part of valour, he had told her what she needed to hear.

"It looks gorgeous. You know you've always been beautiful as far as I'm concerned."

"That's just a nice way of saying anyone else would think I'm a munter but you've got less stringent standards," she said, proof if it were needed that it was impossible to please a woman, and folly to try.

Garin, though, to judge by his appreciative gaze, had not failed to notice how delectable she looked whilst engaged in conversation with her at the bar.

"For some reason, Tommo, your luscious wife seems reluctant to take me up on my offer of a night in paradise, so I'm going to drown my sorrows by trying every one of these ciders and ales instead. D'you want one?"

Tom raised his glass, which was still half full. "I'm fine, thanks."

"Nah, come on. It was your birthday the other day, wasn't it? I owe you a drink, might as well get one in now."

"I'll leave you boys to it," Megan murmured, reaching up to peck a kiss onto his cheek before slipping away to re-join the other members of her team.

"*Penblwydd hapus.* Happy birthday, old bean. Better late than never."

They clinked their glasses together.

It hadn't been a particularly happy birthday this year. In fact, he'd been relieved when it slid past and Megan had stopped going on about it, asking over and over what he wanted.

The only things he really wanted, he couldn't have. Hugh. Greta. *Y Noddfa.* Auntie Jean up and about and well again. His last trip to see her had been so depressing. He'd sat and held her hand, told her about Idris, and Alys getting an award at school, and Dylan's latest escapades. She gaped at him as if he was a stranger.

"So, did Megan do anything nice for your birthday, then?" Garin's eyebrows waggled suggestively.

"Actually, yes. She bought me one of those waterproof video cameras to attach to my surfboard."

"Great! You'll be able to watch yourself falling off, over and over again."

"Yes, I daresay that will be about all I manage to capture." He gave a lopsided smile, well aware that his own surfing skills fell short of Garin's.

"If I were you, I'd film myself and little Meggie in the bath, seeing as it's waterproof. That would make much more entertaining viewing."

"That's a preposterous suggestion. My porn star days are long gone."

"Oh, aye? What porn films were you in, then? *Debbie Does Dowlais? Sheep Throat?* Maybe you could go back to it as a potential income stream once you've jacked your job in: some people will watch any old shit, won't they? Hey, here's an idea: you could get one of those attachments to turn your camera into a bodycam. Now, that could have some very interesting possibilities. It'd bring a whole new dimension to home movies… Just don't put one on while the kids are about."

Tom shook his head. "I really can't see Megan going for that. I'll stick to using it with my surfboard… although it isn't so easy to get to the beach now, without Greta."

Their amusement faded abruptly. Just thinking about his stolen van was enough to snuff out Tom's Christmas spirit. Garin was probably the only person in the world, apart from Megan perhaps, who could come close to understanding what his cheery orange camper meant to him.

"I've been keeping an eye out for her on the VW websites, mate. If you want to send me some pictures I'll add them for you, get people looking out for her. I know you're a bit of a social media phobe, but I don't mind helping you out with it. Have you heard any news about her from the fuzz yet?"

"No. There's been no sign of her."

"Bloody useless, they are. Don't give up hope, though. It's supposed to be the most wonderful time of the year, and you've been a sickeningly good boy since last December, I don't doubt: maybe Santa will bring you some good news."

Tom gazed mournfully into his pint. "I won't be sorry to see this year end. I know now what the Queen meant that time when she talked about her annus horribilis."

"Oh - is that what she meant? I thought she was talking about her arse. You know, Her Maj's *anus* horribilis."

"For God's sake, Garin - surely some things in life should be sacred?"

"Nah." Garin raised a hand to summon one of the bar staff. "The only things that are sacred to me are my cock and my camper van.

Don't take life so seriously, Tommo. After all, you won't be getting out of it alive."

∞∞∞∞

The taxi dropped them home just before midnight, by which time Megan was unsteady on her feet and Tom's speech was slurring from the effort required to produce words with any meaning. It had been, despite their fatigue, a very enjoyable evening. Garin had flirted with pretty much everyone by the time they left, even Sue. He had teased them when they left that they had to go early so that Tom could shag Megan before she turned into a pumpkin at midnight.

Tom did seem to be feeling pretty amorous, judging by the number of times he had declared his undying love for her in the taxi; but Megan had serious doubts as to his ability to stay awake long enough to do anything about it.

They tiptoed into the house, shushing each other loudly, earning themselves an arch look from Bethan, who had been watching television in the living room.

"I take it you had a good time, then," she said, more a statement than a question.

"We did. It was lovely, *lovely* to go out just the two of us. Thank you for babysitting." Megan flung her arms around her sister, only tottering a little whilst squeezing past the coffee table.

"You're welcome. Nia woke up once but she soon went back off to sleep. Apart from that, everything has been fine."

"Aww, thank you so much. Tom, up you get! Say goodbye to Bethan. She's going now."

He had flopped onto the sofa, but hauled himself up obediently for a kiss on the cheek.

"Honestly, what's he like? Last time we both got this drunk, he got me pregnant." She couldn't restrain a fit of the giggles at this, even though she couldn't have explained what made it so funny.

"Thank God I'm firing blanks these days," Tom muttered, lurching off to let Dandy into the garden.

"Somehow I don't think you'd have anything to worry about tonight, even if he hadn't had a vasectomy," Bethan remarked. "He's three sheets to the wind. Right - I'll be off. I wonder what state Matt will be in when he gets home. It seems to be the night for everybody's Christmas parties, except mine."

"You make sure you enjoy yours tomorrow, then. And we'll see you on Christmas Day. Teatime, don't forget! You absolutely mustn't come before teatime. Five thirty, and not a minute earlier. We um… we definitely won't be ready before then."

She held up her forefinger for emphasis, hanging on to the door frame in an effort to remain upright while Bethan zipped up her boots.

"Yes, alright. I get the message. Although it shouldn't take all that long for you to tidy up, surely? It's not as if you're having anyone over for dinner."

Dandy appeared in the hallway and cast a haughty look at them before mounting the stairs.

"He's ready for bed," Tom said, yawning as he followed. "I know how he feels."

Bethan called up the stairs to him, a sharp edge to her voice. "Look, Tom - it's fine about Christmas Day. I can understand you not wanting any family over for dinner this year. And at least I'll get to give the kids their presents at teatime."

Megan felt a cold rush at Tom's confused expression. It sharpened her senses and made her feel suddenly almost sober.

"What's that?" he was saying, frowning.

"Yeah, he really appreciates it. Thanks, Beth." She shoved her sister towards the door. "I'll see you upstairs, Tom."

"But what does she mean? I'm fine with having your family here… Oh, I see." Comprehension and embarrassment dawned simultaneously on his face as her glare and frantic gestures finally pierced his consciousness. "Righto. See you soon, then, Bethan."

Megan faked a smile that she hoped would divert Bethan's attention from her fiery blush.

Bethan's voice was frosty. She shouldered her handbag without taking her eyes off Megan's face.

"You're up to something," she said. "And it had better not be what I think it is."

By Luisa A. Jones

Chapter Twenty-Five

Christmas Eve
Wednesday 24th December 2014
Cardiff

The children were in bed at last, despite being wild with excitement, and Tom surveyed the contents of the fridge while Megan wrapped the last few stocking fillers.

How much food did one family really need for Christmas dinner? Megan had spent a small fortune with her insistence on buying enough to serve a multitude. He had lost track of all the side dishes she planned to serve alongside the gargantuan turkey. She'd even made a traditional Christmas pudding, despite being the world's most reluctant cook. They'd had to google Stir-Up Sunday and queue up to stir the damned thing, each making a wish: after all that, it had better be good.

Those wishes, though… Given that it was too late to wish that she'd never found Idris, or that his own parents hadn't died, he had wished for Greta to be found intact and recovered. As time passed it seemed an increasingly forlorn hope.

Megan hadn't told him what she wished for, but he guessed it would be for Bethan to drop her umbrage over their father's introduction to the family. The strain was beginning to tell on her, especially with the risks she was taking with her arrangements for Christmas Day. He had warned her that it could all go badly wrong, but she'd insisted that as long as everyone stuck to her instructions, there was no reason to fear that Bethan and Olwen would find out Idris had supplanted them at the Christmas table.

Never in his life had he felt less like celebrating Christmas, but it wouldn't do for his own glum mood to spoil it for Megan when she was making such a huge effort. He unpacked the vegetables, dug out a knife and peeler, and set the ubiquitous carols from King's playing through the Bluetooth speaker the kids had given him for his birthday. The tone was pretty good, he thought, as the choristers' voices soared around the kitchen, and carols beat the Michael Bublé album Megan had been blasting out every evening for the past fortnight. Better turn it down a touch, though: the last thing he needed was for the kids to wake now that they'd finally succumbed to sleep.

He had finished peeling the parsnips and moved on to the carrots by the time Megan came down, hair tied back and sleeves shoved up past her elbows ready to join him.

"Ooh, you've made a good start. *Bendigedig*. Do you think those parsnips should be cut into smaller chunks?"

He turned away before rolling his eyes, so she wouldn't notice.

"I think they're about right, but go ahead if you think they need it."

"No, you're probably right. I'll get on with the spuds, shall I?"

"I'm still using the peeler. Why don't you shred the red cabbage?"

"Fine. I'll just find the recipe, see what I need to do."

It was cabbage, for crying out loud – why should she need a recipe? But he held his tongue.

"Shit," she muttered, leaving the book on the table to hunt through the kitchen cupboard. "It needs wine vinegar. Have we got any wine vinegar? Why didn't I notice that when I did the shopping list?"

"I'm pretty sure we have cider vinegar. That will do, surely?"

"It's not what Delia specifies. But I suppose I'll have to make do…"

With the last of the carrot peelings tossed into the food bin, he seized the paring knife and gestured towards the heap of carrots on the chopping board.

"Do you want these cut into rounds or sticks?" he asked, figuring he'd better check with her before making a start, the mood she was in.

"Oh, heck - I don't know. Sticks look more sophisticated but rounds preserves more of the vitamins." He waited while she dithered, frowning over the chopping board. "Hmmm… I'm not sure. What are your thoughts?"

"I don't give a damn either way, I just wanted to check exactly what you want so you can't tell me off later for doing it wrong… But to judge by your expression that wasn't quite the answer you wanted."

"Just do sticks," she said sharply.

"Rounds are easier…"

"Rounds, then. For God's sake, they're only bloody carrots. I don't see why you couldn't have just taken the initiative, it's hardly a major decision."

There was a strained silence while the choirboys trilled out their phrases about peace on earth and joy to the world, punctuated by the chopping of Tom's knife and the slamming of cupboard doors while Megan hunted about for various saucepans and mixing bowls. Suddenly, Tom could hold back no longer.

"I'm also thinking that it's our first Christmas without Dad, and how wrong that feels. And I'm thinking I could really do with a glass or two of wine, or even something stronger, to help me through this evening, but it would be wise to leave off until I've at least finished chopping the veg, because I'd rather not spend Christmas Eve in A&E. And, of course, I'm hoping I can get through tomorrow without saying anything critical of your father or being rude to your mother, because she really does piss me off sometimes and quite frankly I can do without her 'all men are bastards' attitude as much as I can do without his 'I'm right about everything' attitude, because *my* dad was anything but a bastard, or arrogant, and I'd give the world to have him here with us again. And I keep thinking that the last time I spoke to him he asked if we wanted to go to Ludlow for a weekend but I made an excuse because I wanted to take you and the kids camping, and now I'll never get another chance to visit him, and oh, fuck, if only I'd known."

Her arms were already wound tightly around him, holding him against the juddering effort of keeping his emotions in. He set the knife down and turned to clasp her against his chest, his face buried in the softness of her hair while he took several deep breaths to regain his control.

"I don't suppose he'd ever have forgiven you for making that excuse," she said.

He lifted his head, confused. "What do you mean?"

"Well, he'd never have spoken to you again if he'd known you wanted to take your family on a holiday in the van he paid for. He'd have been horrified at the idea of you wanting to spend quality time with your wife and kids."

At last he understood that she was being ironic. It did seem a bit silly, put like that. "Oh," he said, and allowed his shoulders to drop.

She cupped his face in her hands. "You weren't to know. He would have understood. It's only natural to miss him this Christmas. Every milestone during this first year without him is going to be hard, and even afterwards I don't suppose it gets much easier for a good while. I'll cover for you tomorrow if you need to hide away for a bit. I'll even have a word with Mam. You only have to say if it all gets too much; I'm here for you."

He summoned a smile, grateful for the depth of love in her eyes.

"Sorry. I should probably stick to thinking about carrots and put on a more cheerful tune than *In the Bleak Midwinter*."

She hugged him again, then reached past him to pinch one of the sticks of carrot, munching on it.

"Not *Blue Christmas*, then. Or anything about being lonely this Christmas, or homesick, or broken-hearted."

She scrolled through the playlists on his phone while he chopped, feeling calmer now that he had admitted his grief.

"Hey," she said, interrupting his thoughts. "It was our anniversary last week, and we completely forgot about it."

"Our anniversary? But we got married in April."

"Ten years since we first met. December the eighteenth."

Of course. He smiled, remembering.

"Wow. Ten years since you first pounced on me and tickled my tonsils with your tongue in the lift."

She gave him a playful shove that could have had serious consequences if he hadn't paused his chopping for a moment of nostalgia.

"Ten years since our first dance, too. There can't be all that many couples who can boast that their special song is by Jive Bunny and the Mastermixers. Wait, I bet it's on YouTube."

He laughed aloud at that, even more when she put his phone down on the counter and the opening bars of Swing the Mood blasted from the speaker.

"Does this bring back memories?" she asked, tossing his knife aside. Seizing his hands, she started rocking his arms to and fro in time with the music. "For old times' sake," she said, spinning on one foot and back again.

"Your dancing seems to have improved since that night."

"Probably because I'm sober, and wearing my slippers. Less likelihood of falling over my own feet."

"True. But there isn't really room in the kitchen... Oh, sod it."

He grabbed her around the waist and whirled her around. They bumped into the cupboards and trod on each other's toes, and they'd never win any ballroom dancing competitions, but by the end of the song his spirits had lifted and he felt a surge of genuine happiness such as he had not felt in a while.

"Ten years on, we've still got it. I do love you, Meg," he told her, in case the unabashed adoration on his face hadn't already made it sufficiently clear.

Her answering smile changed to a startled look and he turned to see Nia barrelling through the doorway.

"He's here! He's on the roof! I heard him!"

Nia's eyes were round with excitement as Megan knelt to catch her, almost bowling over backwards in the rush.

"Who's here?"

"Father Christmas! *Sion Corn*! I heard the reindeer on the roof. He's here now!"

"Oh, *cariad*. He isn't here yet."

"He *is*. Tell her, Daddy. I heard him!"

Tom caught Nia up in his arms, his heart brimming, and carried her into the living room, where three red stockings lay against the hearth.

"You must have heard him flying over, darling. He won't come until all the mummies and daddies have gone to bed. Look, your stocking is still empty."

"Go to bed then, so he can come."

"We will, as soon as we've finished the veggies. He'll come, don't you fret."

She nodded trustingly and allowed him to carry her back up to bed. Tucking her duvet around her, making sure her teddy was safely nestling under her chin, he felt a moment of sheer contentment. Whatever else had happened in the past year, life was still good. It was going to be a wonderful Christmas.

Chapter Twenty-Six

Christmas Day
Thursday 25th December 2014
Cardiff

The day started early, as it did every year, with their bedroom door bursting open, jolting Megan from sleep. Groggily, she reached for the alarm clock and peered at the display with one unfocused eye.

"Oh, God. It's only half past five. It's not time to get up yet, Nia."

But Nia was already clambering onto the bed, knees and elbows sharp against Megan's shins, making her gasp. Shielding her eyes from the glare of light from the landing, she elbowed Tom, who had barely roused yet. He merely groaned and pulled the duvet up higher.

"Look, Mammy. Wake up, Daddy. He's been! He's filled our stockings and it's Christmas Day!"

It was pointless to suggest that Nia should go back to bed. She'd be much too excited to rest now that she knew her presents had arrived. Besides, Alys was stumbling in now, eyes still clearing the blur of sleep and the beginnings of a smile lighting up her face as she dumped her bulging stocking onto their bed.

"Merry Christmas, Mam. Merry Christmas Dad and Nia. Shall I go and wake Dylan up?"

Tom stirred at that. "No! No, don't. He's only little; let him sleep a while longer."

Dandy scratched at the door downstairs, woken by the noise.

"I'll let him out and fetch the camera," Tom volunteered, his voice still gravelly with fatigue. He lumbered off, shrugging his arms into his dressing gown for warmth. The central heating hadn't come on yet, and Megan pulled the duvet up to her chin while the girls opened the gifts from their stockings.

Luckily, it didn't take long, and they were soon despatched back to their own beds to play with their gifts.

"I'd better put the turkey in the oven," Megan said, yawning, and swung her feet out of bed with considerable reluctance.

"Another hour won't hurt, will it? You've got plenty of time. Set the alarm, we'll get up at seven to prepare everything. I'll help you."

Such a tempting offer. Tom's body radiated warmth, and the duvet was soft, and the floorboards they had painstakingly sanded and varnished were cold under her bare feet.

She awoke again at half past eight, thanks to Dylan poking his finger into her eye socket.

"Open your eyes, Mammy. Wake up."

"Oh, God. Oh, no – Tom, we need to get up. The turkey… I have to take it out of the fridge to bring it to room temperature, and warm the oven, and shove butter under its skin, and put bacon over it, and stuff the neck – at least, I think it's the neck. Or is it the other end? And I have to check what to do with the bag of giblets. Delia will tell me…"

"Don't panic. I told you I'll help. Happy Christmas, Dylan. Let's go and see if your stocking has presents in it, shall we?"

There followed an hour of rushing to and fro between the kitchen and living room, trying not to miss any of the children's excitement at their gifts whilst simultaneously preparing the gigantic turkey.

"I'm sure I didn't order one this big," Megan muttered, her arm half frozen, shuddering at the sensation of the pale, goose-pimpled flesh against hers as she rubbed butter underneath the skin. In previous years, when they had gone to Olwen's or Hugh's for dinner, she had only had to take a dessert or starter as their contribution to the meal. This was too grown-up for her liking. She might have three children to care for, and a job helping to prepare future generations to step out into the world, but preparing a Christmas dinner somehow seemed altogether a much heavier responsibility. Perhaps they should all turn vegetarian. At least she wouldn't have to thrust her arm up a nut roast's gaping orifice.

By the time Celia and Idris arrived, Dandy was drooling onto the kitchen floor from the meaty aromas coming from the oven, but the turkey was still not cooked and despite Tom's attempts to keep her calm, Megan felt she was spiralling into a vortex of stress. She'd wanted everything to go smoothly, and had ruined it with her lack of willpower. Stupid, *stupid* of her not to get up earlier. It took a huge effort to assume a cheery and unruffled demeanour to greet their visitors.

Celia was laden down with gift bags, a bright but brittle smile on her face, while Idris seemed more than a little tense. He kissed Megan's cheek and pulled her in for a hug readily enough, which still gave her a little pop of warmth in her chest; but as he settled on the sofa she couldn't help feeling there was something strained about the atmosphere between them.

Celia chatted away to the children, oohing and ahhing over their presents: "Well, that's lovely, isn't it Idris? It's adorable. Isn't it adorable?"

He barely grunted acknowledgement, his attention on his mobile phone.

She could only assume they'd had a row. It explained everything. Celia was trying to cover it up by overcompensating, and he was still in a mood. Megan's own tension grew.

"Let's open these presents from your Tadcu and me, then," Celia gushed.

They were beautifully wrapped, with co-ordinating ribbons and bows; Megan and Tom's were swathed in hessian, with little sprays of holly tied on. Even Linda, doyenne of domestic good taste and creativity, didn't go that far. When wrapping presents herself, Megan usually dropped them into a gift bag that had been saved from last year, and stuck the top down with a bit of tape. How long must it take to wrap everything as perfectly as this?

The children each had Lego, and a quick glare made Alys express her thanks with more enthusiasm. Nia needed no such encouragement, but hurled herself at both Celia and Idris.

"Manky sometimes gives us Lego too, but not such a big set," Nia said as she clambered off Idris's lap.

"Who's Manky?" Idris asked, mystified.

"Oh - she means Mam. Tom claims to be unable to pronounce Mamgu, so he calls her Manky instead."

Tom shrugged. "I can't help it. I find Welsh pronunciation tricky at times." It was a line he had stuck to ever since Alys was born, even though he knew it infuriated Olwen. He'd never openly admit that it was his small act of revenge for her dislike.

He opened his present: a coffee table book about Welsh rugby. "Ah. Thank you both very much." He managed to sound grateful, despite supporting England.

She hid a smile and turned to her own present, the first she could remember receiving from her father, even if Celia had probably been the one to wrap it. Excitement flushed her cheeks and made her heart flutter as she peeled back the wrappings and opened the box. Then it faded. Inside the box was a silk scarf in shades of yellow and peach.

"Celia chose it," Idris said. "I've no idea what women want. I've spent a lifetime trying to work it out, but am no further on than I was when I met your mother."

She dredged up a smile. "Thank you both so much. It's beautiful." It was, and probably very expensive; but it showed how little they knew her. She never wore scarves, except for woolly ones when she went outside in the cold. As much as she envied people who could tie a scarf in stylish ways to complete their outfit, she found whenever she wore one that it just got in the way. And yellow wasn't a colour she would ever wear. Greens, teals and blues were more her style.

What had Tom said to the children earlier? *It isn't the gifts, but the love behind them that counts.* But it wasn't only love: it was the knowledge of the recipient's likes and preferences, an understanding that came from familiarity built over time. That was what she imagined Tom had been thinking of when he remarked that there weren't so many gifts under the tree this year. It wasn't that they missed Hugh and Jean's generosity, so much as what their gifts used to represent. The care that had gone into their presents mattered infinitely more than the monetary value or any amount of exquisite wrapping.

She fought down the lump in her throat. The relationship with her father was still new. She couldn't expect him to know their likes and dislikes just yet – that would come in future years.

It was time to hand over their gifts. Idris seemed pleased with his bottle of Penderyn Welsh whisky, and Celia with her cookery book and expensive hand cream.

"Will you be seeing your son later, Celia?" Megan asked.

"Oh – no, not this year. I'll pop round and see him tomorrow." If Megan wasn't mistaken, her smile seemed somewhat forced, while Idris's looked like a cynical smirk.

"Do you think there's something going on?" Megan whispered to Tom when they retreated to the kitchen to baste the turkey.

"I'd hazard a guess that Celia's son isn't too keen on Idris. He didn't come when we were all invited to her house. And she didn't give the impression that Idris would be going with her when she visits him tomorrow."

"Oh, no – I don't think it can be that. You must have it wrong. Celia is obviously very happy with…"

Her voice tailed off. Was Celia happy? She was bright and bubbly, and polite enough to be friendly and welcoming, but there had definitely been an atmosphere when they arrived this morning. It was a perplexing thought. What possible objection could her son have? Idris was perfectly pleasant and personable, and Celia seemed to dote on him. Perhaps that was the real reason: her son was jealous of another man being close to his mother. How selfish her son must be.

Dinner went reasonably well, although the lumpy gravy was embarrassing. Tom came to the rescue by making a new batch with some granules and Megan was grateful to get away with this lapse of culinary skill. She hadn't much of an appetite by the time dinner was finally served, having wound herself up to a fever pitch with wanting everything to be perfect; after it was over, Tom sent her to sit in the living room while he tackled the washing up.

With Alys and Nia playing upstairs, and Celia insisting on helping Tom despite his protests that guests shouldn't be working in the kitchen, Megan and Dylan were alone with Idris. Sinking back into the sofa, she reached for the remote control and turned the volume down on the Thomas the Tank Engine DVD just enough to be able to relax, but not so far that Dylan would explode in outrage.

Without the din of whistles, dramatic music and chuffing engines, she could take the opportunity to chat to her dad. But he had taken his mobile phone out of his pocket and seemed deeply absorbed. She waited a while, and was about to express her pleasure at finally being able to spend Christmas Day with him when he looked up and tucked his phone back into his pocket.

"I could fancy a walk," he said. "Blow away a few cobwebs, like."

"Oh! That's a good idea. We'll come too. If you don't mind, of course? Fresh air will do us good, won't it Dylan?"

He hesitated. "I would have thought you'd be glad of a rest after all that cooking?"

"I can rest later. It'll be nice to have some quality time together." A glance at the clock on the mantelpiece showed she still had two hours before Olwen, Bethan and Matt were due to arrive.

Idris waited at the end of the driveway while she strapped Dylan into his stroller, tucking a blanket around him to fend off the damp December air. It seemed to take forever, and she felt compelled to apologise as she joined her father, falling into step as he set off.

"Sorry to keep you waiting. Everything is such a major undertaking with kids, isn't it?"

He grunted, turning towards the park. Perhaps he didn't get it, not having lived with young children for so many years. She must make more allowances for that.

"I lived not far from here for a while," he said, making her chin jerk up in surprise. Had they been living near each other, without knowing it?

"I was seeing an Italian girl. Stunning, she was. Mad as a box of frogs, mind, but definitely a beauty."

"What makes you say she was mad?"

"She had a terrible temper. We had this magnetic rack on the kitchen wall with a set of cook's knives hanging on it. One day I said something she didn't like and she grabbed a whole handful of knives in one go, pointed them at my throat and told me to get out. I didn't hang around after that." He chuckled. "She was fiery, that one. We had a lot of fun when we started out."

"She sounds unhinged, not just fiery."

"Nah, she'd just lost her rag. I expect I deserved it. It's quite funny, looking back – not so funny at the time, maybe."

"Did you live near here for long, then?"

"Only a few months. I've moved about a fair bit. I lived in France for a while, then Spain. The world's too big to stay too long in just one small part of it."

She frowned and huddled into her coat. Her hands were getting cold on the stroller handle, as she'd been in too much of a hurry to remember her mittens.

"You're settled now, though? Celia seems lovely, and Sully is a nice place to live."

He made a sound that could have meant anything.

"It's just… I'm so grateful to have the chance to finally get to know you, but the way you're talking, you've got me wondering if you'll be up and off again."

Her footsteps flagged and he paused, watching her with those blue eyes that had seemed so much like Tom's when she first met him, but suddenly seemed too cool and dispassionate to be like his at all.

"I don't really do permanent, *Cyw*. Who knows how long Cee and I will be together? She's alright for the time being, but… Anyway, whatever happens, there's nothing to stop you and me keeping in touch."

"Like you do with Delyth? She said she phones you a couple of times a year. Is that really enough for you?" She couldn't keep the hurt and disappointment from her voice.

He smiled, as she would smile at one of her own children if they were being silly about something, and briefly pulled her close against his shoulder.

"You'll be fine. You've always managed, haven't you, and you've got Tom to look after you. He seems a steady, dependable sort of bloke. Come on, now: chin up. You look as if the world's coming to an end. Dry those pretty eyes, I'm not planning on going anywhere just yet."

The numbing chill in her fingers was as nothing compared with that in her heart as they continued their walk around the park and finally turned towards home. Dylan had fallen asleep, rosy-cheeked and snug under the bright colours of his blanket. How blissful it must be to feel so safe and secure, immune to the turmoil adults felt. She hardly registered what her father was saying as he remarked on houses they passed, commenting on their extensions or conservatories, on house prices and the best ways to improve a property on a shoestring. It seemed he was oblivious to her misery even as her hopes crumpled, smaller and smaller with every step.

∞∞∞∞

It was obvious to Tom the moment he walked into the hallway that something was wrong. Idris seemed relaxed enough, and Dylan was sound asleep in his pushchair, which was probably unwise this late in the afternoon; but there was something about the weariness of Megan's movements as she hung up her coat that showed she wasn't happy.

"Are you alright?" he whispered.

Her shoulders had slumped as if they bore the cares of the world, and her voice sounded flat and defeated.

"I'll explain later. They're going in a minute. I've told him Mam is coming over, and he doesn't want to see her any more than she'd want to see him."

Celia had followed Idris obediently from the living room, swapping her handbag from one arm to the other to reach for her coat.

"Thank you so much for having us," she said, kissing them both on each cheek. "You've made us so welcome, and the dinner was delicious. I must get your bread sauce recipe next time we come, Megan." If she noticed how wan Megan's face was, she was too tactful to comment.

Tom shook Idris's hand, but his searching gaze uncovered nothing in his father-in-law's bland expression.

They watched from the doorway, Tom holding Megan close against his side, as their visitors walked to their car. She seemed even smaller than usual, as if she was shrinking into herself.

Having safely deposited their presents inside the boot, Celia closed the lid; but neither she nor Idris made any attempt to get into the car. Instead, they seemed to be having some kind of argument.

"What are they doing?" Tom muttered after a minute or two had passed waiting politely on the doorstep. "It's freezing out there, we'll lose all the heat from the house."

Detaching himself, he strode down the driveway. "Is everything alright?"

"She's only gone and locked the keys in the boot. And not for the first time. I'm always telling her not to put them in there, but she never listens."

Celia was apologising over and over, hunting vainly in her handbag. "I can't believe it. I put my bag down on the floor of the boot while I laid the presents down flat – I didn't want Idris's bottle of whisky to smash. My keys were on top of my bag, but now they're not in there. Oh goodness, how embarrassing."

"Do you have a spare key?"

"Yes, but it's at home – and my house key is on the same keyring as the car key, so I can't get into the house either. Do you have your house key, Idris?"

"No. I didn't think I'd need it. I wasn't to know you were going to do this again, was I?"

In the front doorway, Megan was looking at her watch. The hairs rose on Tom's arms. Celia and Idris needed to get going if they were to avoid Olwen and Bethan's imminent arrival. There had to be a simple solution.

"Does your son have a key to your house, Celia? If so, perhaps he'd be able to bring your spare key here? If your car wasn't blocking the driveway I'd gladly take you home to meet him there, but..."

"I'll call him. Just give me a moment."

While she rummaged in her bag, Tom went back to confer with Megan.

"We've got to get them away from here," she whispered, pale with anxiety. "Bethan and Matt will be bringing Mam in less than half an hour."

"Don't worry, we'll sort it – even if I have to call a taxi to take them home to fetch the key. You'll just have to make up some explanation for the flashy car blocking the driveway…"

"How will I explain that away? And a taxi from Cardiff to Sully on Christmas Day will cost a fortune, even supposing we can find one. It's ten miles away."

He'd have paid anything to clear that look of panic and despair from her face.

"Could you phone Bethan, get her to come an hour later?"

"I'll try, but it might be too late. Oh God, why did I think this would ever work?"

She vanished into the house to use the telephone.

"David can't come," Celia said. "He's had a couple of glasses of wine, so he can't drive."

Idris made an impatient noise. "Always an excuse."

"What about a taxi? If you come back inside, I'll call the local firm and they could take you back to fetch the spare key from his house."

She nodded gratefully and he sidestepped to usher them back in. Megan had reappeared in the doorway, but instead of moving aside, she seemed rooted to the spot, eyes wide with dismay.

"Ooh, hello!" came Bethan's familiar voice from behind him. "What are you doing out here in the cold? Already had visitors, have you..?" Her question tailed off and she stopped so abruptly that Matt only narrowly avoided bumping into her back.

Before Tom could move to greet them, Olwen squeezed past, peering myopically from under the hood of her black coat like a mole.

"*Nadolig llawen*, Tom. Happy Christmas," she said, then paused as she spotted Celia and Idris behind him.

"Let's just go, Mam. We can come back later – they obviously have guests." Bethan clutched at her mother's arm, but it was too late.

"*You!*" Olwen hissed.

Idris thrust his hands into his pockets, a cocky smile spreading amidst his beard. "Hello, Olwen. The years don't appear to have been kind to you."

"I don't need to ask what you're doing here," Olwen said, snarling with contempt before turning to Megan, who had run down the frosty driveway towards her in her stockinged feet. "What were you thinking of?"

"I can explain –"

267

"After *everything* I said. You knew how I felt, and yet you not only contacted him, you brought him here on Christmas Day of all days."

Bethan yanked at her mother's arm. "Leave it, Mam. Let's go back to mine. Come on."

"Beth, Mam – please, there's no need for you to go. Come inside, have a drink and open your presents…"

"Come in? You must be joking! I wouldn't be able to bring myself to speak to you, you selfish, conniving, disloyal bitch. You didn't listen to a single word I said. You had to do it your way, didn't you, even though you knew it would cause nothing but hurt to Mam? Well, now you'll have to live with the consequences. Here – take these." Bethan dumped her bags of gifts on the ground. "I'll look after Mam. You've got *him* now. You won't be needing us any more."

"Don't be like that, Beth! You know why I needed to get to know him. It doesn't mean I don't still need you as well!"

Tom had a sense of vertigo, as if everything was falling away from him. This couldn't be happening. One glance at Megan's stricken face spurred him to follow as she chased after Bethan along the pavement.

"Bethan, please. Don't be hasty," he urged. "You're all welcome to come in – there's no need for an argument. Let's discuss it in a civilised manner."

She had climbed into the passenger seat of Matt's car and slammed the door.

"Matt, tell her – please! Don't go!"

Tom caught Megan's arm to stop her wrenching the door open in her distress. The glare on Bethan's face through the glass suggested it would be folly to try to convince her now; Olwen, in the back seat, was facing the other way, as if she couldn't bring herself to look at Megan at all.

Matt opened the driver's door. "I am sorry. I'll try, but you can see how upset they are." He shook his head, looking as stunned as Tom felt, and sent them a sympathetic look before slipping into his seat and starting the engine.

"Tom, don't let them go," Megan pleaded. She hammered her fists on the car windows, but Bethan only scowled, and the car pulled away.

He caught her in his arms: distress made her stagger, her shocked face a contorted mess of tears and mascara. "Come on, now," he murmured, trying to calm her before the children could witness her anguish. "It'll be alright. They'll come round, you'll see. Just give it a couple of days."

Dazed, she allowed him to shepherd her back towards the house.

Celia was twisting a handkerchief in her hands, almost in tears herself at the scene that had so suddenly erupted. Idris, however, merely scratched his beard and raised an eyebrow as they passed.

"Well. After all that palaver, I suppose I'd better call our taxi myself," he said.

Chapter Twenty-Seven

Boxing Day
Friday 26th December 2014
Cardiff

The house was quiet at last. Nudging the bedroom door open with his foot, Tom stepped into the darkened room and, guided by the light from the landing, set a mug of tea and a handful of biscuits down on the bedside table. Megan lay on the bed, curled into a foetal position, her straggly auburn hair vivid against the pale sheets. Dandy snored at her feet, as if he understood that she was miserable and needed the comfort of a warm companion.

"Are you awake?" He spoke quietly, unsure of his reception, and she stirred with a whimper. She'd been in bed ever since they'd got back from Rob and Linda's, after trying repeatedly without success to get Bethan to answer the phone.

"The kids have had supper and I've put them to bed. I told them you were asleep. How are you doing?" It was a stupid question, he knew, but he had to say something. She couldn't just lie here in the dark for ever. She'd been quiet all day, not rising to any of Linda's barbed remarks. In fact, she'd been remarkably biddable: she'd even told Linda that she admired her culinary talents. It had taken the wind out of Linda's sails, made her look at Megan as if she had suddenly shed a lizard's skin and emerged as a fairy princess.

Boxing Day had passed much more pleasantly thereafter, so Tom wasn't complaining; but he was nevertheless unsettled by the way Megan's usual fieriness had been snuffed. Usually, everything she did or said was done with verve. She gave of herself impulsively and freely, without holding anything back. It was one of the things he loved about her: the honesty in her passionate nature. Seeing her passive; diminished, even… it worried him.

She snuffled into a tissue. "I'm sorry I spoiled your Christmas."

"What? Don't be silly." Without Hugh, his Christmas had already been spoiled. There had been no chance that he'd really enjoy it, apart from the opportunity to see the children's excitement. And she had behaved impeccably at his brother's. Although her plan for Christmas Day had backfired pretty spectacularly and given their neighbours material to gossip over for months to come, he felt only sympathy for her, not disappointment. Her intentions had been good, setting out to try to accommodate everybody, even if the execution of her plan had gone awry.

The bed dipped as he sat down and rested his palm on her shoulder. "Have a sip of tea," he suggested, but she grimaced.

"It will take more than a cup of tea to make me feel better."

"Of course, but you don't have to be dehydrated on top of everything else. I brought you some shortbread, too. Come on, low blood sugar won't help either."

She uncurled and sat up against the pillows, sagging as if completely drained. He couldn't recall ever seeing her look so awful, even yesterday, when she'd alternated between distress and rage. Tonight her face was puffy from crying, eyes little more than slits amid streaks of mascara, her skin blotchy and dry. He handed the mug over and she held it with both hands, as if it was too heavy, then waved the biscuits away with a shake of her head. His heart sank: if she wouldn't eat shortbread, the situation was even worse than he'd thought.

"I've tried and tried to ring Bethan, but she isn't picking up the phone and she's turned the answer phone off so I can't even leave a message. I wish she'd talk to me, let me explain."

He sighed. "Let the dust settle; give her time to sleep on it. I'm sure she'll come around, given time."

"She might not. She never understood why I needed to see him. She warned me he was a deadbeat, that he'd never amount to anything as a father. And I'm starting to think she was right. When

271

we went out for a walk yesterday, he as good as said he won't be staying around here for much longer. He said he doesn't do permanent."

"Where does that leave Celia?"

"I get the feeling she's the latest in a long list of women he's stayed with just as long as it suited him. 'I don't do permanent'. What does that even mean?"

Tom thought back to the telephone conversation he had overheard at Celia's bungalow before Christmas. He knew Idris had been speaking to a woman, because he had called the other person Chick in Welsh; and he'd talked about telling Celia something unpleasant once the holiday was over. Perhaps he was planning to leave her?

His lips thinned. If he had Idris in front of him now, he'd be sorely tempted to land the punch he'd wanted to throw the first time they met.

Megan looked up mournfully. "In the beginning, I thought I just needed to satisfy my curiosity about him. I thought that once I knew what he was like, it would be enough. But I let myself be dazzled by him, didn't I? I've come to realise I need more than that. I need a father who would move mountains for me. One who'll listen – really listen, because he's genuinely interested, and advise me. I need a dad who's proud of me, and shows his pride, and who looks at me with more than just a bit of tepid curiosity. I need him to adore our kids, to know he misses us when he can't be with us. I wanted Idris to be the father I'd always missed out on, so like an idiot I saw what I wanted to see. I've been waiting to get the feeling that being reunited was something he'd always longed for, but I haven't had that sense from him at all. I suppose what it boils down to is this: I needed him to be like your dad. I hadn't realised how much I missed Hugh. He didn't make a fuss, but he didn't leave us in any doubt of our importance in his life, did he?"

He nodded, choked that she also felt the loss of his father so keenly. Hugh had been everything Idris wasn't. But then, even a shadow had more depth than Idris Parry.

"I've realised I'd go to Uncle Rhod before I'd go to my dad for anything, because I just can't see Idris as solid or reliable. Am I being unfair..?"

A wry hitch of an eyebrow was enough to express his own view.

"I denied it to myself, for a while, but I can see it now. I threw myself into trying to make a relationship that could never exist. And it was so stupid, because now I've lost my sister, my best friend in the world after you; and I've lost my mother too, and for all her funny ways she's still my mam and I do love her, honest I do." Her voice cracked.

"Of course you do." It didn't matter that he couldn't see much to love in Olwen. He could feel Megan's shock and grief as if it were his own. More than anything, he wanted to make it better. "Come on, don't cry. It will all calm down, you'll see." He rocked her and murmured soothingly until her sobbing turned to hiccoughs.

"What will I do without them? Why can't they understand?"

Inwardly he seethed, helpless in the face of her distress. As much as it ran contrary to his nature to wish ill on anyone, he wished Idris had died years ago. Perhaps then Megan could have come to terms with the relationship she'd never had, instead of chasing after a futile dream. He wavered between wanting either to shake Bethan and Olwen until their teeth rattled in their heads, or to carry Megan off somewhere safe and cosset her until she felt better. He stroked her hair, loving its silkiness under his hand, and made himself ignore the uncomfortable way his tear-soaked shirt front had stuck to his chest.

"Give them a few days, they'll see sense," he murmured, hoping this would turn out to be true. The Parry women were a feisty bunch, quick-tempered and stubborn when set on something. "I'll speak to Matt and see if he can calm Bethan down. Or maybe I'll speak to your mother."

He didn't relish the prospect of contacting Olwen, but it might provide the best chance of sorting things out.

"Bethan hates me," came the muffled, agonised voice against his breastbone. Another paroxysm of crying overcame her, and she shook her head at his automatic attempt at denial. "You saw the look on her face; you heard the way she spoke to me, as if I was some kind of traitor. Bethan bears grudges. When she falls out with people, she's intractable. Do you remember when she fell out with her neighbour? That was years ago, before Alys was born, and they still don't speak."

He raised his eyes to the ceiling and gave himself a moment to adjust his voice. It wouldn't do to show his anger, could only make things worse. Bethan could be a bitch when crossed. He'd faced her criticism himself in the past, and the atmosphere had never entirely thawed between them since. But for her to treat Megan so harshly, to cut her only sister out of her life... that would be taking a grudge to a whole new level.

"We all say things in the heat of the moment that we don't mean."

"But what if she keeps to her word? What if I never see her again? She isn't just my sister; she's my best friend. And now I've lost her."

"You haven't lost her. She'll miss you too much to keep it up for long, you'll see." He patted her back.

At last, no doubt wearied by crying, she lay quietly against the wet patch she'd left on his chest. Her shoulders heaved as she took in a great, shuddering breath.

"Well. At least all this has helped with one thing," she said, her voice hoarse but strangely calm. He had the sense that she had resigned herself to despair.

"What do you mean?"

"There's no point in carrying on as we were."

He frowned and waited for her to explain.

"Send the forms in to HR," she said, wiping her eyes.

"The redundancy forms?"

"Yes. Take whatever redundancy package they offer you. I'll do it, too, if you want. We'll move to West Wales. Or to the moon, for all I care. There's nothing to keep us here if my own sister hates me so much she won't even pick up the phone when I call, and my dad obviously doesn't plan on sticking around."

He caught his breath. She was offering everything he'd wanted. But it wasn't supposed to be like this, when she was too overwrought to know what she was doing. To take her up on this offer - this gift that he hadn't even dared to dream of… it wouldn't be right. He'd be taking advantage of her in her moment of weakness. It wouldn't be fair.

Cautiously, he said: "I think you should probably sleep on it. There's no hurry to make decisions about any of that now…"

But she sat back and shook her head. Her eyes were so red and swollen, she looked as if she'd been in a fight.

"I won't change my mind," she said. "Bethan isn't the only one who can be stubborn. As soon as the estate agent opens on Monday morning, I want you to ring them. I want you to make an offer for *Y Noddfa*."

Chapter Twenty-Eight

Monday 29th December 2014
Cardiff

Megan stared blankly at Tom, who slid the laptop across the table.

"What do you mean, it's gone?"

The estate agent's property listings filled the screen, and she scrolled up and down to hunt through them for *Y Noddfa*. He was right: it wasn't there.

"When did you last look?"

He looked sheepish. "About a fortnight ago."

So he'd carried on looking at it after she'd refused to move. She let it pass.

"Maybe the vendors took it off the market over Christmas. They won't have wanted any viewings during the holidays, will they? That'll be all it is. Ring the agents at nine, when they open, and I bet they'll let you book another viewing in a week or so."

She wiped the mushy Weetabix off Dylan's chin before it could set, then released him from the highchair straps. He slipped to the floor like an eel being released from a net and darted off to play, energised now that he had eaten his breakfast.

"Shit," Tom muttered behind her.

"What's up now?"

"I just clicked the box to include properties that have been sold."

Her heart skipped. Leaning over his shoulder, she peered at the screen and there it was: a photograph of *Y Noddfa*, the whitewashed stone fresh and clean against the deep blue of the sky and the lichen-spotted roof slates. A black rosette marked SSTC was stamped in the corner of the listing.

Sold, Subject to Contract. No wonder Tom had covered his face with his hands.

She sank into her seat. This was a blow. Now that she had decided to support his idea of buying *Y Noddfa*, it didn't seem fair to have it snatched so cruelly from their grasp.

He clicked through the photos, looking wretched.

"Phone the agent anyway. It's only subject to contract, after all. There's loads that could go wrong. Property sales fall through all the time. Offer them more money, if you have to: Rob said you'll have your inheritance by the summer, so we would probably have it by the time the purchase goes through."

"You think I should try to gazump the buyers?"

This wasn't a time for scruples. "Why not? Other people do it."

But he shook his head. "It wouldn't be right. And besides, we're not in a position to proceed. We haven't sold our house, or even put it on the market. We don't have the money in the bank yet to go ahead, or a mortgage agreed. If I put in an offer, they'd be within their rights to laugh in my face."

Her jaw clenched. Why couldn't he see solutions instead of problems?

"Well, at least tell them you're interested, and to get in touch with you if it comes back onto the market."

Cross, she gathered up the breakfast dishes and marched out to the kitchen with an expectant Dandy at her heels.

"Alys ate all her toast, for once, so I only have two crusts for you today," she said, dropping them into the dog's waiting jaws like a zookeeper feeding fish to an alligator.

A glance towards the dining room revealed that Tom was still gazing at the laptop as if he could change things by the sheer force of wishing. She tutted and looked around the kitchen. He had been right about one thing: they weren't in a good position to make an offer, either on *Y Noddfa* or on any other property. Well, that was easily rectified. A week of the school holiday remained and they could get a lot done in seven days, even with the children around.

She made a start as soon as the dirty dishes were stowed in the dishwasher, barely noticing when Tom reached for Dandy's lead and headed out, stooped like a man with the cares of the world on his shoulders.

By the time he returned, with rain dripping from his hair and his nose red from the cold, she was crouching with her head in the depths of the saucepan cupboard and most of its contents spread out on the floor behind her.

"Do we have mice, or something?" he asked, draping his coat over the back of a chair to dry.

"No - what makes you ask that?" She examined the shelves in alarm, but there was no sign of any droppings: only a light layer of sawdust at the back, where the cupboard was starting to crumble with age.

"For the first time since I married you, you appear to be spring cleaning. I couldn't think of any other explanation."

She huffed at the implication that her domestic standards weren't up to scratch.

"I'm just making a start on getting the house ready for sale. If we clear some stuff now, there'll be less to pack when we move. Besides, the number of pointless items in this cupboard is ridiculous. Why did we keep this electric knife, for a start? I don't think it's ever been used in nearly nine years of marriage. It could probably win a prize for Most Useless Wedding Present."

"Auntie Jean gave us that. It might come in handy one day."

"No - I'm making an executive decision. If we haven't used it by now, we never will. It's going to the charity shop, along with all of that lot." She pointed towards the items she had stacked to one side, listing them like a contestant on the *Generation Game*. "Mexican dip bowls; rice cooker; ice cream maker; pasta machine; fondue set.

Honestly, this house is like a collection point for Unnecessary Gadgets of the World…"

He thrust his hands into the pockets of his jeans, frowning. "You're worrying me. This isn't normal behaviour."

"Are you being sarcastic? I know I'm not the most domesticated, but…"

"No, I'm not. Genuinely – this is unnerving. Ever since Christmas Day you've been either manic or miserable."

She bobbed up like a meerkat from the depths of the cupboard. "You're exaggerating. And besides, you should be glad I'm doing this. With less stuff in the cupboards, we'll be able to clear some clutter off the worktops to make the estate agent's photos look better. Do you know, we have twenty-seven mugs! And only five of them match. Four of them say World's Best Teacher, three are for Liverpool FC, there's your favourite one with the photo of the kids on, and most of the others are just – well, completely random. Who on earth needs that many mugs?"

As she spoke, he picked his way across the gadget-strewn floor and grasped both her hands, looking down at her with such seriousness that she had no choice but to stop.

"Why don't you ring your mother?"

She shook her hands free, but he had her cornered.

"I couldn't. Not yet."

"You could."

"Didn't you see the way she looked at me?" She bit her lip, wrapping her arms around herself as if to shield herself from turbulent memories of Christmas Day.

"So apologise."

He made it sound so simple, but it wasn't. If she spoke to Mam, she'd have to explain why she'd gone against her wishes, and she wasn't sure she'd have the courage to do it. Olwen had been so definite and uncompromising about Idris, and her inability to view the situation from a daughter's standpoint made Megan feel there was a gaping chasm between them. It would take more than a simple "sorry" to bridge a gap like that.

"Go and ring the estate agent," she said, to deflect him. "Find out what's happening with *Y Noddfa*."

But his expression told her he had seen through her ploy.

"Tom, I know you're trying to help and I appreciate your concern. But I'll be fine. Really."

She tried to sound as if she meant it. As if her heart wasn't breaking at the thought of losing her mother and sister's love and approval. As if she wasn't grieving Bethan's loss as fully as if she had died. In fact, in a funny sort of way her sister's death might have been easier to cope with. It would certainly have been less complicated. She wouldn't have been caught up in this confusing turmoil of shame mixed up with the need to be true to herself. If Bethan had died, at least Megan wouldn't have been the cause of her own bereavement.

She blinked back tears and ducked back into the cupboard to reach for the slow cooker she hadn't used in a couple of years, wiping the dust off the lid with her sleeve like Aladdin invoking the genie. Behind her, a sigh marked the moment when Tom gave up trying and, to her relief, left the room without another word.

∞∞∞∞

By mid-afternoon, the car was loaded up with boxes and black sacks filled with items for the charity shop. Tom had given up trying to make Megan see sense: to do so was like trying to persuade a tornado to change its course. Although he was pleased that she had made such a good start at the mammoth task of decluttering the house, her motives still concerned him.

She'd been even worse after he called the estate agent and learned that *Y Noddfa* had indeed been sold a week before Christmas. He couldn't bring himself to enquire about the selling price, and he certainly wouldn't stoop to setting off a bidding war. What was the point in fighting against Fate? He should be growing accustomed to loss, and was surprised how much this one hurt, even though the property had never been his.

He'd been in a foul mood all afternoon, angry with himself for not making an offer sooner, with Megan for making him delay until it was too late, and with life itself for being so relentlessly shitty. Surely he was due a break? But no, as if things weren't already bad enough, he now had cause to worry over Megan's state of mind and her increasingly bizarre behaviour. He had thought her numb passivity and lack of appetite odd enough on Boxing Day, but her unwillingness to sort things out with her family was even more out of character. After all, he was the one with the track record of avoiding confrontation and running away from his problems. She usually tackled difficulties head-on, the way she was unexpectedly dealing with their kitchen gadgets. As he slammed the tailgate down over the pile of unwanted belongings, he decided enough was enough. As much as he disliked running the risk of an argument, if she wouldn't take action he would have to do so on her behalf.

The drive to Bethan and Matt's house didn't take more than ten minutes, and he was out of the car and on the doorstep before he could have time to talk himself out of it.

To be fair, Bethan looked terrible. Her hair was lank, her eyes were smudged with indigo, and she was slumped on the sofa in a grubby sweatshirt and leggings. She glared at Tom when he arrived, sending a verbal shot across his bows before he could even cross the threshold into the room.

"I suppose *she* sent you? Too cowardly to grovel in person, is she?"

"Actually, no. Megan didn't send me. She didn't think there'd be any point in either of us trying to talk to you, because she knew how pig-headed you would be about this mess. I made my own decision to come, because I was naïve enough to hope that you might listen to reason."

"Reason? I gave her plenty of reasons not to contact him, but she went ahead anyway. So if anyone's pig-headed, I don't think it's me."

He gave up and addressed himself to Matt. "Talk to her, would you? Maybe you'll be able to get her to see that life is too short to bear grudges like this."

Matt shrugged, his grimace suggesting he was equally sick of the situation.

He rubbed the back of his neck, unsure of the best way to proceed. Perhaps a more conciliatory approach would be more effective.

"Bethan, I've heard the arguments on both sides, and there's no point in going over them again. If it helps, I understand your point of view, and I'm afraid your concerns about your father's character will prove to be right. But Megan did what felt right for her, and I have to support that."

"You're as *twp* as she is, then."

"I may well be as daft as you say, but at least I've never allowed a quarrel to come between me and my only sibling. You've only got one sister, Bethan. Don't throw away everything you've had for the past thirty-eight years just because on this one occasion her needs are different from yours."

He drove to the charity shop and handed over the stack of black bags, brushing off the fulsome thanks of the elderly volunteer who directed him where to leave them. He felt a satisfying sense of a mission accomplished, like the shedding of a skin. They had made a start. They were one step closer to moving. And Megan was on board.

If only he had been equally successful with Bethan. He'd hoped Olwen might still be staying with her and Matt, but she had returned to Carmarthenshire. The rush of adrenalin from his confrontation with Bethan had dissipated with the physical effort of lugging the bags into the shop; but his pulse stuttered again at the prospect of dealing with Olwen. Should he call her? Would it do more harm than good?

Before he could find a reason to back out, he had found her number in his contacts and made the call.

Breathe, he told himself. He'd tackled bigger and stronger people than his mother-in-law on the rugby pitch - and yet the idea of offering a direct challenge to her was much scarier. He half hoped she wouldn't answer; at least he could say he'd tried...

Shit. Her strong Welsh accent cut through his musings and he sat up straighter, mentally preparing for a battle.

"Olwen. It's Tom."

"What's wrong? Has something happened to one of the children? Is Megan alright?"

Of course – he never rang her himself. The concern in her voice about their welfare was touching. That was what he needed to tap into: even this fearsome Welsh dragon could be vulnerable where her family was concerned.

"The children are fine, thank you. Megan, though - less so. This business over Idris..." He left the words hanging, and could sense her guard being wound up like a drawbridge.

"It could all have been avoided if she'd listened to me in the first place."

"Olwen, I've never seen her the way she is. She's either full of manic energy or hardly able to speak for despair. It's like a kind of grief; as if she's broken. I know you and I haven't always seen eye to eye, but I can't believe you want her to feel this bad."

"Do you think I want to be on bad terms with my own daughter? She's brought this situation on herself, remember. When she brought *him* back into her life, she had no thought for how I'd feel. No consideration there; no sympathy. If she had any idea what that man was like..."

He pressed his point. "And whose fault is it that she didn't? Did you ever explain what sort of man he was?"

"I told her enough that she should have been able to work it out for herself. But I didn't go into all the gruesome details, no. And I stand by that decision. No child should know that one of their parents doesn't love them."

"But by withholding that knowledge, you allowed her to grow up dreaming of some idealised knight in shining armour, a hero who would come back one day and love her, when in fact we both know that Idris Parry is as superficial as the skin on a custard. By shielding her from knowing that, you forced her to find out for herself. The hard way. I'm not saying she's blameless in this, but please – have some empathy for her situation."

There was a pause. When Olwen spoke, her voice was trembling in a way he had never heard before. "It's obvious that you think I'm the villain in all this. Well, I'll tell you something I've never told anyone about Idris, and then you can judge me however you see fit. He never wanted children. We only married because Bethan was on the way. When I told him I was pregnant with Megan, he was so furious about it, he threatened to push me down the stairs to make me miscarry. Do you honestly think I should have told her that? What sort of damage would it do to a child to feel so unwanted? What good could it have done?"

He sighed and scrubbed his hand over his eyes. What a fucking mess. He pictured Olwen as she was in Rhod and Jayne's old photos: a girl, small and overwhelmed by the weight of responsibility landing on her young shoulders. How different her life might have been, if not for Idris Parry. For the first time since he'd met her ten years earlier, he found himself feeling some warmth towards her.

"I'm so sorry you went through that, Olwen. I can't imagine how hard it must have been for you, dealing with a bastard like that and then bringing up two children on your own."

Her voice softened. "No, you can't. Promise me you'll never tell her. She doesn't need to know. I'm not looking for your sympathy - I only told you so you'd know the sort of person he is. How little he cared. That's what I've been trying to protect her from."

Through the window of the car he watched people scurrying in and out of the shops, huddled into their coats against the cold. How complicated people's lives were, when you scratched below the surface. Keeping things from Megan had never gone well in the past, but he knew Olwen was right about this. It would be cruel to tell her the depths Idris had been prepared to stoop to.

"I promise," he said.

"When I warned her not to involve him in her life, I'll admit part of me was worried that she and Bethan might be taken in by his lies and blame me for the difficult times we went through when they were little. We never had any luxuries, and I worked every hour I could to keep a roof over our heads. They didn't have it easy, and I feel guilty about that. But more importantly, I didn't want them to end up getting hurt again. I was scared that he'd worm his way into their affections and then let them down again, because unless Idris has had a personality transplant or some kind of Damascene conversion, he's not someone any sensible person would want hanging around."

"I've no reason to disagree with you, or to believe he's changed very much. I suppose he has some superficial charm. He turns on the smiles and makes a show of listening, but I get a sense that he doesn't have much real interest in Megan or his grandchildren. And she's picked up on that. I want to help her in this, but if I'm honest, I don't really know how."

There was a pause before Olwen spoke again. "Look. I'll admit that I didn't take to you when Megan first brought you home to meet me. I thought you'd get bored and tire of her when you realised she didn't have a background like yours, with your private education and your stable family life. Even when you married her, I wasn't sure if it was just because she was expecting Alys and you felt you had to do the decent thing. I feared you might be as shallow as Idris; but in fairness, you've stuck by her and proved me wrong over the years. So I'm glad you haven't been deceived by that surface charm you've described, because you can take it from me – Idris is a leech. Over and over he drained me dry, then dropped away until he was hungry again. I can imagine what went through his head when he met you both. Nice house; decent cars; good jobs; you with your posh English voice that smacks of money in your background. He'll see you as someone to attach himself to when all of a sudden the river isn't flowing his way any more. So my advice about how best to help Megan is to shake him off. Extricate yourselves before he can have a chance to get his hooks in. Because believe me, he'll take and he'll take until you've nothing left to give; and then, when he's exhausted all your supplies of emotional energy and money, he'll disappear without a backward glance. I'm glad you want to help, Tom. Please, don't let him hurt my girls again."

Chapter Twenty-Nine

Wednesday 31st December 2014
Cardiff

New Year's Eve. And what a year it had been: one Megan wouldn't be sorry to put behind her. Usually they'd go to a party, or spend the evening with Bethan and Matt, but neither she nor Tom had the heart for celebrating with friends and as far as she knew Bethan was as implacably angry as she had been on Christmas Day.

She wasn't even sure if she'd bother staying up to see the New Year in. What would be the point in celebrating? There was no reason to suppose that 2015 would be any better than 2014 had been.

Alys had made a fuss, pleading to be allowed to stay up until midnight.

"You're eight, Alys. If I let you stay up that late, you'll be evil the next morning, and frankly I'm not prepared to put us all through that. There'll be plenty of New Year's Eve parties when you're older."

"But Millie's parents let her stay up for New Year. She told me."

"Maybe Millie isn't like a bear with a sore head when she hasn't had enough sleep."

She tucked the blankets around Alys's shoulders, ignoring her scowl.

"You're so mean! Millie's mum bought her a phone for Christmas, too. Why won't you let me have a phone?"

"We've been over this. You don't need one yet. Not until you go to high school."

"But it's so unfair! I hate you."

Megan sucked in a deep breath. If she was like this at eight, what would her daughter be like as a teenager?

"That's right. I'm a wicked, horrible mother, and you're very unlucky to have me. But even though I'm so incredibly cruel, I still love you very much."

She stroked Alys's hair back from her forehead and watched the conflicting emotions cross her face: resentment and frustration melting into amusement as she realised she was being played.

"I love you too," Alys said at last, and Megan smiled, turned out the light and blew another kiss from the bedroom door. Padding downstairs with Dandy at her heels, she pretended she hadn't heard the rustle indicating that Alys already had a book in her hand, ready to read by torchlight under the duvet.

A sudden outburst of barking from behind her almost made her fall down the last couple of stairs. Dandy raced past and launched himself at the front door, where the shadow of a tall figure loomed behind the stained glass.

"What the hell? Hush, Dandy! That's enough." Emerging from the living room, Tom flicked on the light switch and peered through the glass.

"Who is it?" Megan asked, now that that her heart had stopped threatening to leap out of her throat.

"It's Garin," he said, surprised, and opened the door keeping a firm hand on Dandy's collar. "Hi, mate. What are you doing here?"

"And a Happy New Year to you, too," Garin retorted, stooping to kick off his shoes. He nudged them neatly into a corner of the hall, an action that struck Megan as surprising. She wouldn't have expected him to be house-trained.

Now that he was inside and patting Dandy's head, the dog had obviously decided he was a friend, and shook a cloud of white fur over Garin's uncharacteristically smart trousers. Luckily, he didn't seem to mind.

"I guessed you two saddoes would be stuck at home tonight. There was a time you'd have been out partying with the best of them."

"That was BC. Before Children."

"Little buggers don't half cramp your style, eh?"

It was hard to argue with that.

"Anyway, unlike you, I'll be out getting hammered in a bit. I'm on my way to see Shaz. She's got a bunch of mates coming round for a piss-up. Should be a right laugh – we'll all be twatted by ten, if I play my cards right. But I spotted something today that I thought you two would be very interested to see. Very interested indeed. So I thought I'd call in and show you on my way, before I get so rat-arsed I forget all about it, like. I don't plan to see much of tomorrow, and this can't really wait."

Megan and Tom exchanged a mystified look.

"Lead me to your internet," Garin commanded, arm outstretched as if heading a cavalry charge.

"The laptop's in the dining room," she said, and busied herself making them each a cup of tea while Tom booted it up and signed in.

"So what it is, see, is I've been keeping an eye out on all the buying and selling sites to see if any camper vans like Greta came up. And earlier today I spotted this one…" Garin typed ponderously into the search box with one long index finger, then hit the return key with a flourish and rubbed his palms together. Excitement seemed to hang about him like an aura: Megan felt it catch, and realised Tom was feeling it too. She set their mugs down on the table and sat down.

"Here we are: look at this ad, now. 'VW Rare six-berth Viking conversion; blah blah blah.' The seller's based in Swindon. Not much previous feedback to speak of. Asking price thirteen and a half grand. So – does anything look odd to you?"

Megan frowned. She must be missing something. The only discrepancy she had noticed was the misspelling of "berth" on the advertisement, the seller's use of "birth" seeming faintly ironic considering Dylan was born in their own van.

Tom seemed equally confused. "I'm not sure what you're getting at. It can't be Greta: it's blue. And that isn't Greta's registration number. It's not even the same year."

"Look closer," Garin said, his smug grin growing ever wider as he clicked through the photographs. "Look at the doors. What colour are they on the *inside*?"

"Orange," Megan and Tom said in unison, peering at the screen.

"Very good. And the engine bay?"

"Orange," they repeated.

"Go to the top of the class."

Megan was still mystified. "I don't understand. What difference does that make?"

Garin eyed Tom expectantly, as if putting him to the test.

"She's been resprayed," Tom said slowly. "But not very well. They've only done the outside, not the interior metalwork. A full respray would mean taking everything out, and that takes a lot of time and work. This one's been done the lazy way."

"Bingo. Now, look really closely at the photos of the interior. Can we zoom in any further?" He fiddled with the settings, enlarging the photographs. The interior cupboards and seats were just the same as Greta's: 1970s brown checks, designed in the decade that had somehow managed to bypass good taste altogether.

Tom went quiet, intent on the screen. "That patch in the roof canvas. It's exactly like the one I put on Greta last summer."

Garin nodded. "Anything else?"

"There's a bit of a scorch mark on the inside of the cooker lid. And some of the laminate has come off the corner of the fridge unit."

"Mightn't they all have those sorts of marks, though? These vans are ancient, after all. They're bound to have suffered similar damage from thirty-odd years of use." She could see where this might be leading, but surely Garin wasn't seriously suggesting that this blue van was Greta?

"I checked out the history of this blue Viking," Garin said. "Thought I recognised the reg number, did some digging and found it in one of the online forums I belong to. It was advertised for sale for spares or repairs at the end of October. Hadn't had an MOT in fifteen years. It didn't run. And the interior wasn't complete. Yet someone has supposedly managed to source an engine, do a full restoration job, and find all the missing bits from inside – including the correct fridge, which must be as rare as unicorn spunk - *and* change the paint inside the engine bay and doors to orange, which only a fucking lunatic would do. All of this in less than three months. I'm telling you now, if that van turns out to be what the advert says it is, I'll eat my pants. In fact, I'll go further: I'll take a vow of celibacy, go vegan and join a commune with a load of hairy hippies."

"You're serious about this, aren't you?" Tom couldn't tear his gaze from the screen, the rekindled hope in his face painful to see.

Garin sat back and folded his arms. "That, my friend, is what's commonly called a ringer. Your Greta, all done up in a cunning blue disguise. I'm off to Shaz's now to celebrate my own genius by getting shit-faced. But if you've got any sense, you'll get on to the fuzz before the night is out, and get them to take a little trip to Swindon."

∞∞∞∞

Tom's grin threatened to split his face in two. "They're going to pass the details on to Wiltshire police," he said. "By this time tomorrow, maybe they'll have gone round and checked it out. We might actually get her back, Meg. We might get her back!"

Megan flung her arms around his neck and he danced her across the kitchen, finishing with a twirl and a kiss so impassioned she nearly fell over backwards.

"I can't believe it," he said, for perhaps the fifth time since Garin left.

"I know. It's fantastic. Amazing."

"We need to celebrate." He opened the fridge, excitement galvanising him into action. There was a bottle of prosecco that would do: he let the cork fly out into the garden and laughed as Dandy scrambled off the step to follow it. Joy bubbled over in his chest like the wine. Megan had found a pair of champagne flutes and he poured with a bit too much enthusiasm, making the prosecco fizz over the rim of the glasses.

"Steady. You don't want to waste it. It's not so often we get something to celebrate. To Greta," she said, lifting her glass in a toast.

"To Greta. And to this being a good omen for the coming year."

They clinked glasses and he kissed her again.

He had been planning to go to bed well before midnight, but found himself too excited to sleep, so snuggled with Megan on the sofa. It was funny how much closer he felt towards her, now that he had something to be happy about. The rekindled sparkle in her eyes and her beaming smile reminded him that she, too, would be gladdened and relieved by this unexpected turn of Fortune's wheel. Too restless for bed, they scanned the television channels, but were unable to find anything that suited their mood.

"*Love, Actually*, or *The Holiday*?" she asked at last, waving DVDs under his nose.

"Seriously? That's like asking if I'd rather tear my hamstring or my Achilles."

She poked her tongue out and he shrugged, resigned to his fate. He wasn't a fan of Christmas movies – with the exception of *Die Hard* or possibly *Gremlins* – but if it would make her happy...

"You choose," he said.

She didn't hesitate. "*Love, Actually*, then. I'll set it up. You fetch the crisps."

The funeral scene hit him with a jolt – he had forgotten about that part. He watched it misty-eyed, and to his surprise found that he was able to get through it without breaking down. Megan squeezed his hand, and he lifted hers to kiss it.

"You know, I used to think it was quite sweet the way that guy calls round to tell his best friend's wife that he's in love with her – but these days I find it a bit… well, stalkerish, don't you?" she said. They had started a second bottle of wine by then, and set up a tray with crackers and cheeses left over from Christmas, and she was sucking in her cheeks over a sharp pickled onion. "I mean, Garin can be a bit overly flirtatious, but even he wouldn't go that far."

"You weren't worried when he turned up on the doorstep, then?"

"No! Were you?"

He shook his head. "I don't see Garin as a threat. He isn't your type."

"He definitely isn't. Mind - if Hugh Grant turned up, looking for his sexy secretary, I might experience a strange compulsion to drag him inside and distract him from his quest…"

He couldn't help but laugh at her wicked grin, glad to be joking with her again. The wine and the elation that had come from hopefully finding Greta had made him feel more relaxed than he had felt in months.

"Pass the stilton," he said peaceably. As she did, the doorbell rang, making Dandy bark ferociously again.

"I'll get it," she said, looking as surprised as he at their second unexpected visitor of the evening.

Frowning, he wrapped the chunk of stilton up and called after her. "If it's Hugh Grant, tell him to get lost. You're already spoken for."

The front door opened, then closed again, followed by the murmur of two voices; but the identity of the caller was impossible to establish above the sound of Dandy's skittering paws.

Megan reappeared in the doorway, looking bewildered.

"Who was it?" he asked.

She stepped aside.

Behind her, wrapped up in a scarf and beanie hat, and with a suitcase in each hand, was Idris.

"Apparently Idris and Celia have had a row. It'll only be for a couple of days, while he sorts out somewhere else to stay."

"Thanks, *Cyw*," Idris said, then eyed the tray. "Well, look at that, now. I couldn't have timed it any better. I've arrived just in time for supper."

Chapter Thirty

Sunday 4th January 2015
Carmarthenshire

Megan helped herself to another of her mother's posh chocolate biscuits, one of her few concessions to the Christmas season. Olwen had stopped putting up a Christmas tree when her daughters left home; the only visible clue to the time of year was a limp poinsettia and a small pile of cards on the mantelpiece.

"Honestly, I don't know which of you is dumb, and which is dumber. And I've said the same to your sister. I didn't keep your father out of your lives for all these years for you two to fall out over him now."

"I know, Mam. It's not what I want, either. I'm hoping she'll come round, given a bit of time."

"How's your little game of Happy Families working out with your father, then?"

Megan wasn't sure if her mother's tone implied malice or concern.

"It's fine," she said, reluctant to go into detail.

"Really?"

Olwen was eyeing Tom, whose mouth had hardened into a thin line. She had been remarkably friendly towards him today, hugging him with every appearance of sincerity when they arrived, and – strangely – even smiling at him now and then. More surprising still was the way he smiled and hugged her back, with genuine warmth. It was as if something significant had happened to alter the dynamic between them. Positive though this was, it left Megan wondering if something had happened without her knowledge.

"Tadcu is living on our sofa," Alys piped up, oblivious to her warning glare.

"Oh, yes?"

"Yes. He says our house may not be as big as Celia's, but at least he isn't being nagged from dawn to dusk."

"It's only temporary," Megan said hurriedly. "Just until he finds somewhere else to stay. Why don't you go and let Dandy out into the garden, Alys?" Hopefully the dog would distract her from making any further embarrassing revelations.

"Nah. He's already been out." Alys reached for one of the biscuits and smiled happily. It seemed she was determined to share in the adults' conversation.

Megan cleared her throat. "So, anyway – how have you been, Mam? Tell us what you've been up to since we last saw you."

Olwen's arch expression showed she saw through Megan's attempt to deflect the conversation away from Idris, but to her relief she went along with it and filled them in on her news. Megan only half-listened, her mind preoccupied with thoughts of her father. On New Year's Day, a tearful Celia had turned up on their doorstep with more of his possessions packed in black bags. Fortunately, Tom and the children had been out at the time, else Alys would doubtless be regaling Olwen now with tales of her grandfather's scandalous love life. Megan had eavesdropped, dismayed, as Celia demanded back the keys to her house and car.

"Just give back what belongs to me, and then I never want to see you again, Idris. I had thought, at our age, that we'd be past this sort of thing. You can tell your other woman that she's welcome to you. And good luck to her – I hope she knows what she's letting herself in for."

A whole new side to her father had been revealed. The way he smirked at Celia's pale, dignified face had made Megan cringe. Celia had been so kind and generous in the short time they'd known her. His lack of remorse for the distress he had caused her was shocking.

Shutting the front door in Celia's face after tossing the keys into her outstretched hand, he had noticed Megan in the living room doorway and shrugged, as if such painful rifts were inevitable.

"What can you do? She stifled me. Life's too short for that sort of intensity. And I've been thinking of getting a car of my own, anyway. A BMW would be nice."

Megan was forced to tell Tom about these latest developments that night, when he spotted the extra bags shoved behind the sofa.

"So he did have someone else. I thought so," he said grimly. He told her about a conversation overheard during their evening at Celia's house, when her father had called someone else *Cyw* and discussed plans to tell someone bad news after Christmas. The thought of it made Megan feel nauseous. She'd lain in Tom's arms after he told her, fighting the urge to cry. She wanted so much to feel proud of her father, but how could she when he behaved like this?

Since then, Idris had moved on bewilderingly quickly, parking his gleaming new BMW on their driveway without any concern that this meant Tom had to park out on the road. Nor did he seem to feel any need for discretion, now that his relationship with another woman was out in the open. That morning, Megan had brought a plate of croissants to the breakfast table and found him showing Alys and Nia a picture of his "new girlfriend" on his mobile phone.

"Isn't she pretty? Much prettier than Celia," he said.

The confusion on Alys's face had made Megan's discomfort grow. She didn't want her daughters to grow up believing that a woman's worth was solely based on her looks, or that they should compare themselves to one another.

"We don't use mobile phones at the table in this house," she reminded him. She and Tom were always careful to reserve mealtimes for talking as a family, not staring at their phones.

He ignored her, and went on composing a message, so she repeated the rule as if he hadn't heard.

At last he glanced up and sent her a smirk over the top of his handset. "Rules are made to be broken, aren't they kids?"

She had let it go, but his challenge to her parental authority had rankled. As a father, she had expected him to back her up about family rules. Hugh would have done. But then, the differences between Idris and Hugh were becoming more obvious every day.

Olwen's voice cut through her reverie, bringing her back to the present. "I think that's enough biscuits for now, Dylan," she said, putting the lid firmly back on the tin. "We don't want you to be sick, do we? Come on, Megan: help me make some sandwiches. Don't you ever feed these children?"

The blood rushed into Megan's face. Making sandwiches would mean that she would be alone with her mother in the kitchen and the simple apology she had offered on their arrival would have to be followed up with an explanation. She looked at Tom, hoping he would offer to help instead, but he merely smiled and moved his feet so that Olwen could pass.

"Good idea. You two could do with some time on your own," he said, annoyingly.

Megan buttered slices of bread while her mother cut cheese into slices so thin they were almost transparent, just the way she remembered from her childhood.

"I've never been able to cut cheese as thinly as that. It's a rare talent you've got there."

Olwen shrugged. "Old habits die hard. When you have no money and two children to feed, you learn very quickly how to eke out the little you have. I used to know what every penny would be spent on. There was this one time when the only wearable shoes I had were a pair of flip-flops. Your dad hadn't been home for a while and I didn't have two ha'pennies to rub together. Rhodri and Jayne noticed me wearing them in the rain and dragged me off to Stead and Simpson's… They were always very good to me, but it killed me to have to accept their charity. Another time, I remember crying in the supermarket because the price of a dozen eggs had gone up by three pence. It meant I couldn't afford to cook the meals I'd planned. I had to go home and work out a whole new menu for the week."

Megan paused. She'd spread the butter generously, as she always did at home, not even thinking about how much she was using. It would be alright – Olwen earned a respectable wage these days, after all her years of studying and hard work. She could cut her cheese as thickly as she wanted, if she let herself. But her story had made Megan think.

"I've probably never told you how much I admire the way you held things together over the years, Mam. It can't have been easy."

"No, it wasn't. But it was worth it, wasn't it? Look how you and Bethan have turned out. When you're not arguing, of course."

Olwen arranged the cheese slices carefully on the buttered bread, so that they didn't overlap. How many sacrifices had she made over the years, to be so conditioned to economy? How different might their lives have been if her husband had provided the financial support Olwen had been entitled to expect?

"I am sorry. I know you didn't want me to contact him. He let you down, and I completely understand why you wouldn't want any links with him now…"

Olwen put her hands on her hips. "It wasn't about *me*, you silly girl. I didn't want him hurting *you*. Your father was probably the worst thing that ever happened to me. But good did come from it, because you and Bethan are far and away the best thing."

A tear rolled down Megan's nose and she brushed it away with the back of her hand, feeling like a child again.

"Oh, Mam. It's all such a mess."

For the first time in years her mother abandoned her customary reserve, held out her arms and offered the comfort of a long, loving hug.

Chapter Thirty-One

Saturday 17th January 2015
Cardiff

T om lined his knife and fork up on his empty plate, patted his full stomach and leaned back in his chair to watch Megan polishing off the last of her Welsh lamb *cawl*. Date nights were a rare treat, but for once Idris had made himself useful by offering to babysit. He'd even tried to press a twenty pound note into Tom's hand, urging them to make the most of the evening and not to hurry back. "It's the least I can do," he had said, a sentiment with which Tom wholly agreed; but he'd refused the money, knowing Megan would be cross if he took it.

"That was delicious," she said, scooping the last of the rich gravy off her bowl with a hunk of crusty bread. "And such a treat, not having to cook. I'm almost too full for dessert."

"Almost? Still, I'm sure you'll manage to force one down."

She shrugged. "What can I say? I have two stomachs, like a lobster. Even when my main course stomach is full, my pudding stomach still has room."

The waitress came over to clear the table and show them the dessert trolley.

"You could always share with me if you don't have room for a whole portion," Tom suggested, eyeing the lemon meringue tart she had chosen.

Predictably, she responded with a glare. "I've told you before. I'll share my money with you…"

He laughed. "Your debts, you mean?"

"…As I was saying - before I was so rudely interrupted - I'll share my money; I'll share my body with you; my hopes and dreams; my future. You can have half of everything that's mine. Everything

300

except my pudding. That is sacrosanct." She sucked her spoon clean and waved it at him.

It felt good to tease her. He tilted his head to one side, pouting, and made his eyes big and sad. "Not even a tiny bit? A teeny weeny little bit, just for me, the love of your life?"

"You're crossing a line, Field. Keep away from the meringue."

With her next spoonful she taunted him, using the tip of her tongue to lick the cream in a manner calculated to arouse an appetite for more than just dessert.

"You know I'll get my own back," he said, looking forward to doing just that.

"You can try. But I can't lie to you. I might be a bit too full for a while."

The back seat of the taxi home gave him the perfect opportunity for revenge.

"What's that?" he asked, feigning concern as he peered at her ear.

Her hand flew to it, fumbling with her earring. "I don't know. What is it? Oh God, it's not a spider in my hair..?"

"Here - let me see…"

Before she had time to put any defences up, he dipped his head and nuzzled at the sensitive skin on her neck. Her gasp, quickly stifled out of embarrassment as the taxi driver glanced towards them in his mirror, was as gratifying as her giggle a moment later when he slipped a hand onto her thigh. By the time the taxi pulled onto the kerb outside their house, Tom was feeling smug. Even after ten years, it seemed he hadn't lost his ability to set his wife's pulse racing.

He waited on the pavement while Megan paid the driver, rolling his shoulders to stretch his muscles after an evening of sitting for too long. Then, looking up, he frowned. Nia's bedroom light was on. She should be asleep at this hour. He started down the driveway, only to hear raised voices. Just as Megan's high heels clicked behind him and the taxi pulled away, the front door swung open and a woman stormed out, clutching her coat.

301

"Excuse me – who are you?" Tom demanded, but she brushed past him without stopping and headed off down the street.

"What the…?" Megan's uncomprehending expression must surely mirror his own.

He arrived at the front door at exactly the same time as Idris, whose dishevelled appearance was at odds with his usual style. With his shirt undone and his belt hanging loose, hair rumpled and bare feet, he looked as if he had been interrupted in the act of getting dressed. Or undressed, he realised with a jolt, remembering the woman who had raced past him.

"Why is Nia crying?" Megan asked from behind him.

"It's nothing, *Cyw*. She got up and I sent her back to bed, that's all."

"It doesn't sound like nothing." She kicked off her shoes and made a beeline for the stairs.

Tom weighed his options, then quietly closed the door and waited for his father-in-law to finish tucking his shirt into his trousers.

"I'll let Megan sort out whatever's upsetting Nia. And while she does, you can tell me what the hell is going on."

∞∞∞∞

Megan squeezed her eyes closed and put her hands over her ears, but it was no good. She couldn't blot out the memory of Nia's distress as she'd flung herself into Megan's arms and sobbed incoherently. It had taken nearly an hour to work out the gist of what had happened and settle her back into bed.

"Just stop. I know you're right, but stop," she pleaded.

Tom had pressed pause on his tirade at last, but his fists were still clenched, his mouth a thin line as he held his rage in check.

"He has to go. He said he'd only be here a couple of nights, and it's been more than two weeks. And as for tonight…"

Her stomach twisted. "What am I supposed to do, kick my father out onto the streets at midnight?"

"There must be somewhere he can go. And if there isn't, he should have thought of that before he screwed his bit on the side in our living room while his grandchildren slept upstairs."

"We don't know that he did. Not for sure."

It was like watching a controlled explosion as, even in his fury, Tom hissed rather than shouted, long parental habit making him avoid disturbing the children any further.

"Nia saw them! You heard what she said. When she had stopped sobbing and could finally get her words out, I mean. 'Tadcu was on top of the lady, and he was tickling her, and then he said rude words and shouted at me to get back upstairs.' What other possible explanation could there be? When will you *finally* see the man for what he is?"

"Alright! Just – please, don't keep on about it."

"I can cope with him taking advantage of our home. I can handle him drinking our wine and eating our food without offering to pay for anything and without lifting a finger to help with the shopping or the cooking or even the washing up. I've buttoned my lip and kept my thoughts to myself out of deference to your feelings when you've done his laundry, even though you barely get a moment to yourself. I can put up with having no privacy and with not being able to relax in my own living room while he treats it like some kind of squat. But when the first bit of consideration he shows turns out to be a ruse to get us out of the house so he can bang some tart-"

"Stop!" She pressed her hand against his mouth to shut off the torrent of words, knowing he must be able to feel her trembling. Then she sank onto the edge of the bed and hunched over with her fingers laced into her hair.

Everything he said was true. She couldn't deny that Idris was unhelpful, or that he had taken advantage of their hospitality. Having him to stay had held very little pleasure. He left the living room messy, even messier than Megan left it herself, and made no effort to pick up his dirty coffee cups or plates, but left them on the sofa like a trail to be gathered up by someone else. His dirty clothes were strewn across the floor for her to collect, when it wouldn't cost him much effort to pop them into the laundry basket in the bathroom.

The truth was, Idris was selfish. He objected to the children watching kids' programmes on TV, insisting on watching the news instead on a continuous, tedious loop. If one of them dropped something, he muttered that they were clumsy; if they made a noise, he huffed and tutted and turned the television up to drown them out. He'd finish off food without replacing it or even noting it on the shopping list: the other day he'd used up all of the cheese while she and Tom were in work, and she'd only realised halfway through making a lasagne that she'd need to go out again to the shop.

Instead of showing appreciation for the extra housework involved in cleaning up after him and cooking for him, he had a habit of dropping criticism into their conversations. He found fault with every meal: the food wasn't salty enough, or they should have warmed the plates before serving, or the portion was too small. If she helped herself to a biscuit with a cup of tea, he'd raise an eyebrow and ask "should you be eating that, do you think?" And it was a funny thing, because when he said those things, that drip-drip-drip of meanness said with a smile as if he was only trying to be helpful, she took it like a lamb. Since her challenge over using his mobile phone at mealtimes had been so openly defied, she had avoided any further confrontation in front of the kids. Why was she so weak? If Tom spoke to her like that, she wouldn't stand for it. She had accepted rudeness from Idris that she wouldn't tolerate from anyone else.

These were little things. Niggles. She could have borne them as the price to be paid for having her father in her life. But tonight's transgression eclipsed them all. If Idris wanted to entertain guests, why couldn't he see that he should ask before inviting strangers into their home while the children were asleep?

She couldn't stop picturing how Nia must have felt, frightened after one of her bad dreams and confused at the sight of her grandfather 'tickling' a strange woman – the thought of it made Megan's skin crawl. Her little girl should have been met with sympathy and gentleness, not hard words. It wasn't as if a child could fight back…

The thought struck her hard. Megan hadn't been able to fight back, either. When she was with her father, she went right back to her familiar role of rejected child, like an actor in a soap opera who'd been playing the same part for so many years they could slip into it without thinking. She couldn't stand up for herself against Idris because she was too absorbed in quashing the feeling that she wasn't quite good enough in his eyes. Not good enough to stick around for. Not good enough to praise.

Tom sat down beside her, his muscles still taut with anger when she rested her head on his shoulder.

"I'm sorry," she said.

But he wasn't having it. "Why are you sorry? You're not responsible for his behaviour. He's a grown man. And after the little he's done for you over the years, he should be looking after you, not the other way round." He bundled her into his arms, holding her close, and she burrowed against his neck, as if by doing so she could somehow absorb his solidity and strength. "You owe him nothing, Meg. Not a bloody thing."

He rubbed the small of her back, his hand warm and comforting, melting the tension in the muscles around her spine until she sagged against him. The knot in her stomach slowly unravelled. God, she was a mess.

"I'll be the one to tell him to go, if you want. I can understand why you wouldn't want to risk a rift with your dad."

She thought about it. Tom hated confrontation. He was more likely to run away than face an uncomfortable conversation. Yet he was offering to do this out of consideration for her. A rush of gratitude filled her at this reminder that she did have someone who was prepared to make sacrifices for her. The knowledge gave her strength.

"Thank you," she said. "I appreciate the offer more than you'll ever know. But this is something I need to do myself."

Chapter Thirty-Two

Sunday 18th January 2015
Cardiff

After a sleepless night, Megan couldn't bring herself to get up and face the day when Tom got up for his Parkrun. It was still dark, and she was exhausted, so she lay her cheek on the warmth of his pillow and breathed in the faint lingering smell of his aftershave for a while. Still her brain refused to shut off and let her sleep.

Annoyed with herself, she reached for her book. It was hard to concentrate on the pages, so when after an hour or so Nia and Dylan stumbled in, bleary-eyed, for cwtches under the duvet, she was glad of the distraction and the company.

"Is Tadcu downstairs?" Nia asked, snuggling a little closer against Megan's side when told that he was.

"He's sorry he shouted at you," she told her, despite having no idea whether he was actually sorry or not. "He's not really used to children, so he finds it hard to understand how scary dreams can be."

She pulled herself up short. Why was she defending him? If Nia thought badly of Idris, he had brought it upon himself.

"I like your skin, Mammy," Dylan said, stroking the inside of her wrist where her arm curved round him. The change of subject was welcome, making her smile.

"Thank you, *cariad*. I like yours, too." She buried her nose in his mop of fair hair, relishing the still-baby smell of him and wishing she could bottle it to savour for ever.

"You look very thoughtful this morning, Nia." Her face was so pensive, Megan could almost hear the gears in her brain turning.

"I was thinking about Tadcu," she said, making Megan's heart sink. "Is he with that lady now, not Celia?"

"I think so."

Nia took a moment to digest this new information. "Was Daddy with other ladies before he picked you?"

It was funny how her children could always come out with a surprising new angle on any topic.

"Yes, of course. He was thirty-three when I met him, so he'd had girlfriends before."

"He didn't like skinny ladies, then, did he? He picked you instead." For a few moments, Megan was speechless as Nia's words sank in. "I'm glad he picked you, though. I never want any other mammy but you."

She couldn't put off the moment of confrontation with Idris for much longer. After extricating herself from the tangle of her children's arms, leaving them giggling together under her duvet, she slipped on her dressing gown and headed straight to the living room before she could change her mind. She drew the curtains, letting milky winter daylight wash over the mess on the coffee table: wine glasses, an empty box of chocolates and a torn condom wrapper, inadequately disguised by a crumpled tissue. Her mouth twisted downwards in disgust. The air smelled stale: she opened the window and shivered at the freezing draught that immediately rushed in.

Idris sat up, cocooned awkwardly in his sleeping bag, and scrubbed his hands over his eyes.

"This isn't working," she said.

"What isn't?"

She made herself look at him. "You being here for this long. We agreed to let you stay on the basis that it would only be for a couple of nights."

"Oh, for God's sake. He's put you up to this, hasn't he?" He unzipped the sleeping bag and swung his feet out onto the floor.

"Who?"

"Tom. He's never liked me. This is obviously his way of getting me back out of your life. I think he must be jealous or something."

"Actually, we're in agreement about this."

His eyes narrowed. "Is it about last night, then?"

"Partly, yes." Her fingers itched to reclaim the room and dispose of the wine bottle, at least, but she made herself stand still.

"You know, there wasn't really a monster in her bedroom. It was just a stupid, childish dream. If she saw stuff she shouldn't have... well, she shouldn't have been sneaking downstairs in the first place. Sending her back to bed was hardly an unreasonable response at nearly eleven o'clock at night, was it?"

He really didn't get it. How could anyone have so little empathy for a five year-old? Their own flesh and blood. Although, come to think of it, he was only behaving according to past form. The real question should be why she had ever expected anything different.

She spoke slowly, as if explaining a difficult concept to one of her pupils. "We very rarely go out without the children. When we do, it's important to know they're being well looked after. But your attentions were obviously elsewhere last night." His gaze followed hers to the condom wrapper, but if she'd hoped to see any guilt or embarrassment, she was disappointed. "Anyway, it's immaterial. You can stay until Friday, but we need the living room back to normal by then."

"Friday? That doesn't give me much time to sort something else."

"Can't you ask the woman who was here last night?"

"Tessa? No way – she's married. And besides, I've only known her for a week. It's a bit soon for talking about moving in together, I would have thought."

"A week? I thought you left Celia for someone else. I naturally assumed she was the one..."

"That one fell through. It all got a bit intense. You know how it is."

It wouldn't be so appalling if he showed even the slightest bit of regret. What did Mam say? *He took no more responsibility for you and Bethan than a tomcat does for its kittens.* An accurate analogy, it seemed.

Idris was as promiscuous as a tomcat, and equally lacking in any kind of conscience.

"Well, whatever – I'm afraid we need you out of here by Friday evening." Fingers twitching, she picked up the wine glasses and carried them to the kitchen. She mustn't say sorry – he had been given more than enough time to sort himself out.

He followed her. "What's so special about Friday, then? You haven't mentioned a deadline before."

She ran the tap until the water heated up, then added a splash of washing up liquid to the bowl. Perhaps she should remind him that he'd already outstayed his welcome by two whole weeks, and that allowing him to stay until Friday could be regarded as remarkably generous… but then, he should have been able to work that out for himself.

Then, as she washed the glasses, it came to her: a way to kill two birds with one stone. She could give Idris a deadline he couldn't argue with, and take control of the future.

"I've got an estate agent coming on Saturday," she said. It was only a white lie: she'd arrange it on Monday morning, as soon as the office opened. With all the progress they'd made at decluttering before Idris arrived, it wouldn't take much to get ready. And even though Y Noddfa had sold, there would be other houses. When their own house was under offer, they'd be in an ideal position to clinch a deal.

"Oh?" He didn't offer to dry up the wine glasses, but folded his arms and stood watching while she rinsed them and stood them on the draining board.

"I need the house looking its best, ready for photographs, so I'll have to tidy up and clean. We can't have your bags of stuff and your sleeping bag and pillow in the living room, making it look like a dosshouse."

"I didn't realise you were planning to put your house on the market. You never said."

"Well, now you know. As a matter of fact, we've decided to move closer to Mam."

His silence spoke volumes, souring the atmosphere still further. Perhaps he thought she'd back down if he stood there sulking like that instead of helping her clean up? It showed how little he knew her. Fuming, she started emptying the dishwasher, but looked up as Alys appeared in the doorway.

"What's herps?" Alys asked, frowning.

"I beg your pardon?"

"Herps."

"What is she talking about?" Idris asked.

"It's written on your car, Tadcu, in big red letters."

He shoved past her before she could finish the sentence.

Megan set down the cutlery basket and followed, her heart beating faster with the dawning realisation of what she was likely to find on the driveway. Sure enough, someone had sprayed a message along the side of Idris's immaculate silver-grey BMW in bright red paint:

I'VE GOT HERPES.

"You go back in," she said to Alys, not wanting her to be exposed to her father's blistering tirade of swear words. Although they were in Welsh, not English, it wouldn't do for Alys to hear and repeat any of them.

At last he paused for breath.

"Dear, oh dear," she murmured as he stamped back to the house. "It looks as if you must have upset somebody."

Chapter Thirty-Three

Easter Saturday
4th April 2015
Newquay, Cornwall

Tom joined Garin at the hotel window and patted his shoulder sympathetically. A gale had whipped the sea into a frenzy, sending towering waves and foam crashing against the shore. The plan for Garin and Shaz to marry on the beach and surf that afternoon had had to be abandoned, and he felt obliged to offer some comfort in the face of his friend's disappointment.

Garin groaned. "Look at it. It's howling like that shite Shirley Bassey impersonator in the rugby club last weekend. Of all the bastard bad luck."

"The function room was still nice, though. And Shaz's dress looked great."

"She wasn't going to wear a dress for the weddingy bit, only for the party after. We were supposed to get hitched in the water, in our wetsuits, and then surf, along with any guests who fancied joining us." Garin threw up his hands and growled in frustration.

"Come on, let me get you a drink. You're married – you're supposed to be celebrating. Your family is here, and all your best mates. That's what's important."

Although Garin allowed Tom to lead him to the bar, he seemed uncharacteristically tense. Tom set a pint in front of him and waved some friends over to keep him company while he sought out Griff, Garin's brother, and pulled him over to a quiet corner.

"What's up with Garin? I've never seen him like this before. He's practically tearing his hair out over the weather."

Griff shrugged. "He's reeling from the shock of getting hitched, I expect. Maybe that wedding ring feels like a shackle on his finger already?"

Garin's face did seem mournful as he stared into the depths of his pint. But he couldn't be having regrets already, could he? He'd only been married for an hour or so. He and Shaz hadn't even had time to have their first tiff yet.

Tom tried to look on the bright side. "At least we managed to do the camper van convoy this morning, as planned. The day hasn't been a complete disaster."

"Yeah, that was cool. He was telling me your van was stolen last year, you were lucky to get it back?"

"I probably wouldn't have it back if it wasn't for Garin. Luckily the thieves weren't all that clever: although they sprayed her blue and changed the number plates, they didn't change the chassis plate, so the police could tell she was mine. I bought it back from the insurance company. One of these days I'll get the paintwork redone, so she'll be orange again."

Griff whistled through his teeth. "That'll cost you. I know a few people, though – just let me know when you're ready, and I'll pass on a couple of names. You want it done properly, windows out and everything, not some crappy bodge job."

"Thanks. That would be a big help. It's not at the top of our list of priorities at the moment, though. Maybe next year. I'm taking redundancy at the end of this academic year, and last week we sold our house. We'll have to put all our resources and energies into finding somewhere to live."

"Gaz mentioned something about that. Setting up a campsite, aren't you? Heading west, he said."

"We haven't got all our ducks in a row quite yet, but that's the hope…"

His voice tailed off as he spotted Megan hesitating in the doorway, her hair like burnished copper against the deep, rich blue of her dress.

Even after all these years, she could still make the blood surge in his veins. Today, she looked particularly stunning. All the more so when she noticed him and lit up with a smile that made him feel ten feet tall.

"Shaz sent me to find Garin," she said in passing. "Apparently the meal will be ready in ten minutes. I hope you've finished composing your speech?"

The speech. Her reminder sent the butterflies flapping in his stomach again. He patted his pocket, reassured by the rustle of folded paper. At least he hadn't lost it.

He ran through the main points in his head. First, thank Garin and remember to say how stunning Shaz and her sister look. Joke about how he's punching well above his weight. Throw in a couple of anecdotes about his embarrassing escapades, not forgetting the time he stripped off his wetsuit and stood stark naked in a Gower car park just as David Hasselhoff and his Welsh girlfriend drove past. Then propose a toast, sit down, and shut the fuck up before everyone could get bored.

He took a deep breath. Why was it that he could happily stand up in front of hundreds of assembled teenagers, yet thirty or so adults had his knees quaking and his forehead prickling with sweat? He dashed for the gents' toilets to splash cool water on his face.

"Stop being such a dick," he admonished his reflection in the mirror.

"I know. I'm being stupid. But I can't help it." Garin's deep Welsh voice boomed from one of the cubicles, making him jump.

Garin emerged with a mournful sigh. He hung his head over the basin next to Tom's, like a condemned felon on his way to his own execution.

"Is it too soon to be considering a divorce?" he asked.

"Too soon? Five minutes in, you mean? Surely you should wait at least twenty-four hours, for the sake of courtesy."

Garin groaned. "This was such a mistake. I should never have gone through with it. It was supposed to be a bit of a laugh, just a party at the beach – nothing serious. But once the olds got involved, suddenly it had to involve suits and speeches and flowers and wedding favours and a first dance. I didn't want this posh nosh they've got planned. A Cornish pasty and a pint would have done me."

"What about Shaz? Does she feel the same?"

"I dunno. I can't exactly tell her I'm hating our wedding day, can I? I'm not a complete arsehole. Not all the time, anyway."

"Look, if you want my advice – for what it's worth – I think you should be honest with her. Phrase it nicely, obviously. Be kind. But ultimately a marriage should be based on truth, not pretending something suits you when it doesn't. Start as you mean to go on, mate."

Garin nodded bleakly.

"Today is just one day, Gaz. And remember, life is like a dick – even yours can't be hard all the time."

"Cheers, Tommo. I s'pose a dose of your clichéd bullshit was just what I needed today."

Chuckling, Tom followed him to the door, almost crashing into his friend's back as he stopped without warning.

"There you are!" Shaz's voice rang out excitedly.

Tom ducked into the shadows, unwilling to witness whatever Garin might say next. But from this position he still had an uninterrupted view of her slender arms wrapping themselves about his friend's scrawny neck. She was tall, brimming over with confidence, and she couldn't have clung any closer to him if they'd both been covered in Velcro.

"I've been looking for you everywhere," she was saying. "I was thinking… why don't we leave them all to it? Let's just lock ourselves in our room and order room service while the others do the meal and speeches and stuff. I can think of things I'd much rather do – can't you?"

She nuzzled her face against his neck and Tom hid a grin. They were obviously made for each other.

"We can't do that… can we?"

The door closed behind them and Tom waited discreetly for a minute or two before adjusting his expression to something more serious and heading back to the bar.

Megan appeared at his elbow looking puzzled. "Did I just see Garin and Shaz disappearing upstairs?"

One look at his face was enough to make her raise an eyebrow. "Surely not?" she asked, obviously amused.

"I don't think I'll be needing my speech after all," he said.

∞∞∞∞

"I still can't believe they had the balls to do it," Megan said, kicking off her high heels with a groan of relief. "And you, making that announcement. 'Ladies and gentlemen: the bride and groom offer their apologies as they find themselves indisposed, but they insist that we all enjoy the meal without them.' Everybody knew exactly what you really meant. Shaz's dad's face was a picture."

"I hope I didn't sound quite that pompous."

She grinned wickedly, knowing he found her ability to mimic his English accent annoying, especially as he still hadn't managed to master a Welsh accent in over twenty years and had no hope of being able to retaliate in kind.

"Pompous? Only a teeny bit."

She sent him a seductive glance over her shoulder, knowing full well he wouldn't fail to respond with boyish eagerness. One calculated look could generally have him panting like Dandy begging for a treat.

"Would you mind unzipping me?" she asked, scooping her hair off the back of her neck with both hands.

Predictably, he didn't need a second invitation. She shivered with delicious anticipation as he slid the zip downwards, slowly and smoothly, and kissed the skin at her nape. Softly he slipped the dress from her shoulders and she turned to undo his tie, tugging it out from under his collar.

"May I say you look particularly ravishing today, Mrs Field. That new underwear is very nice. Very nice indeed."

"You may, Mr Field." These days she often felt as if she needed a miracle, not just a bra, but her new lingerie set did make her feel good. Unlike her usual everyday underwear, it hadn't yet reached a greying, saggy stage; it hoisted her tits up a good couple of inches more than usual and squished them together in a manner guaranteed to attract attention. Worth every penny, judging by the way his pupils had widened, turning his Aegean blue eyes almost black.

"Do you remember our wedding night?" he murmured, holding her gaze while she popped open his shirt buttons one by one.

"How could I forget? Garin and Shaz had the right idea, locking themselves in their room before anyone could get in there and set up any pranks."

She pressed herself against him, tilting her chin upwards for a kiss and relishing the sensation of his hands on the bare skin of her back. Something hard dug into her tummy.

"Mmm... Is that a mobile phone in your pocket, or are you just pleased to see me?"

"That is a mobile phone, but I'm also *very* pleased to see you." He reached into his pocket and pulled out the handset, ready to toss it onto the bedside table. "Bugger," he said, weighing it in his hand. "There's a voicemail notification."

"You'd better check it, then," she said, flopping onto the bed and reaching for her handbag to retrieve her own phone. "It might be

317

about the kids. Although I would have thought Mam would have rung me first if anything had happened."

While he held his handset to his ear and drifted over to the window to listen, she scrolled through her notifications. Olwen had texted a couple of times.

The kids are fine. They've helped me make chocolate cornflake nests with mini eggs.

She raised an eyebrow. Her mother had never been one for creative cookery. That was more Bethan's style. The next message explained it.

Bethan came. She says she's missed the kids. And you.

A lump rose in Megan's throat as she read the words over. She'd missed Bethan, too. Whilst there had been some positive developments in her life in recent months, like the thawing of Tom's relationship with Olwen and the return of Greta when she had been thought lost for ever, she hadn't managed to shake off the pain of the break with her sister. Like a broken bone that wouldn't set, it left her feeling incapacitated. She pretended to function as she had done before, but really she was just hiding the hurt.

Was she reading too much into this message, or was it an opening? Could Olwen be signalling that Bethan might be receptive to a reconciliation? She should ask Tom if he thought her instincts were true. She rolled over to look at him.

He had set his phone down and tucked his hands under his armpits, hugging himself and staring at her with a wide-eyed look of… what? Alarm?

"What is it? What's wrong?" She sat up, worried.

"Wrong?" he repeated, as if the word made no sense. "Nothing's wrong. In fact, everything's right." He broke into a smile that made his eyes sparkle and tugged her to her feet.

"Tell me," she urged, delighted and mystified in equal measure as he danced her around the floor of their hotel room. "What was your message about? Don't keep me in suspense."

"*Y Noddfa*," he said, the unbridled glee in his voice making her heart leap. "It's back on the market, Meg. The chain has broken down. And so… if we still want it… Oh, God – I can hardly believe it! As long as we match the previous offer, it's *ours*."

Epilogue

Friday 28th August 2015
Y Noddfa, near Cardigan

The nights were drawing in, shadows dimming the vivid colours of summer as the last daubs of yellow, orange and scarlet faded in the sky. Dandy lifted his head, long ears twitching as he listened, and gave a gruff bark to warn some unseen creature that this garden was his territory now.

Here and there, birds fluttered to find a roost for the night in the hedgerows. Apart from the faint sounds of a few restless animals, a gentle breeze, and Dandy resuming his obsessive snuffling across the lawn, the quietness was remarkable. No cars. No sirens in the distance. No neighbours talking or television soundtracks to disturb the peace of the evening.

"Listen to that, Meg. It's so quiet. Even after a week, I still can't believe this place is really ours. Can you?"

Megan smiled and patted the bench next to her. It shifted as he sat down and passed her a mug.

"Funny looking cup of tea," she said.

"I thought we deserved a glass of wine, but I haven't managed to find the glasses yet. They must still be in one of the boxes."

"Remiss of us to leave the most important things still packed."

She took a swig, relishing the tart fruitiness on her tongue. It wasn't the same from a mug, but it was still good, and with the second mouthful the aching knots in her shoulders started to ease. She was fatigued after the exertions of the week, but in a good way: the pleasant weariness of muscles well used and a mind refreshed.

She sighed, shifting to lean her head on his shoulder. "A perfect end to a lovely day."

Earlier, they had set aside a few hours to escape the heaped boxes, and explored the path towards the coast. Tom carried Dylan on his back, pointing out anything they saw that might catch the children's interest as they tramped along the narrow country lanes and footpaths. Dandy left no hedgerow unsniffed. Megan couldn't help laughing at how impressed Tom and the girls had been by her knowledge of animals and wild plants; when she identified a Red Kite wheeling overhead, he couldn't have looked more amazed if she'd taken off to the skies herself. Clearly he had forgotten she grew up in the country, so accustomed was he to seeing the city as her natural habitat.

She wasn't sure yet how she felt about being back in rural West Wales. It was undeniably beautiful, and peaceful. Easy to see why it appealed to a dreamer like Tom, who had always been drawn to the sea and the outdoors. But there was still a part of her that saw it as a backwards step, as if by coming back she had retreated towards her roots instead of forging ahead and making her own path. Still, with the warming of her relationship with her mother, perhaps living nearer to her wouldn't be too great a strain.

The girls competed to spot the sea first, and were excited to see it long before they reached the coastal path. The headland of Mwnt, jutting from the coastline like a conical hat, was too tempting to resist, and after much puffing and panting they reached the top and settled on the scrubby grass to take in the panorama below them.

The Ceredigion coastline brushed its lush green fingers into the Irish Sea, sweeping away to their left past Cardigan Island and to their right higher up the bay towards the north-west. From their rocky vantage point the slope down to the cove was perilously steep, so Megan kept a firm hand on Dandy's leash and was glad when Tom left Dylan safe in his backpack seat rather than risk letting him scramble about on the lichen-covered scree.

"See if you can spot any dolphins or basking sharks," Megan suggested to the girls, delving in her rucksack for bottles of water to refresh them after their climb. Her calves ached, and she kneaded them with her thumb while she drank.

Alys nestled closer against her side. "I like it up here. It's peaceful. The rest of the world feels far away," she said.

"Isn't it beautiful? And just think - living so close now, we'll be able to come here pretty much whenever we want."

It wouldn't do to betray her own reservations about their new lifestyle to her sensitive elder daughter, who would probably find it harder than any of them to adjust to the change.

"Will I be able to invite Millie to stay? I'm going to miss her."

She swallowed her instinctive unwillingness to spend more than a couple of hours in Millie's company. Millie was spoiled, and had a tendency to home in on Alys's weak spots. "Of course," she said brightly, as if she wasn't aware that this would lead to fresh demands for ear piercing, and a mobile phone, and make-up. "You can invite her as soon as we've unpacked everything and settled in."

Alys nodded, but said nothing, gazing pensively out to sea.

"What's up?"

"Nothing, really. It's just... Well, I don't know anyone yet. And it will be strange, going to a school where they speak Welsh all the time, because I don't know all that many words."

She nodded, kicking herself for not sending the children to the Welsh medium school in Cardiff, and for allowing her own schoolgirl Welsh to go rusty instead of making more of an effort to speak it at home. How would she have felt as a child if she hadn't been able to understand what the other kids were saying in the playground, or hadn't understood the teacher's instructions? No wonder Alys needed reassurance.

"You know, you're amazing, Alys. Clever; hard-working, with a lot of determination; you're kind-hearted and helpful, and of course you're talented with your violin playing and your singing. You can throw yourself into the school orchestra and choir, and we'll find some ballet lessons you can join locally, just like you used to back home – I mean, back in Cardiff."

She'd have to get out of the habit of referring to Cardiff as home. Taking a deep breath, she started again and hoped Alys hadn't noticed her mistake.

"You'll soon make friends at school. They won't be able to resist you. And they'll help you with the language. It's bound to seem strange at first, but you'll be surprised how quickly you'll pick it up. I'll help, too. Then you can teach your dad. Just you wait, you'll be making fun of him by Christmas, because he'll still be stumbling over his words while you'll be fluent. You'll be able to call him all sorts of rude names, and he won't have a clue what you're saying."

Alys had blushed at her mother's praise, but now grinned, as Megan had hoped she would. "I wouldn't be rude to Dad."

They spotted Nia waving and poking her tongue out at them from further down the slope, where she had dragged Tom and Dylan to look for seals on the rocks below.

"Nia will, though," she added.

∞∞∞∞

Tom rested his cheek against the top of Megan's auburn head. She was right: it had been a perfect day. He'd loved every moment of their walk to Mwnt, his head full of plans for future guided walks and running routes for the customers he had to believe would stay at *Y Noddfa*. He couldn't have chosen anywhere better to create a sanctuary where people could take a break from the stresses of their everyday lives.

His favourite bit of the day had been visiting the tiny church at Mwnt. Pure in its whitewashed simplicity, it nestled in its ancient graveyard in a dip at the base of the hill as if nothing had changed for centuries. Tom had paused to admire its stark beauty.

"Why don't you go inside for a look?" Megan suggested, shielding her eyes from the sun. The girls had started pleading for ice creams, and she sent them a stern look to halt their pestering. "Go on – you'll like it. We'll meet you at the kiosk when you're ready."

He dithered, then seized his chance for a moment alone. Megan took Dylan's hand and Dandy's leash, and he slipped the baby carrier off his back, feeling suddenly lighter and freer without little hands pulling off his hat and little feet kicking his ribs. He wouldn't stay long, knowing the children would soon nag to descend the steps to the beach, where dogs were not allowed during the summer months; but still, even a few snatched moments of quietness and contemplation would be good for the soul.

Crossing himself out of long habit, he dipped his knee before sliding into one of the wooden pews, its varnish worn in places from the touch of a multitude of hands across the centuries. Gazing around, he was struck most of all by the simplicity of the white stone walls and oak roof, lit by just a few plain glass windows. It was so unlike the lofty grandeur of the church he'd attended as a boy; yet he still felt touched by the same sense of awe.

What a year it had been. On Monday they'd raised a toast to his dad, marking the first anniversary of his death. Perhaps somewhere, somehow, Hugh might know what they had achieved since that terrible day. Maybe he had even been a part of the workings of Fate that had made their move happen.

Lifting his face towards the sunlight spilling through the window beside his pew, he felt a rush of gratitude. He had come through this first year. The recurring image of his father's body lying in the woods plagued him less often, and had started to give way to happier memories of his parents. Whilst it still hurt to acknowledge their loss, he had a sense that they would be proud of him.

He left the church to meet the others feeling comforted.

In the evening, sipping his mug of wine as he surveyed the garden, his head brimmed with ideas and plans. Where should he put each of the glamping pods, making sure that they didn't overlook each other or the house? A playground and space for ball games would be essential, visible from the house so that Alys, Nia and Dylan could play there, either by themselves or with visiting children.

He'd get the barn cleared first, turn it into a base for people to come and exercise. That way, he could set up his fitness business while the campsite was still being developed. People would come, he was sure of it. The tranquillity, proximity to the sea, and the chance to engage with the outdoors would draw them.

There was so much to think about, so many regulations to check and research to do: he mustn't rush into it, but set goals and deadlines to make sure he kept everything on track. He'd apply the same principles to himself that he recommended to his pupils... Not that he'd have pupils any more. The first of September would be just another day from now on. A strange thought. He wanted to burst with the euphoria of possessing this idyllic place and the excitement of dreams and goals yet to be realised.

"I need to find somewhere to buy a new blind and a bigger cabinet for the bathroom," Megan was saying, bringing him back to the present. "It won't be quite as easy as it used to be, when Ikea was just across town."

He hadn't thought of that. Damn. No more Swedish meatballs on evenings when they couldn't be bothered to cook. Still, this view, on an evening like this, was more than adequate compensation… He owned a barn. A strip of woodland. He owned *fields*.

"I'll need a ride-on mower," he said, eyeing the unruly grass.

"Ha! Boys and their toys. But yes, it would take forever to mow that lot with our old Flymo. I'd suggest a goat, but we know as little about livestock as we do about setting up in business. And they have weird eyes."

Her face seemed serene in the half-light, but he couldn't help but wonder if her remark about setting up in business was a hint that she still had doubts.

"Are you scared?" he asked. "I know I am. I'm scared shitless, to be frank. But I'm loving it. I can't wait to get cracking; my head is fit to pop with ideas and lists of things to do. It would be easy to feel overwhelmed, I suppose… but they say fear and excitement are two sides of the same coin, don't they?"

She scuffed her toe at weeds in the gaps in the paving.

"I'd say I'm trepidatious, more than scared. It's a long time since I started a new job. Eleven years was probably too long to stay in one school, but it suited me while the children were little. Perhaps this is the shake-up I needed to move my career on… In a year or so, once I'm used to working full-time again, I'll start looking for a department head post. And then we'll both have our dreams fulfilled, won't we?"

She peeped up at him, past the veil of hair that had swung down across her face while she spoke, and there was something in that nervous determination to push on and try that made his throat close up. He was so remarkably lucky. The knowledge that she had left behind a job and lifestyle she loved to support him in achieving his ambitions made him all the more determined to succeed. He'd prove to her that he was up to the challenge. However exhausted or daunted he might feel in the coming weeks and months, he'd remind himself of the strength of her commitment, and how she'd helped him through the past year.

Y Noddfa already lived up to its name, providing the sanctuary he had needed: their haven from the world. And although Megan occasionally referred to it as the Field Family Funny Farm, he knew she'd find it equally restorative. She'd be able to retreat there at the end of each busy day in her new job and find peace.

"Thank you," he said, his heart too full to say more.

She held his gaze as if she was looking into his soul. He could only hope she could discern the depth of emotion there. Whatever she saw seemed to content her, as she snuggled closer again.

"What is it Polonius says in *Hamlet?* 'Above all: to your own self be true'. I tried to do that when I looked for my dad. And I came to understand that you were doing the same in pursuing this dream of yours. Whatever happens here - whether your business succeeds or fails, whether I love the new job or hate it - we'll be fine. We'll keep going, as long as we keep going together."

He raised his mug and bumped it against hers, making a dull clunk.

"To us, Mrs Field. To us, and to our dreams."

Acknowledgements

Firstly, I'd like to thank you for taking the time to read this book. If you liked it, please take a moment to leave a review or rating on Amazon or Goodreads. I read every one of your comments, and love to hear from you. You can email me at **luisa@luisaajones.com.**

Follow me on **Facebook @LuisaAJonesauthor** and **Instagram luisa_a_jones_author**.

I hope you enjoyed finding out what happened to Megan and Tom in this next stage of their story. Sign up to my email newsletter at **www.luisaajones.com** to receive a free prequel short story and updates on new releases.

Once again, Martin, I thank you for your unwavering love, your pep talks, your help with plotting, your feedback, and your expertise in the field of VW camper vans. You are my rock, my light on dark days, and my inspiration.

To my parents. I know you would move mountains for me. Thank you for all your love and encouragement. I've been truly blessed.

To Lisa, thank you for your gorgeous cover design. You took my vision and then made it so much better.

To David, my writing buddy, thank you for your feedback on an early draft. You helped me to keep ploughing on through the Swamp of Self-Doubt. I like your idea of a spin-off series for Garin, but I suspect he's one of those people who is better in small doses.

To my other beta readers: Ciara, Pauline, Meryl and Julia. Your constructive, insightful feedback was invaluable.

Thanks are also due to Chloe, Ben, Anna and those already mentioned above who helped me when the problem of a title got me in a fix.

To Andrew, whose advice about molehills and balconies provided inspiration, and to Sam, who inspired Sharpiegate. Thank you.

By Luisa A. Jones

To John, thank you for offering insights into the mysterious workings of the male brain, and inadvertently inspiring a crucial aspect of the plot involving Greta.

There are others whose invaluable advice helped with research. If I've made any mistakes, they are my own. I couldn't have created this story without all of you. Thank you to:

Claire (via Sara) and Tony, for advice regarding police procedures for missing persons and unexpected deaths.

Liam (via Louise), for insights into medical conditions which might kill off an apparently healthy 76 year-old man without warning.

Clive, for expert advice regarding probate and inheritance.

Maria, for confirming my memories of HR processes.

Sara and Gareth, and the wonderful VW Camper Chicks on Facebook, for suggestions and information about stolen vehicles and especially ringers.

About the author

After narrowly avoiding being born in the back seat of a Ford Cortina, Luisa A. Jones was perhaps destined to have a keen interest in popular vehicles of the 1960s and 70s. She and her husband are the proud owners of Gwynnie, a classic Volkswagen camper van. They enjoy nothing more than camping with Gwynnie and like-minded friends.

Luisa and her husband live in Wales. Besides their camper van, T4 and two Beetles (apparently one old VW is never enough), they also have three children and two spaniels, who are arguably cheaper to keep and less troublesome than classic vehicles.

Luisa studied at Royal Holloway and Bedford New College, University of London, and the University of South Wales, Newport. Becoming an author fulfilled a lifelong ambition.

She hopes you have enjoyed this book, the sequel to *Goes Without Saying*. If you have, please recommend it to your friends, and consider posting a review on Amazon or Goodreads to encourage others to read it too.

Also by Luisa A. Jones

Goes Without Saying

"Most people run away from home when they're in their rebellious teenage phase. But not you, Tom. Oh, no. You waited until you were a forty-year old father to do it."

Tom Field promised his wife Megan he'd never leave her. So when she finds his note saying he's gone away, she can't help but wonder if that's the only vow he's broken.

Following him and his treasured camper van to the beautiful coast of North Devon, she has plenty of time to reflect on what's gone wrong between them. Time to decide whether their marriage is worth saving.

But all too soon reality threatens to catch up with them. Can Tom make things right before it's too late?

Goes Without Saying is the first book in the *Dreams of Field* contemporary romance series. If you like heart-warming, poignant tales with relatable characters and plenty of witty humour, you'll love this first novel in Luisa A. Jones' page-turning series.

Sign up for Luisa's email newsletter at <u>www.luisaajones.com</u> for a free short story and updates on new releases and special offers.

Making the Best of It

Printed in Great Britain
by Amazon